Praise for Julia Fenton's previous novels:

BLACK TIE ONLY

"An engrossing tale that will take you be[illegible]e scenes of the most glamorous gala of the dec[illegible]"

—Eileen Goudge

"Passion-and-fashion garnished with royalty . . . hot sex . . . deadly secrets."

—*Booklist*

"Entertaining!"

—*Publishers Weekly*

"Glitz, glamour, sex . . . an instant summer hit!"

—*Library Journal*

BLUE ORCHIDS

"A dazzling page-turner."

—Maureen Dean,
bestselling author of
Washington Wives

"Fenton is a born storyteller and this delightfully decadent tale kept me turning pages late, late into the night."

—Rex Reed

Now the bestselling author presents her newest, most unforgettable story—a stunning novel of royal intrigue and ruling passions . . .

ROYAL INVITATION

Also by Julia Fenton

BLACK TIE ONLY
BLUE ORCHIDS

ROYAL INVITATION

JULIA FENTON

JOVE BOOKS, NEW YORK

ROYAL INVITATION

A Jove Book / published by arrangement with the author

PRINTING HISTORY
Jove edition / February 1995

ISBN: 0-515-11548-7

A JOVE BOOK®
Jove Books are published by The Berkley Publishing Group,
200 Madison Avenue, New York, New York 10016.
JOVE and the "J" design are trademarks belonging to
Jove Publications, Inc.

PRINTED IN THE UNITED STATES OF AMERICA

10 9 8 7 6 5 4 3 2 1

For Rick,
whose love carries me through. . . .

For my family who have remained supportive and close to me all these years—Ben, Stella, Ed, Dolly, and Manny. And, Mary dear, I'll never forget you—not ever. God bless and keep you all!

For Cynthia and Robert, Jr., and Aileen, three really thoughtful and considerate children, who are wonderful individuals in their own persons. Thank you.

And for my friends, Dorothy Simon, Mary Stephanie de Freitas, and especially Marcia Ann Fennell; also all the "early birds" at the Franklin Fitness & Racquet Club.

Then a special thanks to the incomparable Sheila Clifford, a person so kind and giving that she was cast in an extraordinary, solitary mold.

And to Nancy Coffey, a dear, wonderful new mom who knows how important she is to the "dream team." Thanks for all your inspirational efforts.

ACKNOWLEDGMENTS

Leslie Gelbman, my editor, has never failed me! She's always been there for me and given her enthusiastic support.

A real big note of appreciation to the following individuals who have assisted the *Royal Invitation* family during the writing of this manuscript: Academy of Motion Picture Arts and Sciences, Hollywood, California; Ginny Borowski, Manager, Special Services, American Airlines, Chicago, Illinois; Mary Kathryn Boyer; Keith Crain, President, Crain Communications, *Automotive News,* Detroit, Michigan; *Daily Variety,* Hollywood, California; John and Marion Dodge; James Donnelly; Barbara Dorda; Sonny Eliot, radio and television personality and syndicated columnist, Birmingham, Michigan; Joann Fairchild; Ozzie and Dede Feldman; Richard Feldman, M.D.; John, Marion, and Peter Ginopolis; Philip Gross, former Special Investigator, U.S. Treasury Department; Ernie Harwell; the Meg Harrison family; Jean and Will Haughey; *The Hollywood Reporter,* Hollywood, California; David A. Kott, D.D.S., M.S.; Kenneth Jay Lane, New York, New York; Bayard Lawes, Great Lakes Helicopter Corporation, Pontiac, Michigan; Mickey and Joyce Lolich; Sammy Locricio, Arriva's, Warren, Michigan; Robert and Aileen Magill; Robert McCabe, President, Detroit Renaissance, Inc., Detroit, Michigan; J. P. McCarthy; Mike and Peggy Miller, West Palm Beach, Florida; Armand Molino, Tennis Pro, Franklin Fitness and Racquet Club, Franklin, Michigan; Marsha Narramore; Dorothy Powers, WJR Radio, Detroit, Michigan; the Bruce Rosen family; the Louis B. Rudolph family; Richard M. Saffir; Catherine E. Schaffer, Public Relations Executive,

Atheneum Hotel Corporation, New York, New York; Edna and the late Joseph Slavik; the late Craig Smith; Jerry Solomon, ProServ Agency, Inc.; Rick Stober, M.D.; Steven Schumer, M.D., Southfield, Michigan; Variety Clubs International, New York, New York; Greg and Kathy Wendt; Harold Wienik; Tom and Linda Wilson, The Palace, Auburn Hills, Michigan.

A big acknowledgement to Jack, Bruce, and Tony Milan of Jax Kar Wash fame, great guys and good friends, Bloomfield Hills, Michigan; also thanks to dear friends Donald, Richard, and Randal Golden, owners of D.O.C. Optics Corporation.

Very special thanks also go to Robert L. Fenton, entertainment attorney, Hollywood film producer, and, most recently, producer of the NBC-TV movie, *Woman on a Ledge,* and to Julia Grice, author of *Suspicion* and *The Cutting Hours.*

Julia Fenton
December 1994

May 1994

The SLEEK BLACK BENTLEY DROVE SLOWLY ALONG the Champs-Elysées, passing the Arc de Triomphe, the Rond Point, and the Place de la Concorde. Dusk was falling, and the wide thoroughfare glowed with hazy light. The famous street, one of the renowned sights of Paris, was lined with beautifully proportioned, classic buildings that had witnessed France's noble and sometimes bloody history.

Behind smoked-glass windows the distinguished-looking passenger gazed coolly at the well-known buildings. His mouth was dry. He swallowed, suppressing his nervousness. Even Claude, his driver, did not suspect how tense he was, how much depended on this meeting.

As the elegant car pulled up to the ornate marble government building, it turned down a narrow passageway that led between ancient walls and stopped at a discreet side door once used by governmental ministers for easy escapes or assignations.

A pair of security guards appeared, walkie-talkies fastened in their ears.

"Sir, you will follow us, please."

They flanked him on either side as he ascended four

shallow steps and entered the building. It was a warren of high-ceilinged corridors. Marble echoed under their heels as they proceeded deep into the building.

A secretary, hurrying somewhere with a file folder, eyed him with a glimmer of recognition. As she passed, she nodded to the gray-haired man with the deepset, dark eyes, a thin, mustached lip, and aristocratic nose. He frowned at her, not liking the attention, and she scurried away.

A wide flight of marble steps led upward, slight depressions in the steps marking where previous generations had trod. At last he was being ushered into a palatial anteroom, papered in a dark red wallpaper, and filled with red brocaded furniture. On the walls hung dozens of large, dark portraits of the great French statesmen of the Second Empire and the Third Republic. Four-foot-tall arrangements of flowers stood scattered on ... of carved tables.

The man covered up his nervous excitement.

One of the guards spoke into an intercom, then opened the double doors. The gray-haired man walked inside, and the doors clicked shut behind him.

The inner office was even more magnificent than the waiting room. It was huge, its walls gray silk, its portraits of France's kings even more distinguished. The tricolor flag, with its panels of blue, white, and red, stood in a gold pedestal, and one wall was covered with photographs of George Bush, Margaret Thatcher, King Juan Carlos of Spain, Queen Elizabeth II, and others. Windows looked out on a formal garden.

"Ah," said the other man softly. He rose briefly, offered greetings, then sat down again behind his fine, granite-topped mahogany desk. "My friend."

They exchanged pleasantries for a few moments, these two men who, each in his own way, controlled the destiny of a country.

"The weather . . . our gray, Paris weather. Not nearly as temperate as your own climate."

"*Oui,* Costa is amazingly sunny. Always lovely, actually."

Finally the man behind the desk was ready to talk business. He cleared his throat, touched his closely clipped, light brown Vandyke, and remarked, "You really don't have much time left if what you told me about your brother and his three children is correct. Situations change; emotions are not written in stone. I want to secure these commitments now. I will go along with your plan as you have outlined it to me, your arrangements with Monsieur Skouros, but in return, I ask that you do one thing for me."

"Of course." He nodded.

"I need an additional fifty million francs to hold everything in readiness with my political friends."

"Fifty million . . . ?" The gray-haired man kept his face expressionless, but inwardly he was churning from shock. It had been extremely difficult to raise the money he'd already provided. Now this, another fifty million? Impossible!

He said, "It is not that easy. There are certain checks and balances. . . . My spending must seem quite appropriate—"

"It is what I need, and I intend to have it, or all your plans will be for nothing, do you get my drift? You cannot tweak the tail of the French lion and then run."

"*Oui, oui,*" said the man, nodding reluctantly. "*Mais certainement,* it will be done."

ONE WEEK LATER . . .

Gusts OF RAIN SWEPT SIDEWAYS ALONG THE RUE de Rivoli, battering the tubs of flowers, harrying loose papers at a newspaper kiosk, and tugging at the big black umbrella the doorman of the Meurice Hotel held aloft for arriving guests.

The ancient Paris taxi pulled up in front, and Teddy Warner jumped out, grabbing with both hands the shopping bags that lined the backseat.

"Paris in the rain," she said with a smile as the uniformed doorman escorted her to the front entrance. The blond braid that had been woven at the nape of her neck was dappled with rain, and even her eyelashes sparkled with silvery droplets.

She rushed into the lobby of the famous hotel, once patronized by Salvador Dali, Maria Callas, and Winston Churchill, buoyed by her shopping spree on the Place du Marché St-Honoré and the Avenue des Champs-Elysées.

She was going to see him again. And this time maybe she wouldn't make a mistake. Maybe—

She hadn't been able to shake Prince Jac from her mind over the past five years. But two days from now she would see whether her fantasies had any chance of coming true.

She was tall, with the slim, toned yet curvy body of an athlete. Her sunstreaked hair was plaited into a thick, golden braid, her cinnamon-colored suntan made her eyes look even more azure, and her full, sensuous mouth held both humor and determination.

At the elevator she set down her shopping bags emblazoned with the famous linked C's and the black, red, and pink of St. Laurent and glanced at the front page of the sports section, which featured her picture. She was shown hugging her father and her coach, her face aglow with the exhausted joy of winning. The picture flattered her, but had caught her father starting to blink, she noticed. The headline read: *Teddy Takes Steffi! Golden Girl Wins French Open from Graf after Close Match; Thanks Father for Inspiration.*

Teddy finally proceeded into the elevator, juggling her bags, its doors whispering shut behind her. As it moved upward, she leaned against the wall, some of her exhilaration receding. Yes, she and her father had been invited to the famous Blue-and-White Tournament at Costa del Mar, but she might have been a little presumptuous in buying clothes for the gala, three-day charity event in the tiny, Monaco-like principality. After all, her father hadn't yet agreed to their going.

But we have to go, she thought desperately. *I have to get Jac out of my head . . . one way or another.*

Teddy hurried into their suite, dropping her packages, purse, and the newspaper. Her father, L. Houston Warner, the CEO of WarnerCo, a publicly-listed software company, looked up from a table where he had been going over a contract with Teddy's agent from ProServ, Russ Ostrand.

"A good practice session, Teddy, I take it?" Houston Warner smiled warmly at his daughter. He'd been ranked one of the twenty best tennis players in the world in 1955, and he still looked as if he could give John McEnroe or Auggie Steckler a run for their money.

"The best. And then I went shopping. I bought the most fabulous things. Dad—"

"How did the practice go? Did you power up those ground strokes? You beat Steffi, but it was damn close, and next time I want you to put her on her ass, honey. Make her sweat. Terrorize her."

"Dad—I *always* do a power practice. You taught me always to give two hundred percent," Teddy said, smiling as she went over to hug her father and nuzzle a kiss on his ear.

"Hi, Russ," she said, greeting her agent, who'd taken her on when she'd first turned pro at fifteen after winning her first Virginia Slims in Dallas. "The contracts are here?"

"All twenty pages of them. I'll be back later, and we'll get them signed."

She eyed the low table where the contracts were spread out. A Paris firm, Marithé, wanted to market a line of sportswear in her name, a deal that would bring her earnings from endorsements alone to over $8 million annually. All of that just for playing a game she loved.

But did she love tennis quite so much today? The morning's phone conversation with Princess Kristina still echoed in her ears. *"You will come, won't you, Teddy? We need you for the charity event, and . . . Jac really wants to see you."*

The three-day event, which would raise money for AIDS research, would feature a tennis tournament with a first prize of $100,000 and a Formula One auto race in which the best drivers in the world would compete, including Jac. To cap the star-studded weekend, there would be a spectacular ball aboard the Nikos Skouros yacht. Teddy was dying to go.

After the agent left, she said, "Dad . . . , I've been working *so* hard, I need a break."

Houston Warner sighed, putting down the contracts. "Teddy Bear, I hope this isn't about Costa del Mar."

"It is. Dad—"

"You're too tightly scheduled, honey. You've got three tournaments next month, and then there's Wimbledon."

"But it's just a three-day break. . . . All the Costan royals are going to be there, Dad. Princess Gabriella, and Kristina, and Jac, even Prince Henri himself. And Elizabeth Taylor and . . . You know how Nikos Skouros loves American movie stars—his ship is going to be crawling with them. And we've got to go!" Teddy finished emphatically.

For some reason her father didn't seem at all eager.

"Baby doll, it would take you out of serious practice right in the middle of the tennis season, and—"

"I need some fun," Teddy argued. "Remember fun? I'm not just a tennis machine, Dad. I've worked hard, I've sweated. And besides, it's a good cause that we should all be concerned about."

"Honey—" he began.

"I *want* to go," Teddy said firmly.

Warner hesitated. "You deserve the world, baby," he finally conceded. "So I guess you can have Costa del Mar."

Georges, brother of Prince Henri, ruler of Costa del Mar, eyed his surroundings with suppressed rage. The bedroom was spacious and possessed an ornately carved and gilded four-poster bed. There were priceless seventeenth-century tapestries of hunters and stags hanging on the walls. Rich, but not rich enough. Palatial, but not palatial enough.

"Sir," said Émile, his personal valet, coming forward with two tailored Costan military uniforms draped on wooden hangers, holding both out for his inspection. "The dress or semiformal uniform? I have pressed both for you, and your royal sash is being dry-cleaned."

"Good, good," snapped Prince Georges. "But where are your brains, Émile? You know I need formal attire. Hang the uniforms in my dressing room and leave, please. But before you do, call down and order me some wine."

"Yes, sir."

The appellation should have been not "sir," but "Your Highness."

Prince Georges, ten years younger than his brother, Henri, and fifth in line of succession, walked out onto the balcony that overlooked the blue harbor of Costa del Mar. He stood at the stone balustrade, gazing down at the stunning view.

Another charitable function, he thought bitterly. *As usual, I will attend, standing in the shadows of my brother, the Royal sovereign. I'm no better than the Duke of Windsor! A supernumerary, more overlooked than respected.*

A detested role.

A jealous fury engulfed him.

The muted hiss of a fax machine printing out documents mingled with the discreet trill of telephones and the voices of executive secretaries and assistants as they completed the final details for the Blue-and-White Sports Celebrity Weekend.

"Your Highness," said one of the secretaries, hurrying up to the dark-haired young woman who sat at an antique desk, studying the guest list for the ball on the Skouros yacht. "We've just had a call from Hollywood. Kate and Steven Spielberg *are* going to attend. He was able to clear his schedule at the last minute."

"Then please do add them to the list," said Princess Gabriella, taking off her reading glasses. The older of the two Costan princesses was twenty-six. Glossy wings of black hair framed her pretty, oval face, but violet smudges of tiredness marked her huge, brown eyes. She had just flown in from New York after another publicity tour to promote her jewelry designs and was suffering from jet lag.

"But there are only twenty-five master staterooms."

"Remember, the Duchess of York had other commitments," said Gaby, who like her sister spoke perfect, idiomatic English, learned while attending school in the United States. "So her suite is vacant."

"Of course, Your Highness."

Across the room at another desk, Princess Kristina, the younger princess, blond and stunningly beautiful, with five Hollywood movies to her credit, was watching as a clerk scrolled through financial figures on a computer screen.

Neither of the princesses had spent more than a few hours a day here in their office at the Vendôme Palace, but they had organized the weekend and would receive all of the credit.

"I wish I knew computers," Kristina murmured to the assistant. She raised her voice. "Oh, Gaby, I think we're going to make a profit of over one million. Maybe even a few hundred thousand more. And best of all, Teddy Warner *is* coming. Her agent just called."

"Do you think Jac is still interested in her?"

"Who knows. He's so fickle!" said Gabriella.

"Well, there were sparks before, Gaby. But, of course, she is a tennis player, and you know what Papa would say. He is so—"

"Papa never bends, does he? I wish—"

"I don't want to be a princess! I don't want to be a princess!" The angry cries of a small child running through the hallway suddenly pierced the air.

Princess Kristina stalked out into the hallway and caught the rampaging three-year-old in her arms. The little girl kicked and wriggled, aiming sharp jabs into the princess's thighs as she was carried back into the room.

"Charlaine, Charlaine," she said, soothing her daughter. "You're hurting me, darling. What *is* wrong?"

The red-faced child was a ravishing copy of her mother, down to her ash-blond curls, rosebud mouth, and perfect, tilted nose. "I *don't* want to wear a pink dress! I don't!"

"Then you shall have a blue dress to match your pretty eyes. You have to help hand out the prizes at the tennis tournament, and you must look your best. Adrienne," added Kristina, calling to one of the secretaries, "would you please phone for Charlaine's nanny? It's time for her nap."

When the child had been taken away, the princesses shared a knowing look.

"Remember that tantrum you had when Papa and Mama were on French television?" asked Gabriella. "*Royal Brat,* the tabloids said."

"I was a brat. But you were just as bad," giggled Kristina. "Remember when you dunked my head in the toilet, saying you didn't see why you had to have a little sister anyway?''

"You were only a baby. How do you remember?"

"Mama told me."

At the mention of their mother, both princesses fell silent. A Swedish beauty and international film star, the fabled Princess Lisse had died in a skiing accident before the horrified eyes of her husband and children ten years earlier. Princess Lisse haunted each of them in a different way. Kristina feared she could never live up to Lisse's glowing star aura. Gaby was ravaged with guilt. Her mother had died for her, trying to rescue the young princess when the avalanche roared down the mountain.

"Well," said Kristina, taking a sip of coffee as she renewed a previous discussion, "what do you think about Nickey Skouros? He isn't donating the *Olympia* for the ball out of the goodness of his heart. He wants something. Probably you."

Gabriella flushed. "He *is* charming, but he's too old. Besides, I have . . . other interests."

Kristina said dismissively, "You mean Cliff Ferguson. That Texan. Well, that doesn't matter to Nickey—he never gives up."

"You mean, Nickey never gives up on *you*. You know Nickey has always wanted you, Kristina, not me. . . ." Gaby paused. "Yes, Cliff is from Texas, and his family are Scottish Jews, and he is terribly rich with his big, American department-store chain. What's wrong with that? I don't know why—" She stopped. "I don't want to argue with you. I'm dead tired, I haven't been to bed since I arrived, and all I want to do is take a nice, long nap."

"Dream of Nickey Skouros," Kristina said, her laugh tinkling.

The ruling monarch of Costa del Mar popped a nitro-glycerin pill under his tongue, waiting a few seconds for it to take effect as he stared at a telegram from the Paris offices of Citibank. They would let him know in two weeks if they approved his formal application for the money to underwrite the public sale of $100 million of Costa del Mar's treasury notes.

Prince Henri thrust it into a pigeonhole in his desk among several other documents and correspondence. Despite the income from its world-famous Casino de Palais, his country's economy hung delicately balanced, under threat from rapacious French officials who wished to reannex it to France, using any legalistic excuse they could devise. Making matters worse, foreign investors had quietly begun to buy up the country's public debentures and parcels of land, urged on by Costan officials who, it was rumored, had accepted bribes to permit dummy corporations to move into controlling positions in the country's economic structure. There had to be a number of individuals involved, but he just wasn't sure who.

Thus far, with loans from Nikos Skouros, he'd managed to maintain the country's financial stability, but each month it grew more difficult. He hoped the international publicity for the charity weekend would give positive signals to the world banking community that his country was still financially strong . . . as well as a sound investment.

Thank God for Nickey Skouros!

Rising, Prince Henri paced the room, which was hung with photographs of himself and his father, Prince Jacques, with various world dignitaries, including Charles de Gaulle and Presidents Eisenhower and Kennedy. Not for the first time, he began to consider Nikos Skouros as a possible son-in-law.

It made sense.

The third-richest man in the world, Skouros exercised power on the highest level. But more than that, Nickey was the sort of man who could deftly handle either one of the princesses.

Henri frowned, his mind ranging to his firstborn. Gabriella needed to be pulled back into the affairs of Costa

del Mar, and Skouros was the man to do it. Henri didn't
consider the nearly thirty years' difference in their ages a
detriment. Skouros would cherish her, give her children,
help her become a strong yet motherly figure—the vibrant
Princess Gabriella that the citizens of Costa del Mar longed
to see.

If they married, Skouros's financial resources would
help solve all the monetary problems of the country, help
refurbish its image. Over the years some of the principality's glamour had eroded, and the casino no longer attracted
the world-famous players. Tourism, with all of its related
business, had fallen off by an alarming twenty-five percent.

Henri frowned again. It always came back to that, didn't
it? Money. But he loved Costa del Mar almost as much as
he cherished his children.

This weekend he would have to make sure that Gabriella
was very attentive to Nikos Skouros.

Aboard the *Olympia*, anchored in the harbor of Port-
Louis, Costa del Mar's capital city, the German banker sat
stiffly on the edge of his seat, his hands splayed on his
knees, as he watched the man seated at the desk scrawl his
quick, slashing signature on several documents.

"Ah. And ah," said Skouros, flicking rapidly from one
page to the next, initialing each one. "Excellent work,
Müller," he said, smiling the rakish grin he was famous
for. "These people will love our generosity. Perfect."

Müller nodded, thinking about his thirty-year relationship with Nikos Skouros. Twice divorced with no children,
Skouros was almost a self-made man, having taken his father's modest shipping business and built it up, tanker by
tanker, into a financial empire that dwarfed Aristotle Onassis's, then branching out into banks, hotels, and real estate. Women adored him, hostesses craved his presence at
their dinner tables, and powerful men boasted that he was
their friend.

The two men began to discuss a new business venture

at length, Müller giving his opinions on what should be done, to which Skouros listened with full attention. Then the phone rang again, interrupting them.

"Yes? Skouros here," said the shipping magnate, picking up on the speaker phone.

It was Sotheby's, in London, calling about his $9.5 million bid for a large Renoir.

"Three quarters of a million more? I think not."

Müller watched as the Greek deftly negotiated. The owner of the painting, a flashy American realtor, owned a huge hotel in Atlantic City that was reputedly in financial trouble.

"Gaming revenues are down because of the recession, everyone knows that, and McGarry himself has just undergone some rather spectacular financial reverses. His bank has reduced his line of credit. . . ."

Skouros began to doodle on a pad of paper, his pen creating quick, deft pyramids locked in other pyramids.

"All right." Nikos Skouros's voice became crisp as he gave his final offer. "I don't believe that nonsense about the Japanese being interested. McGarry is playing games. Tell him I've reduced my offer to eight million, and it's good for twenty-four hours." The Greek financier hung up, smiling. "And now we have a delightful weekend ahead of us. I love American movie stars, don't you? They're so predictable. I expect you to be there, eh, Kaspar?"

Müller nodded.

"I was going to cruise north into the Adriatic," said Skouros, getting up from his desk and going to stand at the raft of windows that overlooked the tiny, picturesque harbor. "But then I decided I couldn't deny the princesses their charity weekend. Costa is a beautiful country, don't you think? So old-world."

SIX DAYS LATER . . .

The SKY WAS DEEPENING TO INDIGO, AND GOSSAMER scarves of salmon-and-fuchsia clouds were stretched, in layers, across the horizon.

Geneviève Mondalivi, thirty-nine-year-old columnist and reporter for *Paris Match,* sat in her car parked near the royal quay, watching as the guests were ferried out to where the *Olympia* was anchored. Each couple had contributed $10,000 for the privilege of rubbing shoulders with Hollywood stars and a plethora of royals, one of whom was a movie star in her own right.

A huge blue helicopter emblazoned with the insignia of the Royal Costan Navy hovered overhead. The stars themselves weren't taking the launch; they would be landing on the yacht's helipad.

Elizabeth Taylor and Larry Fortensky. Joan Collins. Teddy Warner, the golden girl of the tennis courts. Luciano Pavarotti, Gérard Dépardieu. . . . The list went on, encompassing dozens of glitterati and royals, including Princess Stephanie of Monaco and Princess Beatrix of the Netherlands. And the Costan royals, of course, since it was their party, that larger-than-life family who lived their lives under the relentless scrutiny of international publicity.

Geneviève dictated a few notes into her portable recorder, narrowing her eyes at the ship that floated tantalizingly beyond her grasp.

It was the most luxurious ship of its size in the world, 325 feet long, with a grand ballroom, three dining rooms, two kitchens, twenty-five master suites that were the epitome of sybaritic, European luxury. A private screening room seated thirty, and the communications center rivaled that of the U.S. President's plane, Air Force One. The art collection alone was insured for $100 million. A twin-engined, turbo-jet helicopter was carried onboard, along with forty lifeboats, and two twenty-five-foot twin-screw speedboats.

More than 125 crew members served its guests, from epicurean chefs to hairdressers, security guards, masseurs, and secretaries proficient in six languages. Blackjack, roulette, and chemin de fer dealers staffed the ship's glass-mirrored gambling salon.

Another launch, laden with women in chiffon gowns and men in evening jackets, took off from the quay. Genie Mondalvi put the mike of her recorder to her mouth. But instead of dictating more notes, she snapped, *"Merde! Merde!"*

She'd give anything to be aboard tonight.

An orchestra had begun to play, its honeyed violin music drifting in the soft wind. Teddy Warner breathed deeply. It was nearly five years since she'd first been in Costa among the royals, but the feeling was as heady and thrilling as she remembered. She wondered why her father didn't act as thrilled as she was.

"Isn't Princess Gabriella gorgeous?" she whispered, excitedly nudging her father as they stood in the receiving line to greet the owner of the *Olympia,* Nikos Skouros, and their host, Prince Henri.

Teddy glanced down at her own St. Laurent celery-green gown, its hemline daringly slit up her thigh. She had piled her sunstreaked hair high on her head, securing it with pearl clasps.

"Dad"—again she nudged Houston Warner—"look— there's Liz and Larry. God, she *is* beautiful. And I'm sure I saw Ted Turner and Jane Fonda. And I think Randolph and Veronica Hearst."

Suddenly they had reached Skouros, and the Greek shipping magnate reached out both of his hands to encircle hers, his face wreathed in a dazzling smile. Teddy had seen magazine photos of him many times, but in person he was even better looking. A full head of wavy, silver hair. Suntanned skin. Deep blue eyes. A hawkish nose. He projected an energy that reached out to envelop her.

"Teddy Warner, how delightful you could come aboard. The number-one tennis lady in the world. I've followed your career. Thank you for coming."

Charmed, Teddy smiled back.

"And Houston, are you still involved in that project to raise money for the next Olympics? I read about your work—it's wonderful and so vital to the games."

"Yes, yes," said Warner, impressed.

Slowly they moved down the line.

"Teddy," said Princess Gabriella, reaching out to take Teddy's hand. "It's wonderful to see you again. Congratulations on your win today. You really had Eberhardt in deep trouble all day. And thanks—having you play really made the tournament a huge success."

"Thank you."

In a few minutes they were through the receiving line, and a staff member took them to the smaller lounge, where a bar had been set up. People were drifting in and around, the women in gowns designed by every major European couturier, their throats, ears, and wrists glittering with priceless jewels.

Teddy began looking around, searching for Prince Jac. She could hardly wait to see Jac. . . . Had he changed much? Would there still be feelings between them or at least a spark?

She was suddenly nervous.

"Teddy!" cried Princess Kristina, appearing from the lounge, looking glorious in a white crêpe gown that showed off her toast-colored suntan. A choker of diamonds glittered at her neck.

"Kristina!" Teddy was delighted to see her old tennis partner.

The two women hugged. "I missed you!" Kristina

laughed. "I haven't talked to you in so long—I thought you'd forgotten all about us."

Teddy grinned. "With all those wonderful movies you've made? I saw every one three times. Every time I go to a newsstand, you're on a cover, and if it's not you, it's Gabriella."

"Oh, the films were fun to make but I wouldn't call them wonderful. Fortunately, they all made money, so the studios are happy." The princess shrugged modestly. "Have you seen Jac yet?"

"No. . . ."

"Well, he'll be happy to see you. He almost didn't come tonight after all. Something about business—a prototype racing car his company is building."

Teddy nodded, feeling a pang of disappointment. Jac must have known she would be there, but he still had considered not coming to the ball. Not very flattering to her!

Houston Warner mingled with the glittering crowd, noting the faces that had become familiar to him during the past few years, when he'd taken a consuming interest in the Costan Royals. Their politics, their intrigues, their scandals . . . and the aura of danger that seemed subtly to surround them.

Why had he brought Teddy here? Suddenly he wished that he'd discouraged her with a little more firmness. Teddy was the most important person in his life—he hadn't remarried after his wife's accidental death eight years earlier—and now he was wondering if he had done the right thing in bringing her aboard the *Olympia*.

He knew that the girls had become quickly drawn to each other since they'd both had mothers who died tragically in accidents, but he still had reservations about the cruise. Just a sixth sense foreboding.

Teddy's fantasy about Prince Jac had no chance of coming true, he assured himself, but if it ever did, it would mean the end of her tennis career. A tragedy as far as he was concerned. Besides, Warner wasn't at all sure he wanted his beautiful Teddy connected in any way with the Costan royals. He'd learned some things about one of them—

He froze. Approaching from the Grand Salon was a tall, aristocratic figure, Prince Georges, Henri's younger brother. *Even his walk is arrogant*, Warner thought. He moved like a man who believed that he outranked almost everyone else in the world.

Georges was talking to another man in a low voice when his glance briefly fell on Warner, but then flicked coldly away.

Warner continued to make his circuit of the elegant deck, but his thoughts kept returning to Prince Georges. Warner had kept his interest in the royals secret, not even telling Teddy about the obsession that had grown over the years until now he possessed an almost encyclopedic knowledge of Costa del Mar. Recently, however, he'd begun to feel a faint, pricking sensation that perhaps someone did know. . . .

Prince Henri walked slowly along the bridge deck, slightly flushed from the forbidden drink he'd permitted himself. Under Costa's law of succession, if the ruling monarch had only female children *or* if his firstborn was a female, the monarch could appoint any one of his children as the heir, but the latter had to consent to the appointment. Unless Henri could convince one of his children to assume the duties of heir apparent *within the next two years,* Costa del Mar would be acquired by France, and its colorful, glittering tradition of over nine hundred years would be absorbed by the larger country.

Henri felt another stab of chest pain and quickly swallowed another nitroglycerin tablet. What if he were to die before proper arrangements could be made to prepare one of his children to rule the politically troubled principality? Jac had already stated that he did not want to rule—an announcement that had devastated Henri.

Gaby had become a businesswoman, focusing her efforts outside the country. There had been that ugly whispering campaign about her parentage, the controversy, then the attempted attack on her. Would the Costans accept her?

And Kristina—his beautiful, strong-willed Kristina—she preferred being a Hollywood star to seating herself on the throne. Of course, Henri reflected, his brother, Georges, who had recently turned sixty, was vigorous enough to rule, and, Henri suspected, desired to do so very much. Perhaps too much.

Never, thought Henri, feeling the pain again.

Leaving the party hubbub behind, Prince Jac took the stairs near the bridge deck two at a time and headed to Skouros's shipboard office.

"Good evening, Your Highness."

"Good evening. Are there any faxes for me?"

"Yes, sir. Here they are."

Jac flipped through the pile until he spotted a personal message from Gilles Aveyron, the general manager of his new racing company.

Prototype car crashed today at Saint-Tropez. Fuel tanks exploded. Test driver killed.

Jac looked at it in disbelief, then left the office and walked to the opposite deck rail, where he stood staring out over the moonlit harbor. He shuddered; he seldom thought about danger, believing it was bad luck. For some minutes he stood brooding, grieving for the dead driver he had known so well.

"Jac?" said a soft voice behind him. He turned to see Teddy Warner, a light fichu pulled around her shoulders. With her blond hair up, she looked stunning, her eyes huge and feathered with dark, spiky lashes. With an effort Jac drew himself out of his dark mood.

"Teddy Warner," he said, smiling. "How nice to see you. I've . . . thought about you so often."

She had a glowing smile; her beauty struck at him, causing his throat to squeeze.

"I read about you and your racing," she said after a moment. "I've kept up on everything. Even French Morocco."

Jac nodded. Morocco was his most recent win. They began talking awkwardly about Formula One racing, then tennis, sounding more like two strangers on a plane than a man and a woman who had once been lovers.

"This is really a beautiful yacht," Teddy said after a pause. "Do you know Nikos Skouros well?"

"He is an old friend of the family," said Jac stiffly. "A good friend."

They stared intently at the waves again.

The dinner had been fabulous.

Now a rock band pumped the younger couples into a dancing frenzy. Elsewhere on the ship, guests were gambling, playing cards, watching first-run movies, or deep in conversation.

Houston Warner filled in as a fourth at a bridge game in the magnificent, teak-paneled game room, sitting down at a table that included Prince Henri, Nikos Skouros, and Omar Faid, the Egyptian actor who had starred in many American movies in the sixties and seventies.

Warner, partnering with Prince Henri, winced as Henri lost the ace-king finesse to Skouros, giving up a crucial trick.

"You are too quiet tonight, my old friend," Faid smiled toward Henri.

"Ah, between politics, some peculiar business activities, even the . . ." Henri muttered something half under his breath. Hearing his words, Houston Warner narrowed his eyes. So, he thought, some of his information was correct.

"Now, Your Highness, surely you are not referring to a few businessmen like myself?" remarked Skouros smoothly. "After all, I do have a considerable interest in Costa."

"Not legitimate concerns like yours, Nikos. I'm referring to unscrupulous developers—those with no concern for the environment," said Henri, his perfect English only slightly accented. "We are a small country rich with tourist trade and gambling money, and yet not so rich. I have begun to suspect I may have traitors in my own cabinet, my family . . ."

The table fell silent, electrified, as Henri muttered several names. Houston Warner could not hide his amazement. Obviously Henri's tongue had been loosened by his drink, causing him to hint at the most confidential governmental matters.

Suddenly he realized that Nikos Skouros had noticed his elicited interest. Hastily he looked down at his cards, waiting for the prince to begin playing again. *Politics,* Warner thought. So insidious, so circuitous. So dangerous.

At the end of the rubber Warner made an excuse to leave the game and went to his room. He wanted to write the prince's remarks down word for word while he still remembered them. Then he phoned the prince's secretary and left a message that he wished to meet with Prince Henri as soon as possible.

This shipboard cruise was a golden opportunity for him to talk to the prince and warn him in case he did not already know the extent of the conspiracy surrounding him.

"You dance like a young animal," said Jac. It was after three in the morning, the *Olympia* was cruising out at sea, and only the overnight guests remained on board. Prince Henri had long since retired to his suite with a headache, and no one dared to disturb him; his messages would have to wait until morning.

Teddy grinned. "What kind of animal?"

"Oh . . . perhaps a puma. Are there still pumas in America?"

"A few, I think," she said, adding, "but I really don't know," as she seemed to float with the movements of his body.

Jac pulled her close when the orchestra finally slowed down for a romantic ballad, and she was caught up in the heady, delicious sensation.

"I'm going to get some air, hon." An out-of-breath Houston Warner waved to his daughter as he walked off the dance floor.

He wandered the length of the lower deck and finally settled on leaning against the railing and staring out across the water. The moon had an unearthly beauty, casting down silver splashes on the waves.

Gazing at the moonlight on the water, he thought about Prince Henri. He'd left the message, but the prince had gone straight to his cabin. He would try to talk to him early tomorow. Perhaps the prince really didn't suspect the lengths to which—

He sensed more than felt a movement behind him.

"Pardon—" he began politely, turning.

Hands gripped him tightly under the crotch and buttocks, lifting him upward. Startled, Warner let out a yell and clutched desperately at the railing, but he was already going over, pitching downward, and the weight of his falling body tore his grip away.

He landed in the swell of a wave, plunging downward, drenched in so much black water that he could not see which way was up.

Wildly he kicked, the urge for air crushing his lungs. He struggled to the top, swallowing water.

"Teddy!" he shouted.

He kept struggling, but the ship sailed farther and farther away, its deck lights sparkling and winking like a diadem of jewels.

*   *   *

The orchestra was playing a slow ballad.

"You seem distracted," Jac murmured in her ear.

"Well . . . yes," Teddy said. Something had given her a cold feeling, causing a shiver along her bare shoulders.

Flushing, she said, "My dad is wandering around on deck somewhere, or maybe he's gone to his room. I always say good night to him. He has to leave for New York in the morning."

She excused herself and hurried along the deck. A crewman in white duck pants strode past her, brushing her arm so hard that she staggered backward a little.

As she reached the base of the stairs, she thought she heard a muffled shout. Was it her name being called? She turned toward the noise, but when she gazed out over the water, she could see nothing but the enormous silvery swatch of moonlight that danced on the waves.

"Teddy!" She thought she heard it again, even fainter. Then the band started up again, its pulsing beat drowning out all night sounds.

She reached her father's stateroom and knocked on the door, then quietly pushed it open. The lights were out, and the empty room smelled faintly of her father's aftershave. Some papers lay scattered on the floor, unusual for her meticulous father. Again she felt that damp cold, and an uneasy shiver crept over her.

"Daddy!" she gasped. Had he been calling her from—

Gasping with fright, Teddy hurried to the telephone and punched the clearly marked number for the bridge.

"Bridge."

"My father," she screamed. "He's— I think he's fallen overboard!"

"Madame . . ." began a placating male voice.

"He's fallen overboard! Hurry, damn you! Hurry and look for him!"

* * *

The *Olympia* had turned and was circling back over her previous route, floodlights illuminating every deck and the surrounding waters, crewmen scanning the eerily lit waves through binoculars. Every room on the vessel was being searched, in the event Houston Warner had collapsed somewhere and was lying ill or injured. Nikos Skouros stood on the bridge deck with an electronic megaphone as he directed the two support boats in the search.

Powered by twin turbines, the Augusta 109 helicopter clattered overhead, its powerful searchlights probing the distant waters.

"This can't be allowed to happen." Prince Henri shook his head sadly. His heart was hammering. Even two nitroglycerin pills hadn't helped. "Nikos, tell your captain to radio to Admiral Maurer at the Royal Naval Base."

"Certainly, Your Highness." A nod from Skouros and a crewman at his side headed to the bridge.

"How could he have fallen overboard?" Henri muttered, his eyes still on the waters.

"An accident," said Skouros. "Or perhaps he jumped. There is always that possibility. Perhaps he had overwhelming business problems. . . . One never knows."

Exhaustion suddenly flooded Prince Henri. A vicious angina pain clamped down on his left arm, radiating downward from his chest and neck. Henri gasped, stiffening until it was over.

"Your Highness?" said Skouros in concern.

"It's nothing," Henri said hoarsely. "Just . . . continue to search. *Please.*"

Long lines of clouds stretched over the shoreline, now blazing with dawn colors. Houston Warner had not been found.

On board the *Olympia,* Teddy covered her eyes. How could she live without her father?

Teddy was numb.

                    *   *   *

"I've brought you some breakfast," said Kristina. The youngest Costan princess carried a tray from the *Olympia*'s galley, bringing it herself to Teddy.

"I couldn't."

"Teddy . . . I don't know how to say this. . . . Nikos asked me to come and talk to you."

"I don't want to hear." Her eyes glazed with tears, Teddy turned her face away. "I wish we'd never come on board this ship."

"Teddy, they have searched more than eight hours. Your father is nearly sixty years old. The odds are . . . well, that he couldn't stay afloat that long. Skouros and the Royal Navy are going to continue the search for a day longer, but even the Navy believes that your father is gone."

"No. *No!*"

"I'm very sorry," Kristina said in a shaking voice. "If there is anything any of us can do, just ask and it will be done."

Teddy stared out at the smoothly cresting waves, on which sea birds rode. *Dad,* she thought, staring at the waves. *I love you, Daddy. You gave me so much. More than I ever appreciated. In a way you made me who I am.*

Too stunned to think, she pushed away the vague image of someone in white almost knocking her over the night before . . . but hadn't that person been running away from the deck area?

Her mind hardened. Her father had been reluctant to come aboard, she remembered now. And that time in New York, didn't he tell her he thought he was being followed? She'd discounted it then—this *was* real life, not the movies—but now the idea worried her.

As they entered the beautiful harbor of Port-Louis, nestled at the bottom of the pink, wedding-cake casino, and saw the magnificent yachts flying multicolored flags from all over the world, all the grief in Teddy coalesced into certainty.

Suddenly she knew.

Someone had pushed her father overboard, she thought, her heart hammering with grief and rage. But who? And for what reason?

MAY 1988

Teddy WARNER TROTTED OUT OF THE WOMEN'S dressing room, her short, swirly tennis skirt flipping in the warm breeze.

She ran to the waiting area near center court, which was grass, manicured to a thick, velvety green. Overlooking the courts were the buff-colored walls of the palace of Costa del Mar, its graceful towers rising at varying levels, each tower flying a blue-and-white pennant.

"Your first time playing against royals?" said Auggie Steckler, grinning at her as he shoved his forelock of white-blond hair away from his deeply tanned forehead. At twenty-four, he was the "bad boy" of tennis, famous for throwing tantrums on the court.

"Yes. How did you guess?"

"Somehow I knew." August Steckler leaned close to Teddy, managing to brush up against her. "Do you want some advice? Don't give an inch to them—the fans will like you better and the royals will too."

Teddy straightened her spine. "I wasn't planning to."

"That's my girl."

"And I'm not your girl," she said.

To Teddy, Costa del Mar seemed a fairy-tale setting, more like a Hollywood movie set than a principality with seventy thousand citizens.

Canopy-shaded bleachers were packed with spectators for this special Pro-Am, each of whom had paid $1,000 for the privilege of watching Teddy and Prince Jac play doubles with Auggie Steckler and Princess Kristina in a charity match to benefit handicapped children.

Teddy swallowed nervously as she waited with Auggie for the two young royals to arrive.

There was an excited buzz in the crowd, followed by a burst of music as the band suddenly struck up the Costan national anthem.

A young man and woman, dressed in tennis whites, had appeared and were walking down the pathway, grassy and bordered with flowers, that led from the Vendôme Palace. Escorting them were two stone-faced, blue-uniformed Costa del Mar soldiers. Prince Jac was tall, lean, and sun-tanned, and the D.O.C. wraparound sunglasses he was wearing could not hide his handsome face. Kristina was small, lithe, with a mane of champagne-colored hair.

As the two royals progressed, the applause grew, and the crowd in the bleachers began to stand.

"My gawd," Teddy couldn't help muttering.

"You must be Teddy Warner," said Princess Kristina, walking up to Teddy and extending a hand to her. Her hand was small, smooth, and warm.

"Yes, I—I'm Teddy, Your Highness."

Kristina's laugh was casual and rippling. "Oh, call me Kristina. All my friends do. Thank you for being here."

"We've followed your career for a long time," said Prince Jac, looking down at Teddy. He had a square jaw, and even though he was still two months short of being eighteen, he had the rangy, muscular build of a man of twenty-five.

A referee was motioning them onto the court preparatory to starting their match.

Bedazzled, Teddy and the others walked onto the court, to another round of applause.

As soon as she was on the court, Teddy's apprehensions about playing with a prince fell away. She knew her father, seated in a front-row box seat, would be rooting fiercely for her to win. He always did.

Now, with Prince Jac as her partner, she began to experience a competitive burst of adrenaline.

They took the first two games.

Across the net, Auggie Steckler was playing his usual fierce, individualistic game, battering the ball, running with tight-muscled ferocity, virtually ignoring Princess Kristina, who missed many of the balls aimed at her side of the court.

"Sorry," Kristina called at one point as the ball sped past her.

"Move your ass, dammit!" Steckler snapped.

"Don't be so crude," Kristina snapped back, putting a spin on her next serve, her blond hair flying, a light patina of sweat gleaming on her face.

Teddy played her best game, running quickly up to the net and putting the ball away with a blazing passing shot for game, set, and match point.

Teddy and her father cabbed back to their hotel, the Crillon, a fantastic pile of aqua stucco that was famous for its gingerbread ornamentation. On the way Teddy mentally ran through her wardrobe for dinner at the palace that evening, wondering whether she'd packed an appropriate gown.

"Oh, Dad, I always look like a tennis player. And my hair . . ." Anxiously Teddy touched the thick golden braid she wore hanging down the middle of her back. "I had no idea this would be so . . . European, so regally formal."

"Your hair is wonderful, and you look wonderful. If you want, we can send out to one of those exclusive little shops for a more fabulous dress."

"Something beaded and glamorous," Teddy decided. "And I want a hairdresser, Dad. Does my braid look too old-fashioned?"

"Darling"—Houston Warner smiled at his daughter— "didn't you notice?—some of the women in the stands were wearing their hair just like yours. You've started a trend, honey. Be yourself tonight—I'm sure that's what they are all looking forward to."

A limousine arrived promptly at eight to pick them up. Teddy wore an off-the-shoulder white silk petal gown with silver-beaded sequins that made her look as ethereal as a filmy white cloud. Her blond hair was pulled back at her temples, brushed out to hang in rippling curls down her back, the remainder braided and strung with iridescent pearls.

They drove through a gate in a fifteen-foot-high wall guarded by sentries, then passed two more blue-and-white-striped sentry boxes, before proceeding into a bricked courtyard edged by a lawn and formal manicured gardens. Stone nymphs and cherubs gamboled in a gushing fountain.

"This is fantastic," breathed Teddy, looking around her.

"Much more glamorous than the palace at Monaco," commented Warner.

"Poke me. Pinch me. I think I'm dreaming this."

All around them soared the ancient walls of the Vendôme Palace. Home of the Bellini dynasty since the 1400s, the palace had had many additions in the following centuries. Mullioned windows looked down—hundreds of them. The palace was said to have more than 120 rooms, many of them no longer in use.

The car pulled under a porte cochere, and the driver parked. A doorman hurried forward to let them out. Two sentries stood at duty here as well, their handsome faces young and expressionless.

"You are expected in the entrance hall, where the majordomo will take you to the small ballroom in the east wing," said the driver.

"Whoa," exclaimed Teddy, giggling nervously.

As they progressed deeper into the palace, Teddy's curiosity changed to awe, then to a stunned feeling that gradually gave way to awe again. The Bellini palace had been "modernized" several times in the past centuries, and its interior now was a rococo mixture of Versailles and Belle Époque.

The ballroom was endless, its length marked off by two rows of ecru-colored marble colonnades. Its windows were draped with pale raspberry silk draperies, its walls hung with stunning Impressionist paintings. A mural overhead showed nymphs flying among clouds, their flowing robes highlighted with gilt. Chairs covered in deeper raspberry lined the walls, and a small orchestra played on a dais. Banks of flowers were everywhere, emitting fragrant wafts of perfume.

"If this is the 'small' ballroom, I wonder how huge the 'big' one is," Teddy whispered to her father, as they were being announced.

A long dinner table had been set up for twenty, glittering with silver, crystal, and exquisite Limoges china place settings.

"You're here—I'm so glad to see you off the court, Teddy, and to meet your father," said Princess Kristina, coming forward.

Kristina wore a strapless teal gown that revealed her golden, tanned skin and her perfect shoulders. Around her neck was a gold chain, on which hung a circlet of diamonds framing the hugest blue sapphire that Teddy had ever seen. Although Teddy knew that Kristina was only nineteen, her own age, she seemed ageless tonight, brushed with a glow of European sophistication.

"I love the palace," Teddy blurted nervously. "But how do you—that is—do you really live in such . . . such . . . I mean, how do you relax here? I mean . . ." She subsided in embarrassment.

Kristina threw back her head and laughed. "The rooms you saw are formal rooms—we only use them when we are entertaining heads of state. Our family quarters are much smaller, and far more intimate. If you wish, I'll show you later. We even have an indoor swimming pool and a screening room, and Jac has a weight room. And I have a whole room full of dolls that I collected when I was a little girl. Come—I want you to meet my sister Gaby.''

Princess Gabriella, in ice blue, extended both hands to take Teddy's, her smile revealing white, perfect teeth. ''You and my brother made quite a team, Teddy Warner. Jac refuses to play with me—he says I don't run hard enough.''

Gabriella was stunning in a slim, exotic way.

''Your necklace,'' Teddy exclaimed. ''It's just beautiful!''

''I designed it myself.''

''You did?''

Gabriella flushed with pleasure, fingering the breathtaking woven necklace of multicolored, semiprecious stones. ''I've been working with a jeweler here in Costa del Mar, but it is difficult. My being there attracts crowds to his shop and interferes with his business.''

Teddy and her father circulated among the other guests, Prince Alexander of Greece, Costan officials and their wives, some of the other tennis stars: Auggie Steckler, Martina Navratilova, Steffi Graf, and Ivan Lendl.

''Have you heard that the princesses are at each other's throats over a man?'' asked Karen Roth, one of the top women players on the circuit.

''What man?'' asked Teddy curiously.

''Jean-Luc Furnoir. Gabriella was engaged to him first, and after breaking up with her, he's now got a hot thing going with Kristina.''

''But''—Teddy shook her head in bewilderment—''I just saw both of them together and they were wonderful together.''

Karen threw back her head and laughed. ''Oh, that's just their public personality. The tabloids say that they argue a lot behind closed doors. They say Gabriella is jealous because Kristina is so pretty, and Kristina is jealous because

Gabriella has a real talent, something she can do with her life.''

Prince Jac arrived late, casually sauntering into the ball-room wearing impeccably tailored evening clothes. Teddy's heart began to pound—he *was* so attractive—but before she could even smile at him, the young prince was taken in hand by a beautiful young woman. Over her shoulder he shot her a rueful look and shrugged, as if to say, *I can't help it.*

Prince Henri entered the ballroom next, wearing a blue uniform that blazed with medals, a white sash angling across his chest, a silver scabbard dangling from his belt. He was a dark-eyed, handsome, elderly man with a full head of snow-white hair and a perfectly chiseled nose, and looked every inch the old-world monarch. Since the death of his wife five years earlier, he had remained single.

Gabriella went over to greet her father and, on his arm as his hostess, began receiving a long line of guests, greet-ing each one with a few gracious words. Someone handed her a bouquet of deep pink roses and Gabriella leaned for-ward and kissed the man on both cheeks, handing the bou-quet to a servant.

When Teddy was presented to him, Prince Henri gave her a warm smile. "You set a good example for my younger daughter," he told her. "Perhaps you would be willing to stay in Costa del Mar for a few days and give her some tennis lessons? If there is time on your busy schedule," he added politely.

"I'd—I'd love to," Teddy said, electrified with surprise.

Prince Georges, dressed in a gray Savile Row suit that displayed his still-well-proportioned, fifty-five-year-old body, despised the obvious curiosity of the American tennis stars. *C'est stupide.* Naive, that's what they were.

He was standing with Étienne D'Fabray, the Costan fi-nance minister.

"My brother is on borrowed time," he murmured to the

minister, glancing at Prince Henri, who reigned over the far end of the room, receiving his guests.

"Ah," said D'Fabray noncommittally. At fifty-two, he had held his position only ten years, making him practically a newcomer in the bureaucratic government.

"He is getting old. He has been having angina attacks for years. He has concealed this medical condition from the rest of the country, but I have my very good sources; I even have access to his EKG reports. Not much escapes me."

"I see," said D'Fabray, looking interested. Instinctively the two men withdrew into a small alcove.

"He could keel over at any time, throwing the country into disarray," Georges went on. "And who will succeed Henri? Prince Jac? A *jeune homme* still in his teens? In six months, Jac would have roulette wheels in the palace, race-car drivers in the throne room, and nude girls in the swimming pool. Plenty of those."

The minister cleared his throat. "Perhaps you are right."

Georges moved closer, lowering his voice. "Henri himself disapproves of Jac, I have been told. He does not like having a playboy for a son. In the past, you know, Costan rulers have petitioned the Parliament to alter the line of succession—"

"Not in seventy years," said the minister.

"But it could happen. If it does, I could be chosen. . . . I am far better suited to run this country than a recalcitrant youth," Georges said contemptuously. "But this cannot come from me, naturally. You have Henri's ear, your advice is well received by him."

The minister frowned. "I am loyal to my prince."

Georges drew back, his expression congealing. "But my dear D'Fabray," he said, "you have certain gambling markers outstanding at the casino—markers you have had trouble repaying. Your markers at Casino Royale total more than five hundred thousand francs."

The minister's eyes widened slightly.

"Further," said Georges, "you are using your wife's inheritance, aren't you? Without her knowledge. Very, very dangerous."

"Yes, yes . . ." The minister began shifting uncomfortably. "Tell me what it is you want, Your Highness."

Georges spoke in a low voice. "I want to . . ."

He paused, swallowing his words. L. Houston Warner had come up beside them and was addressing Georges.

"Pardon me, could you tell me where I might find a telephone?" the entrepreneur asked in his American-accented French.

"One should ask a servant, of course," snapped Georges, turning away rudely. Warner looked startled, then walked quietly away.

"I want to be number one in this country," Georges continued. "Do you understand, D'Fabray? If anyone helps me, he will be handsomely rewarded . . . and his wife will never learn that he is embezzling from her accounts."

D'Fabray hesitated. "Whatever you wish, Your Highness."

Houston Warner backed away with embarrassment and more than a touch of anger. What had those two narrow-nosed specimens been talking about? It had sounded very much to him as if one was trying to bribe the other.

He asked directions twice, and finally was told by a servant that a telephone could be found in the men's cloak-room located down the corridor to the left.

"Could you tell me who those two gentlemen are?" he asked. "The ones standing in the alcove near the blue painting?"

"That is Prince Georges, sir, and Monsieur Étienne D'Fabray, the minister of finance."

"Of course," said Warner.

The cloakroom, its walls covered in dark red silk and hung with hunting paintings, looked unchanged since 1815. Warner discovered a modern, Touch-Tone telephone along with a fax machine, apparently for the use of guests.

Swiftly punching in numbers, he was connected to his New York office, but all the while he kept thinking about Prince Georges and the whispered conversation.

A bribe? Costan politics was a real snakepit, Warner had read, and obviously Georges was one of the players.

"Oh, yes, and Mary Katherine," he said abruptly at the end of his call, "go to the library and look up Costa for me, will you? Especially Prince Georges, that's the younger brother. Just get everything you can on him, okay? I've suddenly got a curiosity about him. Make up a file, eh? I'll read it when I get back to the office."

After the two-hour, eight-course dinner, Princess Kristina dragged Teddy away from a group of tennis players, insisting on showing her the family's private quarters.

"You *are* going to stay and work with me on my tennis game, then?" she asked Teddy as they were walking through the long corridors again, passing door after door. "I hoped Papa would ask you."

"I'd love to! After the tournament here, I do have a ten-day hiatus before I have to go on to the next one. The only problem is I practice six hours a day, run an additional two hours, I lift weights, then do aerobics for another hour. I can't stop my training schedule."

"*I'll* practice with you," declared Kristina. "I'll be your hitting partner. And I can run with you. Have you ever done any beach running? It's wonderful for the legs."

"Great! It's a deal."

The family quarters were as warm and welcoming as the rest of the palace was intimidating.

Kristina's bedroom had been decorated in Belle Époque by Karl Lagerfeld, who owned a villa nearby. The walls were covered with stenciled leaf-green satin. There were several furniture groupings, chairs and couches upholstered in a pale chintz. Charming window seats were deep enough not only to sit on but also to curl up and read in.

Lying on one of the window seats was a copy of the French edition of *Vogue*.

"*I* was going to be on the cover," Kristina explained, a note of disappointment entering her voice. "But Papa wouldn't allow me to sign the contract. He said he didn't want me to be involved in the modeling world."

Her bed, with carved posts and a canopy, dominated one end of the room. Nearby was a stereo system and shelves stocked with a vast supply of CD's of French, English, and American rock groups. Dozens of fashion magazines were stacked on bookshelves, along with books about Hollywood.

"Here is one of my dressing rooms," said Kristina, striding on ahead of her through a doorway. "There's also a Jacuzzi. I had it installed last year."

"I love it," enthused Teddy.

"Gaby's suite is at the other end of the hall," Kristina said. "There is a secret tunnel in this wing. In fact, there are four secret rooms in the palace and two tunnels. Isn't that wonderful? I use one of the tunnels when I wish to go out discoing and don't want the sentries to know."

"Oh," said Teddy, amazed.

"Shall I show you? One of the tunnels isn't far from here—it's a little dirty and musty, but if we're careful, we won't ruin our dresses."

Kristina lit a candle from a box that was kept near the entrance of a large, cool wine storage room that held more than two thousand bottles of French wine, carefully stored in racks.

"We have to use candles because the tunnel isn't lit," the young princess explained. She walked over to one of the wine racks, pushed down on a particular bottle of wine, and the entire rack swung aside, exposing a long, dark space that stretched into the night.

"My ancestors had to keep escape exits here in case the palace was ever overrun by enemies," Kristina explained.

"During World War II they hid Jews and members of the French resistance here. They sent them out through this tunnel to the sea, where submarines were waiting to take them north along the coast of Bretagne and then across the English Channel. If Papa knew I was using the tunnel to sneak out, he'd probably have it boarded up."

Bending over slightly, they crept through the tunnel, which slanted downward, finally branching off in two directions. The chill of damp stone made Teddy shiver.

"If we go that way, we'll reach the beach," said Kristina. "The other way leads toward the boardwalk. From there it's only a five-minute walk to Hippolyte's—that's my favorite disco. Do you dance, Teddy?"

"A little."

Kristina's eyes seemed sparkling and eager in the candlelight, her face ethereally beautiful. "You must come dancing with us, then—tonight! It will be such fun! And in a few days, after you win the tournament, we'll start playing tennis."

Teddy hesitated. The tournament's quarterfinals for women were beginning tomorrow.

"Please?" begged Kristina.

Teddy thought of all the long hours of practice that had begun when she was six years old, the constant traveling, the high school friends she'd never had, the prom she'd never attended because she had to play in a tournament, the college courses she had to take by correspondence, so as not to interrupt her career. Now a princess wanted to be her friend.

She couldn't help it; she started to laugh. "I'll come with you," she said. "I have to warn you, I haven't danced much."

"I'll teach you," promised Kristina.

The disco was packed with beautiful people and celebrities, as well as a few tennis players who'd already lost their matches.

True to her word, Kristina taught Teddy the latest dance moves, which she picked up quite easily. She had phoned her father to tell him where she was, and tried to ignore his angry protests.

Teddy danced with a succession of partners, a French *coiffeur* renowned for his unusual haircuts, a famous race car driver, and the son of a prominent French actress. Dancing, whirling, she felt a giddy sense of freedom and happiness.

At 2:20 A.M, Prince Jac showed up.

"Do you like my country?" he asked her as they moved rhythmically to the loud, pounding band music, which never seemed to slow its beat. He had a natural, animal sensuality that came alive when he danced, and Teddy could hardly tear her eyes away from the young prince's gyrating, sexy body. He seemed much older than seventeen. Well, he was going to be eighteen soon, she reminded herself. And she was nineteen, so the age difference wasn't that great.

"I love it!"

"Would you like to see more of it?"

She felt a burst of excited pleasure. "I'd love to."

"I'm going out in a glider tomorrow—the cliffs around here are perfect for hang gliding. Maybe you'd like to come. The views are breathtaking."

Teddy reluctantly shook her head. "Not until after the tournament is over, and even then I can't afford to risk getting injured. But . . . I'd love to see Costa del Mar," she added.

Jac gazed at her with his deep blue eyes that held an inner spark of laughter. "I'll show you the *real* Costa del Mar—not the one they write about in the magazines."

Teddy moaned as the alarm clock buzzed, and with her eyes still closed she groped for the shut-off button. She blinked her eyes open. It was another perfect, sunny Costa del Mar morning. In the courtyard below her hotel room she could hear the splashing fountain and the muffled roar of a hedge clipper.

She sat up, throwing aside her sheets. Her head was throbbing from all the wine she'd drunk, both at the palace and at Hippolyte's. Getting out of bed, she spotted a tabloid she'd purchased yesterday after practice.

Did Princesses Fight Over Furnoir? screamed the headline, over a photo spread that juxtaposed two pictures of Kristina and Gabriella facing each other. Between them had been placed a photo of a man with dark good looks and a dazzling smile. Teddy had seen him last night in the disco, dancing with Kristina.

Teddy settled down to read the story, which wasn't nearly as scandalous as its headline implied. Apparently Gabriella had been engaged to the man for less than a month; then the couple broke up, refusing to talk about their relationship to the press. Almost a year later Furnoir and Kristina began seeing each other.

Now palace sources say that Furnoir and Kristina will be announcing their engagement within weeks. . . .

Typical media hype, she thought. The princesses faced it every day of their lives.

Her bedside phone rang, and Teddy picked it up.

"Well, you're finally up," came her father's voice. "I was beginning to wonder—after dancing all night it's a miracle you're awake at all. I hope you can manage to drag yourself down to the court for a practice session."

"Dad . . . , there won't be any problem."

"There *is* a problem. You've got your first match tonight at seven-thirty, Teddy, have you forgotten? You can't afford to blow it."

"I won't blow it."

"I can't believe you could be so careless with your career, Teddy. Discoing until nearly dawn—it was totally irresponsible. I hope you don't pay for it tonight. Now I suggest you get up and get some breakfast and get down to the court. Manuel is already waiting for you."

Manuel Muñoz was her hitting partner, a tennis pro who traveled with her.

Teddy sighed. "Don't worry, Pops, I'll win tonight. As for my being out late, don't you understand? I was out with *Princess Kristina*. And I'm going to stay here for a week or so, and . . . well, give her some tennis lessons."

"*Tennis lessons?* Teddy, you haven't got time to—"

"I'll make time."

There was a long pause. "Teddy, tennis doesn't forgive mistakes. You have to have one goal, and one goal only. You have to—"

"Dad—"

"If you allow this fantasy thing with the royals to interfere with your game, Teddy, you're going to regret it."

"Dad, I like Kristina, I love Costa del Mar, and this is something I want to do. I'll win the tournament, I promise. And after that, a few days here aren't going to hurt anything."

The forty-room, sand-colored villa was perched high on the crags overlooking Costa del Mar, reached by a winding road that switchbacked several times. It was built in Spanish-style architecture, its roof tiles a muted, dusty red. An enormous flagged terrace overlooked the glittering Atlantic.

"I won't be upstaged by my spoiled nieces and irresponsible nephew," said Prince Georges, speaking sharply.

"Of course, I can understand that," said Nikos Skouros. He had just emerged from his sixty-foot lap pool, rivulets of water running down his hard, compact body. Georges eyed his host's physique with some envy. His own body, although still slim, was not quite as firm as it had been a few years ago. The only exercise he got now was an occasional hunting trip in the Pyrénées.

"It is ridiculous to entrust a country to wild juveniles who are more interested in parties, tennis, modeling, and car races than they are in financial matters. Kristina is a disgrace, dancing in the discos until dawn, and Gabriella is just a pretty young girl. As for Jac, he is growing up into a reckless playboy.''

"Of course you are right."

"Whereas I . . ."—Georges paused to give weight to his words—"*I* could do something with Costa."

"Indeed you could," said Nikos Skouros, toweling off his silvery hair, which glinted in the bright sunshine. "But these are extremely private thoughts you're sharing with me; I am sure you would not wish your opinions on such matters known to others. They must be held in the strictest of confidence, and I, of course, will honor the trust you place in me now. Why have you come to me?"

"I think we could work something out that's of mutual benefit."

"Ah," said Skouros, raising a quizzical eyebrow.

"You are interested in developing the country. You have attempted to obtain a gambling license and were turned down."

Skouros nodded. "Your brother Henri believes that I would flood the country with Mafia-type gamblers. He wishes to appeal only to those certain few, the international jet set, to whom price means absolutely nothing. But that group comprises only a relatively small number of people. Thousands with modest incomes would rush to buy condos here. Many more thousands would stay in newer, less expensive hotels. Henri does not realize the huge financial possibilities inherent in this country."

"*I* realize them," said Georges. He leaned forward, speaking earnestly but in hushed tones. "If I were to become ruler here, many things would change. I would be much more open to, ah, say investments by outside individuals. Even gambling as it is encouraged in Las Vegas and Atlantic City."

"If you become ruler," said Nickey Skouros, narrowing his eyes reflexively.

The men continued to talk until a drift of clouds blew in from over the Pyrénées and rendered the terrace too chilly and breezy, whereupon they moved into the villa and talked for several hours more.

Houston Warner sat in the first row of box seats. It was the final match.

As Teddy raced around the court, forcing Monica Seles to fight back with her powerful groundstokes and drive volleys, he leaned forward tensely, calling out a running monologue throughout the match. "Come on, Teddy, hit the ball.... Power it.... Oh, nice shot!... Smash it through.... Oh, yes!"

Once, when Teddy seemed briefly to lose her concentration and skid on a slick place, Warner tensed, banging his fist onto his knee. She was losing her edge.

Tensely he watched Teddy use her strength to run the tough Yugoslav around the court, controlling every big rally. In less than an hour the score was 6–2, 4–2. Cheers rose from the royal enclosure, echoed by the rest of the audience.

Teddy was going to win this one after all—she was a true champion.

"Your Highness, my shop is much too small for you, and it is ridiculous that someone as creative as yourself should waste her time attempting to make individual pieces of jewelry. Really, Your Highness, it is completely impractical."

Monsieur Épinalle owned the jewelry shop established by his great-grandfather, which had held the royal warrant for more than one hundred years. She adored making her sketches and trying to see if she could bring them to glittering life. But she'd begun to realize that she had no skills as an artisan. His remark stabbed Gabriella with disappointment.

"I suppose you are right, monsieur," she said in a low voice, putting down the makings of the elegant bangle she'd been attempting, rather unsuccessfully, to set with rubies. "It's just that I like doing these things. . . ."

"But Your Highness!" The jeweler stared at her in surprise. "I didn't mean that you should stop. You have a true gift of design. Your conceptions are stunning. But there should be a staff of jewelers working to execute your designs."

Gabriella rose, moisture filling her eyes, tears that she carefully blinked back.

Épinalle went to a small office and began flipping through a Rolodex until he had located a telephone number, then jotted it down on a sheet of paper. "This is the number of Kenneth Jay Lane in New York, an old friend of your family."

"Of course," said Gaby, taking the paper. Kenny Lane was a brilliant designer of costume jewelry, owner of a chain of deluxe boutiques, patronized by Elizabeth Taylor, Gloria Vanderbilt, and most of society's beautiful and wealthy women. But more than that, he had known the family for years, since he had first begun designing costume jewelry for Princess Lisse.

"I know he doesn't work with *others* ordinarily, but for you, he might make an exception."

Gabriella stared down at the number. The jeweler's remarks reverberated in her mind. Her conceptions were stunning? She had talent? She sank back into her chair again, her heartbeat slamming up into her throat.

Teddy stood proudly tall as the Costan national anthem played, and Prince Henri presented her with a check for $50,000 and a gold statue of a female tennis player.

"You were *wonderful*," cried Princess Kristina, hurrying up to her as she left center court to the loud patter of applause. "Take a quick shower and change, and then we're going to have a party at Hippolyte's. We've rented the whole place just for tonight."

Teddy nodded and agreed. She wanted to laugh with pleasure. A week ago it had been nothing but dull practice.

Now she was partying every night!

The pink stucco nightclub, emblazoned with neon signs, had been built into a rocky hillside. Its parking lot was jammed with Ferraris, Alfa Romeos, Mercedes, and a few limos.

The chef had prepared a feast of langoustines and shrimp, various salads, and a huge selection of pastas and cassoulets, along with French pastries. About sixty young people crowded around the buffet table, many of the girls wearing dresses so abbreviated that most of their glowing skin showed. Teddy recognized Monaco's Princess Stephanie and actress Nastassia Kinski. But she did not see Jac.

"I envy you," said Princess Gabriella, who had come to stand beside Teddy. Her cheeks seemed flushed with excitement, her dark prettiness striking. "You travel all over the world to play tennis—you are so free."

Teddy turned to look at the older Costan princess, who was wearing a miniskirt and bandeau top under a gauze blouse, her wrists jangling with dozens of gorgeous bracelets of hammered silver set with colored stones.

"Free?" said Teddy, laughing. "If you only knew! Every minute of my day is accounted for. It's tennis, tennis, and more tennis."

"It sounds wonderful," said Gaby, her eyes shining. "I'd love to be that devoted to something."

Teddy stared at her. "But I thought—I mean, you're a princess."

Gabriella held up her arm, so that the beautiful bracelets fell toward her elbow. "Yes," she said a little sadly. "I am a princess."

Just as the rock band began to play, a late-arriving guest appeared, a good-looking man in his late thirties. Teddy recognized Jean-Luc Furnoir, the darkly tanned man whose picture she had seen in the tabloid.

Teddy saw Gabriella catch her breath, her face flushing a dark shade of pink. For a frozen moment it looked as if

Gaby might actually run toward Jean-Luc. But it was Princess Kristina, instead, who ran toward him, holding out both of her arms eagerly.

Gabriella turned and stalked toward the door, her face ashen. As she reached the door, where *paparazzi* had gathered, flash bulbs suddenly popped.

In the ladies' room Kristina was back-combing her mane of champagne-colored curls, fluffing them into a wild, tousled torrent.

"Now she's done it—created more scandal," Kristina muttered, as Teddy stood beside her at the mirror, reapplying her lipstick. "We agreed between us—we agreed that he wasn't right for her. Now she makes a public display of her jealousy. The *paparazzi* just wait for something like that to happen, then they sell their pictures to the tabloids and Papa becomes furious with us."

Teddy stared at the princess. "You agreed? But I thought—I mean, it said in the paper that she was originally engaged to Jean-Luc."

"Of course, she was!" Kristina said. "But they had a quarrel, and Gaby really didn't love him. She only wanted him because Papa thought he would make a terrible husband. Ah, Gaby only hurts herself. She said she had no real feelings left for him, and we decided she would publicly drop the engagement after only three weeks. And now . . . just because I have been seeing him, suddenly she thinks she loves him again."

Teddy shook her head, imagining the field day the tabloids would have tomorrow.

"Anyway," said Kristina, smiling brilliantly, "what does that matter now? I'll talk to Gaby tomorrow morning. Let's go and dance. I *love* to dance."

"My sisters have always been at each other's throats," explained Jac the next day, as he took Teddy for a ride on a minibike through the streets of Port-Louis. His English was flawless.

"For a short while after Gaby was born, she was the heir to the throne and was treated as Her Serene Highness. Then Kristina was born, and I came along later, and Gaby wasn't the heir apparent any longer. Besides which, there were . . . rumors about Gaby's birth. My mother had a problem getting pregnant, and she visited a fertility clinic in Switzerland. My father visited her there, and while he was visiting her, she became pregnant. They did not want information about the clinic visit to be leaked to the world, but naturally people talked anyway."

Jac gave an eloquent Gallic shrug. "They said Gaby was the same as illegitimate—a bastard child not belonging to my father."

"But how terrible for her," remarked Teddy.

"Yes. After a while the whispers mostly stopped. But some people still believe they are true. Poor Gaby has enemies, and it has been hard on her."

Teddy frowned sympathetically. "Then your mother died. That must have hurt her very much, too."

Jac nodded. "Gaby idolized our mother. Mama was trying to push her out of the way of the snow when it happened. Gaby feels as if the whole family blames her for this, as if she alone is at fault. And sometimes I think my sister Kristina *does* blame Gaby for causing Mama's death. Who knows? All I know is that one minute they love each other; the next they are fighting like—how do you Americans say?—cats and kittens."

"It's 'cats and dogs,'" Teddy said, giggling.

It was a wonderful day. The sky, blue-washed, was dotted with white, billowy clouds, and everywhere flowers blazed, growing in beautiful and lush green *jardinières*. Teddy felt a burst of pleasure and energy. No practice today. She was just going to be a tourist, enjoying the sights, like any other nineteen-year-old American girl lucky enough to be in Costa del Mar.

The capital city of Port-Louis was a pretty town with winding, hilly streets lined with stuccoed old-world hotels painted in pastel colors, and shops that sold everything from designer beachwear to perfume. Every few hundred yards there was a blue-and-white-striped sentry box, manned by a huge, immaculately uniformed sentry.

"Why do you have so many sentries?" Teddy asked Jac when they stopped for a lemon *glace* at a snack bar.

"It's just tradition, like the Queen's military guards around Buckingham Palace." Then he added, "Anyway, let's get out of here. I know a wonderful beach I can show you—the kind they don't have in America."

They jumped back on their motorized bike and sped down the cobbled streets, past cafés, a butcher's shop that sold joints of mountain lamb and plump, juicy rabbits, and numerous seafood bistros that advertised *"fruits de mer"*—shrimp, lobster, and crab meat—as well as *glaces* and *galettes* for dessert.

The boardwalk, the Boulevard de la Croisette, stretched along a mile of white sand. They motored to the end of it, weaving in and out of groups of strolling pedestrians. Some of the women were topless, and others wore little more than a thong.

"Here, we'll leave our minibike now," the prince said, and they leaned the bike against a tree and continued to walk on the beach, where thousands of bathers sunned themselves or sheltered under striped beach umbrellas. A mile-long row of cabanas was ranged behind them, in vivid greens, blues, and oranges.

"This is fantastic," sighed Teddy.

They took off their shoes and waded in the surf, holding hands as they ran. Within seconds, Teddy's sarong skirt was wet, and she peeled it away, revealing a pair of brief shorts and her long, slim, sun-darkened legs.

She saw Jac looking at her. "You're different from the girls I know," he told her.

"How's that?"

"You're more . . . sure of yourself. Not so silly."

"I'm also nineteen," Teddy said after a hesitation.

Jac shrugged. "So? I have been with women of twenty-five. Come—we have to climb over these rocks now. *Faites attention!*"

A tumbled outcropping of rocks blocked the beach, extending out into the water. They clambered onto them, Jac leading the way.

On the other side of the rocks there were no rows of cabanas. This beach was even more breathtaking, the surf crashing in white sprays onto the sand.

Teddy caught her breath. Two couples were approaching them strolling hip to hip—totally nude.

"Whoa," she said.

Jac did not seem embarrassed. "I just wanted to show you this beach. It's my favorite. I often come here to go parasailing. Would you like to go? I've already arranged for the boats to meet us here. Unless you're afraid," he added, giving her his bright, brash smile.

"Why not?" she agreed recklessly.

Teddy screamed in delight as she soared high over the waves, suspended sixty feet in the air from a harness that was attached to a blue silk parachute towed by a ski boat.

Beside her another boat towed Jac. His parachute was red, and he was soaring even higher than she was, bouncing just beneath fluffy clouds, or so it seemed. The faster the boats raced, the higher they sailed into the sky.

She gasped, clutching at the support straps as her feet dangled. Wind rushed past her face. This was as close to flying like a bird as she would ever get.

"Did you enjoy it?" Jac murmured.

"It was wonderful," sighed Teddy, bracing herself against the bounce of the waves that slapped the prow of the thirty-foot speedboat, spraying droplets across the windshield.

He'd dismissed the driver, taking over the wheel himself, and they'd motored far out on the water, finding a tiny cove behind the lee of a small, rocky islet. There was a picnic lunch in a wicker basket, and hungrily they'd devoured chunks of cheese, smoked sausages, and more than half of a *baguette* of wonderful, crusty French bread, along with beautiful, blue Agen plums, and a bottle of red Bordeaux wine.

The warmth of the sun on her shoulders, the rhythm of the waves, the wind and salt air, and the deep red, rich wine were making Teddy feel lazy and sensual. She stretched out on one of the cushioned seats, stripping down to a bikini, little more than two wisps of black.

Jac casually removed his shirt, revealing a lean yet muscular chest and wide shoulders. His skin was almost baby-smooth and tanned to the color of medium toast. Watching him, Teddy felt an involuntary thrill.

"You're beautiful," he told her, giving her a long, smoldering look.

"Not compared to Kristina," Teddy managed to say, suddenly becoming nervous. "Kristina is really, *seriously,* major league Hollywood beautiful."

"Kristina *is* beautiful, but she never thinks," Jac said shrugging. "She just goes for what she wants at the moment sort of like an existentialist. Will you take off your top?"

Teddy shifted nervously, involuntarily crossing her hands in front of her chest.

"I don't—" she began.

"I'm going to take off my things," Jac said, and casually began to peel away his shorts and the tight, string briefs he wore. She moistened her lips, unable to stop staring. Prince Jac had a beautiful body.

"I don't know," Teddy said again, looking miserable. *A million girls would kill to be in my position,* she told herself, trembling.

"I have *une capote anglaise,*" said Jac, pulling a condom out of the pocket of the shorts he had discarded. He was already reaching for her, his smooth skin smelling wonderfully of sea and salt. "Please, Teddy. . . . Please."

"I'm not sure—" His lips tasted of the wine they had drunk and a sweetness that was wholly Jac. Her heart pounding violently, she put her arms around his neck and felt his hands plucking at the back fastener of her bikini top.

Within seconds, it had fallen away. Then, deftly, Jac slid the bikini bottom away, too, and they were both naked, their arms and legs wrapped around each other. Jac's breathing was deep, his hands caressing up and down her flanks, cupping her buttocks. She could feel his urgent hardness against her stomach.

Her panic melted, to be replaced by a wild, primitive yearning. He was so wonderful. She wanted him. She wanted to experience this. . . .

They lay on the seat cushion, which somehow had fallen to the bottom of the boat, wrapped in each other's arms. The waves rocked them, and the sun beat down on their nakedness.

"I want to be inside you," he whispered, raining kisses on her mouth.

They made love three times while the boat rode at anchor, pausing only once to throw a towel over themselves as a police helicopter briefly dipped over the island.

Jac was a tender, demanding lover, who kissed and caressed every inch of her. It had hurt a little, the first time, but then the pleasure had begun to build. Her first, sweet, gasping orgasm stunned her.

"I love being with you like this, and I am pleased to be the first," Jac whispered, kissing her neck. "You're so—I didn't expect . . ." He kissed her again.

Teddy lost herself in the kiss, which inevitably led to more. When they finally pulled apart, she said, "Do you often bring girls out in your boat like this?"

Prince Jac lay with his arms folded behind his head, his face relaxed. "Occasionally. But you're so pretty, so different—I really like you."

"I like you, too," she said, wondering just how many wealthy young countesses and beautiful actresses and models Jac had already had. Now she was one of them.

A breeze had begun to blow from the shore, chilling her skin. She sat up and pulled on her shirt, thinking that it had been a wonderful afternoon—a perfect one.

Well, almost perfect.

Teddy and her father were sitting on the tiled terrace in front of their hotel, gazing out at the ocean as they sipped their drinks, Warner an Absolut martini, Teddy a Perrier. The water gave off dazzling sparkles of light from the setting sun. The sound of pounding surf was punctuated by the sound of an orchestra and voices drifting from the nearby outdoor bar.

"You did what?" said Houston Warner. "You went up in a *parachute*? Attached to a speedboat? Have you completely lost your senses, Theodora?" he said, calling her by her proper name because he was irritated.

"I wanted to go. It was fun—it was like flying," she said stubbornly, hoping her father would not see the slight whisker-burn where Jac had crushed hundreds of kisses onto her cheeks and mouth. Her pelvic area felt tender as well. She knew she'd never forget today if she lived to be a hundred.

"What if there'd been an accident? My God, what if you'd broken a leg or an arm?"

"But I didn't."

"But you could have. I'm going to call a travel agent and get our tickets changed. It's time we left here and went back to Connecticut, where you can concentrate on your tennis game instead of on jet-set princesses—or is it a prince?"

The accuracy of her father's guess made Teddy flinch.

"Dad! I'm old enough to travel all over the world and play tennis. Please stop treating me like a baby," Teddy cried. "And what did it hurt for me to have some fun? Fun and tennis *don't* seem to mix, at least according to you."

Houston Warner reddened, staring down into his drink. "I've never heard you talk that way, Theodora."

"Maybe I've never felt that way. I love tennis, Dad, don't get me wrong, but I don't want it to rule my entire life. I want . . . a lot more than just tennis."

"Two million dollars a year in endorsements alone is a great deal, Theodora—and that's just for starters. You're still green."

"I know. And I appreciate it."

"Not to mention the fame. You're known all over the world, darling. You're going to be tennis's golden girl in a few years . . . my golden girl."

"I know, Dad." Feeling suddenly contrite, Teddy patted her father's hand, then clasped it tightly. "You've done so much for me, and I do appreciate it. I love you so much . . . but I have to have my own life."

After a long pause Warner said, softening again, "Look, Teddy, I have to fly back to New York tomorrow. I have important meetings scheduled all week. We're acquiring a new manufacturing company, and I want to be there for the negotiations. Will you be all right here?"

Teddy gazed at her father, touched. He was telling her that he trusted her enough to stay in Costa del Mar alone.

"Yes, Dad," she cried. "Oh, thank you!"

"Thank you for what? If you slack off on your training, you'll be the one who pays the price," Warner warned gruffly.

Back in his spacious, elegantly furnished New York office, Houston Warner shuffled through stacks of mail, already sorted by his executive assistant, who had efficiently divided the papers into piles labeled important, pressing, and extremely urgent.

When he came upon the manila envelope filled with photocopied newspaper and magazine articles about the Costan royals, he paused. Then, thoughtfully, he pulled out the clippings and spread them across the gleaming mahogany surface of his desk.

The material covered everything from Costan politics to fluff pieces about the casino. But Prince Georges's name was mentioned in every article, and there were a number of photographs of him. Apparently the aging Georges possessed more than thirty-five titles of various kinds, from Knight of the Royal Palace and Duke of Longchamps, to Prince of the Seven Seas.

Warner stared at the elongated, frowning face, the steel-gray hair, and discontented eyes, wondering how it must feel to be an almost-ran, the brother to the ruler, a man who held dozens of empty titles but possessed no power of any significance.

Did Georges chafe over his position? Did he plot and plan? Warner shook his head, thinking that European history was rife with rivalries and *coups d'état* culminating in bloodshed. According to one of the clippings, an early Bellini prince also named Henri had slain his brother Étienne in a vicious struggle over the tiny seaport country, which in the 1500s had earned most of its money by piracy.

"Mr. Warner, I have Anton Tewes on line six," said his assistant, buzzing through on the speaker phone.

Reluctantly Warner turned away from the fascinating clips vividly depicting Costa's turbulent history.

Still, as he attended meetings throughout the rest of the day, his mind returned several times to Prince Georges and the conversation he'd overheard. He possessed a piece of insider information, but there was nothing that he could do with it.

Besides, it was Teddy who was really important. He just hoped that being among the royals didn't turn her head too much. She was all he had. Without her, his life would be worthless.

* * *

A week passed—days full of sun and tennis practice, evenings full of parties, discoing, and moonlight boat rides on the royal yacht, the *Belle Lisse II*. Teddy became better acquainted with both princesses, especially with Kristina.

Gabriella left for New York at the end of the week, saying that she planned to visit an old school friend, Sydney Mellon, whom she had met when both princesses attended the exclusive Miss Porter's girls' school in Farmington, Connecticut, for two years. Teddy was surprised when she realized that the twenty-one-year-old princess traveled with her own entourage, including a bodyguard, a personal maid, and a press secretary.

Teddy kept waiting for Jac to invite her to go parasailing again, but he didn't, and then he left for Cannes and another car race, returning at the end of the week.

At the beginning of the second week, Jac eyed her again with that slow, tender, flirtatious look he had perfected, and began teasing her in the palace swimming pool.

They sneaked past the servants and went up to Jac's apartment, a suite of four huge rooms including a small kitchen with light oak paneling and windows that overlooked the sea.

"I love holding you. I love sex with you," Jac murmured into her neck, as he filled her body with strong, urgent thrusts.

"Jac . . . Jac . . ." Gasping, she felt her pleasure building, and she exploded against him, her body bucking in wild bursts of ecstasy. He came almost immediately afterward, crying out hoarsely.

They lay on Jac's extra wide bed, with its dark, intricately carved posts, and Teddy felt a sudden urge to cry now that the sexual excitement was over. . . . Sex? Was that all their lovemaking meant to Jac? She pressed her face against Jac's sweat-damp shoulder.

"What's wrong?"

"Nothing."

"Something's wrong—I can feel your tenseness."

"It's nothing," she said, sitting up. "It's just that—Jac . . . I . . ."

"I'd like you to have something," Jac said, striding naked across the room. He opened a drawer and pulled out a small, beautifully wrought pink seashell. "I picked it up once when I was diving off St. Tropez, and then I had pearls set in it. It's for you, Teddy. Perhaps you can use it for a necklace."

"I will," she promised confusedly, trying to smile as she turned the beautiful shell over in her hands. Somehow she knew it was his way of saying good-bye gently. Still, she was angry, and before she left Jac's room, Teddy put the pearl-encrusted shell back in the drawer of the armoire. She just couldn't accept a gift from him under the circumstances.

"There! And there!" Kristina swung her racquet, lobbing a ball over the net, and Teddy slammed it back to the other side of the court, forcing Kristina to run.

The princess overextended herself and stumbled, missing the shot, and the ball bounced out of court. Perspiration was pouring down her face, soaking her headband, but in spite of that, she looked beautiful and glowing in her goldenrod-yellow tennis shirt and shorts.

"Kristina! You have to be more aggressive, attack the ball more," Teddy began, pausing before the next lesson.

"Yes, yes, yes," sighed Kristina. "I know all that, but I don't think I'm cut out to be a tennis pro, Teddy. I don't know what I am, actually, other than just a better-than-average weekend player."

The two girls walked over to the edge of the palace's court, where a table held a pitcher of lemonade and a plate of fresh fruit.

"My life is on hold," declared Kristina, throwing herself into a chair. "I'm *so* bored all the time. Having you here for a few days has been wonderful, but it's not enough.

After all, when you leave— Oh, I don't know!''

"What do you mean?''

"I told you about my short-lived modeling career. I had a composite photo portfolio made and the Wilhelmina Agency in New York was anxious to sign me. They were going to have a huge party to celebrate the new contract. I was even going to be on the cover of *Vogue.* I flew to New York and looked over the contract, and was getting ready to sign it when I received a phone call. Papa forbade me to sign. He demanded that I return home immediately. He said modeling was not suitable for a princess.''

"Did you?''

"Of course. I am a royal. I must obey.''

"That must have been difficult for you.''

"I disappointed so many people—people who'd invested money in promoting me. And I disappointed myself,'' said Kristina gloomily.

During the days she'd been in Costa del Mar, Teddy had come to realize that Kristina constantly skittered from one social event to the next, unsatisfied with anything for very long.

"But you have so much,'' Teddy said.

"I do . . . but spontaneity is not part of a royal's lifestyle. I'm supposed to marry some titled man, someone rich, someone Papa approves of. Attend official engagements, groundbreakings, state dinners—that dreary, endless routine. I'll support three or four charities. I'll have a huge wardrobe of designer dresses, and I'll look wonderful at palace balls and parties. And, of course, I am expected to have at least two children and bring them up in an appropriate manner. . . .'' Kristina sighed. "But I'm supposed to do it all *here,* Teddy. Within this country, within sight of the palace, all according to prearranged rules and regulations. I'll never really have an adventure . . . or a life of my own choosing.''

Teddy didn't know what to say. At first she'd thought the life of the royals seemed glamorous, but now, looking at the problems that the young British royals were going through . . . First Fergie and Prince Andrew, and now there were rumors about Princess Anne and Captain Mark Phillips . . . and especially about Di and Charles going their separate ways.

Thunder rolled ominously, rain spattering against the windows of the limousine.

Princess Gabriella leaned forward in the backseat of the limousine, her eyes riveted on the sea of black, bobbing umbrellas that surged up and down Fifth Avenue.

"We haven't moved more than fifty feet in the past ten minutes," complained Marie-Paule Coty, Gaby's press secretary. Her bodyguard, Pierre, was seated next to Marie-Paule, along with a security guard assigned to her by the U.S. State Department at Henri's request.

"But it's all so *alive*," said Gaby. "I love it."

Officially she was visiting an old school friend who lived in Manhattan. But beside her on the seat rested a leather portfolio that contained several dozen sketches of her jewelry designs, the best of her work culled out after days of agonizing decisions. Nervously she wondered if she should have included the cat pin series she'd been thinking about. But she still hadn't really finished working out the concept. Everything had to be perfect—stunning. More than anything, she wanted to impress Kenny Lane.

After more traffic delays the limousine pulled up in front of the address they had been given, on West 37th Street off Fifth Avenue.

The driver came around to open the door, and Pierre got out of the limo first, unfurling a huge black umbrella to shelter Gabriella from the pelting rain. The other guard and the press secretary followed.

Gabriella took the umbrella away from Pierre and hurried ahead of all of them, suddenly impatient with her entourage.

*   *   *

The building had a tiny, old-fashioned elevator that could only hold four people. It took them upward to the sixth floor, where they entered a small foyer. A receptionist, Blanche Davinger, who'd been with Kenny so long that she was an institution, sat at a desk.

She welcomed them effusively. Marie and the two bodyguards waited in the foyer while Gabriella walked on through to a large showroom, filled with long drawers that contained samples of Lane's jewelry. A desk, covered with black velvet, offered space for the samples to be displayed to retail buyers. On the walls were photographs of Lane's most glittering creations.

Gaby looked around, her heart pounding with anticipation.

"My dear," said Kenneth Jay Lane, looking up from the carefully rendered sketches of opulent rococo necklaces, chokers, bracelets, and dangling earrings conceptualized in a variety of stunning, semiprecious stones. "My dear, these are fabulous."

"They—they are?" Gabriella's flush was so deep that she felt its heat burn her cheeks. They were in Lane's tastefully furnished office hung with family photos. Lane was in his early fifties, very British in appearance. His graying hair was combed straight back, and he wore a powder-blue shirt with white collar and cuffs, blue-and-white polka-dot tie, blue blazer, and gray slacks.

"You are gifted, Gabriella. Your talent is quite extraordinary. Women are going to love the details you work into your pieces. What did you plan to do with them?"

"I want to sell them," she said firmly. She was astounded, astonished, deliriously joyful.

Lane gazed at her for a long moment. "May I say this? Ordinarily I would never dream of entering into a licensing agreement with any other company or person. I've built this business from nothing myself, and really prefer to do it my way. But because I know your family and because your designs are so wonderful, I'd like to propose something like a joint venture to you.''

Gabriella smiled, tamping down her delirious joy into the calm behavior suiting a princess. "Yes?"

"We'll call our creative efforts the celebrity line, *Princess Gabriella*," said Lane. "We are going to capture today's most lucrative market—the working woman with her own paycheck. You'll come back to New York for a few weeks and work with me and my designers until we've all agreed on the designs and number of pieces that will go into the new line. I'll furnish you with a small office and a secretary in both my showroom and my manufacturing facility. To start off with, I'll give you a minimum of five percent of the gross sales of the line, and if it reaches certain financial goals—we'll work all of that out—it would increase to seven and a half, and eventually ten, percent."

Gabriella stared at him. "But . . . ten percent of what?"

"Possibly the first year the sales could be between eight and ten million. The second year, ten to twelve million, and in the third year, if the line is extremely successful, we could have sales somewhere around fifteen million dollars."

Gabriella hesitated, rapidly doing the calculations. She'd never negotiated anything before in her life, but now, recklessly, she decided to try.

"Kenny," she said, "if I sign this contract with you, I'm going to be giving up most of my privacy, and I'll become very visible. I could even possibly be the target of—well, a kidnapping or a terrorist attack. I want a three-million-dollar guarantee over the terms of our agreement *and* a contract for five years, the first million on signing, the rest to be paid in equal installments over the next four years—whether or not the line is successful."

As she spoke, Lane's expression changed from that of shock to hardheaded business. "Even if the line isn't successful? That hardly sounds—"

"I am putting my entire life and my country, too, behind

it, and we expect to be properly compensated."

Lane nodded. "Make it two million one, with seven hundred thousand on execution of our agreement, and we have a deal. But you must commit yourself to promoting the line at your own expense, and that should be about a hundred fifty thousand a year. The Princess Gabriella line should engender a tremendous amount of media. There will be the talk-show circuit—Donahue, Oprah Winfrey, Letterman, 'The Tonight Show'—all of the big ones. You'll need a full-time publicist. I assume that presents no problem for you?"

Gabriella knew that Prince Henri might not be overly pleased at the idea of his oldest child traveling all over the world to market a line of jewelry. Even if he allowed it, he might put so many conditions on her activities that she would be severely hampered. Still, the prospect dazzled her. To have something real to do—something she loved—to be more than just a princess with a pretty face, this was what she desparately wanted.

"There won't be any problem with my father," she assured Lane nervously. "I myself will talk to him as soon as I arrive home. I'm sure he will—" She stopped, uncertain of what Prince Henri's reaction might actually be.

Lane smiled. "Gabriella, you must listen to me very carefully when it comes to marketing and public relations, because I know this business better than anyone. Your first sales job will be on your father."

"What?"

"It's very simple. All you need to do is convince him that your selling this fabulous line of Princess Gabriella jewelry will enhance the image of Costa del Mar—that you'll be a spokesperson, not just for the jewelry, but for your country."

"Of course," Gaby said, a grin spreading across her face.

"Listen to me. I know it will work."

* * *

Teddy was on the telephone to Jamaica DuRoss, her best friend in tennis, who had come up the ranks with her.

"Jamie, it's just incredible. I feel like I'm wandering around in a Hollywood movie or something," she enthused to her friend. "This is just a wonderful country. It's so clean—and there are flowers everywhere. You never see any poor people—the Costan government pampers all of its citizens like you wouldn't believe."

"Okay, but are there any men?" asked Jamaica.

"Everywhere," sighed Teddy. "Even the sentries are hunks . . . and Prince Jac is the most incredible hunk of all. Only—" She hesitated, a wave of caution holding her back. *Prince and Tennis Star.* She could imagine the tabloids.

"Teddy . . . ?" Jamaica was saying. "Come on, tell me all. What's Jac like? Is he a good dancer? Did you get a chance to dance with him at all? Does he have a lot of girlfriends the way they say in the magazines? Is he arrogant?"

"I guess he does," Teddy said slowly. "Have a lot of girlfriends, I mean. But he isn't arrogant. He's very nice."

Prince Jac had been using the NordicTrack machine in the palace exercise room, and thinking about Teddy Warner, when he was called to the telephone by a servant who added that his father also wished to see him in twenty minutes.

The woman on the other end of the line was practically crying. Panic filled her voice as she spoke in rapid-fire, Parisian French. "Prince Jac, I don't know what to *do*. I wasn't going to call you, you've been so very generous— but I don't know where else to turn. My daughter—it's Cécile!"

"Suzette, what's wrong?" Suzette Moulin was the wife of his school friend, Joël Moulin, who had recently been injured in a car crash while Formula One racing.

"I know you helped us when Joël was hurt—but now

our little girl was terribly burned in an automobile accident yesterday.''

Jac felt a twist in his stomach. ''Suzette, I'm so sorry. Try not to worry. I will send a plane to pick Cécile up, and she will be flown here to the hospital in Costa del Mar. We have one of the best burn centers in Europe. Meanwhile I will have plastic surgeons who are specialists with burned tissue flown in; they will be waiting for her. The best in France.''

''But we can't afford—''

''I'll pay for everything, Suzette.''

He comforted the hysterical young woman for a few more minutes, then hung up and telephoned his secretary, asking her to make the arrangements. Finally he walked into the small bathroom that adjoined the workout room, and stripped for a shower.

Another matter concerned him right now—his father's sudden, peremptory message that Jac was to appear in the breakfast room. Turning under the spray, Jac wondered what Henri wanted.

The palace breakfast room had been used as a weaving room two hundred years ago, when a staff of weavers and seamstresses had provided all the royal garments. It still contained ancient carved cupboards that once had held bolts of cloth. Now, round tables had been added, and enormous tropical plants, growing in tubs, gave the room a more modern look. Henri sometimes used the room when he had architectural plans he wished to spread out on tabletops.

Jac, his hair slicked back from his shower, heard an angry voice behind the double doors, apparently Henri speaking on the telephone.

''No!'' the old prince snapped. ''No, I have told you! I will not. . . . I don't care how much he is willing to pay, the gambling rights of Costa del Mar are not for sale. I repeat, *not* for sale. And even the suggestion I find insulting.''

Jac felt uncomfortable eavesdropping any longer and quickly knocked.

"His Highness is waiting," said the secretary, opening the doors for him.

Jac walked in. Henri was seated at a table, glaring down at a stack of the huge plat books that marked off property lines in Costa del Mar. It was apparent that he was deeply worried. But his father had always dealt with conflicts, Jac quickly assured himself, and would continue to do so for many, many years. At least Jac fervently hoped so.

"Papa? You wished to see me?"

Henri looked up. It was as if he had to bring his thoughts back from a very long distance. "Yes, my son."

Jac waited. One did not rush his father.

Finally Henri spoke. "President Clinton and his wife, Hillary, are making a state visit here next week. I want you to be available to them; Monsieur Dupré will give you their schedule. You have been running off to entirely too many car races and speedboat races, neglecting your responsibilities."

Jac flushed. He disliked state visits, with their endless receptions, interminable ten-course meals, and long speeches. As a rebellious fifteen-year-old, he had once been caught exiting the palace through the tunnel when he was supposed to be attending an important dinner with Queen Elizabeth II—a slight of major proportions. Prince Henri had cut off his allowance for an entire year.

"Papa," he said quickly. "I am planning to leave for Torino next week. There is a new sports car I want to inspect—"

Fire sparked from Henri's eyes. "You will not be rude to the Reagans."

"As you wish," said Jac, flushing.

"We have international relations to see to. It is important to keep up our connections with heads of state, especially the Americans."

Jac nodded politely as Henri continued to speak at length

about Costa's relations with other countries, and why the country's delicately balanced financial condition needed a new, fresh boost. "We haven't the luxury of the Americans' huge tax base," intoned Henri. "Unfortunately we have the French sharks slavering to take us under their 'protection.' . . . They would love to eradicate all of our privileges and slap heavy taxes on our citizens, nationalizing our hospital and museums."

Jac frowned. There'd been talk, of course, but he'd assumed that's all it was.

Finally Henri wound down his lecture. "Enough, enough," said the prince impatiently. "You are not really interested."

"I am interested," protested Jac. "I care a great deal."

"Maybe it will all be your problem one day. We'll see."

Walking through the palace corridors again, Jac shook his head, a twinge of anger moving through him. If he were Henri, he would hire his own "shark" to deal with the various encroachments. Then he cut off the thought. Why should he think about ruling, when other young men of his age were doing exciting things like serving in the armed forces, driving race cars, or acting as stuntmen in movies?

Of course, he might one day change his mind and want to rule—but it would be a very long time from now, if ever, he assured himself.

Geneviève Mondalvi was thirty-four and diet-thin. In France, her gossip column was feared as much as Liz Smith's syndicated column in New York's *Daily News* or Suzy's in the fashion world's *W*.

"You know that the tabloids have published photographs of you with Prince Jac." The columnist began to interview Teddy as soon as she was seated in her hotel suite. "Have you seen them?"

"Photos?" Teddy shook her head.

Genie Mondalvi pulled a folded newspaper out of her bag and handed it to Teddy. *Jac Plays with Blond Tennis*

Star, said the headline in French.

Shocked, Teddy stared at the photographs of herself and Prince Jac. Some of the photos showed her and Jac playing tennis and parasailing together, Jac's hand familiarly on her shoulder as she was being strapped into the harness-chair. Another showed her in the speedboat with Jac on the day they had first made love. The two of them were locked in an embrace, kissing passionately. The grainy, black-and-white photo made Teddy, clad only in a bikini, seem nearly naked.

"How long have you known the prince?" the reporter wanted to know.

"We're just friends," Teddy blurted, blushing, wondering what Prince Henri would think when he saw the photographs. So much for their plan to keep things quiet.

"Friends?" The older woman looked skeptical.

"Yes," Teddy insisted.

"Well, the tabloids love Jac," said Genie Mondalvi, pursing her lips. "You aren't the first girl he's been linked with romantically, you know. Our young prince already has quite a reputation as a ladies' man. I understand he's seeing Camille de Borély as well. She is a countess, and has a wealthy family—it would be a very good match for him."

The columnist waited expectantly, as if hoping to see Teddy react, producing yet more sensational fodder for her column.

"I doubt if he plans to marry anyone anytime soon," Teddy said evenly. "Why should he, when he's having such fun playing the field?" Her face flushed to a deep pink.

"Have you been practicing?"

"Every day, Daddy," said Teddy, hot from a tiring jog along the beach following her five-hour practice session. She balanced the telephone on her shoulder as she attempted to unplait her long, blond braid so she could shampoo her hair. "Don't worry, I'm lean and I'm mean."

"You haven't skimped on hours, have you?"

"Full practices, I promise you. Kristina's been my hitting partner."

"Kristina isn't a strong enough player for you, honey. I wish we hadn't sent Manuel home. You know you need—"

"*And* I've been hitting with Prince Jac," Teddy added. "He's a very strong player. He could have played professionally if he'd wanted to." Her hair was loose now, and she shook it around her shoulders, wishing the obligatory phone call was over. She had to hurry—Kristina and Gabriella were taking her shopping in half an hour.

"Prince Jac?" The note of worry in Warner's voice became even stronger. "I know all about him—two people sent me clippings, Teddy. It's obvious your stay there has involved a lot more than just tennis lessons for the princess."

Teddy flushed at the thought of her father seeing those revealing pictures. "Not anymore. He's . . . seeing a countess now," she admitted.

"Darling." Houston Warner had caught the misery in Teddy's voice. "Teddy, please, remember that you and Prince Jac live in two totally different worlds. He might play with you, but he's supposed to be dating titled women. That's what his family expects. His lifestyle is—"

"Dad," she choked, "I *know* what his lifestyle is. I *know* we're not compatible. No one has to tell me that."

She managed to deflect her father's concern, asking him about a new tennis racquet that was being made for her, and confirming her arrival time at New York's JFK airport the following day.

"I'll be glad to see you, honey. You need to get back on track again. Your life is playing tennis, Teddy, not hobnobbing with royals. Costa is a very political place, more than you realize. It's not for the likes of us."

Five minutes later she hung up, her mood rapidly plummeting.

Well, she wasn't going to fantasize about her future with Jac anymore. He really hadn't said much to her since the last time they had made such wonderful love . . . and that was days ago. So she would take her father's advice. She was going to go back to Connecticut and resume her training schedule. She had two commercials to shoot and the French Open to think about, after she played Melbourne. That was plenty to keep her busy.

Prince Georges paced up and down the drawing room at Royal House, situated five hundred yards from the palace itself and always in its shadow. Anger at betrayal mixed with hate, and they both scorched through him.

He'd just learned that D'Fabray had sided with Prince Henri on the explosive issue of the country merging with France.

"We will never join our forces with France; we would rather perish first," had been Henri's brave words to the press. And the finance minister had added his own sycophantic agreement: *"If France takes us over, we will lose our way of life and become poor peasants and petits bourgeois—which is exactly what they want us to become."*

It was becoming clearer to Georges with each passing day that the people rallied around Henri. They barely noticed *him.* . . . Only recently a gossip column had by mistake reported Georges's age as nearly ten years older than he actually was—the error reflecting the view of many people, he felt sure, that he was old, decrepit before his time.

That image had to be changed—and fast. And to do this, he needed a minister on his side, not the treacherous D'Fabray, but one who would be sympathetic to *his* aims and desires. And he knew just the man for the job, a man with whom Georges had gone to school. François Gérard. He and Georges had been involved as teammates on a boyhood soccer team. Henri liked him and would probably appoint him.

Georges frowned, rubbing his throbbing forehead. There

had to be a way. . . . Didn't Gérard have contacts with certain of the military, men with unusual skills and few scruples?

Yes. It would work. Of course, they would do it through two or three intermediaries. His name would never be known by those who actually did the . . . His mind backed away from actually repeating the word. He was a prince, after all. Royals were bred never to think of such things, always to keep high thoughts and standards . . . whenever possible.

The small, two-engine plane dipped along the seacoast near the Côte d'Azur. It veered over the red-tiled roofs of Saint-Tropez, the beach a curve of gold edged with white lines of surf, the deep blue sea dotted with numerous islets. East of Cannes the coast rose in terraces from the shore and Cap d'Antibes jutted out into the sea, with the Îles de Lérins clustering around it.

Étienne D'Fabray and his wife, Émilie, were taking a much-needed vacation. Émilie, daughter of an immensely wealthy Parisian perfumer, owned a villa near Cap d'Antibes.

"Étienne," she said, cuddling up next to him as he sat glowering at a folder of documents. "Étienne, I am beginning to feel—how shall I say?—very sexy."

Wearily the Costan finance minister turned to look at his fifty-year-old wife. She was typically French in appearance: short, olive-skinned, and dark-haired, and with a sense of style and a vivacious manner that made her very attractive. Her dark eyes, underneath which bluish pouches had begun to form, sparkled with playfulness. She had no idea that her husband had raided her financial holdings. Naively she'd left the management all to him, and he'd shown her several bogus reports showing significant monetary gains. But since then he'd amassed even more gambling debts. He'd visited Atlantic City the previous year when he was in the United States on business. A huge mistake. American

casinos did not wait quietly for their money. He was going
to have to gut several of her money market accounts. If she
ever found out—

God knew she would divorce him, and she would certainly ruin his reputation. He'd have to leave Costa del Mar.

He needed help.

But he and Prince Georges had recently had a serious
disagreement. He'd sided with Henri on an important issue.
After all, what was he to do? Henri *was* the country's ruler.

That was really why he and Émilie were taking this vacation. So Georges could calm down.

"Étienne? You haven't been listening to a word I've
said," complained his wife.

"Of course, I have. You are feeling . . . very desirable,"
he said, running a fingertip softly up the center of his wife's
palm, a gesture he knew drove her wild. "Which, of course,
you are. You're wonderfully desirable."

He glanced significantly at the plane's small bathroom,
which they had used before for impromptu lovemaking ses-
sions. "My darling, should we . . . ?"

"*Oui,*" she whispered huskily.

They rose and walked up the aisle toward the cramped
little room. That was when D'Fabray happened to glance
out the porthole window to his left. An explosion of red
filled the entire window, blooming like a strange volcanic
flower.

Then the fireball roared into the cabin, and D'Fabray felt
a brief spasm of unimaginable pain before the plane, and
its occupants, disintegrated.

Their first stop on the long-awaited shopping trip was a
little boutique that sold antique lace. As a clerk was wrapping up the length of lace Gaby had purchased, two women
entered the shop.

The younger of the two women glared angrily at Princess Gabriella, then hissed a torrent of rapid-fire French to
her friend. Teddy heard the name *Lisse,* followed by an

unfamiliar phrase, *une poufiasse vache salope.*

"Let's leave," Gaby murmured, looking stricken.

But Kristina marched over to the two women. "Your loose tongues aren't appreciated!"

As they were climbing into the Rolls, Kristina angrily remarked, "Life is so good for them here. People like that don't deserve to live in Costa del Mar. They don't appreciate their citizenship. They get free hospitalization and pay no taxes—and then they treat Gaby like that."

"What did the woman say?" Teddy dared to ask.

"Nothing," Gabriella said, biting her lower lip. She still looked stricken, and was clenching both hands in her lap.

"It's just local politics," explained Kristina after a moment. "A few people resent the monarchy *and* the royals and prefer a republican form of government. It is very boring, really. Now let's go to Colombe's. I have a dress fitting, and, Teddy, you are going to love her sexy dresses. You absolutely *have* to buy one."

Sitting in the designer's tiny salon, watching as several models glided out wearing a succession of glorious cocktail dresses, Teddy wondered what it would be like to live like the princesses, to be able to waltz into a designer's shop and order whatever she wished . . . to be billed to the palace.

But as they viewed the glamorous crêpe de chine and chiffon-topped crêpe dresses, she noticed that Princess Gabriella still wasn't smiling, and her face seemed flushed. Obviously the encounter in the lace shop had disturbed her a great deal.

Later, in the fitting room, Teddy overheard the two princesses arguing through the thin walls.

"You didn't have to *defend* me," cried Gabriella. "I don't need *defending.*"

"The woman was being rude," insisted Kristina.

"I could have handled her. I didn't need you to do it."

"Well, you didn't do it, you just stood there and looked

appalled. I should think you'd be grateful for what I did, instead of acting as if I spilled wine all over you.''

"At least I'm not screwing every man in sight. What about that photographer we saw in the car? I suppose you'll want him next—after you're done with Jean-Luc, that is. Or maybe at the same time, who knows?''

Kristina caught her breath in what sounded like a gasp. "At least I'm not a fool who goes everywhere on Papa's arm and stands in receiving lines and seems to think she can replace our mother.''

"What!''

On the other side of the wall, Teddy, too, reacted in shock.

"You heard me. *You're* not Mama, and you can't ever be Mama, no matter how hard you try.''

It sounded as if Gaby was near tears. "He—he asked me to do it. . . . He needed someone to act as his hostess.''

"He uses you,'' snapped Kristina. "Who else would be stupid enough to go to one boring function after another? He's not going to *love* you more if you do all that. He won't even respect you.''

"He will, soon. I have my jewelry now, and I—''

"Anyway,'' said Kristina airily, "*I* have Jean-Luc now, so I don't care about anything else.''

Gaby reacted with horror. "You're not going to—''

"Wait and see,'' said Kristina.

In the fitting room, Teddy, who had been standing with a shimmering organza dress in her hands, started pulling it over her head, beginning to feel guilty at her unavoidable eavesdropping.

That evening the music of an eight-piece orchestra filled the moist night air, as couples in evening wear danced on board the *Belle Lisse II*. Later, Paul Anka and Liza Minnelli were to entertain the prince's 150 guests.

Everyone was talking about the plane crash.

"So tragic. Such misfortune,'' murmured Teddy's part-

ner in her ear. He was a French businessman twenty years
her senior, who talked interminably about his shipping business. "Of course," he said, returning to his favorite topic,
"the price of Middle Eastern oil has affected shipping costs
dreadfully."

"Interesting," she sighed, attempting to follow his in-
tricate foxtrot variations.

"Shipping is very—how do you Americans say?—cut-
throat. In fact, it is a business in which a man must show
his . . ."

Teddy sighed. Her last evening in Costa del Mar wasn't
turning out to be a success. This official party, given by
Prince Henri, with Gabriella as his hostess, was turning out
to be a bore. Most of the guests were older, titled aristocrats
whose names were familiar to Teddy from reading fashion
magazines, along with wealthy businessmen such as André
Chambord, her current partner.

Her eyes, sweeping across the crowded dance floor,
found Prince Jac. Dressed in his smashing dark blue Costan
Navy uniform, his sash pale blue, Jac was just entering the
dance floor, his arm around a stunning black-haired woman.

This must be the countess that Genie Mondalvi had told
her about. Teddy couldn't help noticing that Camille de
Borély's silky black hair was piled high on her head, secured with an antique diamond clip that looked as if it had
been in her family for generations. She looked much older
than her eighteen years. As Jac whirled her around the
dance floor, Camille gazed soulfully into the prince's eyes.

Teddy looked away.

". . . and, *naturellement,* I have bought another four
tankers in order to ship crude oil," her partner was saying.

Teddy gritted her teeth and blinked back sudden tears.
Well, she wasn't going to let it bother her.

She'd been a fool to think that he could ever be interested in her.

*   *   *

Across the floor, Kristina danced with Jean-Luc Furnoir. She had drunk too much wine. The room seemed to tilt around her, dizzying her with sparkling lights, music, and a kaleidoscope of women's dresses and jewels.

She raised both of her slim arms and wrapped them around Jean-Luc's neck, pulling him close. He was a lithe, sinuous dancer who knew how to move his hips—just the kind of partner Kristina liked. And Jean-Luc seemed greedy for fun, a quality that appealed to her, too.

"I want to dip," Kristina whispered to Jean-Luc. "Dip me."

Jean-Luc glanced over his shoulder to the dais where Prince Henri was seated next to Princess Gabriella.

"Now," she ordered.

Obediently Furnoir lowered her down to the floor, as Kristina arched her supple spine, trailing one hand with graceful abandon.

"Everyone is staring," laughed Jean-Luc as he raised her again.

"I want us to do it tonight," Kristina said dreamily.

"Do what?"

"You know—announce it!"

Furnoir appeared startled. They had become secretly engaged several days ago and had agreed to announce their engagement several months from now, after the Catholic Prince Henri had become fully accustomed to the idea of having a divorced son-in-law with two teenaged children.

"Tonight? But I thought—"

"*Tonight,*" insisted Kristina. "Gaby is here, and everyone else, and I'm in the mood to do it now. I'm just smashed enough to have the courage, Jean-Luc." Before he could answer, she weaved her way through the dancing couples, reaching the bandstand.

"I need to borrow your microphone," she said to the astonished bandleader, climbing onto the dais.

"Everyone—I have news—wonderful news!" Her voice was picked up by the mike, causing the dancers to pause and turn their faces toward her.

Kristina jumped down from the dais and ran to get Jean-Luc, grabbing his left hand with both of hers and pulling him toward the stage. "Jean-Luc and I . . . we are getting married! In one month!"

A startled murmur sprang up, and, on the dais, Kristina saw Prince Henri rise up out of his chair, his face turning white. Beside him, Gabriella had blanched, and she clutched her father's arm for support.

In the elegant salon of the royal yacht, Prince Georges sat at a table, staring sullenly into the golden depths of a snifter filled with cognac. Kristina's engagement was a blow to his plans.

He wanted to leap up and hurl the brandy into the girl's laughing face. He had waited too long. How dare she? Kristina was still a child, hardly ready for marriage yet. Much worse, within nine months there would probably be a little royal heir, a baby to assume its place in the royal succession, bumping him down to fifth. The prospect rankled.

"You are not celebrating?" asked Prince Henri wryly as he entered the saloon. His brother's face looked worried, with his forehead etched in deep furrows.

"Of course," Georges said with deliberate vagueness. "It is wonderful news."

"Yes." Henri waved imperiously at a steward, who came scurrying over. "Brandy. My usual," the prince said, and then turned back to Georges. "I need it after the news of that terrible plane crash."

"Yes, a sad matter."

"The children grow up," Henri began, changing the subject and shaking his head in a displeased manner. "There are problems. . . ."

"Ah, yes," said Georges, daring to add, "I am certain that Kristina is not, well, not terribly responsible at this time in her life. Of course, she will make a lovely bride," he went on hastily, as his brother's frown deepened.

"Brides, marriages—I have two daughters and a son," Henri said. "I imagine there will be several weddings within the next few years, perhaps a coronation as well."

A coronation? Georges felt his chest tighten. *Mon Dieu . . . !* The sharpness in his chest was so intense that he wondered if, like Henri, he too had a heart condition. He opened and closed his mouth, forcing out the words. "You plan to . . . abdicate in favor of . . . ?"

"Ah, but not for many more years," said Henri quickly. His eyes rested on Georges, narrowing. "I will not leave Costa without good leadership, you can be sure of that. In time, Jac will take his place as planned."

Kristina stood on the rear deck, leaning over the rail and feeling faintly ill. Since making her startling announcement she'd had three more glasses of wine, and now she could barely remember what she'd said. But the reaction of the crowd was indelibly emblazoned in her mind. They'd been shocked. Even horrified. Jean-Luc, the son of a famous French actress, had lived all his life on inherited income and his own questionable charm. He was not Catholic; his divorce had been messy. In no way was he a suitable husband for a princess.

"I hope you are happy." Kristina turned to see her father approaching along the deck, his face grim.

"Yes, I am," Kristina said in a low voice. "I'm very happy." She was growing more sober by the second.

"You have made a fool of yourself. The international press will write that my younger daughter is marrying a dissolute *cavaleur* more than twice her age. A playboy who has been married once, has children, has never worked, and moreover comes from a barely respectable family."

"In the first place he is thirty-six, not forty," began Kristina, but Henri cut her off with a sharp gesture.

"Don't you realize that I wanted the best for you, not this . . . this Jean-Luc? You need a strong man to stand beside you, one who respects our country and its traditions, not one who isn't even Catholic. What if he refuses to convert?''

"He will, Papa, I know he will. He's a good man!"

Henri said tiredly, "Kristina, when we return to the palace I want you to call him and tell him that you are breaking this so-called engagement—because I forbid the entire travesty.''

"What?'' Shocked, she faced her father.

"I cannot sanction this union.''

"You have to!'' she cried. "I'm going to be married in the cathedral—and if you don't let me, I . . . I'll fly to Las Vegas, and we'll be married in one of those wedding chapels. Would you like that?'' Her voice rose. "All the American reporters will swarm around us, and I'll tell them that you forbade the marriage and I had no other choice.''

"Daughter, you would not dare do such a thing!'' Henri thundered.

Kristina trembled. "I would. This is the nineteen eighties, not the Middle Ages. I can marry whomever I want, and if he's not perfect, well, maybe I don't care. He's the man I want! He cares for me. And I love him.''

Henri was silent for a long time.

"Very well,'' he said at last. He looked at her with remorse and then nodded desolately. "Maybe some children—a family—will settle you down, Kristina. I hope so. But it *must* be a Catholic ceremony in the Church, and there will be a tightly worded prenuptial agreement, of course. And the preparations will take more than a month. We will follow the standard protocol, you may be sure.''

Her father stalked away, leaving her standing at the railing, the wind plastering her dress against her legs and blowing the tears from her cheeks.

The next morning, Teddy felt oddly bereft as she left the *Olympia* on a launch, wind buffeting her hair. Kristina's announcement had startled her and made her feel a sharp sense of loss. Kristina, Gabriella, and Jac would continue to lead their royal lives, while Teddy had to go back to her own world—a world that consisted mostly of tennis.

Not for the first time, she wondered just how long tennis could continue to be enough for her. Yes, she loved winning, and she believed she could continue to win her matches for many more years, making her father happy. But was his ambition the reason she worked so hard at tennis? He'd pushed her . . . she did love him so much— God, sometimes it was confusing!

But recently she had begun to sense that an entire world lay out there for her, if only she could decide what she wanted.

A few hours later, she walked through the crowded concourse at Orly airport, passing a kiosk that sold international newspapers.

As she'd expected, all the headlines blasted out the news of the royal engagement. *Kristina to Marry Playboy. Kristina Shocks Costa with Surprise Engagement.* She stopped and bought a copy of *Confidential,* an American gossip magazine, and began reading it as she entered the gate area.

A close palace source says that Prince Henri is furious at his daughter's sudden engagement to a French playboy, read one article. *Jean-Luc Furnoir has been linked to models and actresses, and rumors say he has also had a liaison with a well-known race car driver. Furnoir has promised to convert to Catholicism and will sign a prenuptial agreement that specifies a settlement in case of later divorce.*

Teddy handed her boarding pass to the American Airlines attendant and walked onto the jetway, pausing for one last look out the window at the brilliant sunlight slanting down onto the tarmac outside. A wave of sadness came over her, so profound that she had to force herself to keep on walking.

Jac. All he'd been was a fantasy, just like the rest of Costa del Mar.

And the two princesses. She'd liked both of them, especially Kristina, who might even have become a close friend if their lives had been different. She wondered why Kristina had become engaged to a man like Furnoir, a man who was basically just a spoiled, self-indulgent playboy. What kind of latent death wish had driven the princess to do something like that?

Teddy found her seat in business class and sank into it, wondering if she'd ever hear from the young royals again.

"Dad," said Teddy, later that week in Connecticut as they ate breakfast on the deck overlooking the woods, "Dad . . . there's something I want to talk with you about. Something important."

Houston Warner gazed at his daughter.

"Yes, what is it, Teddy Bear? Don't you think you should be getting ready for practice? Manuel is waiting at the club for us."

"Can't practice wait?" said Teddy, putting down her croissant.

"Honey, practice can never wait." He smiled to take the sting out of the words.

"I've been thinking," she began. "I would like to take a year off tennis. A year just to relax a little—maybe take some college courses or just kick back and have some fun, become a beach bum for a while."

"What? You can't be serious!"

"Daddy," Teddy said gently, "I know you mean well, and I do love tennis—I truly, truly, do. But I'm burned out. I've traveled all over the globe, I have so many frequent flier miles I can't even use them, and everywhere I go I'm surrounded by tennis people. Tennis. That's all they talk about. I'm expected to live, breathe, eat, and sleep tennis." Her voice quivered. "I work harder than ninety-nine percent of the adult population. And I have less than one percent of the fun."

"Don't be smartass, Teddy."

"I'm not being smartass. I'm getting tired, Dad. Whatever happened to fun? I want to walk on the beach. I want to learn windsurfing. I want to go to a Formula One race. I want—''

''Formula One race? Is that what this is about? Those Costan royals?''

''No . . .'' She flushed painfully. ''It's just one year, Dad.''

He looked at her. ''No, it isn't *just* a year—it's your whole competitive edge. You have momentum now, Teddy. You're strong, you're lean and mean. But in a year, other girls, younger and more hungry, are going to come up behind you, and they'll surpass you. Trust me, you'll hate it.''

''You don't want to listen, do you, Dad?'' said Teddy tiredly. ''You really don't.''

''I am listening. I do appreciate your hard work. Maybe we can swing a couple of weeks of R and R—'' he began.

''But I'll have to practice every day, won't I? So as not to lose my 'edge,' '' she said, her eyes filling. ''Okay. I'll do it your way, Dad. I *am* a tennis player, I do love the sport . . . but why does it seem sometimes as if there's something missing? Something *more* I could have—if I only knew what I wanted?''

Later, on the train to New York, Houston Warner sat stiffly with all the other commuters. He was holding the *New York Times,* but his mind was on his daughter. When had Teddy started sounding like this?

After she met Prince Jac, he told himself. That's when it had started. Damn them—damn those royals. He just hoped that they didn't steal away the few short years his daughter had to be a tennis star.

Gabriella had put off talking to her father, afraid of his reaction, but Lane had called several times and she knew she could not put it off any longer.

''Papa,'' she said nervously one morning at breakfast, ''Papa . . .''

''Yes, yes, of course,'' said the monarch dismissively. He was seated at one end of the long, burnished ebony table in the garden room, eating a brioche spread with pear preserves, while reading *Le Monde*.

"I had a wonderful time in the United States last week."

"Hmmm," said Henri, turning a page.

She blurted, "I met with Kenny Lane, and we're going to have a line of jewelry called 'Princess Gabriella,' and we have entered into a licensing agreement, and I'm going to travel all over to promote it. . . ."

Henri looked up, startled. "What did you say?"

Gabriella's heart was pounding as she went through her carefully rehearsed speech, pointing out to Henri all the advantages of having her own jewelry line. She showed him photographs of some advertisements in *Vogue* and *Town and Country* that illustrated the way that Lane wanted to promote her. She showed him copies of a projected fifteen-city publicity tour, figures on Cable Network, the new QVC channel that sold merchandise via television into tens of millions of homes.

Henri had forgotten all about his newspaper. "Fifteen cities? You? Why should I permit you to cavort around the world like this?"

"Because the Princess Gabriella line of elegant and expensive jewelry—the very best—will get Costa out in front of the international press each and every day. People will be focusing on our country, constantly reminded that we have the best of life—and everything else in Costa." She was warming up now, her enthusiasm growing. "It will promote Costa del Mar as a place of glamour, style, and undisputed luxury!"

"But you are talking about becoming a . . . a salesperson. That is all you would be."

"A spokesperson!" cried Gabriella. "*And* a designer of wonderful, elegant jewelry. These pieces are going to be stunning. . . . Women will kill to have one of my necklaces or pins in their jewelry collection. Don't you often say that you are the CEO of the corporation of Costa del Mar? Aren't those your exact words, Papa? Well, corporations need publicity, and they need—"

"Enough," said Henri, beginning to laugh, and succumbing to her enthusiasm.

"May I do it, then?"

"Yes, under two conditions."

"Yes?" said Gabriella warily.

"You must travel with sufficient security, two bodyguards at least, and every host city must provide adequate security coverage for your needs. This is the late eighties, dear Gabriella, and international terrorists are a real threat, especially to people like us, people who are so visible. Remember when Princess Caroline of Monaco and her husband, Stefano, just narrowly escaped being kidnapped? It is frightening. And secondly . . ." Henri paused.

"Yes, Papa, what . . . ?"

"I want you to remember where your heart is."

"Oh," cried Gaby. "Oh, Papa—" She rushed over to hug her father, and in a rare moment of unrestrained affection Henri permitted her to wrap her arms around him and nuzzle his neck. She laughed happily. "I *know* where my heart is, Papa. It's here in Costa. . . . Always here. . . . Always."

The staccato pop of tennis balls reverberated in the autumn air.

From the window of his study, Houston Warner looked out on the clay court, where Teddy and Jamaica DuRoss were volleying fiercely, neither of them giving an inch.

He watched for a moment, bemused, thinking that Teddy was such a beautiful woman and didn't even know how truly beautiful she was.

The ringing of the telephone interrupted his reverie, and he picked it up, thinking it might be a call he was expecting from Zurich. Instead, he heard a clipped male voice speaking with a French accent.

"His Royal Highness, Prince Jac, wishes to speak to Miss Teddy Warner."

Prince Jac.

Warner felt a burst of astonishment, quickly followed by a strong surge of protective alarm. He wasn't stupid; he knew that Teddy and Prince Jac had had an affair when Teddy was in Costa, and Jac had behaved like countless dozens of royal playboys and dumped her afterward, discarding his daughter as if she were some tarty little dolly bird. Oh, yes, Warner had seen the hurt in Teddy's eyes, the hurt she had tried so carefully to hide. It had infuriated him.

Now Prince Jac wanted to talk to her, probably to take up where he had left off—only to drop her again when he was bored with her. If only Jac were older, and settled, but he wasn't. He was a headstrong royal teenager who didn't know what the hell he wanted. And Teddy was a vulnerable young woman—scarcely more than a girl. The prince would hurt Teddy badly if she ever got involved with him again. A hurt that would be intensified a thousand times because their romance would be played out in the media. For the rest of her life, Teddy would be the woman who was dumped twice by a royal. . . . No, he couldn't let such shame happen to her.

"Hello?" said the voice of the royal secretary. "Hello?"

"Ah, yes," said Warner, thinking fast.

"His Highness wishes to speak with Miss Teddy Warner."

"I'm sorry, but my daughter is hiking in the Adirondacks and cannot be reached," Warner said quickly, wiping a bead of sweat from his face.

He hung up, then sat staring at the telephone, his heart pounding thickly in his chest. He'd done what he believed no father should ever do—interfered with his little girl's life. God, had he done the right thing?

Thinking for a long time he finally reached for the telephone and dialed a number in Paris.

* * *

"Are you sure?" Houston Warner said, his voice rising with excitement. "Are you sure of this, Max?"

Max Bergson was a journalist writing for the Paris office of *Time*. Warner had hired the young newshound to research the Costan royals for him.

"Absolutely. I don't have concrete proof, but I do have impeccable sources at Royal House, and they say Prince Georges made an unusual phone call to a boyhood friend, who just happens to be a guy he used to raise hell with. A guy who just happens to have connections with the military. Enough of the call was overhead—well, most of those aristocrats tend to ignore servants. They're so arrogant they don't even see them most of the time, even though they are there and listening."

"I see."

"Quite a coincidence, wouldn't you say? I mean, that such a phone call would be made, and not a week later, D'Fabray, his wife, and the pilot are killed in an explosion aboard his plane. And now Prince Georges's friend just happens to be the new finance minister."

Houston Warner was feeling an odd, horrific chill, a sensation of the hairs lifting across the center of his back and neck. "You're not saying—you're not accusing Prince Georges of complicity in murder, are you?"

"Listen, I'm not accusing him of anything. There is no concrete proof—the manservant didn't have the balls to make a tape of the phone call, and all we have is his word. Unprintable as far as *Time* is concerned . . . now. The servant may be disgruntled, he may have axes to grind, or maybe he just dislikes his employer. It's just a report without corroboration," said Bergson. "That's what you wanted, isn't it? Reports?"

"Yes," said Warner, shaken. "Yes, thank you. Keep them coming, Max. Whatever you have, no matter how vague, I want them."

"Sure thing, man. But this may be a big story sometime, so be prepared. And it'll be my exclusive."

Warner hung up, feeling disturbed and uneasy. This investigation of Prince Georges had started more as a curiosity, a hobby that had quickly become consuming. The more he learned about Prince Henri, the more he respected him. But Georges . . . And what if he *was* up to some royal double-dealing? Even worse? Didn't Prince Henri have a right to be warned?

He went to the phone and dialed the country code for Costa del Mar. He was glad now that he had decided not to go to his office. There his executive assistant handled his calls for him, getting the other party on the line before he spoke to them, but this was one call that Warner wanted to keep secret.

Because the country was so small there was no city code, and in a few minutes he was connected with the palace.

"This is Houston Warner, the CEO of WarnerCo," he said. "I wish to speak with Prince Henri, please."

The male voice on the other end of the line quickly switched from French to English. "I am sorry but due to security reasons His Highness does not accept unsolicited telephone calls."

"I'm Houston Warner," he repeated. "We've met at the palace. He knows me—"

"You may leave a message, sir."

Two days later, he was speaking to Prince Henri.

"You had a message of some importance, as you say it?" The old prince's voice was deep, still firm and ringing.

"Your Highness, I am not sure how to say this. . . . I have come upon some information, and even though I cannot vouch for its accuracy. . . ." Warner went on to describe what the journalist had told him, but even as he said it, he realized how flimsy it sounded. It was servants' gossip, really, and little more.

Henri spoke slowly, his voice tinged with anger. "I thank you for your concerns, Mr. Warner, and I will, of course, have the matter looked into. But I must tell you this journalist, this Max Bergson, has printed several defamatory articles about Costa in his magazine and would like nothing better than to conjure up an exclusive story for himself, even if he has to base it on little more than hearsay and gossip. Like all journalists, he frequently makes false assumptions. If I were you, Mr. Warner, I would abstain from interesting yourself in Costan matters of state. My country has passed through many centuries of complicated politics, and it is difficult for outsiders to understand us.''

Slowly Warner began to realize that he was getting a royal rebuke—and being told to keep away from Costan affairs.

''I just thought you would want to know,'' he stated, unwilling to apologize for doing what he had thought was right.

''Of course. We will deal with it in our own way.''

The entire country of Costa had been scrubbed and spruced up for the wedding of Princess Kristina and Jean-Luc Furnoir. Its cobblestoned streets were fairly sparkling. The best of the late autumn flowers were massed everywhere, along with ribbons and blue-and-white bunting.

The *paparazzi* had been waiting outside the cathedral since dawn, along with crowds of Costan citizens, tourists, and press. All were eager for a look at Princess Kristina and Jean-Luc as the royal family arrived in a gilt-encrusted barouche that dated back to Napoleonic times.

Uniformed soldiers from the palace formed a mounted honor guard.

Seated in a pouf of lace and pearl-embroidered chiffon designed by Yves St. Laurent, a veil covering her pale beauty, Kristina gazed straight ahead, in a tense world of her own. The engagement period had been tumultuous, with disagreements between Jean-Luc and her father over almost everything: the religious conversion ceremony, the guest list, and even protocol for seating at the cathedral. To add to Kristina's misery, Gabriella had remained silent and defensive, and the sisters had continued their recent quarrel, barely speaking except in public.

Gaby was still angry at Kristina for "stealing" Jean-Luc.

Was getting married a mistake? Kristina was thinking, panic swirling through her brain. *Oh, mon Dieu.* . . . But it was too late now.

Prince Henri, seated in the royal pew in the first row, watched the nuptial mass with damp eyes. He had decided to give Jean-Luc an additional gift, the title of Marquis de Costa—a title, he had shrewdly arranged, that would only last so long as the marriage was intact.

His thoughts turned to the startling conversation he'd had with L. Houston Warner only four days previously. He had already dispatched the head of palace security to talk to Prince Georges's manservant, but the man had flatly denied saying anything to the reporter.

Could Georges . . . ? Henri wondered uneasily. But, no, he assured himself. The explosion on the finance minister's plane, still under investigation, was being blamed on pilot error, and Henri could not bring himself to believe that his fifty-five-year-old, ineffectual brother could actually be responsible for such a heinous crime.

Georges was simply a weak man, that was all. A man who might experience some feelings of envy, understandable envy, but who frittered away most of his days with golf, travel, or various mistresses. Georges simply didn't have the brains or the drive to be a traitor.

Seated between Henri and Jac in the royal pew, Gabriella held her hands clenched tightly in her lap, keeping a smile on her lips. *He was mine,* she thought.

But had she ever been his? Gazing at the couple who knelt at the altar, she found it hard to believe now that she'd actually slept with Jean-Luc, giving her virginity to him. That event, more than a year ago, already seemed like an unreal dream.

Making love . . . blending one's self with another human being—would she ever really find that for herself? Gaby felt a sudden, fierce stab of loneliness. Sometimes it seemed as if she wouldn't. She knew she set up barriers between herself and men, afraid to let them past. Even Jean-Luc had called her "cool."

She thought about that sleazy article in the tabloid. Jean-Luc and his women—and his men. He was going to create trouble, she thought. Couldn't Kristina see that? She'd tried to tell her several times, but her sister had refused to listen.

"I'm making my own decisions for a change," the younger princess had insisted.

Gabriella closed her eyes, feeling a stab of pity for her impetuous sister.

At the reception following the wedding there was a towering, six-tiered wedding cake with two captive doves trapped in a silver cage between the fifth and sixth layers. Wedding gifts included a new apartment for the newlyweds from Henri, luggage, silver boxes, a two-thousand-piece set of silver from the citizens of Costa del Mar, and a Louis XIV desk from Jean-Luc's parents. Nikos Skouros had sent a Renoir.

The receiving line for the nine hundred guests took two and a half hours, and Kristina's gloved hands became sore from being constantly squeezed. She kept smiling, murmuring charmingly when she could not remember someone's name. Princess Diana had attended, but Prince Charles, committed to an international polo match in Vienna, was not with her. There were dozens of other European royals, venture capitalists and heads of international development agencies, as well as a glitter of film people. Nancy Reagan, the Dustin Hoffmans, Richard Gere and Cindy Crawford, Max von Sydow, Isabella Rossellini, and the powerful Hollywood agent Michael Ovitz, of Creative Artists Agency, and his wife Judy were just a few of the notables.

"You're the most beautiful woman I've ever seen," said Mike Ovitz, finding Kristina as she stood talking to several school friends.

Kristina had heard such remarks all her life, but from Ovitz, she was thrilled to receive the compliment. Anyone from Hollywood impressed her. "Thank you," she murmured.

"The Academy Awards are coming up the first week in April. I would like to invite you and your husband to be my guests and to attend the Governor's Ball afterward. I will take care of all the arrangements."

"That would be wonderful. Have your secretary call mine," Kristina responded warmly.

Ovitz pressed her hand in his. "Princess Kristina, I can guarantee you will have a wonderful time. I have a project in mind, a film I'm trying to package . . ."

Kristina was shocked. She stared at the attractive, brown-eyed, confident Ovitz, head of an agency whose huge client list was studded with major stars.

"*A film?*" she gasped.

"Princess Kristina"—his smile was warm—"if you're at all interested, even just slightly interested, just come to Hollywood for a week. I promise you won't be sorry."

"Let's blow this place as soon as we can," said Jean-Luc, gazing over Kristina's shoulder at the wedding guests. He had already had several drinks, and his face was flushed.

"We are required to stay until the end," whispered Kristina. "No one can leave until Papa does."

"Soon," insisted Jean-Luc. "My feet hurt."

Kristina looked at her new husband. As children, she and Gabriella had been trained to ignore such matters as hurting feet, boredom, or discomfort. "But Jean-Luc—"

"I want to be alone with my new wife."

"All right," she agreed. The excitement of a new husband seemed to pale in comparison to the thrill of being approached by Mike Ovitz. *He wants you because you're a princess,* the sensible part of her mind said. She knew it was true, yet she couldn't resist wondering if she could ever really be a movie star.

In the dressing suite that had been set aside on the first floor of the palace for Kristina to change in, Gabriella was waiting.

"You . . . look so lovely," she whispered to her sister. "I don't think there's ever been a lovelier bride in this country."

"Mama was a beautiful bride. You've seen the photographs."

"Not half as beautiful as you."

Kristina looked at her, too exhausted to fully accept her sister's attempt at a truce.

"I wish you luck," Gaby said.

"I . . . Gaby . . ."

"So much luck. I mean it. I know we've argued, I know we aren't perfect sisters—"

"We *are* perfect," cried Kristina.

Suddenly they were hugging, squeezing each other tightly, and Kristina was crying on Gabriella's shoulder, her tears dampening her dress. "I didn't mean to hurt you," sobbed Kristina. "I'm selfish—I thought only of myself."

"You didn't."

"Sometimes I don't even know myself," cried Kristina.

Teddy Warner watched a film clip of the wedding on "Entertainment Tonight," wistfully envying Kristina's lacy gown and the pomp and panoply of the ceremony.

When it was over, she left the lounge of the Regent Hotel in Melbourne, Australia, where many of the players in the Australian exhibition match were staying, and dashed for the elevator. She was in a hurry to get to her room and change her clothes; a few of the women players were going out together for dinner, trying to alleviate the tensions of the week.

The elevator arrived, and she hurried in, jabbing the button for the tenth floor.

"Wait—wait! Hold the elevator," someone called. Just as the doors were closing, a pair of muscular, suntanned hands brashly thrust themselves into the space, followed by the rest of Auggie Steckler, the top-seeded male player for the tournament. Teddy hadn't seen him since they'd played with the royals in the benefit doubles match at Costa del Mar. Amazing . . . that he would risk injury to his hands merely to open an elevator door for a beautiful woman.

"Well, if it isn't Miss Golden Girl," he said, grinning. His blue eyes fastened on her with frank, admiring interest. "How was Costa del Mar? I heard you stayed there for a while."

"Wonderful." Teddy smiled uncertainly. Auggie had a reputation for romancing many of the women on the circuit.

"I heard Princess Kristina got married."

"In style. I just saw it on TV," Teddy said.

"You weren't invited?"

Teddy's smile was a bit sad. "I met the royals, but I don't think I'm exactly in their inner circle."

They rode up together, their bodies placed in close proximity by the small European elevator, and Teddy could smell Brut, the aftershave Auggie wore, along with a whiff of clean soap. He was blond and square-jawed, with a Michael Douglas–type chin cleft.

"Nervous about playing Steffi Graf in the finals tomorrow?"

"No. Should I be?"

Auggie Steckler raised one blond eyebrow. "All I can say is that you're one helluva cool lady. And the funny part of it is, that chilled-out attitude against Graf might be the best defense."

"I don't know," responded Teddy truthfully. "Maybe I'm just lucky and don't choke. I almost never clutch up before a match. I figure what's going to happen will happen. All I have to do is play my best and then a little harder than that. Of course,'' she said with a laugh, ''a little prayer doesn't hurt.''

''Care for a drink in my room?'' he offered.

''I don't think so. I'm meeting some people for a quick dinner and a movie. But thank you for asking.''

''You wouldn't be sorry. I promise.''

She smiled again, but in a dismissive way.

Reaching her room, Teddy walked in and discovered that her message light was blinking. When she called the desk, she was told that her father had called. Teddy sighed. When her father didn't travel with her, he expected her to keep in close touch and wanted to know the blow-by-blow details of every match she played, overloading her with criticism if he felt she could have handled a shot better.

She direct-dialed Connecticut, and within minutes was speaking to her father.

''Dad, it's all going fabulously,'' she told him, summarizing the day's match. He launched into his usual series of incisive questions.

''By the way,'' her father said, after she'd finished, ''I saw on CNN sports that Prince Jac is driving in the Costan Grand Prix. Very risky, very reckless for a young royal. He certainly doesn't have much stability, does he?''

Despite her father's obvious criticism, the mention of Jac caused Teddy's heart to pound.

''He's going to race?''

''Word is he actually drove a car in the time trials and lapped right behind one of the best drivers. The old prince was furious. At this rate he's not going to live long enough to wear a crown, I'd imagine,'' added Warner dryly. ''Race car drivers aren't particularly noted for their long span of life.''

''Oh, but Jac is different,'' she began.

''He isn't, honey, he's too young to know what the hell he wants. Anyway, Teddy Bear, I won't keep you if you're going out for dinner. I just want you to know that I love you and I'm pulling for you. *Good luck!* Call me tomorrow as soon as the match is over.''

"I will," she promised, hanging up.

Restlessly Teddy began pacing her room, too excited now to change her clothes. The maid had left a morning edition of the Melbourne paper on her bedside table, and she rushed for it, hoping to find some mention of the Costan Grand Prix.

Flipping through the newspaper's sports section, she found an article about the time trials, and she down on her bed to devour every word, studying the photograph of Prince Jac. Wearing a driving suit, he looked confident and happy as he stood beside a low-slung race car.

Her heart began to pound. She could call Jac. Right now, this minute.

Painfully Teddy closed her eyes, recalling the warm brilliance of the Costan sunlight, the winding, pastel streets lined with flowers, the medieval castle with its fluttering, blue-and-white pennants. And the way Jac's arms felt around her, the smooth hardness of his young body. . . .

Then she snapped open her eyes.

She had friends to meet. By tomorrow night she could be the tournament winner, photographed in every major paper in the world, appearing on every TV network. She had to quit thinking about him.

Jac didn't need her. If he did, *he* would have called *her*.

The Egyptian sun beat down like a huge, golden furnace, glaring in Kristina's eyes even though she had shielded them with designer wraparound sunglasses especially made for her by the D.O.C. Optics Corporation in the United States. They had arrived by private plane from Cairo some three hours ago. She stepped out of the Jeep Land Rover and gazed at the Nubian village called Gebel Togo, near Aswan, some five hundred miles from Cairo—a collection of crumbling whitewashed hut-buildings with roofs littered with sticks and straw.

Jean-Luc, who'd drunk too much the night before at the

Nile Hilton, then kept her up half the night in frenzied, demanding lovemaking, remained in the Jeep. Even in the heat, he was impeccably dressed in fashionable Italian designer clothing.

"I have a splitting headache, darling," he told her. "So you go look for both of us."

She sighed, already bored with the village, which had remained unchanged for centuries. They'd already visited the Pyramids, gaping at the Sphinx during the day and also at a laser light spectacle in the evening. They'd seen the Temple of Abu Simbel, visited the tomb of Tutankhamen, and the huge temples at Luxor and Karnak. The sights had been astounding, but Jean-Luc, who'd been to Egypt before, hadn't shown much enthusiasm, somewhat spoiling it for Kristina. She had really gotten caught up in this adventure into an exotic and ancient past and even took a short ride on a camel named Yankee Doodle.

She walked around the village for a while, staring at the skinny, almost naked children, the scrawny dogs, and the crumbling, dusty streets.

"For God's sake, will you stop being Mother Teresa? Come on," her husband called. "Get back in the Jeep, will you? These filthy Arabs are boring. I want to go back to the hotel and have a drink and a shower. And you," he added.

Kristina finally climbed back into the Jeep, and the driver restarted its engine, proceeding along dusty roads back to the Hotel Oberoi.

Back at the hotel a group of tourists were just arriving, their voices rising in torrents of fluent, excited French.

"Jean-Luc!" The woman was young with streaked brown hair and huge, brown eyes, dressed in smart Parisian chic. "My God, is it really you? The last time I saw you, you were *bien cuit* . . . very, very drunk!"

"And I could be again," said Jean-Luc, smiling broadly, his sun-drenched lassitude disappearing. He hurried forward and scooped the woman up into a big hug, whirling her feet off the floor. Then he turned to Kristina. "Kristina, I want you to meet Martine Chenonceau. I almost married her once, but she had the good sense to turn me down."

Martine giggled, smiling at Kristina, then turned to Jean-Luc again to speak in her liquid French. "Your wedding was beautiful, I saw the pictures in *Paris Match*. I have just remarried, too. My husband, Étienne, is the one over there arguing with the *concierge*. He is very jealous, hmmmm? So let's not tell him about our 'friendship,' all right? He resents anyone I was involved with before him. I'm sure you both understand."

Kristina looked at the broad smiles that kept breaking over her husband's face as he spoke to Martine.

"Drinks," Jean-Luc announced. "Let's have cocktails in half an hour. We'll meet in the lobby, eh?"

"Wonderful," said Martine.

Kristina nodded.

In the *International Herald-Tribune*, Kristina read that Teddy Warner had beaten Steffi Graf at the Australian Open. She stared at the photo of Teddy caught by the camera, leaping in the air, her skirt flying to reveal flawless thighs.

She felt a flash of unexpected envy. Teddy was a star in her own right, even if it was just tennis. Whereas she . . . Already Kristina knew she'd made a terrible mistake in marrying Jean-Luc.

The two couples, along with Kristina's bodyguard, traveled back to Alexandria, where they had booked rooms at the Montazeh Sheraton, a charming hotel overlooking the Mediterranean Sea and the gardens of the palace. Martine's husband, an importer, had some important business with an Arab sheik, something about an oil refinery operation in Morocco.

Paparazzi had heard about their stay in Egypt and mobbed their hotel. They descended on Kristina and Jean-

Luc and even included Martine and Étienne in their shoot-ing frenzy.

Jean-Luc and Étienne left for a business dinner one night, and Martine pleaded a migraine, saying she had to remain in her suite or she would be desperately ill for at least three days. Kristina decided to remain at the hotel, too. She hadn't slept a full night in two weeks. The long hours of lovemaking every night, catering to Jean-Luc's exotic desires, had left her feeling drained.

She ordered from room service and then went to sit on her balcony, which overlooked a sweeping view of the cres-cent-shaped seafront, lined with majestic palms and stately old houses.

Gazing down at the street, she thought she saw Martine getting into a blue-and-white taxi. But when she glanced again, the taxi had already turned a corner.

She took a luxurious, three-hour nap and woke up feel-ing vibrant again. Jean-Luc *was* a fabulous lover and seemed eternally hungry for her. What woman could com-plain about that? By the time Jean-Luc returned, she was wearing a white lace negligee, his favorite, with lace cut-outs artfully arranged over her breasts and pubic area.

"Darling," she said, greeting him by sliding her arms around his neck and pulling him to her for a long, sensuous kiss.

"Not now," her husband told her. "I have to shower—that stupid restaurant had poor air-conditioning, and I sweated through my clothes."

"We never minded a little perspiration before," she wheedled, starting to unfasten her husband's collar.

"I just want to take a quick shower first," Jean-Luc said, pulling away and closing the bathroom door behind him.

Two days later, accompanied by her security guard, Kristina was leaving the hotel to go shopping at a boutique off Tahrir Square, where Martine had told her she could find wonderful leather goods, when one of the local *paparazzi* stopped her.

"Mademoiselle, mademoiselle," he called in strangely accented French. He was poorly dressed in white pants and shirt, and had the dark skin and melting black eyes of an Arab peddler.

"Please—no pictures today," urged the princess's bodyguard, Lucien.

"It is not your picture. I *have* picture."

"What?" demanded her security.

"This," he said, thrusting several photographs past the guard directly into Kristina's hand. Bewildered, she stared down at a photograph of her husband, kneeling astride a naked woman who had Martine's long, medium-brown hair, while another woman, also nude, knelt behind Jean-Luc, licking his balls. The blurred picture had obviously been taken with a telephoto lens, but was clear enough to reveal her husband's lips opened wide in pleasure.

Kristina stared at it, stunned, then looked at the second photo, which showed the three of them lying on the bed, arms and legs entwined. Jean-Luc was sucking Martine's dark brown nipples.

On our honeymoon, Kristina thought. All her previous reservations about Jean-Luc came flashing over her again.

"Five hundred pounds, Egyptian," said the photographer. "Or I send to Prince Henri in Costa del Mar."

"No," said Kristina, shaking her head and beginning to back away.

"Five hundred pounds—or I send in mail today."

This would enrage her father, and the anger might cause him to have another heart attack. Desperately she dug in her purse, producing three hundred Egyptian pounds, all the money she had on her.

"Your Highness—" the guard began, trying to stop her. But she brushed him aside.

"I—I can get more," she promised. "Please—just wait here, and I'll run up to my room and get the money."

"Money now, or I mail."

"For God's sake! I have to go and get some more money—do you think I carry that much money on me?"

The man scowled. "Money now."

Kristina uttered a cry of exasperation and snatched the two photographs out of his hands, turning and running back into the hotel before he could react. Ditching her guard as well, she raced across the lobby.

Hurrying into the elevator, she pressed the button for their floor, and waited until the door closed. Leaning against the wall, Kristina began to tremble. When the elevator door opened, she walked down the corridor to their suite, deciding that she would call her father and warn him that an Arab photographer was trying to blackmail them using fake photos of Jean-Luc with two other women.

Yes. Henri might believe that. The tabloids had used such bogus photographs before, and Henri had been furious.

She unlocked the door and hurried inside, all thoughts of shopping gone from her mind. Jean-Luc's closet door was open, and his clothes, imported from Italy and England, hung in neat rows. Beneath were arranged his shoes, all made in Italy of butter-soft leather.

Kristina glared at the clothes, and then all her disappointment and pain merged into a crescendo of rage.

She walked to the closet, scooped up an armload of suits, adding several pairs of shoes to the top of the pile, and walked across the room to the balcony. Stepping onto the balcony, she walked to the edge and dropped the armful of clothes three floors below onto the street.

"Why did you do that?" raged Jean-Luc several hours later when he returned, staring incredulously into his empty closet.

"How dare you screw another woman on our honeymoon?" cried Kristina, hurling a room-service napkin at him.

"I didn't screw anyone."

"You did! I saw the pictures! You and that bitch Martine!"

"I didn't. I only had a drink with her—"

"You were *stupide* enough to be photographed by one of those vile *paparazzi*," screamed Kristina in French, following the napkin with a crystal saltshaker. "He asked me for money for your filthy pictures," she said in a quieter tone.

"Please, darling—"

"I despise you! I never should have married you."

Losing her forced composure again, Kristina tossed the entire room service tray on the floor. Finally she threw herself on the bed, sobbing into her pillow.

"*Bébé,*" crooned Jean-Luc, stroking her hair, "I didn't mean to . . . I was just so drunk. I don't know what happened. That bitch Martine was angry because I jilted her. She wanted me to look bad. Oh, darling. . . ."

"I hate you," wept Kristina.

"Don't hate me, darling. Please. I don't know what happened. I love you . . . *ma petite poupée.*"

"Oh, shut up," she sobbed.

"I never meant to hurt you. . . ."

"You did hurt me."

"I never meant it," said Jean-Luc, carefully stroking her shoulders. "Oh, Kristina, *ma petite* . . ."

Spring in Connecticut was a display of white dogwoods glimmering in the woods, and tulips and daffodils everywhere. Houston Warner's obsession with the Costan royals had become a crusade.

He phoned Bergson again, asking him to tap all of his sources to find out just what was happening.

A month later, Bergson phoned him. "Well, Prince Georges has covered his tracks well. I haven't been able to find out much. Nothing of any validity. Now even his servant denies overhearing anything. He's totally clammed up.''

"No rumors?" persisted Warner. "Nothing?"

"Nothing—the well has gone dry," reported Bergson. "But I feel I must say something to you, Mr. Warner. Costa del Mar is a small country, and when one goes around asking questions, people know about it. Word spreads. Maybe that's why people won't talk to me anymore. You're trying to overturn some very ugly stones, and I think you should cool it for a while.''

"Just keep looking, Bergson. I'll pay you well. If what I give you isn't enough, just let me know.''

"It isn't the money, Warner. It's just—'' Then Bergson sighed. "Well—all right, I did uncover something pretty incredible. It seems that about ten years ago one of Prince Georges's servants was killed in an automobile accident. It turns out he was tattling to Prince Henri about Georges's escapades with a servant girl. Henri is pretty conservative, and he came down hard on his brother, making him toe the line. Coincidence? Maybe. But I did hear a whisper that maybe Georges arranged to have the servant knocked off.''

"No," breathed Warner.

"Rumors. Who knows?" Even over the phone Warner could sense Bergson's quizzical shrug. "I'd say that our boy Georgie isn't a very savory guy, though. You really should back off, Mr. Warner.''

"I'll think about it," Warner finally said.

Four days later Max Bergson died. Warner didn't hear about his death for another month, and when a staffer at *Time* told him, she said it had been a tragic mishap—Bergson had been hit by a car while jogging on the quai de Montebello.

It was a misty day, the sun just beginning to burn through the moisture, turning trees and grass an incredible, fresh green.

Teddy Warner loped toward the prestigious center court

at Wimbledon, wearing a stunning tennis dress with a petal-cut white skirt, its collar emblazoned with the Reebok logo, deftly parrying questions from reporters trotting after her, eager for a story. Yes, she'd just signed a three-year contract, worth $350,000, to wear Reebok's clothes and shoes during her matches, and, yes, her new racquet was by Yonex, the result of another multiyear, high-paying deal recently arranged by her agent.

She stood nervously in the center court waiting room, her adrenaline starting to flow faster now; the match could not begin until any royalty present that day had been seated. A huge sign over the door that led to the court quoted Rudyard Kipling: "If you can meet with triumph and disaster and treat those two impostors the same."

A buzz of excitement rose from the crowd. Princess Caroline with her father, Prince Rainier of Monaco, had just arrived in the royal box, taking her place in the front row of cushioned seats. A moment later Princess Diana arrived, clad in deep turquoise and yellow polka dots, accompanied by a giggling group of her Sloane Ranger friends.

Cheers and clapping filled the air as Teddy and Martina Navratilova walked out onto the court. They stopped at the service line, then followed tradition by turning and bowing to the royal box. Princess Di smiled directly at Teddy.

Bowing, Teddy had a deep, excited thrill of anticipation. Wimbledon was the apex of any tennis player's career. She'd worked her entire life for this minute.

Then she glanced up. A late arrival had just hurried into the royal box and was making his way down toward an empty seat in the front row.

Teddy froze. *Jac! Here?*

The young prince of Costa del Mar, wearing wraparound aviator sunglasses, had now seated himself. One of the pretty Sloane Rangers leaned toward him, smiling as she said something, her hand touching his shoulder possessively.

Teddy felt her stomach tighten. Why had Jac chosen *today* of all days to do this to her? To spoil her concentration?

Painfully aware of Jac's eyes on her, along with the TV cameras, Teddy walked toward the opposite service line, her heart in her throat.

God, she couldn't choke up. Not now. Not now!

"Isn't she lovely?" Lady Philippa Hawthorne was saying. "Look at her run. Don't they say that some of the top female tennis players are, well, not very feminine?"

"Teddy Warner is *very* feminine," Jac said.

"Then what is she doing in a competitive game like tennis?"

"Winning, it appears," drawled Jac. He leaned forward as Teddy streaked across the court, her skirt flipping up to reveal her lace-trimmed panties, her blond braid flying out behind her as she slammed the ball across the sideline boundary. The crowd *oohed* together as if exhaling one single gigantic breath, and the sound echoed throughout the stands.

"Well, I'm tired, and I'm thirsty and hot, and I wish we hadn't come," said Philippa grumpily. "Tennis can be an awful bore, don't you know?"

Jac turned briefly to smile at his girlfriend of two months. He said, "Of course, you must be getting tired. But, darling Philly, we can't leave now in the middle of the match. It isn't done."

"Pish tosh. Who cares what they think? I'm much prettier than Teddy Warner is."

"Of course, you are," lied Jac, watching Teddy.

He'd met Lady Philippa at the Grand Prix in Monaco and sparks had ignited between them. Philippa, who was twenty, looked like a younger version of Princess Diana, her English beauty the type that would photograph well, her slim body made for designer suits and ballgowns. Jac had no doubt that if he married her, the world press would glorify Philippa, making her into another Di.

But did he love her? His father had been pressuring him to settle down, and Jac knew that traditionally, royal engagements were often more like legalized mergers between countries than love matches. If that was what one wanted.

Frowning, Jac watched Teddy hit a winning point. She grinned up at the stands once, her smile dazzling. He loved the fierce way she played. And her clean, blond looks. Why had she never returned his call?

He could send a message to her, he supposed, apologizing for his caddish behavior in dropping her after they had become lovers. But what should he say? He wasn't much for writing anything. He almost never wrote letters; secretaries did that for him, but he could hardly ask a secretary to write a love note.

"Will you *stop* staring at that girl," snapped Philippa, tugging at his arm.

Wimbledon had just come apart at the seams. People screamed, laughed, waved United States flags. Teddy had come up from being seeded number 5 to topple Navratilova. Pandemonium ruled even the royal box.

"Dad!" said Teddy, weeping with emotion as she clutched the treasured silver winner's plate and the £175,000 check she'd just been given by Princess Di. "Oh, Dad!"

"Honey, we did it!"

"Teddy! How does it feel? Are you floating on air?" said Fred Manfra of ABC/CAP Cities Network radio, maneuvering Houston Warner to one side so the cameras could focus on Teddy.

"Wonderful! Wonderful!" gulped Teddy as someone thrust a bouquet of roses into her hand.

In the locker room, Teddy finally made her way through the crowd of well-wishers.

"Isn't this the most wonderful week you've ever had?"

chattered Laurette, one of the quarterfinalists as Teddy was
getting undressed. "And I can't believe all those royals.
Wasn't Princess Di just beautiful? But so thin. And Prince
Jac . . . what a hunk! Oh, man, would I ever love to have
five minutes alone with him!"

Still dazed by her victory, Teddy could only nod.

"Too bad he's practically engaged to that English
girl . . . Lady Philippa whatever-her-name-is. They say he
even gave her a necklace from the crown jewels that used
to belong to Princess Lisse. I guess his father really wants
him to get married. I suppose they'll have one of those huge
royal weddings."

Teddy stared at Laurette, feeling as if she'd been
punched in the center of her stomach.

"She's one of Princess Diana's ladies-in-waiting. They
say she's so rich her family owns half of England. . . ."

Teddy turned away, unable to listen further.

Later, in the car back to their hotel, Houston Warner
excitedly began a postmortem, dissecting the match point
by point. Teddy barely listened. *Lady Philippa. A royal
wedding.*

When she reached her room at Claridge's, the old-
fashioned luxury hotel in the heart of London, she saw the
red message light blinking and called down to the desk.

"Miss Warner, an envelope has been left at the desk for
you," said the deskman. "Shall I have a bellman bring it
up?"

When the bellman arrived, she tipped him and then
stared down at the cream vellum envelope bearing the
deeply-embossed Costan crest.

Her heart began to pound as she tore it open. Inside was
one sheet of paper, on which a note had been hastily
scrawled, in unfamiliar, masculine handwriting.

*Teddy, Congratulations on your win. If you still want to
see me, please call.* The message had a telephone number
and was signed *Jac.*

She stared at the note for a long time and then, finally, tore it slowly in half and tossed it into a wastebasket.

That night she and her father had dinner at Chez Nico, in the St. James section of London, where Houston insisted on taking Teddy to celebrate. They encountered Auggie Steckler, dining with his agent and eight or ten others at another table. Auggie had won his match against Ivan Lendl.

After a while tennis's handsome, blond "bad boy" came over to their table. "Congratulations," he told Teddy. "You were beautiful out there."

He gave Teddy a kiss that brushed her cheek, and Teddy dutifully air-kissed him back, congratulating Auggie on his victory.

"I sweated for it," Auggie admitted. "Would you and your father like to join our table? We've ordered champagne, and after this we're going to either the Comedy Store or Stringfellow's for drinks, and catch the late show at the Hippodrome over on Leicester Square."

Teddy hesitated, then agreed. Her first, hot triumph had begun to fade, and perhaps it would be more fun to celebrate with other people.

Waiters scurried over, bringing another table and adding places for Teddy and her father. Auggie began telling a long, involved story about a prank he and John McEnroe had once played.

As the evening passed, and the group adjourned to Stringfellow's for more drinks, gradually she began to forget Jac's note.

At 2 A.M., Houston Warner pleaded exhaustion and an early plane to catch back to the States. As they rose to leave, Auggie said to Teddy in a low voice, "Lunch tomorrow—just you and me?"

"I don't think so," said Teddy, smiling to soften the rejection. "I'm flying back to New York with my father; I have to be in Chicago on Tuesday to do a Reebok commercial.''

''Oh, Teddy, Teddy, Teddy,'' Auggie said, walking beside her as they made their way through the crowded restaurant lobby to the street. One of London's cool, drizzly rains had begun, water on the pavement reflecting back the headlights of passing taxis.

Auggie took Teddy's arm and led her a slight distance away from her father and the others. ''Teddy, why don't you like me?''

''I do like you.''

''You laugh at my jokes, yes, but you hold yourself back.''

''I—I don't,'' she lied.

''You know, I'm not really the lady-killer of the tennis world. Most of those stories are just media hype.''

''Oh?'' Teddy grinned at him. ''What about Natasha Lilova? And Margaux Genelli? And Stacey Gynn? Were *they* media hype? And don't forget Jette Michaud and Orchid Lederer.''

''Enough, enough,'' said Auggie, laughing. ''All right, I'll admit it, I haven't been one hundred percent pure. But it's tennis, my love—the grind'll do it to you. You're all alone in some strange town, stuck in your hotel room with nothing but the four walls and a TV set with cable movies—''

''Poor, poor you.'' Her father had already climbed into one of the cabs, and the driver was holding the door open for her. ''I have to go now,'' she added. ''I suppose I'll be seeing you around.''

''When?''

''Well, I'm playing in the Swedish Federation Cup,'' said Teddy lamely. ''Then I have an exhibition tournament in Japan—''

''Oh, yes, the Fuji?''

''Yes.''

''I'm playing there!''

"Then I'll see you in Tokyo," said Teddy as the cab driver slammed the door. The taxi sped off, its tires spraying water.

In Costa del Mar, touches of spring were everywhere, from the flowers in pots in front of nearly every shop and boutique, to the hordes of the wealthy who were beginning to flock to Costa again, opening their villas for the summer season. Princess Kristina was back from her extended honeymoon, looking oddly sulky, and Princess Gabriella was involved in some mysterious project having to do with her jewelry designs.

Nikos Skouros stood on the jetty at the San Marcos Shipyard, gazing with excitement at the graceful hull of his fiftieth-birthday gift to himself, the ship he intended to name *Olympia*. The huge yacht loomed above him, her lines beautiful, her finish immaculately white. On her decks, workers swarmed. Designers. Carpenters. Shipfitters. Electronic technicians.

He'd been the oldest son of a moderately successful Greek shipping-firm owner. Claudios Skouros believed in strict discipline both in running his business and raising a family. Once he had put his twelve-year-old son, Nikos, in the hospital for a week for missing choir practice at St. Anthony's, the Greek Orthodox church the Skouros family attended.

From then on, it had been constant battles. A welted backside. A broken nose. Blackened eyes.

Nikos did as his father ordered, but behind his back he began cultivating the employees at the shipyard, making friends with them. At seventeen, he entered the family business, quickly proving himself. Within five years he had doubled the firm's business and opened personal bank accounts in Athens, London, and Zurich to expand his own financial network. But he got his way through smiles and friendship, not crude aggression. Charm. That's what it took. And with his charm, Nikos Skouros intended to become a thousand times richer than his father's biggest dream.

His tactics worked. People began asking for young Nickey—they wanted to do business with him. They liked him. The worldwide operations—shipping freight back and forth between Hong Kong, New York, Buenos Aires, and London—created more annual profits than the average man or woman could even dream about in a lifetime.

Old Skouros became jealous and went after his son once more with a strap that had a heavy buckle, but this time Nikos was twenty-two, not twelve, and he protected himself.

Within a year Nickey had forced the old man to retire, taken his entire fortune, and had begun building the new supertankers for worldwide oil transportation. In the next few years he'd become a billionaire. But merely being rich wasn't enough. He was still trying to prove something to the old man.

Fifty, he thought. *I am now older than my father was when we had our last fight.*

The Greek rejected the memories, turning away. He walked back along the jetty with its view of the Costan harbor, where a yacht was just now entering the breakwater. Costa del Mar was a beautiful country. Almost like a fairy tale. Skouros nodded appreciatively.

In the parking lot his driver was waiting for him.

"The Casino de Palais," he told the man, named Johnny Ginopoulis, who had been with him for years.

As soon as the car was underway, Skouros picked up the car telephone and dialed a number.

" 'Allo?" said the deep, resonant voice.

"I am going to the casino," Skouros said smoothly without identifying himself, well aware that car phone transmissions could sometimes be picked up on radio bands.

"Perhaps I will play a little *chemin de fer,* too," said François Gérard, Costa del Mar's finance minister, who had been appointed by Henri after D'Fabray was killed. "In half an hour?"

Skouros hung up and then called another number in Paris, Prince Georges. Following that, he dialed a third number—the palace.

Prince Henri swam slowly through the azure water of the palace swimming pool, his arms parting the clear blue in a leisurely crawl stroke. His doctor had ordered him to get more exercise, and he had increased his daily laps to thirty.

As he swam, he brooded over the letter he had received today from a photographer in Alexandria, Egypt. The contents didn't surprise him, only that it had happened so soon, while Kristina and Jean-Luc were still on their honeymoon. Well, he would solve that today. He had already summoned Furnoir to his office. And there was another, more troubling problem: the threatening letters about Gabriella, hate mail that accused her of not being his flesh and blood. Recently a small group of radicals had sprung up, denouncing Gaby in a dozen ways through a small, garage-printed newspaper. They viewed his older daughter as his favorite, and they wanted to eliminate her from the direct line of succession.

Henri made up his mind to give a carefully orchestrated interview to the *Costa Monde,* the country's daily newspaper, denouncing the group and explaining the true facts. Years ago, Lisse had been convinced that her fears of being infertile were shameful and had insisted on keeping her visit to the clinic in Switzerland a secret. Traveling incognito, Henri had visited her there; invigorated by the mountain air, they had made love repeatedly, and Lisse became pregnant. But now the people needed to be reassured that Gaby was his legitimate daughter.

But Nikos Skouros occupied Henri's mind even more than his worries about his daughters. Cut from the same cloth as Aristotle Onassis and Stavros Niarchos, the handsome Greek was far more charming and a very good friend.

Henri could relate to him. But at times, Skouros made him feel uncomfortable.

Skouros had indicated a willingness to loan the country $50 million for ten years, in exchange for the deed of a one-mile stretch of prime beachfront property. The purchase price, $7.5 million. Not a bad deal!

Henri had wrestled with the dilemma for more than a month now. Costa del Mar desperately needed the $50 million to pay off the German bankers, but Henri knew that Skouros had hopes of building another huge casino and a medium-priced condo development. A vacation mecca for the working man. Mass production. Lots of customers gambling, eating, and reveling twenty-four hours a day. Japanese businessmen flown in from Tokyo with a quick stop to pick up wealthy Chinese passengers in Hong Kong. Junkets from the capitals of Europe and the U.S.A. twice weekly.

Impossible! The entire country was only five miles square, and even one tawdry development could effectively ruin its wealthy tourist trade.

To protect the country, Henri had had his lawyers draw up an agreement that would prevent Skouros from building any hotels, multiple-unit condos, or apartment buildings on the property for ten years. He hated giving up part of Costa to a man like Skouros. But what other choice did he have? It was still better than turning the country over to France.

His trainer, stationed on the pool deck, signaled thirty laps, and Henri pulled himself up over the edge and reached for the towel that the man handed him, woven with the Bellini family crest.

But as Henri was drying himself off before pulling on a terry-cloth robe, another servant came hurrying out to the terrace, bearing a mobile cellular phone on a silver tray.

"Your Highness, a phone call from Mr. Skouros."

"I will take it here. You may leave," said Henri. When they were gone, the prince picked up the phone and spoke briefly into the receiver.

He listened intently for a few minutes. When he hung up, his usually pale face was slightly reddened, and his pulse had quickened.

Nikos Skouros had asked the prince to host a fiftieth-birthday party for him at the palace.

A little presumptuous, maybe, but under the circumstances, Prince Henri had no choice. His friend Skouros had never been known to be reticent about anything.

Jean-Luc Furnoir's splitting headache needled points of pain into his temples; his mouth tasted like stale wine. He rubbed his head, wishing he'd had time to take something for his hangover.

Last night he and Kristina had thrown a beach party, inviting sixty people to frolic with them around a huge bonfire, enjoying a lamb barbecue, while a rock band played in the sand.

"You're ignoring me," Kristina had accused as the fire burned down to a glowing mass of coals and many of the couples had gone off into the dark.

"Why, of course, I'm not, *ma petite*," he'd insisted.

"You're embarrassing me by flirting with that little Italian model. What were you doing out there in the dark anyway?" Kristina had exclaimed angrily. Then she had turned away before he could answer.

"I tell you, Kristina, I'm being perfectly honest. I made a mistake before—I admit it—but now all I want is for you to trust me again," he'd insisted, as he left their apartment the following morning to answer Prince Henri's summons.

Attempting to control the sweating of his palms, Jean-Luc gazed uneasily at the Bellini ancestral portraits that hung on the walls of the prince's anteroom.

"His Royal Highness will see you now," said a male secretary, entering the foyer.

Jean-Luc rose and followed the secretary into a large room completely lined with glassed-in bookshelves that contained rare volumes, including several priceless medieval illuminated versions of the Bible. The ceiling was painted with a fresco of a hunting scene.

Prince Henri was seated in the center of the room at a huge carved cherrywood desk. In front of him sat a manila envelope plastered with foreign stamps.

"Your Highness," said Jean-Luc, covering up his unease.

The prince did not speak, but merely handed the envelope to Jean-Luc.

"What is this?" said Jean-Luc.

"Perhaps you'd care to look," snapped Henri, his eyes blue-gray steel.

Jean-Luc hesitated, then reached into the envelope and pulled out five grainy black-and-white photos. "Why, I— I don't— There is some mistake!"

"Mistake?"

"Yes, I was never—I have never met these women. The man in this photograph is not me."

Henri's eyes hardened. "Interesting. It looks exactly like you."

Jean-Luc pretended to examine each photograph, keeping an indignant expression on his face.

There was a long silence while Henri examined his new son-in-law, staring at him down his long, aquiline nose. The prince finally spoke. "Discreet assignations are not unknown to us. But this is not discreet. If published in the media such photographs would be extremely damaging to the Royal House of Costa del Mar."

"But of course," said Jean-Luc, nodding fervently.

"I have sent an emissary to take care of this matter in an appropriate manner. As for you . . ."

Jean-Luc felt his stomach churn.

"As for you, I expect you to conduct yourself in a way that befits the husband of a Costan princess. If you do not, I will put an end to your marriage, *toute de suite, comprendez-vous?*"

"Yes—yes, Your Highness," Jean-Luc blurted, terrified

that his luxurious living would soon end.

"That is all. You may leave."

The prince's office still smelled faintly of Jean-Luc's imported aftershave. On his desk the incriminating photographs had been neatly stacked.

"Papa!" said Kristina, nearly crying. "It isn't as it appears—you know how the *paparazzi* are! They'll stoop to anything! These pictures have been altered!"

Prince Henri made a sharp gesture, cutting her excuses off. He shoved back his chair and walked over to the window that overlooked some of the palace's original stone fortifications, now less bellicose because of the beautiful landscaping. "Kristina, the photos are really not the issue. Your husband's indiscreet behavior reflects on the entire House of Bellini. It reflects on *you,* Kristina."

"*I* didn't do anything," Kristina whispered, shocked.

"Ah, but you did. This isn't a private marriage. It's a matter of State, and there is much more at stake here than just your private wishes. You must see to it that he behaves, Kristina. It's part of your obligation. If you insist on having this . . . marriage aired in those despicable tabloids and bringing us public notoriety again and again, then I'll have to take drastic actions. Costa can't afford a scandal. You know of our political weakness and the financial instability of our country. There are interests in France and elsewhere that are just looking for an excuse to deliver the *coup de grâce.*"

"But"—she moistened her lips—"but what if he will not?"

"I am sure he enjoys living in your ten-room apartment, driving the two cars I have provided for you, and spending your liberal allowance." Henri's expression softened. Kristina was, after all, his favorite. "I am giving a birthday party tomorrow night for Nikos Skouros, our Greek friend. You and Jean-Luc will attend, of course. Be solicitous of Skouros if you will. It is important."

"Of course," Kristina agreed, trying to smile. She'd already scheduled her trip to Los Angeles; she'd been thinking of nothing else for weeks. If Papa forbade her to go, she would be devastated. "But, Papa," she burst out, "the pictures—they really *were* tampered with. Jean-Luc was not guilty of—"

"Tomorrow night," Henri said, cutting her off. "I will expect you to look your most beautiful."

Princess Kristina floated into the room on the arm of Jean-Luc, stunning in a shimmering tube of gold. Secured in her champagne-blond hair she wore the famous, heart-shaped diamond tiara that had belonged to her mother, Princess Lisse.

Heads turned as she approached the guest of honor.

"Happy birthday." Kristina warmly greeted the Greek shipping billionaire. "It's delightful to be able to celebrate with you."

The Greek's smile was dazzling, his natural charisma reaching out to enfold her in its aura. "It's wonderful to be here. Your father is most kind to remember me."

The eight-course dinner took more than three hours to consume, each course highlighted by an exquisite wine. Nikos Skouros, seated in the place of honor next to Prince Henri, entertained the company with stories of a recent trip he had made to Italy to have a new race car built. When Prince Jac heard the words "race car," he stopped bantering with his pretty blonde dinner partner and began to listen attentively. Skouros liked to dabble in Formula One car racing and even boasted that he had driven a car himself when younger. His anecdotes were witty, urbane. But Kristina noticed that his eyes always returned to rest on her, their look intense.

Afterward, she had walked out onto a balcony, where Skouros followed her, as she'd known he would. "You are the most beautiful woman in the room," he said in his deep, well-modulated voice with its faint Greek accent.

"Am I?" She smiled. "I saw your new ship in the ship-yard. Are you sure you'll be able to get it into the main harbor channel? Our channels aren't very deep or meant for a ship quite so . . . large."

Skouros's eyes met hers. "I have been assured there is sufficient draft for the . . . hull, *more* than sufficient. Are you interested in nautical matters, Princess Kristina?"

"Sometimes."

"Perhaps you would like to have a tour of the *Olympia*. She is being finished off now, and there are some very nice features that will make her the most luxurious private yacht in the world."

"But I know nothing about ship design. Surely others would be far more qualified."

"Your opinion is the only one I want."

"Perhaps . . . sometime."

"Was he coming on to you?" demanded her husband, maneuvering her into a corner.

Kristina shrugged. "Why do you use such silly Ameri-can phrases? Nickey was merely being cordial. After all, my father did ask us to patronize him."

"You were being much more than patronizing—"

"And you are being a fool," she snapped. "I am gath-ering a group to go to Caveau de la Huchette tonight. Why don't you ask Nickey Skouros and his date if they would like to come?"

"If we can go to the casino first," Jean-Luc said sul-lenly.

"You know my father has forbidden Gabriella and me to go there. No Bellini woman ever goes there."

Jean-Luc seemed about to argue, but then, glancing over at Prince Henri, he decided not to. "Fine," he agreed. "I'll invite him. *And* his date."

The royal party spent several hours at the popular jazz club, then adjourned to Cigale, a rock club. Although the weather had turned chilly and rainy, the air inside the club was overheated, and strobe lights flashed across the ceiling to the pounding rhythms of the Rolling Stones.

Gabriella, escorted by a young French count, talked only of her meetings with Kenneth Lane and her jewelry until her date gave her a bored look.

"Such a businesswoman," he drawled, deliberately speaking in a French patois that barely concealed his disapproval.

"Why not?" demanded Gaby. "If Princess Caroline can do it, then so can I."

Kristina swiveled her hips close to Nikos Skouros, who matched her move for move. The Greek's physical energy seemed endless.

Skouros hadn't taken his eyes off her all night. His date, a model named Giselle deBosses, had grown annoyed and was seated at a table in the corner, making conversation with several of her friends.

Jean-Luc, too, looked quite annoyed, his brows practically meeting over his nose.

"I might want to look at your yacht, after all," said Kristina.

"When?" said Skouros hoarsely. "What about your husband?"

"He sleeps late; I will go with you tomorrow morning. Ten A.M."

Skouros shook his head. It was already four-thirty in the morning. "Ten?"

"Ten."

The roar of high-powered cars running the track through the streets of Port-Louis was audible even inside the palace. The qualifying trials of the Formula One Costan Grand Prix—the second "F1" race to be held in the principality, whose winding, hilly roads were ideal—had begun early that morning. The first race had been so well attended by free-spending tourists, Henri had decided to stage another Grand Prix event.

Clad in a pair of skintight jeans and a white crocheted sweater worn over a silk tank top, Kristina stepped into the silver Rolls-Royce that Nickey had brought to pick her up. She had left her husband sprawled in bed and snoring.

"I don't mean to place you in a compromising position," Skouros told her, smiling. "If I have, I'm terribly sorry."

"I do as I please," she lied. "Jean-Luc will be sleeping until at least two o'clock, possibly three. *Cuver son vin,* that's how he always deals with a hangover after he drinks wine."

From the bar in the back of the limo, Skouros poured champagne into a glass half-filled with fresh orange juice and handed it to her. Kristina sipped her breakfast cocktail very slowly.

"What happened to your date?" she asked him.

"I sent her back to Paris."

"So early?"

"She had a TV film shoot. . . ."

Five minutes later they were pulling into the shipyard. The huge, 325-foot yacht dominated the yard, her name already affixed to her hull in elegant, gold lettering.

"*Olympia,*" said Kristina. "It makes me think of the gods in Greek mythology."

"You are the first goddess to board her."

Skouros escorted Kristina down a wooden walkway toward the freight cage that was used to board equipment and fixtures onto the dry-docked yacht. As the cage rose, Kristina could see the Royal Yacht Harbor, a forest of masts, and beyond that the tan turrets of the Vendôme Palace.

The *Olympia* appeared to be almost ready for her maiden voyage. Most of the luxurious fixtures, furniture, and carpeting were in place. Skouros gave her a tour, but after about thirty minutes, Kristina became bored.

"My suite," he said at last, opening a door.

The rooms were huge, paneled with teak, a domed sky-light overhead giving great drafts of sunlight. There was a king-sized bed already made up. An antique marble fire-place mantle dominated one wall.

Kristina started into the room, then suddenly stopped. "I . . . I am married," she blurted.

"My darling princess, but of course you are. Isn't this room lovely?" He began showing her the details, then used an intercom. Within a few minutes a steward wheeled a gold-plated service cart into the room.

"The kitchens aren't really in operation yet, but I thought you might be hungry, so I arranged to have brunch brought aboard."

The meal was simple, yet exquisite: an *omelette piper-ade,* which was an open-faced omelette with Basque gar-nish; a salad of tossed greens, French bread, and *mousse de fraises en coupelles,* a smooth strawberry sherbet served in elegant cookie cups. With it was served a delicate rosé wine.

"Slightly fruity with a suggestion of floral," pronounced Skouros, swirling the wine around in his glass. "A hint of crispness. Wonderful."

He began to tell her about a vineyard he had looked at in the Burgundy wine region of France, going on in detail about the purchase he hoped to make, "just because I love wine." He seemed enthralled with the process of wine-making, the mystique of the grapes, the growing season, the aging of the wine in casks. Kristina relaxed a little, enjoying this new facet of Nikos Skouros.

"Perhaps you will fly over there sometime and look at the vineyard with me, give me your opinion," Skouros sug-gested, reaching across the table to touch her hand.

Kristina felt the tingle again, the sensuous warmth of his skin. And he was smiling at her. He was *so* attractive.

She continued the meal in a kind of daze. This urbane, sexy, charismatic Greek was not at all what she had ex-pected.

"I have something else I wish to show you," said Skouros when the meal was completed, and the servant had brought in a rare, smoothly sweet dessert wine called Coteau du Layon, produced from Chenin Blanc grapes and scented with honey and spices.

"Yes?"

Skouros rose and went to a locked cabinet, where he removed a small, square package wrapped in silk and padded in layers of cotton.

"This is something very rare to have survived for so long—a Tintoretto sketch. It's a preliminary drawing of one of his studies for the Virgin Mary. . . . I've had it authenticated, and it is indeed genuine, sketched by the master himself."

As he spoke, Skouros was unwrapping layers of cloth, finally revealing a cardboard folio. He opened this, revealing a six-by-seven-inch sheet of yellowing paper, on which had been penned in faded ink the outlines of a ravishingly beautiful, oval face. Her hair was pulled straight back from her temples and secured by some sort of cloth. Her full lips, her delicately strong cheekbones, and the curve of her jaw . . . The artist's model looked exactly like Kristina. It was uncanny!

Kristina sucked in her breath, narrowing her eyes at the sketch, which seemed so fragile after four centuries that it might actually crumble. It couldn't be her . . . but it was.

"Do you see the resemblance?" Skouros was smiling proudly. "She's perfect—she's your clone, Kristina. She's you. I couldn't believe it when I saw this. I had to have it. I knew I had to give it to you one day."

"But—but I couldn't possibly take it."

"My darling Kristina, the money I spent on this means nothing, but how could I have let this treasured piece of art go when it looks exactly like you? I want you to have it. I want you to think of me when you look at it."

He put the sketch on the table, his eyes searching hers.

"Nikos," she whispered, reaching out to touch his hand.

He smiled, pulling her close. Kristina went willingly into his arms, her heart pounding. He smelled wonderful—of spice and soap and sweat.

"I must not urge you into something you don't wish to do," he murmured into her neck as he kissed the hollows of her throat. "Kristina . . . you are wonderful . . . even more beautiful than that lovely Madonna."

"Nikos," she whispered again.

Sunlight streaming in through the skylight awoke Kristina with the sensation of heat across her naked hip. She lay for a moment curled up in the animal warmth of being close to another person. *Mon Dieu,* it had been so wonderful. Nikos had made her come alive.

He was a tender yet demanding lover, who had brought her to such heights that she'd cried out, moaning and screaming at the climax of her passion.

"Oh! Damn! It's nearly six o'clock!" she cried, staring at her Piaget watch in consternation. She and Jean-Luc were scheduled to attend a racing party tonight.

"Indeed it is," murmured Skouros, waking up from the satiated nap into which he had fallen. Now he sat up in bed without a sign of sleepiness and reached for the telephone, which had just begun to ring.

"Didn't I tell you not to disturb me?" he snapped, apparently to his assistant. "Very well. Since it's urgent, I will say a few words to him, but next time, please follow my wishes."

Kristina jumped out of bed while Skouros continued his business call.

"I'll be there in ten minutes, Claude," he said, hanging up as she finished showering and dressing.

He rose from the bed, magnificent in his nakedness, and took her in his arms. "My darling Kristina . . . I have no words for what I feel."

She clung to him, feeling more waves of regret.

"You are crying." His fingertip touched her eyelid,

brushing away a slight patina of moisture.

"I don't— I can't—"

"Kristina, my dear girl, my wonderful princess, please don't cry. I can't bear it when you cry. I feel the same as you. I am wondering why we didn't find this earlier—why we only now have discovered each other. . . ."

With all the strength in her, Kristina managed to pull away. She gazed at him sorrowfully. "But we didn't, Nikos, and I took vows, marriage vows before God. I've already broken them. . . . I've sinned, but I can't compound my sin any further by thinking about things that—that can't be. Please . . . I know you'll forgive me."

"Of course. My dear, I didn't mean to distress you." Skouros kissed her lightly. "I will have one of my servants escort you back to the car, my love. Don't forget to take the sketch with you. You do know, don't you, that with it goes my heart?"

She stared at him. She didn't know what to say.

"Go, lovely Kristina. Back to your life."

Car engines roared, emitting the gritty odors of grease, oil, and gasoline. Bleachers and VIP boxes had been built overlooking the place de la Couronne and Princess Lisse Boulevard. VIP tickets were being scalped as high as $800 apiece. The boxes cost $10,000 each but were worth it for the wealthy racing aficionados. Many of the boxes would hold twenty-five people or more, and had specially built portable kitchens and private bathrooms.

Prince Jac entered the designated pit area and drew a deep breath. He loved it all—the noise, the confusion, the crowds, the tang of machines and oil.

He wended his way down the narrow walkway that separated the different pit areas from the spectators, stopping to greet William Davidson, a Detroit auto-glass billionaire who was sponsoring a car with Guardian Industries, Inc. Davidson had attended many parties at the palace and owned a luxurious condo in Costa, which he used fre-

quently in the winter for ski weekends in the French Pyrénées.

"Wonderful day," said Davidson. "We're doing great
on the qualifiers. I hope you can come to the party I'm
giving tonight, Your Highness."

"Yes, of course," said Jac absentmindedly.

He talked with Davidson for a few minutes, then walked
on. He ran into Nikos Skouros, who was dressed for the
occasion in a black silk jacket emblazoned with the name
and logo of Skouros Shipping Lines. Skouros Shipping was
sponsoring two drivers in the races. They exchanged greetings and moments later found themselves discussing the
very essence of racing.

"Racing isn't just a matter of training and then experience," Skouros said. "A driver must have something special in him. It's an inborn talent, razor-sharp reflexes, an
innate competitiveness—almost like a killer instinct.

"Jac, I have been a friend of your family for a very long
time, I have virtually watched you grow up, and I am convinced you are one of those few persons born to race. I
have heard of your desire to race and that you need a sponsor. I would like to sponsor you myself."

Jac flushed. Why would Skouros take the risk of of-
fending Prince Henri in order to do this for him? "But I
cannot put your friendship with my father in jeopardy."

Skouros smiled. "Such a small matter as racing cannot
put my strong friendship with Prince Henri in danger. Our
company, Skouros Shipping, is modifying a Ferrari F92A
with an electronically controlled clutch—you'll be driving
it. I have commissioned the construction of a new, more
fireproof type of racing suit, which you will be wearing,
and I also insist that you undergo two months of training
with Unser. If my judgment of your ability is correct, by
the time your training program is finished, you'll be one of
the top young drivers in the world."

Jac hesitated, feeling a beat of caution. Then rebellion
swept through him. He wanted to live a little before other

obligations surrounded him with a wall of tedium. He knew that with Nikos Skouros behind him, he would have the best car and the finest training possible.

"Well, Your Highness?" asked Skouros cordially.

"I want to do it," said Jac.

The bells of Costa del Mar's cathedral were ringing the hour as Kristina walked into the magnificent apartment Prince Henri had given the newlyweds. Her body still felt warm and satiated from her lovemaking with Nikos Skouros.

"Where have you been?" demanded Jean-Luc angrily. He had been sunning himself on their garden terrace and smelled of coconut oil.

"Shopping. What else did I have to do? *You* were asleep and snoring like *un cochon*," Kristina retorted, taking several hastily purchased bikinis out of her shopping bag. Beyond their patio the palace's swimming pool was visible behind a screen of trees and shrubs. A swim in the heated water would feel good, Kristina decided.

"I've already heard where you were," her husband sneered. "*He* came in a car to meet you."

She did not respond, changing into one of the new bikinis, a tempting wisp of yellow spandex.

"I have my own network," Jean-Luc announced. "Not much escapes me. Don't think your behavior has gotten by me, because it hasn't."

Kristina turned away from him, hiding the flaming blush that had risen to her cheeks. Without protesting further to her husband, she slipped on a pair of thongs and started along the brick pathway edged with brilliantly colored annuals, in the direction of the pool. An ancient stone wall bordered the path, hemming them in from view of the palace itself.

"I *said* I know where you were!" cried Jean-Luc, practically running after her! "I *said*— Listen to me, Kristina! You are my wife. You——"

Kristina turned. "I might be your wife, but you will still speak to me in a civil manner," she snapped. "Now leave me alone, I want to swim in peace. And then we have to get dressed for Billy Davidson's party."

Kristina swam laps for nearly an hour, methodically plowing up and down the pool, thinking about Nickey. By the time she pulled herself out of the pool, the church bells were chiming again. A Catholic marriage was forever . . . or was it?

The Davidson party was being held at L'Aigle, the rooftop restaurant of the Casablanca Hotel, a five-star restaurant of international acclaim. There were swooping views of the harbor, the buoy markers already blinking as the purple dusk fell. A small orchestra played, and there was the discreet buzz of conversation.

Race car drivers, along with their wealthy sponsors, were clustered around a laden hors d'oeuvres table, and groupies sought the attention of these attractive young men, who seemed cloaked in the arrogance of being the best in the world.

Prince Henri had arrived in a flurry of bodyguards, accompanied by the playing of the Costa del Mar anthem. On his right arm was Princess Gabriella, her neck and ears glittering with jewelry of her own design.

"What do you think of this fabulous party?" Geneviève Mondalvi, the columnist from *Paris Match,* queried Kristina. "Aren't all those race car drivers to *die* for? Such power and masculinity. It makes me quiver all over. And your brother, Prince Jac? Isn't it exciting that he's going to join one of the racing teams, too?"

"Jac? Race?"

"Haven't you heard? He persuaded Nikos Skouros to give him a place on his team. What does Prince Henri say?" the columnist probed. "I would imagine he would not be pleased at his only male heir risking his life in such a way."

"I really couldn't say," Kristina responded vaguely.

"I understand that you and Nikos Skouros are 'very good friends,'" the woman continued in a staccato rhythm.

Kristina blanched. Surely her afternoon liaison had not already found its way into the gossip circles! She blurted, "What would make you say that?"

"You were seen dancing with him last night at Cigale in a rather, ah, *intime* fashion. And someone saw you getting into his car, my dear. You know this is a very small country with many eyes."

Kristina stared at the woman, stunned. She knew Geneviève was right. If she snapped at a servant, within hours the press learned of it. If she bought a purse or some lingerie, the shop owner talked about it. Frequently she was forced to order by phone and have a servant pick up her items, to eliminate the chance of gossip. And every man she danced with, talked to, flirted with, made love to— someone knew.

"Princess Kristina?" said Genie Mondalvi. "Are you quite all right?"

"Just a headache," Kristina murmured, moving away.

"You will not join the Skouros racing team!" snapped Prince Henri, maneuvering his son out onto one of the stone balconies that overlooked the famous Casablanca gardens. There they could have privacy from the eavesdropping of bodyguards and other guests. "I told you before—I will not hear of such a thing. You must be insane even to think of it."

"I want to do it," said Jac defiantly. "It's perfectly safe if one knows what he is doing."

"And you aren't even nineteen yet, but you know what you are doing?" Prince Henri could barely conceal his rage with sarcasm.

Jac pressed his lips tightly together, a muscle knotting in his jaw. "Don't worry, Papa, I won't be killed. I will have the best trainers. And I drove very well today," he added proudly.

Henri knew he had to squelch this daredevil trait in his son now. It wasn't just a matter of Jac's personal safety, it was the crown that he was concerned about. All of Jac's upbringing had been directed toward preparing him to rule when he acceded to the throne.

"It doesn't really matter how well you do. Racing is a dangerous activity. Even Ayrton Senna, considered the best in the world, was killed in Italy at the San Marino Grand Prix. You had no right to make such an agreement without consulting me," Henri continued. "I forbid this nonsense. Absolutely forbid it."

Jac faced his father, his jaw tightening again. "I will not back out of my agreement."

"What?" Shocked, Henri stared at his son.

Jac's eyes blazed fire. "There's more to life than the five square miles of Costa del Mar and some official ribbon-cutting ceremonies. I want to take some chances in life! I want to *live*! And I do not wish to rule this country—ever!"

He turned on his heel and stalked back into the main room, leaving Henri stunned by the announcement. *Not wish to rule?*

"Is everything all right, Your Highness?" Henri's body-guard peered through the arched doorway. Furiously Henri motioned him away.

Shaken, he walked to the railing of the balcony. Costa del Mar lay spread before him, washed with moonlight. Floodlights illuminated the circular course of the Formula One racetrack. At the end of the narrow street the lights of the Casino de Palais glittered. Even now, the world's wealthiest people were clustered around the *chemin de fer* and roulette tables, wagering thousands of francs on a single bet. Because of the millions they spent, the citizens of Costa del Mar enjoyed a standard of living higher than any other country in the world.

"I do not wish to rule, ever"?

Gazing at the lights, Henri felt a film of tears rise to his eyes. He, too, when young had once felt as Jac did, but when his country had needed him, he'd been forced to put aside his doubts and his youthful dreams.

Prince Jac would feel that way too, once he had a chance to think it through. But if he didn't . . .

The following day, Henri quietly went to the Privy Council and reinstated a long-forgotten addendum to the Costan law of succession. Only twice before in Bellini history had this rule been invoked, allowing the monarch to bypass the usual male succession and select his replacement from any one of his children.

He didn't want to invoke it, intended *not* to invoke it. But he was too much of a realist not to be prepared.

Teddy was back in Connecticut, trying to come down from the enormous "high" she'd experienced in winning Wimbledon—and in seeing a segment on "ABC Sports" that showed Prince Jac being interviewed while sitting in a race car.

"I love racing more than almost anything," he'd told Curt Gowdy, passion shining in his face.

Teddy, sitting glued to her TV set, had experienced a strange, hard pounding of her heart—and a feeling of intense loss. Then she grabbed for the remote and punched the button, switching to another channel. God, what was wrong with her? She had some kiddie crush on Prince Jac, that's all this was, and she'd better stop it, right now.

She was slightly ashamed of it, but she'd started clipping out articles about both princesses, too—even a tidbit of gossip about Kristina's marriage faltering. And a rather startling article about an incident where Princess Gabriella had been attacked in Port-Louis by a group of dissidents, who were driven off by palace sentries before the princess could be seriously harmed. The four radicals had been sentenced to prison for five years.

It was as if Teddy couldn't let go of the royals, she

thought, couldn't let go of their lives, their doings. And sometimes she sensed from talking to her father that he felt the same way, that he actually was as interested in the Costans as she was.

It *had* to stop. Grimly she marched over to her dresser and pulled out the bottom drawer where she'd placed her Costan clippings, photos of Jac, and other royal memorabilia. Deliberately she gathered all of it up into a plastic garbage bag and trashed it.

Jac, you were wonderful, and you are so handsome, but you are in a totally different world than most other people, including me.

All the major U.S. magazines were hot to do a story on her. "The Young and the Restless" wanted Teddy to do a cameo appearance with Peter Bergman, and "Murder, She Wrote" wanted her to play a tennis star whose brother was murdered. "Good Morning, America" wanted her for a twenty-minute segment on Friday, and Joan Rivers had to have her in two weeks, while CBS Fox Video Company, the same outfit that did the Jane Fonda videos, wanted her to make an instructional cassette for them.

"You're a star, babe," her father enthused. "You call the shots. You're going to get millions in endorsements. Everything is going to go your way now."

"Wonderful," agreed Teddy. "In tennis anyway, I suppose."

"And what's that supposed to mean?" demanded Houston Warner.

She bit her lip. "I mean, the tennis part of my life is going great, but the rest of it is a little, well, lackluster. The personal part—it sucks!"

"Do you mean boys?"

"Boys?" Despite her blue mood, Teddy hooted with laughter. "Dad, I'm twenty years old. I've hardly even had ten dates in my whole life with men *or* boys. I want to meet someone special, someone who isn't all wrapped up

with tennis, someone who has a regular life of his own and does something interesting and exciting.''

"What's wrong with tennis players?" demanded Warner. Then he immediately nodded, conceding the point to Teddy. "All right," he said. "I'll see what I can do. I'll call some of my friends. They probably have sons at Harvard or Yale who would love to meet you.''

"I *don't* want a blind date, Dad. *Ugh*. The thought makes me barf. Anyway, who would I have the time to meet?" Teddy said gloomily. "I have to practice all day, and then I'm too tired at night to do anything but sink in front of the TV set and watch cable.''

"Darling," said Warner, not understanding. "Darling, we could schedule some parties for you—"

"It's not parties I want," said Teddy, sighing.

Later that week Jamaica DuRoss came over to hit balls with Teddy. She hadn't seen Jamaica in several months; not since Jamaica had dropped out of tennis and was all set to enroll at Princeton. "Time to face reality," Jamie said. "I'm good but not great, and I think I can be a great lawyer someday.''

They played at the Weston Tennis Club, where they had first trained, until both women were perspiring and Teddy had trounced Jamaica, 6–0.

"God, it feels terrific to get beat by a Wimbledon winner," said Jamaica, taking the defeat in good spirits.

They broke for Diet Pepsi's and a long gossip session.

"Men," said Jamaica. "I want to know all about the men you've been seeing, Teddy. You haven't heard from Prince Jac, have you?''

"No," said Teddy, flushing. "Jamie, it wasn't anything with him. We just danced a little at the disco, and the press made up the rest.''

"Oh," said Jamaica, disappointed. "Well, what about Auggie Steckler? I heard he talks about you all the time and says he's going to get you if it's the last thing he does.''

Teddy reddened.

"Well . . . it's probably only gossip. But would it really be that bad?" said Jamaica. "I mean, he's cute, and he's rich, and he's the best male tennis player in the world. Also, he's got *great* buns—I mean *totally* great buns!"

Teddy sipped her Pepsi, growing pensive. "Auggie is cute, but—I don't know—I feel so restless," she complained. "I want something, but I don't know what."

"I've been telling you," said Jamaica, laughing. "You want a man."

Jamaica had to leave; she had a date with a pre-law student. Teddy showered and drove home, her mood plummeting again. She'd heard about the emotional letdown that occurred after players won a Grand Slam tournament like Wimbledon, but now it was happening to her. She'd achieved a lifetime dream—now what lay ahead?

Oh, she'd almost forgotten. The exhibition match in Tokyo. It seemed very much an anticlimax.

Tokyo was dampened by a light, fine rain that made the thousand-and-one lights of the glittering Ginza seem even more brilliant.

Their hotel, the Imperial, was located on Uchisaiwai-cho near the Imperial Gardens and government ministries. As Teddy and her agent, Russ Ostrand, who had accompanied her, walked in to register, three or four Japanese women spotted Teddy and came hurrying up with pieces of paper for her to autograph.

Teddy scrawled autographs, surprised when the crowd began to grow.

"They must think I'm Madonna," Teddy joked to Russ.

"Just wait, babe. It gets better."

Her suite was glamorous, combining beautiful Japanese antiques with more Westernized furniture. Teddy left the curtains open so that she could gaze down on the brilliant lights of Tokyo. One electronic sign almost opposite the hotel kept flashing the moving figure of a woman tennis player, along with some red letters in Japanese.

Finally, stunned, Teddy realized that the tennis player was supposed to represent her.

"Holy cripes," she muttered, staring at it.

Her phone rang. She lunged for it, snatching it up off the hook.

"Well, I see that *you* made the big neon advertising sign outside your hotel, not me," came the voice of Auggie Steckler. But he seemed amused rather than jealous.

"Isn't it incredible?" she said, laughing. "I'm in lights."

"How about a nightcap? I'm just down the street from you, I could be at your hotel in five minutes."

"I don't know," she said nervously.

"Babe, let's get one thing straight right now. I'm not going to jump your bones—at least, not unless you want it just as much as I do. I *am* a gentleman, despite what my advance press notices might say to the contrary. I just want to get to know you, Teddy."

"All right," she finally agreed. "But we'll meet in the bar downstairs—the Imperial bar, the one with the famous Frank Lloyd Wright relics. It's off the lobby."

Hoping to avoid hassle from autograph-seekers, Teddy wrapped a scarf around her hair, concealing her distinctive blond braid, and proceeded down to the lobby. The hotel had just celebrated its one-hundredth year as Tokyo's premier hotel and featured impeccable, quiet service.

Auggie Steckler was already in the bar, surrounded by a crowd of eager Japanese.

Auggie looked up, quirking his blond eyebrows at her. "The price we have to pay for fame. I think we'd better go right back up to your room, Tee."

Teddy grinned. *Tee.* She thought it was sorta cute. Entertaining Auggie in her room wasn't what she had in mind,

but she realized there was little other choice if they wanted
any privacy.

Auggie spent time admiring the view from her suite,
which was fifteen floors higher than his own. He didn't
touch her, but sexual vibes emanated from him, causing
little goose bumps to rise on her skin. It was one thing to
be in Connecticut talking with Jamaica about needing a
man, quite another thing to be alone in a hotel room with
the best-looking man in tennis.

"So," Auggie said, when at his suggestion room service
had delivered an appetizer tray of delicate fish dishes along
with some beef tempura and rice. "How do you like your
fame?"

"It's fine," said Teddy.

As they ate, they talked casually about the usual tennis
gossip, and who were the new faces to watch.

Finally he looked at her, his face suddenly serious.
"Teddy," he said, "you're so beautiful you scare me."

"Please . . ."

"I've been attracted to you from the first minute I saw
you on the courts at Costa del Mar. You remind me of
Grace Kelly, do you know that? Something about your
face. . . ."

"I don't look anything like her. I think . . . I think you'd
better go, Auggie."

As she opened the door to send him on his way, Auggie
leaned down and planted a soft kiss on her lips.

"Good night, my golden girl."

The exhibition matches were being held at a posh tennis
club located in the downtown area of Tokyo, near the Air
Express Terminal. It had more than forty courts, each one
in use eighteen hours a day.

As the limousine pulled up, Teddy noticed that there was
a long line of people waiting to get into the club. The limo
had been instructed to pull around to a back entrance, but
found itself stalled in traffic. Suddenly a roar went up from

the crowd, and hundreds of people streamed forward, surrounding the limo. Faces peered in at her, hands waving.

"Your fans," said Russ Ostrand with pride.

Eight Japanese security guards had to help her fight her
way to the players' locker room. Roxanne Eberhardt, her
opponent, was already there, a five-foot–seven-inch, 140-
pound woman of nineteen with rawboned strength, who had
fought her way up the women's circuit and was just coming
back after a knee injury. She'd been seeded number two at
Wimbledon but had to bow out of the competition when
she was hurt.

Roxanne scowled at Teddy as they greeted each other.

"These crowds are amazing," Teddy said, wanting to
be friendly. "I didn't know it would be like this."

"It usually isn't. Not for me anyway," said Roxy, who
was getting only $75,000 to Teddy's $150,000 appearance
fee. They would battle for the winner's purse—another
$100,000.

The match lasted more than two hours, going into over-
time, but gradually Teddy forced Roxy to make mistakes,
and when Roxy lunged for a ball that flew out of bounds,
losing the match by two points, the crowd went wild.

"Teddee! Teddee! Teddee!"

As Roxy flung down her racquet and stalked off the
court, Teddy raised her hands to the wildly cheering stands.
Auggie Steckler jumped out of the box where he had been
sitting with several members of his entourage. He loped
across the court to her, bearing a huge bouquet of long-
stemmed yellow roses.

"Tonight," he whispered to her. "Late dinner at the
Pastorale. It's the most fabulous restaurant in Tokyo, and
it's not far from your hotel."

Caught up in the crowd's excitement, Teddy hugged
him, whirling him around. She loved to win, and suddenly
life looked great again.

*   *   *

Pastorale was located on top of the Ginza Seiyo Hotel building, forty floors up, with a stupendous night view of Tokyo. They ate at a low table, their legs folded under them. The meals here cost an astronomical $250 per person, and the other diners, Japan's wealthiest businessmen, were the only ones who could afford to eat the elegantly prepared French cuisine, considered the best in Asia.

"Do you always throw your racquet?" inquired Teddy. Auggie, too, had won his match, chasing around the court against the volatile McEnroe and heating up the audience as the two "bad boys" of tennis screamed at each other.

"Pretty often," admitted Auggie. "It's gotten to be a trademark of mine. I know I take tennis too seriously."

"But don't you think throwing your racquet is a little, well . . ."

"Rude? Low-class? Probably. But with a name like August, and being the son of immigrants from Bavaria, I don't fit into the aristocratic image of tennis anyway. It's all a show, Tee. A circus. That's why they pay us so much money. That—and the fact that we'd kill to win."

"Didn't I read in *Tennis* that you were married once?" she ventured to ask him.

"For six weeks, back when I was twenty. She was jealous when I had to play out of town. She always thought women were after me."

Teddy grinned. "She can't have been very perceptive."

Auggie grinned back, acknowledging the hordes of women who regularly chased after him. "Yes, but I was reasonably faithful so she really had no complaint."

" '*Reasonably* faithful'? Is that the same thing as 'almost a virgin'?"

Auggie frowned. "Give me a chance, Teddy," he pleaded. "I mean it. I'd never want anyone else if I had you."

She gazed directly at him. "Auggie, I know you mean it, at least for the moment, but . . . I'm not sure I'm ready."

The delicately pretty, Geisha-like waitress arrived to

clear away their plates and bring the next course. Auggie
changed the subject, telling her about the fragrant Cordon
Bleu dish that would be served next. Teddy could see the
slight flush on his cheeks. She knew her words had stung,
but at least she was being truthful. She was a Connecticut
girl with a sheltered upbringing, and she'd already been
hurt once.

Kevin Kline was just arriving, then Geena Davis, nom-
inated for Best Supporting Actress in *The Accidental Tourist*.

Seated in the limousine with Mike Ovitz and his party,
their vehicle flanked by two other cars containing bodyguards, Princess Kristina excitedly gazed out of the smoked
window at the glittering Academy Awards hubbub.

Even Gaby would have adored the jewels on all the
women, but Gaby was in New York again, involved in
more meetings with Kenny Lane and his staff.

"There's Jodie Foster!" Kristina cried.

"Indeed, and she's looking forward to meeting you,"
said Ovitz. "By the way, you look absolutely stunning."

Kristina was wearing a strapless red silk crêpe gown by
Ungaro, its daringly low, pointed bodice embroidered with
gold, a front slit revealing her long, sexy legs. With it she
wore the Sharif diamonds, a triple-strand necklace with a
huge ruby pendant that had been in the Bellini royal collection for 150 years.

Kristina smiled warmly at her host, the most powerful
agent in Hollywood. It seemed as if she had been moving
in a dream ever since she arrived in sun-drenched Los Angeles. It had been decided by her security chief that her
presence at the Oscars would not be announced beforehand.

The limousine pulled up at the entrance, where two uniformed doormen waited. One of them hurried forward to
help Kristina out, and flashbulbs popped.

"It's Princess Kristina!" someone shouted. People began to crowd around, pushing to get closer. The guards in

the first car, who'd already gotten out, began to form a protective line around her. Rather than being frightened, Kristina began to laugh, exhilarated.

Rain Man was the big winner, including Best Picture, and its star, Dustin Hoffman, had been named Best Actor while Jodie Foster won the Oscar for Best Actress in *The Accused*. Mike Ovitz and his party were picked up by their limo again and driven to the Beverly Hilton Hotel on Wilshire and Santa Monica.

They were ushered toward a roped-off area about a hundred feet long, lined with swarms of people who had been waiting all night to view the celebrities who now began to troop past them.

"Kristina! Kristina!" someone shouted.

Delighted, Kristina waved back.

"Amazing," said Ovitz when they were inside. "You created more excitement than Jodie Foster—and she won the Oscar!"

"Oh," said Kristina, shamelessly swiveling her head, "there's Kevin Kline!"

"You're incandescent," said someone beside her. "Just incandescent, Your Highness."

Kristina turned and gasped. It was the legendary Bret Thompson, a star who had started out making "spaghetti westerns." Now at age thirty-four, he commanded more than $8 million a picture and had begun to direct his own movies. He'd been up for Best Director but hadn't won.

"Are the Academy Awards always this exciting?" she managed to say, concealing her thrilled reaction.

"It's nerve-wracking if you're one of the nominees. I can vouch for that," Thompson said, exuding his famous, rakish grin that had caused *People* magazine to name him America's Most Devilish Hunk. He was shorter than he appeared in his pictures, his eyes level with Kristina's, but what he lacked in height, he made up for in charm. She'd read in the tabloids that he was seeing several actresses at the moment, and she had heard the rumor that Bret was insatiable in bed.

"I'm amazed that you're here," he told her. "I thought princesses basically stayed in their castles."

"Not this one. And Mike Ovitz has even promised me a screen test."

"Would you care for some champagne? Just what we need to whisk this evening away on a tide of bubbles."

"That would be lovely."

Later, after he had brought her champagne in a fluted goblet, he pointed out some of the others, filling her in on Hollywood insider gossip. Kristina nodded and made intelligent comments, giving Bret her opinion on Jessica Tandy's performance in *Driving Miss Daisy,* a movie she had recently seen at a private screening. Looking around the big room, filled with women in showy long gowns and men in tuxedos, Kristina felt another burst of pleasure and happiness.

Hollywood. It was where she wanted to be.

Kristina gazed down at the script she'd been handed, a remake of Eugene O'Neill's *Anna Christie,* which had been made in 1930 as Greta Garbo's first "talkie," one of MGM's big moneymakers for that decade. Odd—last night she'd felt strangely queasy and wondered if she'd eaten some bad shellfish, but this morning she felt wonderful.

She'd already had two days to look over the script and memorize the lines. People stood all around them, cameramen, girls in jeans with clipboards, a hovering makeup artist who'd just finished dusting more powder on Kristina's nose. A cameraman waited on a dolly track, looking for a signal from the director. Dozens of grips and gaffers, each busy with their own problems.

"Whenever you're ready," said Lawrence Kasdan, the acclaimed director who'd been asked to do her screen test. Kasdan himself would read the male parts.

"Fine," said Kristina, frowning at the pages again. It

was the torrid love scene originally filmed with Charles
Bickford, who played a sailor. "Here it says we are to
kiss . . . ?"

"Not today. We're doing just dialogue. I'm just reading
the lines so you'll have something to respond to. Now, are
we ready? The body mike will pick up everything you say,
so just speak in a normal voice."

Kristina went to the mark they had shown her, drew a
deep breath, and when Kasdan said, "Speed, action, rolling," she sauntered onto the set, her hips swaying. By the
time she had reached her next set of marks, she could feel
herself slipping into the role of the woman with a shady
past.

They did eight or nine takes, Kristina's low, throaty
voice growing more confident with each take. After she was
finished, the crew applauded. Mike Ovitz seemed flabber-
gasted.

"Veteran crews don't react this way. A very good sign,
Kristina."

The following day, Mike called. "You're a natural,
Your Highness. You project emotions, sex. Even the crew
were practically jumping out of their chairs."

"Now what?" Kristina asked.

"Now I'm going to negotiate a deal for you."

"No," said Henri, glaring at his younger daughter. "I
don't know where your head is these days."

"Don't deny me this!" cried Kristina, jumping to her
feet and pacing the length of Henri's office. She had arrived
only this morning and had not yet gone to bed—she was
far too keyed up.

"I am not denying you, I am just pointing out that your
duty lies here, not in America," replied Henri patiently. He
had been bent over some figures when she came into the
room, his brow furrowed.

"You mean attending a fund-raising meeting at Église
St-Barthélemy?" cried Kristina. "Or opening the new Prin-

cess Lisse wing at the hospital? Or attending a dinner and fashion show at the Princess Royal Gardens, as Gaby does? Is that my 'duty'? Well, I don't want to do my 'duty'! I want to be an actress. I have talent, Mike Ovitz said I could be sensational, he said—''

''My dear daughter,'' sighed Henri, ''I realize that you have reached a restless age, an age when you are ready to reach out and spread your wings. But you are a married woman. What about your husband?''

''Jean-Luc?'' Kristina caught her breath in shock. During all of this, she hadn't even thought of him. They'd barely made love at all in the past few months, except for one or two occasions. They had a marriage in name only. She had never forgiven him for making love to two other women on their honeymoon. She hadn't brought him to the Oscars, and she didn't intend to let him into the Hollywood part of her life at all. That was for her alone.

''Your *husband*—'' repeated Henri. ''What would the world think if you just ran off to another country, leaving him alone? I cannot allow you to set yourself up for public ridicule. Gaby's problems with those hate letters are bad enough. I'm doing this because I love you, darling Kristina. Besides, it's possible that you may be . . .'' He cleared his throat delicately.

Kristina, angry and terribly disappointed, felt the blood rush to her face. ''Do you mean pregnant? Is that what you're trying to say? Well, I'm not! I'm never going to be pregnant by him. Never! And maybe not by anyone!''

Ignoring the shock on her father's face, she turned and rushed from the room.

Kristina was too angry and hurt to phone Mike Ovitz to give him the news that she couldn't act in the remake of *Anna Christie*. Instead, she had her secretary tell him it would be several months before she could accept a Hollywood contract.

Hollywood was a dream she wasn't ready to give up.

* * *

"Your Highness, how would you like your hair today?" asked the talented British hair stylist the Bellinis had just hired away from England's Princess Michael.

"Perhaps pulled back," Gaby said, wondering what was wrong with her sister today. Ever since she'd returned from California, Kristina had been in a feisty, restless mood. One minute she was laughing raucously, the next she was sulky and withdrawn. Maybe it was Jean-Luc? Gabriella had been reading about him in the tabloids. The Honorable Marquis, as Jean-Luc was called, had been cutting a wide swathe across the single women of France, and there were even hints that one of his lovers was male. In fact, one of Gaby's friends had actually asked her about it today.

"Something dramatic would be smashing," suggested the hairdresser. "You have wonderful cheekbones, let's show them off."

"Fine," agreed Gabriella, settling into the chair.

It was "the season" again in Costa del Mar. Crowds of jet-setters had descended on the principality, booking the most elegant suites in the best hotels, renting cabanas at the beach, flocking to the restaurants and discos, crowding around the "chemmy" table at the Casino de Palais. Beautifully dressed young women were on view everywhere, setting fashion styles for the next year.

"There," said the hairdresser thirty minutes later, standing back from her work with blow-dryer, curling irons, and mousse. "What do you think, Your Highness?"

Gaby gazed at herself in the mirror. She saw a strikingly pretty, self-confident woman with soft, dark eyes, her hair pulled upward, secured with pearl pins, a few tendrils trailing along her nape. She didn't have Kristina's shimmering beauty—perhaps she didn't even want it—but she did want to be considered lovely in her own way.

She wanted a man, she knew suddenly. But who?

"Wonderful," she responded politely.

Then she rose to go and dress. She was expected to attend the reception for the Prince's Awards for Achievement at 1:00 P.M., followed by an appearance at the opening of a new hospital emergency center. Gabriella never shirked her duty.

The following day Gabriella looked away from the sketch pad where she had been trying to draw a pin shaped like a cormorant and studded with pearls.

With an effort she forced herself to stare down at the drawing of the seabird, displeased with her efforts. The drawing seemed lopsided and too heavy for the airiness of the bird. She tore off the page from the artist's sketch pad, crumpled it, and tossed it into a wastebasket already filled with scrambled balls of paper. Her eighteenth sketch—and it still wasn't right.

In fact, her ideas, once so plentiful, seemed to have evaporated.

Working women with their own paychecks. The more she thought about such women wearing her jewelry, the more tense Gaby became. What if these women didn't like her designs, considering them too elaborate, too old-world? Kenneth Jay Lane was investing several million in her, and Gaby didn't want to let him down.

She moved to the telephone and dialed the U.S. access code, then the number of Lane's private office.

"Kenny," she said when the jeweler finally came on the line, speaking in his slightly clipped accent.

"Gabriella! How delightful to hear from you!"

"I'm having trouble with these sketches. Nothing seems to be going right. I'm not satisfied at all. I don't like anything I've done. In fact, I *hate* my sketches."

"Gabriella, do you find yourself doing one sketch over and over and over? *Agonizing* over each one?"

"Yes. I draw on it so many times that it's hopeless, then I just throw it away."

Kenny Lane laughed. "It's just stage fright, my dear. That sometimes happens to creative people. They begin obsessing over one piece, so anxious about how their art is going to be received that they become creatively frozen, unable to press on."

"I—I think that's what's wrong with me."

"Then I want you to forget about sending me any sketches for six weeks. During that time I want you to draw at least one sketch a day and just file it away in your portfolio."

"But what will that—"

"It doesn't matter if it's good or not, just draw. At the end of the six weeks, go through the drawings you've accumulated and pull out the ten best ones. Then you can start revising those. By then your stage fright will be gone, and your creative juices will be flowing again. I guarantee it."

"Very well," agreed Gabriella. "I didn't realize that creativity could have so much *pressure*. So much depending on it financially."

"Welcome to the real world, Princess," said Kenneth Jay Lane.

Later that day, Kristina lay facedown on the massage table, drifting into a delicious, oil-scented doze as the Swiss *masseuse* pounded and pummeled her flesh, releasing the knots from her muscles.

Her mind floated . . . to the Academy Awards again . . . and all the stars she'd met there. Especially Bret Thompson. *Sexy* Bret Thompson.

When the massage was over, Kristina noticed that the *masseuse* had brought a copy of one of the French tabloids with her.

"May I look at this?" Kristina asked casually.

The woman nodded, and Kristina picked up the tabloid. The front-page photos showed a smiling Jean-Luc with his arms around two gorgeous women and a shot taken of herself several weeks ago dancing the lambada at Hippolyte's. The headline underneath read, *Princess K. Dances While Hubby Lights Up with Two Flames.*

Kristina frowned, skimming the article, which claimed that Jean-Luc had had affairs with a ravishing, thirty-year-old French rock singer and the nineteen-year-old daughter of a Spanish count. There was also an innuendo, discreetly phrased, about a race car owner-driver called Gilles Roque-bart. Angrily, Kristina read all the way to the last para-graph.

He wouldn't do it to me, not after the way Papa talked to him.

Someone knocked, and the *masseuse* went to the door, then announced her sister, Gabriella.

"Tell her to come in," sighed Kristina. She could see that Gabriella was in one of her intense moods, her brow furrowed with anxiety.

"Kristina, I've been thinking. We have to talk!"

Kristina waved away the *masseuse,* who left the room, and then she looked up at her sister. "What's wrong?"

"You have to do something!"

"Do you mean this?" Kristina held up the tabloid. "It's garbage, Gaby—the usual trash they print."

"No, no, no," insisted Gabriella. "Too many people have seen him. People are starting to talk. Kristina, don't look that way—it's true. And I think one of his lovers is a man."

Kristina felt a burst of nausea as all of her old feelings came flooding back, the quarrel she and her sister originally had over Furnoit.

"You couldn't wait to come to me with these vicious rumors, could you?" she snapped.

"They aren't rumors." Gaby put her arm around Kris-tina's shoulders. "I'm so sorry, I didn't mean to hurt you. But I thought you should know before—"

"Just go now. . . . I have to think."

"Please, Kristina—"

"I have to think!"

When the door closed behind Gabriella, Kristina leaned against it, trembling. She *knew* she'd made a huge mistake in marrying Jean-Luc. They had little in common. He lived a life of self-indulgent idleness. He had never worked. He refused even to manage his own investments or go to official engagements, but preferred to spend his days boating, playing tennis, or sunbathing, and his nights gambling for huge stakes at the roulette tables.

But could he have made love to a man?

She showered in the adjoining bathroom, quietly dressed, and left the exercise room, taking the tabloid with her, folded under her arm. She continued down the corridors until she reached the wing that contained their apartment. Entering the apartment, she stopped short. The delicious odor of garlic and wine drifted through the rooms.

"Jean-Luc? Jean-Luc?" she called.

She stepped into the kitchen. Her husband, naked, stood in the kitchen, stirring an ironware pot that held the tantalizing odor of *coq au vin*. Surprised, she stopped short. She had never seen Jean-Luc cook before. Usually the palace cook prepared their food, or they ate out.

Looking up from the pot, he greeted her with a dazzling smile. "I'm your chef tonight, after which we are going to make love for hours while I kiss every inch of you."

She couldn't help it; she giggled. He looked so cute standing there without a stitch on, cooking for her.

"Jean-Luc?" She held up the tabloid.

"You believe that garbage?" he asked incredulously.

"The—the man they mention here. The implication is . . . you may be a . . . a . . ."

Jean-Luc laughed. "My darling Kristina, there is always an implication in the tabloids. That's how they sell millions of copies. It's meaningless. I only want you. You're my wife, my beautiful love. The only woman I want."

That night they made wonderful love. She wanted so to believe him. The next morning she woke up feeling queasy again and was forced to rush to the bathroom.

She sent her maid out to discreetly purchase a pregnancy test, and then she sat staring at the results, her face draining white. Thank God—she wasn't pregnant. Her periods were always irregular, and she'd been nervous about the Academy Awards and then upset about Jean-Luc and the tabloids. She knew she didn't want a baby with Jean-Luc.

A July sun dazzled the Costan coastline, and flowers bloomed everywhere, saturating the city of Port-Louis with their fragrance. Fashion magazines from all over the world had sent photographers to Costa to photograph the style-setting women who thronged the beaches and strolled the boardwalk.

In her large marble bathroom, Kristina stared down at the pregnancy test tube with a feeling of disbelief and horror.

This time she *was* pregnant. . . . How had it happened? *Mon Dieu,* she'd been so careful! She sank down into a chair, her head pounding. But gradually a feeling of anticipation crept over her, followed by pride. Her baby would be Henri's first grandchild.

As for Jean-Luc, he wasn't going to be a good father, but maybe he didn't have to be.

"No," said Jean-Luc into the telephone. "No, Gilles, I can't meet you this morning. I'm scheduled to fly to Paris with Kristina today."

"I need to see you," begged Gilles. "You know how I feel about you. . . . I hate being pushed aside like this."

"You're not being pushed aside. I'm merely going to Paris for a few days."

"Then I'm coming, too."

"No! No, that isn't a good idea," Jean-Luc said hastily. The news that his wife was expecting a child had swept over the small country like a burst of fireworks. The Costan citizens had adored Kristina since she was a young girl with white-blond hair, and they loved her now even more.

Even Jean-Luc felt proud. True, he already had two teen-aged boys attending school in Switzerland, but he was delighted to be fathering a third child. *A royal child.* Certainly the irascible old prince would look much more kindly on him now that he'd produced offspring.

"What hotel will you be staying at?" demanded Gilles Roquebart. "Tell me, you naughty tease, or I'll tell everyone our little secret."

Kristina had always adored Paris. She loved going to the Marais quarter, home of Azzedine Alaia, Lolita Lempicka, and Paule Ka, Paris's trendiest young designers. But this time she looked forward to her Paris trip even more, because she planned to purchase a complete baby layette.

Today Jean-Luc was being fitted for suits at Charvet, *the* Parisian men's haberdashery. As her limousine drove up to the glittering Place Vendôme, a children's boutique called Enfantin caught her eye, its windows crammed with long christening gowns trailing festoons of rare, antique lace.

"I want to stop there," she told the driver. Her announcement created a small flurry as her bodyguard went ahead to clear the shop and apprise the owner that the princess would be visiting.

"Ah, Your Highness, we are honored. How may I help you?"

The surprised shop owner waited eagerly to fulfill Kristina's every wish. The fact that Kristina shopped here would be a *coup* for the shop, and they could trade on the publicity for years.

Kristina sighed with pleasure. While she could buy everything in the shop if she wished, all she wanted was, perhaps, several of the adorable, white-on-white quilts, in addition to a complete layette.

She could hardly wait to show it all to Jean-Luc.

When she returned to her hotel, the Plaza-Athénée, laden with purchases and with more to be delivered, she was disappointed to find that there was a message from her husband asking her to meet him in Room 1720 of the Inter-Continental Hotel on the rue de Castiglione, near the boutiques in the Place Vendôme that she had just left.

Kristina nodded, wondering why Jean-Luc would ask her to meet him in a hotel room, rather than in the lobby or the restaurant.

The two men lay beside each other on the king-sized bed, their bodies still gleaming with sweat from the energetic lovemaking that had consumed two hours. Jean-Luc had insisted on the protection of safe sex. He tested clean of AIDS, and Gilles claimed he had, too, but one could never be sure.

"*Chéri*," said Gilles, stirring, "I love you."

"No, you don't," said Jean-Luc.

"I do, I really do. I'm tired of barroom liaisons that never lead anywhere. I want to settle down with someone. I want to relax a little, not always be thinking I have to appear hot and desirable to someone new."

"You are very hot," said Jean-Luc, realizing that this was exactly the sort of thing he was forced to say to women.

"But not hot enough, apparently." Restlessly Gilles got out of bed and padded naked across the room to the small refrigerator that held a selection of wines, mixes, and mineral waters. "This room smells of sex," he added as he opened a bottle of Perrier and poured two glasses.

Something about Gilles's body language made Jean-Luc uneasy. He sat up, too, and started into the bathroom to shower.

"No," insisted Gilles anxiously. "Not yet. Let's make love again. This isn't enough—it's never enough! I hate this secret life we lead, always hiding, never sure when we'll see each other."

"But I have to meet Kristina back at the hotel in an hour."

"Let her wait. She has you most of the time, she can damn well give me an hour or two. I deserve at least that," said Gilles sulkily, reaching for Jean-Luc and pulling him close for a long, tantalizing kiss.

Gilles was bent between Jean-Luc's legs when there was a knock on the door.

A few seconds later there was another knock.

"I thought you put out the *Prière de ne pas déranger* sign," Jean-Luc snapped.

"I did . . . but I ordered some caviar for us. That must be room service now."

Gilles got up from the bed, casually reaching for a towel and wrapping it around his waist before proceeding to the door.

"Princess Kristina!" Gilles said.

"Gilles Roquebart? What are you doing here?" Kristina's voice made it clear that she was puzzled and displeased.

"I'm in Paris for a week," said Gilles Roquebart, eyeing Princess Kristina with angry hauteur. He didn't bother to adjust the white towel that was slung precariously low on his narrow hips.

Kristina stared at him. He was holding the door open, so she stumbled into the room, taking in the sight of the form on the bed, guiltily bunched in sheets. Rank sexual odors permeated the room, and a package of condoms lay on the bedside table, along with a phallus-shaped vibrator.

"Jean-Luc?" she whispered, feeling sick.

"It's not as it seems—"

"*Isn't it?*" Kristina was beyond fury, the hurt so devastating that she reeled under its impact. Everything Gaby had told her was true.

She fought back her anger and drew herself up tall, speaking in the chilly, regal tones her father used when he was chastising a cabinet minister. "Get out of bed and get dressed," she ordered her husband. "You're going to have to leave this room with me. That way the maids and hotel staff won't be suspicious."

"But—"

"Just do it!"

When Jean-Luc didn't move fast enough for her, she grabbed up his clothes from a chair and thrust them under his nose, forcing him to dress more hurriedly. All the while Gilles Roquebart watched, his eyes glittering.

"As for *you*," Kristina snapped, whirling on the race car driver. "If you ever show your face in Costa del Mar again, I will have you arrested and then deported! We still have laws prohibiting this kind of liaison."

"You can't do that, not without letting Prince Henri know the reason why," Roquebart gloated. "Jean-Luc is *mine,* he's always been mine, and now I'm going to have him. You can't stop that. We love each other."

"*Love?* Oh, please!"

Jean-Luc was struggling to tie his tie, his hands shaking so violently that he kept botching the knot. Kristina snatched it away from him and thrust it into her purse.

"You don't need a tie," she snapped, handing him his jacket.

Stepping closer to Gilles Roquebart, she said flatly, "If there is one word of gossip spread about what happened in this room today, I guarantee you I will see to it that you never race again."

She led her husband to the door, snapping it shut behind them. She and Jean-Luc started down the long corridor toward the nearest bank of elevators. A room-service waiter could be seen pushing along a cart laden with someone's expensive early meal.

"Put your arm around me," Kristina told Jean-Luc in a fierce whisper. "I meant what I said. There is never going to be one word of gossip about what went on in that hotel room."

The Rolls was waiting for them, double-parked on the entrance drive in front of the hotel. She had a great deal of thinking to do. Right now she was exhausted and just wanted to get back to the hotel for a hot bath. Her marriage with Jean-Luc was over.

*   *   *

The rumors hinting at the end of Kristina's marriage had been in all the newspapers, and several of the seamier tabloids had suggested that Jean-Luc had taken a series of lovers. However, the divorce would not become final until after Kristina's child was born.

Teddy lay on her stomach on a blanket on the warm Santa Monica sand next to Auggie Steckler, a copy of Britain's glossy *Royal* magazine spread out in front of her.

Kristina . . . having a baby.

They were almost the same age. Would *she* ever want a baby?

A short distance away the surf crashed on the sand, endlessly advancing and retreating in doilies of foamy lace, as the glorious California sun beat down on their oiled bodies. The other bathers had left them alone, respecting their privacy, and they lay in the sand, enjoying the rare, sensuous pleasure of soaking up the sun without having to hit tennis balls.

"I'm always rushing off to the next tournament," sighed Teddy. "That's what I was trained to do, but right now I'm wondering why I never stop and just smell the roses."

She couldn't help remembering that the last time she had been on a beach she had been with Jac.

"Did anyone ever tell you that you're glorious?" murmured Auggie. His right hand casually reached out and touched Teddy's bare left thigh. At the warm pressure Teddy felt her insides melt.

"You're not so bad yourself," she murmured.

"Do you really find me attractive?"

She laughed. "Yes, I do, along with ten million teenaged tennis groupies. Of course, you're attractive, Auggie, and you know it."

"Fans are just part of the scenery. Teddy, I've been patient. I've held myself back, I've been gentle and considerate, and it's been driving me crazy. Do you care about me at all?"

Her answer surprised her. "Yes . . . I . . ."

Auggie didn't waste any more time. He sat up, reaching for the cooler they'd brought with them, beginning to pack up their things. "Then what are we waiting for?" he said. "Darling Tee, I've got a wonderful suite at the Beverly Hilton. I want to hold you in my arms. I want to kiss those beautiful eyes of yours. Life is too short to wait any longer."

Teddy's hesitation lasted only a few seconds. "Yes," she whispered.

"Don't be nervous," said Auggie, sensing Teddy's discomfort as they walked toward the elevators of the famous old hotel on Wilshire Boulevard. During the drive back to Beverly Hills, caught in the heavy traffic on the Santa Monica Freeway, her romantic mood had gradually faded. Her father had warned her about Auggie; now she was about to go to bed with him.

"I am nervous. I just—what will my father say?"

"He'll be glad you're finally having some fun."

"But what about—" She couldn't say the word.

"Darling girl, I'm going to take care of everything," Auggie assured her.

The drapes in Auggie's large suite were drawn against the sun, creating a dim, private cave, the bedroom dominated by a king-sized bed. He was tactful enough not to urge her toward the bed right away. Instead, they stood embracing in the sitting room, Auggie's arms tightening around her as he began to press himself against her with mounting passion.

"You're so beautiful," he kept saying. "Teddy, it drives me totally crazy to see you on the tennis court. The way your little skirt flips . . ."

He began pressing kisses on her.

"Baby . . . babe. . . ." He deepened his kisses, encircling her lips with his tongue as he then probed deep within her mouth, tormenting her with his tongue tip. She began to tremble, her body shaking all over.

They were both breathing raggedly, their hands greedily exploring each other.

Auggie began to strip, tossing away his T-shirt and shorts. She stared at him, awestruck. He had a wonderful body, every muscle smooth yet taut, a fine fuzz of blond hair running from the thatch on his chest down across his washboard-flat belly, where it descended to the kingly erection that was demanding her urgent attention.

She managed to pull off her shorts while pressed tightly against him. Then somehow he was helping her with the bikini, their hands bumping and meeting as they tried, in the fastest possible way, to shed the remaining bits of cloth that stood between them.

"Ah, God," groaned Auggie, lifting her up and carrying her over to the bed.

They lay together in total exhaustion, wrapped in each other's arms, Teddy resting her head on the moist skin of Auggie's chest, his blond hairs faintly tickling her nose. The loamy smells of their juices rose around them, a sexy perfume of love. They'd spent more than two hours rolling on the bed in frantic abandon, completely lost to time and space as they ravaged each other.

"You were wonderful," said Auggie, toying with a tendril of blond hair that curled near Teddy's ear. "You're a tiger in bed, sweetheart. You're my little passion pit."

She giggled. There was a warm, quivery feeling at the center of her body, created by the two intense orgasms she'd enjoyed. A wonderful feeling of lassitude was creeping over her. "Did you know this was only my third time?"

Auggie made a mock "oh" with his mouth. "No."

"Really."

"Who were the lucky men that were first and second?"

Teddy turned her head away. "*Man,* and I . . . really can't talk about it."

"I've heard the most amazing rumors," Auggie told her.

"About you and Prince Jac. He wouldn't be the one, would
he?"

"No! Of course not."

"That's good, because I don't think he's good husband
material. He's still got a few years of helling around left
before he settles down and becomes the big honcho. Assuming he ever does. They say he's already told his father
that he wants no part of the throne, and the old boy's furious with him."

Teddy closed her eyes. Auggie had no right to ask her
about Jac.

"I think . . . I'm too sleepy . . . " she muttered.

Auggie's laugh was a deep rumble in his chest. "Then
let's sleep, my sweet Teddy Bear. God, I love you so much.
I'm glad I waited and didn't push you. I was so afraid I
would lose you."

She drifted irresistibly into sleep.

When Teddy woke again, the room was dark. She could
hear the faint rumble of a 747 as it climbed out of LAX
airport. Somewhere a siren whined. Perspiration and body
fluids had dried on her skin, leaving her feeling sticky, and
she was chilled from sleeping without a sheet.

She looked beside her where Auggie Steckler was still
sleeping. He was one of the handsomest men she had ever
seen.

"God, I love you so much," he'd told her.

Had he meant it? Or did he say it to every woman he
wanted in his bed? She bit her lip in confusion, wanting to
believe yet afraid to. Then her Connecticut practicality
kicked in. How was she ever going to know if Auggie had
told her the truth unless she kept on seeing him? He was
going to have to prove his feelings were genuine.

Troubled, she turned over in bed, careful not to wake
up Auggie. Love affairs between players were common on
the tennis circuit, of course. But it was hell on a woman
player to be forced to worry about a dwindling love affair

when she was trying to concentrate on winning a tournament.

"Tee?" Auggie said, suddenly awakening. "You okay?"

"I'm fine," said Teddy, staring into the dimness of the room. "Auggie ..."

"Yes?"

"I don't want this to be just a cheap affair."

"A cheap affair?" Auggie laughed. "Oh, Tee. Really, Teddy. Don't think like that. I love you and I want you, and now that I have you, I'm going to work like hell to keep you."

It was exactly what Teddy had wanted to hear. Reassured, she pushed aside the sheets and slid out of bed. "I'm all sticky. I need a shower."

"I'll take one with you," said Auggie, getting up too.

Standing with him in the shower, Teddy clung to Auggie's slick, wet, muscular body as he began to make love to her again under the curtain of streaming water. She felt a rush of joy. Maybe she could love Auggie. Maybe he was the one for her.

"I don't understand why you are so adamant," said Prince Georges, staring at his brother down the length of the long table where the two were enjoying a late brunch. He wore a British-made tweed sports jacket over a dark burgundy turtleneck and very much resembled Queen Elizabeth II's husband, the Duke of Windsor. "There are many pluses to unifying with France."

"There are no pluses! It's treason even to consider such a thing," cried Henri.

"We will have a much larger army and navy," enumerated Georges. "We will stabilize our economy, we won't be subject to the vagaries of rich tourists who have to be lured to our gaming tables. We can be part of the European Common Market, and we'll have certain trade advantages with the U.S.A."

"Yes, we could have that," snapped Henri. He gazed at his younger brother, his eyes chilly. "But we'll lose our identity, and our citizens will suddenly be slapped with crippling taxes, all of their advantages gone. We'll be merely a sideline to French history. . . . I won't stand for it!"

"I was only trying to persuade—"

"Who put you up to it?"

"What do you mean?"

"Costa is small and rich, the target for many avaricious men." He rose, summoning his secretary with a snap of his fingers. "I have a meeting now. Are you the traitor in our midst, Georges? Are you working seditiously to undermine Costa? Were you involved in D'Fabray's plane crash?"

"No! My God, no! Never. I was merely trying to—to make you see—"

"It is not necessary to *make me see* anything. Georges, even though you are my brother, you don't really appreciate the problems of our country. Please don't bother me again with your opinions. What I do see is a total lack of compassion on your part, and I tell you this, I don't like it."

As the astonished Georges stared after him, the old prince walked slowly toward the door, accompanied by his stiff-spined secretary.

Autumn came again to Costa, icy Atlantic winds sweeping through the tiny principality, creating monstrous breakers that crashed against the famous beach in sprays of steel-gray foam.

Gabriella had made her first publicity trip for the Princess Gabriella line of jewelry, visiting New York and Palm Beach, and the press coverage was astounding. Every major U.S. magazine had run a piece about her, and she'd been on the covers of *Town and Country* and *People*.

Kristina stifled her envy.

It wasn't fair. . . . Gaby was doing everything she wanted to do, and being successful at it.

Kristina celebrated her twenty-first birthday quietly in Costa, inviting only a few friends to her party. She would not allow Jean-Luc to join them, telling her guests that he had a touch of the flu and could not be with them.

"Kristina, I'm so sorry for what I said about Jean-Luc," Gabriella said, trying to make amends, but Kristina felt too hurt to tell Gaby that she'd been right after all.

She and Jean-Luc hadn't had sex since Paris. She couldn't bring herself to touch him. Thank God, he swore he'd always used a condom so at least she and her baby didn't have to worry about AIDS. How dare he put both of them in such danger?

She cried every night. It was her own willful and immature behavior that had led her to marry a *pédé*, which didn't make it hurt any the less.

Curled up on the chintz-covered window seat of her beautifully decorated bedroom, staring out at the moonlight that flooded the stone walls of the palace, she brooded. She'd wanted to make their marriage work, but it was impossible. She was beginning to hate Jean-Luc for what he had put her through.

The weather had broken and a chilly sun illuminated the cobbled streets of Costa.

"You are looking quite skinny," said Prince Jac, giving Kristina a ride on his motorbike to the center of Port-Louis, where she wanted to do some shopping.

"I suppose I am," she said, gripping her brother's muscular back as they negotiated the sharp curves of the winding, cobblestoned streets, passing a series of sentry boxes. Wind whipped her hair out behind her.

"I thought when a woman was *enceinte*, she was supposed to get bigger, not smaller."

"I am dieting," Kristina said to excuse her recent weight loss, which was caused by worrying about her marriage and her nonexistent acting career.

"Well, don't diet too much, darling sister, because we

want a nice, big, healthy baby.''

As they whizzed up Prince Henri Street, passersby stared at the two golden royals. Jac had already driven his new Ferrari, with its state-of-the-art electronically controlled clutch, in two other races at Brands Hatch, in England. He had taken a second and an eighth, and was rapidly becoming a folk hero. He had also gained attention by establishing an emergency fund for the burned child of a racer, and then quickly had expanded this fund so that it would help all handicapped children. He was becoming much more active in the Variety Club, the children's charity. The prince had appeared in over a dozen burn centers and hospitals, personally handing over checks.

A Prince with Heart, said one article, which showed him holding a small, bandaged boy on his lap. Kristina happened to know that Jac had recently traveled around the world, raising more than $15 million for children's causes.

"Voilà!" Jac said, depositing Kristina in front of the shoe salon she wanted to visit. "At your service, *madame.*"

He grinned at her, his smile so warm and kind that Kristina faltered. Surely Jac would understand. . . . But then she stifled the impulse to confide in her brother. Jac would probably one day be the reigning prince. He wouldn't understand.

". . . and after our commercial break, we're going to have Princess Gabriella modeling her own glittering line of Princess Gabriella jewelry. Stay tuned. It's going to knock your socks off,'' said the voice of Oprah Winfrey, who was in the middle of another one of her much-publicized diets.

Watching the program on the TV set in the greenroom, Gabriella swallowed nervously. She'd already briefly met Oprah, who had welcomed her, then rushed off to a preshow meeting with one of her producers, Karen Melamed.

Solicitously, one of the network executives hovered around her. "Princess Gabriella, can I get you some coffee or a soft drink?"

Gaby shook her head. She didn't want to ruin her makeup.

"It should be only a few more minutes before they come to get you. Just remember to look right at Oprah, rather than at the camera. We're all friends here at ABC, we're just a big family, you should do fine."

Gaby swallowed again. "What questions will Oprah ask?"

"About the jewelry and your life. She doesn't have a prepared list, she just gets all excited and asks whatever she's interested in," said the producer. "Oh—there they are now to escort you onto the set."

A plump young woman led Gaby down long, chilly corridors, escorting her into a huge cement soundstage, which contained the set for the show and chairs for the studio audience. Someone rushed up with a body mike on a wire.

"Your neckline is too low to clip anything to," the young man informed her. "Would you mind if we put it up your hemline and clipped it inside your side seam?"

Trembling, Gaby helped to run the wire under her own clothing.

"It's time, Princess Gabriella. Be careful, don't trip on those cords," said the young man, escorting her toward the chairs that had been set up in front of the audience. Oprah, in a dark blue silk suit, was waiting for her. The popular host winked at Gaby, smiling broadly. In her hand she held a portable mike.

"Thirty seconds . . . twenty . . . ten . . ."

Suddenly a red light winked on, and Gaby realized she was on camera in front of twenty million people.

"If we ever have a day when we want to glitter, now we know just what jewelry to wear," began Oprah. "Flash and glitzy glamour, that's what Costa's Princess Gabriella has designed for us. Today we're all gonna feel like a princess."

* * *

First, Gaby modeled the five jewelry designs that she and Kenny had selected to appear on the program, while explaining the background of each. As she put on each one, the audience gasped.

When the audience applauded and cheered her third piece, a magnificent choker, Gaby felt a thrill.

Finally she was sitting in a chair again, talking to Oprah.

"How do you feel when you sketch out a design? Do you imagine yourself wearing the piece?" questioned Oprah.

"Always," said Gaby, her voice gathering strength. "I've loved jewelry ever since I was a little girl and my mother used to allow me to try on her necklaces and bracelets."

"Your mother being the Swedish beauty and movie star, the incomparable Princess Lisse of Costa del Mar," said Oprah. "Tell me, Princess Gabriella, do you have a favorite piece of jewelry that your mother left you? And do any of your own designs reflect her taste at all?"

Gaby smiled. "My favorite piece is just a simple pearl necklace that she gave me when I was seven. I treasure it and plan to pass it on to my own daughter one day. That's why I put it in the collection." Her eyes grew suddenly misty. "As for her taste . . . I suppose that everything I do, really, has part of her in it. She was a warm and lovely woman. As beautiful inside as she was on the exterior, and I always admired her so much."

"And then she died," said Oprah, "killed in the avalanche while trying to rescue you. . . . Is it true that you've always blamed yourself for her death? I don't mean to put you on the spot, Princess Gabriella, but could you tell us how you felt on that terrible day?"

Gaby brought her hands tensely to her face, then put them in her lap again. "I was so young. I didn't know what was happening, there was just the snow, so much of it, and I never even heard her scream. The sound of the snow was so thunderous, I'd never heard anything like it before. Then

I was buried—I could hardly breathe. And then people were digging me out, and I called for her but she—'' She stopped, for a few seconds unable to go on. "No, I don't blame myself,'' she added. "I was only a young girl—how could I have controlled what happened? I miss her terribly and always will . . . as long as I live.''

The studio audience was visibly caught up in Gaby's emotions.

"And now you are commemorating her with your beautiful jewelry,'' said Oprah. "Do you think that somewhere she knows what you're doing?''

"I'm sure she does.''

"And the Princess Gabriella line *is* definitely very, *very* royal,'' said Oprah.

Devoting the rest of the hour to Gaby, the talk-show host went on to ask probing questions about Gabriella's love life.

"I have men friends, of course, but no one special in my life right now,'' she told Oprah.

"Princess Gabriella, you are in the line of succession to the throne of Costa del Mar. Do you think you would ever want to rule? There are some who say you are your father's favorite, and since Prince Jac doesn't want to rule, your father may select you.''

Gaby hesitated, feeling a light flush rise to her cheeks. "I would do my duty, of course. I—''

"But how do you *feel* about it?'' persisted Oprah. "Does the idea, well, make you happy, or does it kinda give you the shivers? I mean, don't they say that running Costa del Mar would be like running a wealthy corporation?''

Gaby laughed. "I'm becoming a businesswoman now, so I suppose . . .'' Then she shook her head. "I don't think I'll ever rule. I'm not sure I want to. No, I don't think so.''

"And one last question, Princess, before we have to conclude. Anyone who reads the papers knows that you and your sister, Kristina, have had—well, just a touch of sibling rivalry. How do you feel about Kristina at this time in your life? Are you both in competition with one another?''

Gaby hesitated so long that Oprah was forced to speak up to fill in the empty air space. "She needs some time to think, folks." The studio audience laughed appreciatively.

"We are sisters, but we are also very different," Gabriella finally said in her low, soft voice. "That's all I can say. Kristina is a beautiful person. Beautiful and talented. I think she will go a long, long way."

"And I think so will you, Princess Gabriella," said Oprah, ending the interview to the sound of applause.

Back in the greenroom there was a commotion; it seemed that three men had attempted to force their way into the studio, carrying placards that said *Gabriella Will Never Rule Costa.*

As her security guards and the others in her entourage milled around, Gaby sank into one of the chairs, both stunned and embarrassed. Why did they harass her like this? She had just gone public with the news that she didn't wish to rule Costa. Maybe the crazies would now go away and leave her alone.

"Honey?" said Oprah. "You all right? This publicity stuff can be a killer sometimes."

"It's just politics," Gaby managed to say, keeping her smile.

From Chicago, Gabriella flew to New York to do "Good Morning, America" and then to Los Angeles for "Hour Magazine" and "The Tonight Show." She gave press interviews and posed for more fashion photographs. There would be more appearances later, Kenny told her. His jewelry boutiques all over the world were being flooded with new customers. Already orders were pouring in faster than his manufacturing company could fill. He was in the enviable position of having to scramble around to hire dozens of additional artisans.

"I think we're going to be very, very rich," he told Gabriella.

Teddy's romance with Auggie Steckler had continued, often long-distance, but Auggie phoned nearly every day and spoke soft love words to her. She was beginning to depend on him, to daydream of much, much more.

A September heat wave had turned the U.S. Open, held in Flushing Meadows at the National Tennis Center not far from La Guardia Airport, into a sauna. The opening rounds, the quarter- and semifinals, stretched out over a period of ten days, had been played in crippling heat. Tempers flared.

Teddy had sailed through the semifinals and was slated to play Roxy Eberhardt the next day in the finals. Still chafing from the humiliation of her defeat in Japan, Roxy had boasted she was going to pound Teddy Warner into the court.

"Then I'm gonna celebrate by getting *very* close to Auggie Steckler," she declared one day in the locker room after a practice session.

"What?"

Roxy grinned at her. "You heard me, girl. I *don't* take defeat lightly."

Teddy lifted her chin, going into the shower area and deliberately turning the water faucet to maximum volume until she had drowned out the rest of Roxy's taunts.

"This heat reminds me of the Amazon," said L. Houston Warner, who had come to the locker-room entrance to take Teddy out to dinner. Her father's upper lip was covered with a thin line of perspiration, and he fanned himself continuously with a copy of the *Wall Street Journal*. "But, Teddy, it might be a stroke of luck for you. Roxy tends to get emotional; this hot weather might make her crack."

"I hope so," said Teddy. "She's such a strong player, Dad."

"Teddy Bear, last year at the Australian Open it was

beastly hot and she got frazzled and began yelling and curs-
ing at a linesman because he called her ball out. She was
fined more than five thousand dollars. You can beat her
with no problem if you just stay cool.''

Teddy frowned. ''Dad, I think I see Auggie over there,
on the other side of the club. Would you mind if I ran over
there and talked to him for a second?''

''Of course not, honey. I'll wait for you.''

Teddy threaded her way through the milling crowds that
flooded the club, many of whom had gathered to watch
André Agassi practicing his giant serve.

She found Auggie standing by the court entrance, watching his opponent with grim, total concentration.

''Auggie! Auggie! My dad is taking me out to dinner,
but I just wanted to catch you before we left.''

''What? I'm not invited?'' Auggie smiled at her, but she
could see his eyes already sliding back to the tennis court.

''My dad wants it to be kind of a father-daughter thing,''
she explained awkwardly. ''Look, it's like this. Roxy Eberhardt has been kind of throwing your name around, if you
know what I mean.''

''No, Tee, I don't think I do.''

''She's saying that you and she—well . . .''

Auggie finally looked at her. ''Spit it out, Teddy. You
think I've been playing around with Roxy, don't you?''

Teddy turned beet red. She hadn't meant to say that at
all. ''No . . . of course I don't. . . .''

''Well, I did, but not recently. It was last year in Australia. I was bored, she was bored, and we both said what
the fuck. So we slept together. But it didn't mean anything,
Teddy, I swear it didn't.''

Teddy was shocked, then desperately hurt. She hadn't
expected such a confession.

''Well, now when I play against her, I'm going to be
forced to think about the two of you,'' she exclaimed angrily.

"No one is forcing you to think about anything, Teddy."

"But I will!"

"That's your problem, then," said Auggie, turning away.

Teddy froze, horrified. She felt the sting of tears and hurriedly blinked them away.

"I'm sorry," she said, wrapping her arms around him. "It's just that I love you so much. I don't like to think about all the women you had before me."

"Then you mustn't think about them, Teddy." Auggie wasn't smiling. "Darling, you knew what kind of a man I am. I've never lied to you about anything. I've been a womanizer, I admit it. But I love you now, and I'm not like that anymore. At least I'm trying hard not to be."

"I want to believe you so much," she whispered.

"Then believe me." He pulled her to him and kissed her warmly in full view of a group of young tennis players and their coach who were trooping past. Several of the boys whistled.

As Teddy stood leaning into Auggie's shoulder, relief flooded over her, and her confidence came flowing back.

Her father took her to the "21" Club, a legendary four-star restaurant on 52nd Street off Fifth Avenue, with classic American cuisine that has a continental influence and an intimate club atmosphere. A real fun place. But first they did a little window-shopping, while discussing Teddy's strategy for tomorrow.

"Dad," Teddy suddenly said. "This is crazy, but it almost looks to me like a guy is following us."

Warner turned, gazing over his shoulder. "Do you mean that dark-haired guy in the jeans?"

"No, that large man over there—the one in the Italian suit."

Both of them eyed the man's window reflection. He was big, and his suit was carefully tailored to hide muscular bulges. But then he walked into a store without even glancing at them.

"For a minute there you really gave me a turn, Teddy Bear," her father said, smiling. "No, honey, the man is just shopping like we are. Whatever made you say such a thing?"

Teddy frowned. "I don't know. I just saw him watching us, that's all. I had a funny feeling."

"Maybe he was watching you. You are a beautiful young lady, you know."

Teddy nodded, and they continued into the restaurant, the incident forgotten.

Waiters in black tuxedos with starched white shirts and black bowties hovered over their table, and the maître d', Walter, came over to ask how they were enjoying their food.

As they were being served their desserts, an excited ripple at the entrance of the restaurant attracted their attention. A couple was entering the dining area, accompanied by four bodyguards in dark business suits. The woman, ravishingly beautiful, wore a dress discreetly designed to conceal an early pregnancy. The man was dark, sulky-looking.

"Dad, that's Kristina! Princess Kristina! And he must be her husband, Jean-Luc."

The princess settled herself in her booth seat. Despite her burgeoning pregnancy, her beauty was so luminous that the entire restaurant seemed galvanized; people were discreetly staring. She was even more lovely than when Teddy had seen her last.

Teddy felt a flush go over her skin. She'd liked Kristina so much. Should she go over to the princess's table? But Kristina solved the problem by looking directly at her and smiling.

In a few minutes one of the bodyguards appeared at their table, inviting Teddy and her father to join the royals.

"We're in New York to do some shopping," said Kristina warmly, when they were sitting down. Beside her,

Jean-Luc nodded politely, but Teddy noticed that he seemed angry.

Brightly Kristina went on. "And then we're flying on to Las Vegas. I thought it would be fun to see what Vegas is like. And after that, we'll stop in Los Angeles, I want to see some people there. I *love* Hollywood, you know."

Kristina was so natural that instantaneously, it seemed, they were friends again, and Teddy was eager to reconnect to the *Gulliver's Travels* kingdom she'd fallen in love with the previous year. "But how is Gabriella? And your father? Is Jac still racing? When is your baby due?"

Kristina's laugh was musical. "March—if I can wait that long."

They caught up on Costan gossip, and Kristina told Teddy about Jac's latest racing win at Albacete, in Spain. "Papa was furious."

"Is Jac . . . seeing anyone?" Teddy dared to ask, then immediately regretted the question.

Kristina looked at her penetratingly. "He is seeing Lady Philippa Hawthorne. They are . . . fairly serious, at least for Jac."

Fairly serious? What did that mean? Well, that chapter of her life—no, it had been a paragraph, thought Teddy— was done.

Finally Teddy and her father rose, excusing themselves, pleading that Teddy had to get up early to practice the next morning.

"Do you have tickets to the Open?" Teddy wanted to know. "If you don't, I'll have some waiting for you."

Kristina looked at Jean-Luc, who was glowering again, obviously not pleased with the spontaneous invitation. "I'm afraid Jean-Luc is in a hurry to get to Vegas," she said regretfully. "But I'll promise to watch you on television, Teddy—and I'll say my prayers that you'll beat that horrid woman, Roxy Eberhardt. And Teddy . . ."

"Yes?"

Kristina leaned forward. Her eyes suddenly glazed with

moisture. "Please call me when you can. I—I miss you. Call me soon. I'll be back in Costa in a week, maybe sooner. Remember . . . call me!"

The following morning dawned breathlessly hot, humidity saturating the air, and Teddy was already perspiring during her practice session even though it was only 6:30 A.M.

By noon she was sitting around watching the men's finals, as Auggie lost to Agassi. Sweat ran off Auggie's face, soaking his shirt, and he hissed at the stands angrily when one of his balls was called out of court and the spectators seemed to agree with the call.

Later, when she went up to console Auggie, he seemed moody and angry, and would barely hug her. "I get so pissed when I lose," he told her intensely, moving away from her.

"I know, but losing is only a matter of learning from what happened and correcting your—" she began, but he cut her off.

"For God's sake, don't lecture me, and don't feed me platitudes. I need to be alone for a while, that's all."

Teddy walked away, thinking that Auggie hadn't even wished her luck, and her own match was due to start in less than thirty minutes.

Teddy crouched low, both hands on her racquet, waiting for Roxy Eberhardt to power another ball in her direction. Deep in her concentration, she barely heard the screaming of the audience, the ready sound of the public-address system.

Roxy was playing a fierce, almost manic game, pumped up with a herculean drive.

But Teddy was the Terminator, she was a tennis machine, and all she needed was another burst of energy . . . just one more solid hit . . . then another . . .

A moment later, Roxy aimed a forehand pass. As it

banged past, Teddy lunged, her sneaker landing on a small, slick spot.

Suddenly her right ankle wrenched, knives of pain stabbing up to her knee.

No, she moaned, catching herself. She tried to keep her momentum, but the pain skewered her bone all the way up to her hip, and then her ankle simply would not hold her.

"Baby, baby, Teddy, you're going to be just fine," said Houston Warner, the tone of his voice raw and tense after conferring with the orthopedic surgeon, Dr. Richard Feldman, present at all U.S. Open matches.

Teddy lay on the sun-heated hard court, amazed at how warm it felt, as EMS attendants, tournament officials, and photographers swarmed around her. In the background she heard the excited buzz of the stands as they began to realize that one of the top woman players in the world had just been seriously injured.

"Dad . . . it happened so fast. One minute I was running and then I just lost it."

"Honey, I'm with you."

But where was Auggie?

She fought back tears of pain. A broken ankle!

"Now we're going to put something on your ankle. This is artificial ice. It will help the swelling go down," a female EMS attendant said in her ear.

"Will I— Is the break bad?"

"The doctor will have to X-ray it, honey. We're going to put a splint on now, then we'll run you over to the hospital. You're going to be just fine."

Teddy sagged back onto the court, determined not to cry. *Auggie,* she thought in desperation. She wanted him to be here with her, she wanted him to hold her and reassure her that the injury was nothing, that she'd be playing again in three months.

Then just as she was being put on a stretcher, Auggie pushed his way through the crowd.

"Teddy, my God, this is terrible." He put his arms around her.

"Auggie—"

The EMS people were already carrying her away on a stretcher, brushing Auggie aside.

Sitting on a treatment table while the doctor wrapped sheets of gauze around her light, plastic cast, which extended from below her knee to her toes, Teddy closed her eyes to the throbbing pain.

"Doctor, with this kind of break, about how long will I be out of competition?" she asked.

"I don't know exactly—it depends on your individual recuperative powers. You need to baby that ankle for a long while. Remember, you tore some ligaments, too. You'll use crutches for about two weeks, so don't put your weight on it until I tell you to. When we do finally take your walking cast off, you'll need a cane for another week or so. Your ankle is going to be very swollen, perhaps for several more months."

"You mean . . . six weeks in a cast, then *several more months?*"

"For playing professional tennis, even longer. I imagine you can keep up your skills by watching videos of yourself," the doctor rambled on.

Teddy slumped back on the table. She couldn't believe it. *Sidelined for four months or even longer?*

As she was being wheeled back out to the main lobby of the emergency room in a chair, a hospital attendant came hurrying up to her carrying an enormous bouquet of white roses—four dozen at least, by the look of the huge, green florist wrap.

Teddy took the flowers, dully glancing at the card. *Love, Auggie,* it said.

Auggie had not come to the hospital, but Teddy could understand that: He had previously agreed to do several network and foreign newspaper interviews that could not easily be canceled.

"Honey," said her father, wheeling her out to his car, "we're not going to let this lick us. As soon as you're out of that cast, I'm hiring the best physical therapists. And we'll use videos to—"

"Videos. Right," sighed Teddy. Auggie's roses were in the backseat, filling the entire car with their scent.

"Now, honey. I'll have the cook make us some gourmet dinners, and we'll go out to eat, too. You can call Jamaica, she's back at Princeton but she's called several times. I'll set up a room full of exercise equipment so you can start working your upper body right now."

"Great," said Teddy.

Her father awkwardly continued trying to make her feel as if the bottom of her world hadn't just dropped out. "I'll even introduce you to a few nice young men who—"

"Daddy . . . *please.*"

They drove back to Connecticut along the beautiful parkways lined with towering trees and shrubs which shielded the quaint New England villages that were now expensive suburbs.

As they pulled into Westport, Teddy blinked back tears.

Home . . . the exact place she did not want to be.

Her father made phone calls, canceling her schedule for the next four months.

Everyone sent flowers and telegrams. Princess Kristina had called twice, and Gaby sent her a wonderful pink-coral bangle studded with amethysts, from the Princess Gabriella line. Auggie had bombarded her with roses, a new arrangement arriving every day.

But even their sweet perfumed scent couldn't cheer Teddy up. She wanted Auggie himself, not roses.

Teddy wasn't a very good patient, she discovered. But she and Auggie got in the habit of having long phone calls every evening. Auggie would phone her from whatever city he was currently playing in, giving her a stroke-by-stroke account of the match he had played that day. He would fill her in on all the gossip, the insider information on each player's game, sexual preference, and current love interest.

"You should write a tennis column," Teddy told him, half joking. Actually, his recitation of the tennis gossip made her feel somewhat left out of the tennis world . . . her world.

"Babe, it isn't nearly as much fun as playing. Oh, sorry, Tee. I didn't mean to make you feel bad."

Teddy began telling him about the problem she had with the cast—how difficult it was to take a shower with a plastic garbage bag pulled tight over it.

"Ugh," exclaimed Auggie. "Please—I don't even want to think about it. Could we change the subject? Guess what, Tee. I'm going to be in New York again next week for some more TV spots. And—ta da!—I've got four or five days free."

"What?" She was incandescent with delight.

"I had to bend my schedule a whole lot, and my agent is royally pissed at me. But I want to see you, Teddy. God, I haven't seen you in weeks."

That same week, an advertising firm, J. Walter Thompson, threw a party in New York for Gaby at Lutèce. The private party room was thronged with the agency's clients and potential clients and with ABC network television executives, who hoped to convince Gaby to do her own nighttime talk show.

She was deep in conversation with Roone Arledge when she looked up and her entire body vibrated with awareness of the tall, suntanned man who had just entered the room. He was about thirty-five, with a craggy face and deeply cleft chin, and he wore a dove-colored business suit, impeccably tailored. On his feet were cowboy boots of light tan snakeskin.

"Who is that?" she finally asked.

"Oh, that's Clifford Ferguson, he owns Ferguson's, the department store chain. It's based out of Dallas, but they have branches everywhere."

Everyone had heard of Fergie's. "Of course," murmured Gaby, remembering that Kenneth Lane had been elated when his director of sales had sold a large order to the central buying office.

The Texan was approaching them, and Dan Burke, recently retired chairman of Capital Cities–ABC, introduced her.

"Princess Gabriella, your line of jewelry is stunning. I've already purchased several pieces for different friends and members of my family," he told her, shaking her hand warmly.

"Oh?" She felt a stab of disappointment. He was married, then.

"But mostly for my young daughter, Rebecca. Becky just had her thirteenth birthday. Her mother died two years ago, and I wanted to give her something different. She's a very special girl."

Gaby smiled. "Which piece did you choose for her?"

"The pretty pearls. The sophisticated jewels can come later, don't you agree?" His eyes held hers. "Rebecca is a pairs skater—she's hoping to make the Olympics in 1992. I must confess that I told my daughter over the phone that I was coming to this party, and she begged me to get your autograph. Could you possibly help me?"

Gaby was intrigued by the down-to-earth charm of this man. "I'd love to . . . but I don't have anything to write on."

Ferguson grinned. "I've come prepared." He produced a three-by-five card from his jacket pocket and held out a gold pen for her to take.

Dear Rebecca, Warmest wishes in all that you do, Princess Gabriella Bellini, Gaby finally wrote, after thinking for a moment.

"Thank you," said Ferguson, taking back the card and

returning it to his pocket. "She'll be thrilled, Gabriella. . . . Sorry, maybe I shouldn't have called you that. It seems so strange here in America to refer to anyone as Your Royal Highness."

"Of course. Please do call me Gabriella."

"Gabriella, would you like to have lunch with me tomorrow, if your schedule permits? If a commoner can look at a princess, so to speak. Or is it, 'If a cat can look at a queen'? Whatever."

Gaby giggled. "I'd love to, but I'll have to check with my secretary first and then my security people. I'm supposed to fly to San Francisco to meet with some jewelry buyers—"

Ferguson raised an eyebrow. "Then I'll fly you there. And I'll check with my security honcho. He's a big German shepherd named Jesse, which is short for Jesse James."

"Jesse James?"

"Jesse James is one of our cowboy folk legends, I guess sort of a good guy in some parts of the West. I'll tell you all about him tomorrow at lunch, assuming your security people and my security people can manage to get their heads together," he said with a large attractive grin.

Ferguson spent most of the plane trip on his private jet closeted in an office with a secretary and a fax machine, while Gaby studied her drawings and sketched, feeling close to Cliff somehow because they were in the same plane. To her amusement, he'd actually brought the dog, Jesse, a kingly-looking 110-pound animal with black-and-tan markings. His staff would look after Jesse while they were eating lunch.

After Gaby's meeting, they ate at La Folie, on Polk Street in San Francisco. The dining room, a pretty "folly," had clouds painted on a blue ceiling, and monkeys and parrots cavorted on yellow drapes hung at double rows of windows.

"Call me Cliff," he told her over ravioli of sea scallops

and shiitake mushrooms that chef Roland Passot had wrapped in cabbage and sautéed with citrus butter and chives. "Everyone does. And a few people even call me Fergie, but I don't encourage it; sounds too much like the Duchess of York." He eyed her mischievously. "You aren't very intimidating, or are you?"

Gaby laughed. "I don't think I could intimidate anyone."

"Oh, yes, you could. I saw the way some of those people were watching you at that party. We Americans aren't accustomed to rubbing shoulders with royalty, and I'm afraid some of us go too far in the direction of adulation, while others, well, perhaps they are a bit more reserved."

"And which are you?"

Ferguson's laugh was warm. "I'm somewhere in the middle, but I still can't help admiring your lovely face, Gabriella. You are a beautiful, doe-eyed woman, and there is a gentleness about you, a sweetness. Honestly . . . it's almost like a fawn's, so innocent and trusting."

Gaby looked down at the table, her heartbeat speeding up into her throat. *Mon Dieu* . . . this man really liked her. And she found him exciting, too, charming and warm and wonderful. But something in her insisted on holding back. He was American: He lived across an ocean from her, and he was extremely Texan. Even today he wore a Western-style bola tie with his suit, and he had on another pair of expensively tooled cowboy boots, which, she speculated, were probably his uniform of choice. Also, he had a teen-aged daughter of thirteen, and he wasn't Catholic.

"You have a ranch near Dallas?" she queried.

"About a hundred miles away. Down in Texas, we call that 'near.' It's a beautiful place. My great-grandfather settled it, and we still have more than ten thousand head of cattle on fifty thousand acres. Great-granddaddy was real enterprising when he came over from Glasgow in the early 1900s. He bought forty choice acres of real estate down in south Texas near the Mexican bordertown of Juarez. Folks today refer to it as downtown El Paso. He was the first Jewish cowboy, I think.'' Ferguson smiled ruefully. ''Our original name was Fuerstein, but my grandfather David found it was easier doing business as a Ferguson. When I have time, I still ride fences and rope steers. Of course, there hasn't been a lot of time recently. Ferguson's commands all my attention nowadays. I've recently expanded to London, Tokyo, and Paris, and have put out feelers about opening stores in Moscow and a few other cities.''

They talked business for a while, Gaby intrigued with the idea of a Jewish cowboy who ran a huge department store chain, the finest in the world, comparable to Lord & Taylor or Neiman-Marcus. She did like him . . . so much. But there were going to be big problems, she could see. Surely Ferguson wouldn't even consider coming to live in Costa, and she didn't know if she could ever live in Texas.

Mon Dieu . . . what was she dreaming about?

The waiter brought a telephone to their table, and Ferguson excused himself, taking the call. When he had finished, he hung up, apologizing. ''A small business emergency,'' he explained. ''I hate to cut this short, but I'm going to have to fly us back to New York. You don't mind going back earlier, do you? I was planning to take you sight-seeing but now there really isn't time.''

Gabriella nodded, regretting that the day was ending.

Seated in the large living room of the Warner house, Teddy heard gravel crunching under car tires.

''There's Auggie,'' she cried. ''Right on time.''

Houston Warner, reading his *Wall Street Journal,* didn't look nearly as pleased. ''Teddy Bear, I don't want you to get your hopes up, dear. The man is terribly busy, and you know how some players are about injuries. They think that if they're with a player with a broken ankle, then it's almost like a jinx. . . . All athletes are terribly superstitious.''

Too excited to listen, Teddy was already stumping on her cast across the room. Reaching the hallway, she stopped in front of the gold-burnished antique mirror that once had belonged to her mother. "Do I look all right, Dad? My hair . . ."

She'd tried a new style, perming her hair into ringlet-like crimps that flowed in ash-blond riotous masses down her shoulders, dwarfing her face and making her blue eyes look huge. For tennis she would have to tie it back or braid it, but right now its wildness made her feel sexy.

"He'll love your hair," said Warner. "If he doesn't, we'll toss him out. Maybe we should do that anyway."

"Daddy . . ."

She reached the door and threw it open.

"Auggie!" she squealed. He'd had his own sun-streaked hair trimmed, too, in a short, trendy buzz cut that made him look most appealing.

"Baby, baby, baby," said Auggie, opening his arms and scooping her in.

Teddy bent her head into his wide chest. "Auggie," she whispered, her eyes stinging, and then she was laughing, hugging him, and crying all at the same time.

"Hey, aren't you even going to invite me in?"

"Oh, I got so carried away. Please come in. Dad's taking us out to dinner tonight at the Three Bears Inn—it's the most wonderful old place—and tomorrow we'll go out driving. The fall colors are glorious here, and I want you to see—"

"Hey, talky girl," said Auggie, putting a finger over her mouth. "One thing at a time. First you. I have to give you a *real* kiss."

He proceeded to do just that, enfolding her in a full-body embrace, his hands deliciously roaming her back and buttocks. Teddy clung to him, her heartbeat thumping as she gave herself up to the glorious sweetness of being held again after three long weeks of worrying.

"Teddy," called her father from the upper living-room level of the big house, "is that Auggie?"

Teddy giggled at her father's effort to be tactful. "It

certainly is, Dad. I'll bring him right up. We're going to
have him for *five whole days.*"

The Three Bears Inn, a 150-year-old, low-ceilinged New
England inn, had applewood logs crackling in its fireplace.
Well-to-do Wilton, Darien, and Westport residents filled
every table.

"I just adore this place," sighed Teddy. "We used to
come here when my mother was alive. I used to love the
name, because it always made me think of the nursery
tale."

Auggie and Houston Warner began talking about the
stock market. Auggie said he tracked all of his own investments and was considering buying a large apartment
development in Westport, which was one reason he was in
Connecticut.

"So I do have a few meetings tomorrow," he told
Teddy apologetically. "I hope you'll understand. Maybe
you'd like to come along with me, both of you. I could use
some good advice."

"Of course we will," she agreed, but with disappointment in her voice. She'd planned to spend the morning in
bed with Auggie, then go for a ride through the wonderful
New England villages with their pretty white-clapboard
churches and homes, many of which dated back to the early
1800s, a few even earlier.

Auggie's hand came out to cover hers. "But meetings
are only during the day—we'll have the evenings together,
darling Tee."

As Teddy was crossing the parking lot toward their car,
after leaving the restaurant, the heel of her walking cast
slipped on a scatter of damp, fallen leaves. Skidding awkwardly, she grabbed at Auggie's arm for support, but he
was stepping ahead, and her fingers didn't get a strong grip.
She pinwheeled her arms, then suddenly sat down hard on
the pavement.

"Tee!"

"Teddy!"

Both her father and Auggie called out at the same time, bending over her.

"I'm fine," cried Teddy, tears of chagrin in her eyes. "Damn this cast!"

"Here, help her up," ordered Warner, and both men reached for her arms, assisting her to her feet again. But looking at Auggie, she noticed that his mouth had tightened, and when they were walking again, he didn't reach out to touch her.

"I want to show you our family photographs," said Teddy, proudly leading Auggie to the upstairs hallway, where more than 150 black-and-white family pictures hung in a wall display begun by her mother when Teddy was a little girl.

Warner had added to them, and now the pictures were like a catalog of her life, showing her as a small girl with her hair pulled back in two fat braids, holding her first tennis racquet. Then as an eager eight-year-old junior girls' winner, on up through the Australian Open and Wimbledon.

"You were a great kid," said Auggie, looking at them. Then he looked at Teddy. "Tee . . ."

"Yes?"

"Oh, never mind," he told her. "God . . . I guess I just let that broken ankle of yours get to me for a little while. I'm a weird, superstitious dork. I do love you, Tee. I can't begin to imagine life without you."

The next three days were heavenly. They drove everywhere, and Auggie even met with her physical therapist and told her what he thought ought to be done to get Teddy back in tournament shape. But Auggie cut his visit short, leaving on the morning of the fourth day, explaining that his agent had just called saying he had to meet with some people in New York.

"Before I leave, I have something for you," Auggie whispered as they stood in the hallway where he had put his suitcases.

He reached for his briefcase, opened it, and pulled out a small jeweler's box.

Teddy stared at it, her heart giving a huge thump.

"Aren't you going to open it? It's just a little something I picked up for you. I hope you like it."

Her hands shaking, Teddy reached for the box and pulled off its lid. Inside, nestled on blue velvet, was a solid gold tennis racquet on which their initials had been engraved. She looked at it, then looked at it again, her thumping heart doing slow, incredulous rolls. She'd thought it would be an engagement ring . . . and it was just a tennis racquet. *A gold one, though,* she added in her mind, fighting back the hot tears of disappointment that flooded her eyes.

"It's a pin to hang from a gold chain," said Auggie, picking up the racquet. "I had it made so you could wear it around your neck all the time. It's a . . . pre-engagement gift, Tee, for good luck. I hope you don't mind that I didn't get you the ring yet. I still have some anxieties over the big 'M word,' and I'm trying to kinda ease into it."

Teddy took the tiny racquet from him. "It's lovely," she said. "Very beautiful. It's the most beautiful pin I ever had."

Auggie took her in his arms again. "I know I'm probably not as wonderful as you deserve, and I have a feeling your father doesn't like me all that much, but, Tee, I love you, and I care, and I want you to *play tennis again,*" he added, laughing. "Now with your new good-luck charm you can't miss. Tell that therapist that she'd better put you through your paces, or she'll have to answer to me."

They clung together.

"I'll tell her, Auggie."

"Good. Hang in there, Teddy."

Auggie backed his car out of the long driveway, as Teddy stood on the lawn, watching until his car disappeared on Wolf Pit Road, around the corner by the woods. She didn't know whether to laugh or cry. She was "pre-engaged," with Auggie's gold tennis racquet to prove it . . . almost like a fraternity pin.

"Good night, Mr. Warner," said Mary Katherine, Houston Warner's executive assistant, giving him a weary wave as she finally walked out of his office after putting in a thirteen-hour day, standard for his staff and himself.

"Good night, Mary," he called.

The minute she had left his outer office suite, Warner walked to the door and threw the lock, then began pulling his tie loose. He walked back into his inner office and threw himself on a couch, weariness pounding through his body. He could feel a burning band of tight muscles across his back.

His eyes flicked to the wall, hung with tennis pictures of Teddy, along with several taken of himself in his own tennis days, serving as a proud reminder of who the Warners were.

Teddy, so blond and beautiful, such a tennis natural. He frowned.

Teddy's romance with the hot-tempered Auggie Steckler bothered him. The man was so selfish he could scarcely be bothered to visit her. He was a classic tennis stud. Why couldn't she see that? He was going to drain her energies and hurt her, damaging her chances to become the biggest woman tennis champion the world had ever seen.

But he didn't think Auggie was going to last very long. He recalled a number of small disagreements that he and his daughter had had the previous week.

"Dad," Teddy had said as they both pored over the *New York Times,* "did you read that Prince Jac is doing just great on the Formula One circuit? He's going to be better than Ayrton Senna was. All he has to do is prove it."

Warner had given a short laugh. "Since when do you

follow car racing, Teddy? I thought tennis was our sport."

"It is. . . . Oh, Dad, it's just that I know Jac, and I'm
interested in how he does. . . ." Her voice had faltered, and
Houston Warner, who knew his daughter's every mood, felt
a chill center in the pit of his stomach.

"Teddy," he said, "you don't have a schoolgirl crush
on Jac, do you?"

"No—no, of course not!" But her denial had come too
fast.

"Good," he said quickly. "Crushes are a waste of time
for a tennis player, honey—they drain your energy from
the sport. That's one thing you're going to have to be very,
very careful about, Teddy. You need to concentrate totally
on tennis. You've already got one boyfriend in Auggie—
how many do you need? There will be plenty of time later
for a husband and children. Hopefully you won't even consider having children for about ten years. You'll still be
young enough and—"

"Daddy!" she cried angrily. "Daddy, you sound as if
you have my whole life planned."

He immediately felt a rush of guilt and backtracked.
"Maybe I *was* being a bit of a tennis father. It's an old
habit of mine. Forgive me, Teddy Bear?"

She hesitated. "I forgive you."

"Good," he'd said.

But now as he replayed the conversation in his head, he
realized that Teddy *did* have a crush on young Jac, whether
she would admit it to herself or not. It made him even more
anxious to keep an eye on the Costan royals—to indulge
in what had become his unusual hobby—royal-watching.

Warner rose from the couch and went to a filing cabinet,
where he pulled out a thick folder. Taking it to his desk,
he sat down and began to turn the pages, rereading bits and
pieces of the old reports he'd paid Max Bergson for, and
the newer reports that a journalist for *Paris Match* had sent
him.

Prince Henri, a benign despot, seems to be ruling his

country with blinders on, Bergson had written in one of his early reports. *The aging monarch, who rumors say is plagued by bad health, is besieged on all sides with problems. Dwindling financial resources. Investors, some of a shady nature, wanting to move in on his country. Citizens who wish to turn the country over to France. And there are also rumors, which I have not yet been able to substantiate, that Prince Georges, Henri's brother, is scheming to take over the throne.*

There were more speculations, linking Georges with Nikos Skouros, the Greek shipping magnate, who manipulated power with Machiavellian skill.

Warner frowned, rereading this paragraph, then turned the page. *Georges has had a checkered past—officially concealed from the public for years. In his school years a classmate died in a mysterious prank, killed while walking on the hood of a moving car. Some said that Prince Georges was among those youths involved, perhaps even the instigator, but the scandal was immediately hushed up by the palace.*

Finally Warner put the reports aside. He'd uncovered more than he should have, he knew, and sometimes he wondered if that man in the suit outside the ''21'' club *had* been following him.

But no, he assured himself. God, he was really being paranoid, wasn't he? As chairman and CEO of a large corporation, he'd become too security-conscious, he thought.

SPRING 1990

Six MONTHS HAD PASSED. TEDDY WARNER WAS back on the circuit and had won an exhibition tournament in New Orleans, beating Sabine Appelmans of Belgium. *People* magazine ran a photo of her slamming the ball, her short skirt swirling to reveal the high-cut, lace-trimmed panties she wore underneath, which had now become her trademark.

Kristina had gazed at this picture enviously, rubbing her own enormous belly.

She tossed the magazine down and stumbled to her bed, where she threw herself on the embroidered coverlet, tears streaking from her eyes. Her morning sickness had lasted for months, and even when she wasn't being sick, all she could keep down were dry crackers, toast, fruit, and cola.

Wiping her eyes, she contemplated her position. Here she was, trapped in Costa del Mar, pregnant and sick . . . losing weight everywhere except her stomach, which was getting more rounded every day. Even if Papa *had* allowed her to work in Hollywood, she couldn't now because of her pregnancy. Worse, she was married to Jean-Luc, and would have to remain so at least until after the child's birth.

Gabriella was free as a bird, flying to the United States to promote her jewelry, *permitted by Papa to do so. It isn't fair,* Kristina fumed. Why was jewelry more acceptable than modeling or acting?

Getting off the bed, Kristina moved to a shelf where she kept a collection of books on Hollywood. These included six published about her mother, Princess Lisse. Picking up one of the books called *Princess Lisse: A Fairy Tale Come True,* she stared at the cover photo of her mother, shown wearing the heart-shaped tiara.

She began to turn pages. Papa had permitted Mama to

act in two pictures after their marriage, she recalled. She began flipping through pages, wondering just how Lisse had accomplished this minor miracle.

Lisse presented her Napoleonic husband, Prince Henri, with his Waterloo when she flew to Hollywood and signed with Frank Capra to do Tuesday Girl *with Cary Grant. . . .*

Smiling, Kristina closed the book. "Thank you, Mama," she whispered.

"Papa permits *you* to go all over the world, but he wouldn't let me model because he said it wasn't suitable," Kristina remarked to her sister later that evening, unable to hold back her jealousy. "But you were on the Oprah show, and some of Oprah's guests are pretty raunchy. Transvestites and men who beat their wives, women who have affairs."

"Not the day I was on. I was the only guest. Anyway, you know I'm representing Costa," insisted Gaby. "I'm going to build up publicity for our country as well as my jewelry. In fact—"

Kristina gave a bitter laugh. "You *always* want to represent Costa, don't you?" Her cheeks had gotten red. "It's so obvious, Gaby, what you're trying to do."

"What am I trying to do?"

"Why, you want to sit on Papa's throne instead of Jac, so you're trying to get a lot of positive publicity. It's just disgusting."

Gaby stared at her, stung and wounded. "I didn't . . . I never thought of that."

"Well, you *know* Jac told Papa he didn't want to rule."

"Kristina, please. . . . I know Papa treated you unfairly—"

"*Unfairly!* That's hardly the word to describe it. I can't just stay here in Costa del Mar, fat and pregnant, doing what he tells me to. As soon as the baby comes, I'm going to Hollywood."

"What?" Gaby stared.

"I'll get a divorce—the terms are already provided for in the prenuptial agreement, there'll be no problems. Then I'll take the baby, and I'll sign a movie contract—and Papa won't dare to stop me."

"But that's not true, Kristina. You know he will stop you. . . . He is our prince."

"Don't be so scared of him," fumed Kristina. "I'm not. After all, he is our father, too! He doesn't worry me at all. What is he going to do—lock me in a dungeon until I'm forty? I'll have long, gray hair hanging to my feet, and I'll let my fingernails grow into claws."

Gaby couldn't help it; she giggled. "You could be like Rapunzel and let down your hair to some fair prince," she suggested.

Kristina hooted. "I can think of one fair 'prince'—oh, he's very fair—but by the time I'm forty, he'll be over seventy, so he probably won't have the necessary strength—"

"Who?" cried Gaby.

"*I'll* never tell you," said Kristina, grinning. "I'm a married woman, remember? Oh, so married," she added, rubbing her stomach.

The Royal Costan Hospital was getting a face-lift, scaffolding erected along its south wall, where workmen were sandblasting the ancient, wind-pitted stone.

Prince Jac strode past a newsstand where an issue of *Sports Illustrated* showed Teddy Warner on the cover. He couldn't help it; he slowed a little to get a better look at the lively photo.

Teddy. Pictures of her appeared nearly weekly in the international press, and each one hit him with a small blow to the center of his stomach. He couldn't help hearing about her romance with August Steckler, and often he wondered just what she saw in a temperamental, selfish man like Auggie. Of course, he told himself, Auggie was very handsome.

Even Philippa—Lady Philippa to most people—had

sensed his interest and brought up the topic of Teddy more
than once, discussing her in a taut voice and referring to
her as "that awkward tennis player."

"She isn't awkward." Jac had been driven to defend
Teddy. "How can you possibly say that, Philippa? She's
amazingly graceful. Most women tennis players seem all
muscle and sweat, but Teddy is the most feminine woman
ever to play at Wimbledon."

"You fancy her, don't you?" accused Philippa.

"No, of course I don't."

"Why don't I believe you?"

Now he hurried into the hospital to begin visiting the
child burn patients he sponsored.

"Would you like to ride in my race car with me? When
you're better, of course?"

Prince Jac, stifling his sympathetic anguish, knelt beside
the wheelchair of an eight-year-old boy called Didíer, who
was so covered with bandages that only his eyes peered out
through slits in the cloth. He had been burned on eighty
percent of his body when a space heater in his family's
home in the Costan suburb of Notra Patria had exploded.

"*Oui,*" said the child, his voice barely audible.

"You must be strong," said Jac, smiling. "I will come
to see you again, and I'll bring you pictures of my new
Ferrari, the one we're going to ride in, you and I."

The child nodded, and Jac smiled warmly. He handed
the boy a small replica of a Ferrari. "For you, Didíer."

Then he got to his feet. Today he had talked to forty
children, and he was emotionally exhausted from the effort.

"You have made a tremendous difference, Your Highness," said the nurse, a woman in her thirties, as they
walked out to the lobby.

"What about that boy, Didíer?"

"He's going to have severe facial scars," said the nurse
reluctantly. "Very severe."

Jac told her he would arrange for a plastic surgeon to
be flown in from the United States.

The woman nodded. "Your Highness, these children just light up when you come to visit. It makes them feel special to think that their prince is interested in them. They'll remember it all of their lives."

Jac didn't know what to say. He wasn't doing this to get flattery or praise or even to please his father, although Prince Henri had been begging him for several years to do his part to fulfill the royal family's official engagements. Visiting hospitals was the most difficult thing he had ever done, but since he had assisted his first burned child, he had become obsessed with easing the pain of these poor tormented youngsters.

As he walked out of the hospital to the Yamaha motorcycle he'd left parked outside, he was already thinking of ways to raise money. He knew he could depend on his sisters.

But he had another source of possible funds, too: Lady Philippa, whose vast fortune grew larger daily. Straddling the Yamaha, he glanced at his watch. He had scheduled the palace plane to leave at 4:00 P.M. for London.

Gaby and Kristina, their quarrel mended, sat over lunch in the palace solarium, debating what sort of entertainment to devise for Jac's charity concert for the Burn Center.

They had already booked New Kids on the Block, and had tentative commitments from Bonnie Raitt, Smokey Robinson, and Natalie Cole. The Broadway singing star Valentina had phoned with a definite acceptance, and they had placed several calls to the agent of Johnny Coates, the British rock star whose husky tenor voice had been compared to Rod Stewart's.

"I'm sure it will all come together just fine," said Gaby.

Kristina looked at her sister, and suddenly her mood was down. She didn't want to be here. She wanted to be on location, making a movie. She *knew* she could do it. Even in that short screen test last year, she'd sensed her own power. She was convinced she had real acting talent.

"I'm going to have my secretary make some calls and see if she can find me an acting coach," Kristina said casually. "I'll fly someone in from California if I have to, and put him or her up at the Casablanca Hotel."

"Acting coach? Kristina!" Gaby was shocked.

"Don't tell Papa," Kristina begged. "I *have* to do it, Gaby, or I'm going to go quite mad."

A light March mist had dampened the cobbles on the streets of Port-Louis, creating a wet, slick patina.

Kristina fidgeted, unable to settle with any comfort into the back of the Rolls-Royce, despite its spaciousness. She'd just been visiting her couturier for a fitting on her gown for the charity concert, a concoction of filmy, floating chiffon meant to conceal her pregnancy. She felt so bloated. Her doctor had told her that she would deliver within the next fifteen days or sooner. Actually, Papa had asked her not to attend the concert, but she had promised Jac.

"I want a drink," complained Jean-Luc, who had accompanied her, enduring the long wait at Madame Aumont's.

"You always want a drink," sighed Kristina. "Ouch!"

Jean-Luc, busy staring at a young girl sauntering past on the sidewalk wearing a micro-miniskirt, didn't hear her.

"I think . . . Oh, *mon Dieu*—Jean-Luc!"

He turned to look at his panic-stricken wife. "No. You're not supposed to have it now. You told me you wouldn't."

Kristina's laugh turned into a groan. "I think this is it!"

Jean-Luc spent five hours pacing the VIP lounge on the royal floor, chatting with one of the staff doctors and watching television. Now he was bored and tired and wanted to go back to their apartment for the drink he'd been denied.

A doctor clad in greens hurried in to tell him that mother and baby were just fine.

She'd had a girl. He had really hoped for a boy. A boy

would have cemented things much better than a girl . . . but maybe there would be a boy next time. Maybe. If he could ever convince his wife to sleep with him again. He had the gloomy feeling that once the baby arrived, his marriage with Kristina would be toast.

He walked down the hallway to Kristina's suite.

"I thought we would name her after my mother, Nicolette," he began.

Kristina stared at him as if he had gone mad. "She is Princess Charlaine Lisse."

Jean-Luc didn't argue. He gazed at his new daughter, who weighed six pounds four ounces. The newest Costan princess was breathtakingly tiny and already very alert, her slate-gray eyes showing signs of becoming deep blue. She had an adorable tuft of light hair and quizzical eyebrows shaped like tiny wings.

"She's so beautiful," Kristina whispered. *"Mon Dieu."*

"As pretty as you," said Jean-Luc. He hovered over her bed, reaching out to touch the baby's miniature curled fist. "Kristina, I know I wasn't much help. . . . These things bother me—woman things."

"Jean-Luc," said Kristina, looking at him contemptuously, "I guess the only thing about our marriage that I can think about fondly is Princess Charlie. Now I'd like to rest. I'm very tired."

Jean-Luc nodded and obediently left the room. His tenure as husband was over. The Bellinis would arrange the divorce, and they would make it look good with the Church, too.

Prince Georges and Prince Jac stood shoulder-to-shoulder as squadrons of Costan soldiers marched past them, raising and lowering their rifles in crack precision. A military band played the Costan anthem. Church bells were ringing, and there had been a twenty-gun salute.

It was all to celebrate the birth of another princess. Henri, thrilled beyond belief, could not do enough.

"We have such good-looking soldiers," murmured Prince Georges as line after line of young men marched past.

"Indeed," said Jac, feeling a thrill of patriotic pride. Jac's own blue serge chest was covered with hereditary medals, as well as three or four he had earned himself in the eighteen months he had undergone naval pilot training.

Later, after the troops had marched back to their barracks, Jac and Prince Georges returned to the robing room of the palace to change out of their uniforms. A boot room held rows of polished leather boots, and there were display cases to hold medals, some dating back four hundred years. On the wall hung swords once carried by Bellini men, many with elaborately damascened scabbards.

"I have been wanting to discuss something with your father," began Georges, clearing his throat. "The plans, I mean."

"What plans?" Jac, unbuttoning his high-collared blue tunic, paused.

"Nikos Skouros's magnificent ideas for Costa. He is going to make the entire country sparkle like a diamond. His idea for hotels and casinos is wonderful. It will bring in a whole new influx of tourists—"

"Casinos? In the plural? But Papa has forbidden outsiders to build hotels or casinos without his permission."

"Nikos Skouros is hardly an 'outsider,' as you call him. In fact, I believe that he has applied for Costan citizenship, which will make him very much one of us. He is a great friend of Costa del Mar, nephew. Perhaps you do not realize just how much Nikos Skouros loves our country or how much he is willing to do for it."

"I see," said Jac.

"Skouros has rescued us financially more than once. Without him, we would be in disastrous circumstances. And you know that his wealth is more than that of many countries. He could do so much more for us . . . if only we would permit it. I thought you might wish to mention this to your father.''

"I'll think about it," said Jac hesitantly.

After he had changed, he walked along the corridors of the palace to visit Prince Henri, his mind turning over the conversation he had just had with his uncle.

He wasn't quite sure he trusted Nikos Skouros, that "great friend" of Costa del Mar. In fact, he decided, he would talk to his father about it and ask him to be very cautious. He knew his family had its hands full, with Kristina's divorce looming on the horizon, and felt a strong pang that he suddenly recognized as concern . . . for Costa. He still didn't plan to take over the reins—God, he just didn't think he ever could—but he cared about his country, and he was worried about it.

"Eight hundred people . . . just to watch one baby being christened," said Kristina, scribbling another name on the guest list she was making up.

"And eight thousand more would willingly attend," said Nikos Skouros, who had come to pay her a visit in the hospital before flying to Greece on business.

He went on. "It will be a monumental event. Henri's first grandchild. And she'll be, what, fourth in line for the throne?"

"I want little Charlie to be happy," said Kristina.

"Ah."

"Happy," Kristina repeated. Motherhood had affected her oddly. One moment she was high on adrenaline and surges of soft love. The next she was gloomy and brooding. What could a baby do with a useless father like Jean-Luc? Did she herself have enough mothering ability? She hadn't really ever held a newborn before, and she'd been shocked at how small they were. Fortunately, there would be armies of servants to take up the slack. Mary Abbott, the princess's old nurse, was warm and competent.

She went on, "A twenty-gun salute . . . eight hundred

people attending her christening . . . and more messages arriving from Papa every hour on what we are to do next. It's going to be a circus. And all of it for a sweet little girl who only weighs six and a half pounds.''

Skouros leaned forward in his chair, fixing her with his sharp blue eyes. "You want something, don't you?'' he said gently. "I mean, for yourself.''

She was startled at his penetrating remark. "Of course, doesn't everyone?''

"You want something specific.''

"I don't know. Yes. And no. I don't know! I've never had any adventures. I don't even know how to have one. Now I'm a mother. I'm not sure I know how to do that either.''

Nickey paused. "*I* could provide adventure for you, dear Kristina. You only need to say the word.''

Kristina looked at the handsome, silver-haired Greek, who was smiling at her with deep affection. She found herself drawn to the warmth of his personality, but she had had to face the truth about her present marriage, and now she was wary about future commitments.

Encouraged because she hadn't stopped him, Nickey continued. "And I'm offering you my loving companionship—you already know I adore you, Kristina. I'd be the best husband . . . and father, too. We could travel, anyplace in the world you want to go. From the Taj Mahal to the Himalayas and the Seychelles. Anyplace you want. We can even cliff-dive if you want—''

"Cliff-dive?'' Kristina's silvery laugh echoed. "That would be fun, yes. . . . Nickey, you *are* wonderful, more than wonderful. But I want—'' She opened her arms, gesturing widely. "I just want it all. I want everything!''

As his private jet hummed along to Athens, where he had a series of business meetings, Nikos Skouros went into the office section of the plane. A secretary was seated at a computer, typing up an agreement for one of his offshore corporations to purchase additional property along the Costan shoreline.

"Almost finished, Jeanne?" he asked.

"Ten more minutes, sir."

"Good. Bring it in to me when you're finished."

He strode on past her into the inner office, closing the door behind him. He sat down at his desk, picked up the telephone, and began to direct-dial a number in Costa del Mar, then stopped halfway and put the phone down again.

Kristina. He had never seen a woman with more breathtaking beauty. She far surpassed his first two wives, and they had been stunning. Even she didn't know the full impact of her elegant looks.

Obviously marriage to that dissolute playboy had been a failure. Already the Vendôme Palace was releasing discreet publicity that arrangements were under way for a divorce. He would be there to pick up the pieces.

Satisfied with his thoughts, he picked up the phone. Within minutes he was connected to one of the Costan ministers. *His* minister.

"I want more land," he said without preamble. "Perhaps that nice section two miles from the boardwalk, near Pointe-à-l'Aigle. And tell Georges to call me when it is convenient."

"Yes, sir, of course."

The small party walked into the main hall of the palace, the baby carried by her head nurse, Mary Abbott. Kristina, tired from her five-day hospital stay, stopped still in astonishment.

All of the servants had gathered to greet them, lined up along the great hall in two rows, two hundred fifty people smiling and clapping and applauding. The entire staff of the palace.

"Oh!" said Kristina, smiling brilliantly. "Thank you!" She took the baby from the nurse, carrying her toward Prince Henri, who waited at the end of the row, smiles wreathing his face. As they progressed, she held up the infant princess so all could see her face.

There were more smiles, and some of the older staff members had tears in their eyes.

Prince Henri couldn't wait for her to reach him, but came hurrying forward.

"My first grandchild is home," he said with choked emotion, looking down at the baby. He reached out a forefinger to touch the infant's hand, and the miniature fingers closed around his.

"She looks just like your mother," he said through tears of pride.

Kristina smiled radiantly.

Later that evening Gabriella paced up and down her suite, repeating the same path on the rose-and-cream Aubusson carpet. She was playing a CD by Mariah Carey, but the pounding music didn't assuage her badly aching heart.

The baby was beautiful!

Her skin was so pink. Her eyes already turning from slate to blue. Her hair a delicious wisp of light brown. Someday she might sit on the throne of Costa del Mar.

Gaby was ashamed of herself, but she couldn't help experiencing a few painful stabs of a less noble emotion. Charlaine had arrived as a legitimate heir, with no questions attached to her parentage, no whispers that she "might not be a real princess," whereas she herself was still subjected to the rumors about her parentage.

Gaby drew in another choked breath. Things hadn't really been going right since she met Cliff Ferguson. He'd been calling almost every day, and he'd even suggested that he fly into Costa del Mar, pick her up, and take her to lunch in Paris. She'd refused.

Papa had heard about the calls. "My dear Gabriella," he had said one morning at breakfast, "could you select your friends from people who are closer to Costa?"

"Do you mean men who aren't Texan? Men who aren't

also Jewish?'' she'd responded sharply.

"Our country saved thousands of Jewish lives once,'' he told her. "Think about it very carefully, Gabriella, think about who you are and what you represent. I will not say anything more. I will leave it to your discretion. I am sure you will behave sensibly.''

Now she shook her head from side to side. If he'd only forbidden her outright—then her indignation might have carried her to defiance. But he had left it up to her. That made matters ten times more difficult. Clifford Ferguson was not a man to be toyed with. She would have to be decisive with him.

He was a man who would like to start a second family, or at least he had hinted at that when they had lunch in San Francisco that day months ago.

She just wasn't ready! Gabriella put both hands to her face, rubbing at her throbbing temples. At this moment she didn't feel very happy with herself.

The telephone rang, and when Gaby picked it up, she heard her secretary's voice. "Mr. Ferguson is on line three, Your Highness.''

"Tell him I'm—that I . . . Put him through, please.''

"Well, hello, beautiful princess,'' greeted Cliff, his telephone voice smoky and husky. "I just called to tell you that I'm going to be in Paris in two days . . . and my lunch invitation *definitely* still stands.''

"Lunch? In Paris? I'm not sure. . . . I was planning to work in my studio, and then there is Charlaine's christening.''

"I won't interfere with that. I'll have you back in plenty of time if that's what you want. Gabriella, I know I've perhaps been presumptuous in calling you so often. I don't want to intrude upon you if I'm not welcome, but I did sense certain feelings between us. Certain very strong feelings. Correct me if I'm wrong.''

Gabriella hung on to the telephone, her panic telescoping into terror. "I would imagine—I think. . . . Yes,'' she finally admitted in a low voice.

Cliff's laugh was warm and triumphant. "Well, then. The only thing for us to do is have lunch again."

"And would you like to come to the christening?" she heard herself say in that same, low voice.

"I'd be delighted."

Gaby hung up, her heartbeat thumping. She walked into her large dressing room and stood staring at her reflection in the full-length, triple-wall mirror. What was it about her that Cliff Ferguson found so appealing?

Her looks? Gaby considered herself to possess above-average prettiness and an excellent figure, but surely there must be thousands of other women—models, actresses—who were far more stunning. Weren't women in Texas reputed to be particularly pretty? A man like Ferguson could have his pick of them.

Or was it just that she was a princess? Just the inescapable attention and adulation she had been receiving since she put on her first long dress, from the too-many men who gravitated to her royal title?

Gaby turned quickly away from her own reflection. She would just have to trust her own instincts, she decided.

The warm *foie gras* salad latticed with sheaves of truffles was exquisite, and the lobster in vanilla sauce was divine. Unfortunately, Gaby could hardly consume a bite and only pushed the delicious food around on her plate.

"You seem quiet today," said Cliff, reaching across the linen tablecloth to take both of Gabriella's hands. He had left off the cowboy boots today and was dressed in a double-breasted, pinstriped suit of dark blue worsted, a blue-and-white foulard at his neck, with a white button-down custom shirt. "And you've barely touched your wonderful lunch."

They were dining at Lucas-Carton, one of the great restaurants of Paris, with its month-long wait for dinner reservations, its monumental prices, and magnificent Belle

Époque decor. Dark brown banquettes were separated into
individual dining spaces by carved wood and frosted glass
dividers, and the ambience was enriched by tall, beveled
mirrors and huge floral arrangements.

At another table, three Costan security guards were eating their lunch, trying vainly to give the princess some
modicum of privacy at the same time that they were watching out for her safety. There had been more terrorist threats
recently, and Henri had insisted that she take three of the
palace guard with her.

"Do I seem quiet?" Gaby hedged. His hands felt so
very warm and strong.

"Yes, my dear, you do. By the way, I love your accent,
you speak English better than most American girls do."

Gabriella gave Cliff a faint smile. "I'm just tired, I suppose," she admitted. "All the travel—I have another trip
to Florida coming up in a few weeks, I am going to do an
appearance at Kenny Lane's boutique in Palm Beach. And
attend a party at Mar-a-Lago, I suppose. Word-of-mouth is
just as important as the talk shows, Kenny says."

"Is that all?" inquired Cliff. "I mean, is that it? Gaby,
perhaps we'd better be honest with each other. It's hard to
carry on a friendship, even a long-distance one, when there
is something hanging between us."

She stared at her wineglass, the delicate crystal beaded
with small droplets of moisture. Then she looked up at him
and was immediately caught in his intent blue gaze. "Cliff,
we are so very different, we are worlds apart," she murmured.

He nodded, but she could tell by the flush that rose to
his cheeks that he was slightly taken aback. "I know that.
I'm a brash American, you're a European princess—and
never the twain shall meet, right?"

"I don't know," she mumbled. Her flush increased, heat
stinging her cheeks. He was so warm, so appealing, she
was even beginning to think she loved him. *Mon Dieu,*
what a mistake that would be.

His pressure on her hands increased slightly. "Gabriella. I admit before I met you I wasn't well informed about your country, and I haven't really been a royal-watcher. I've been much too busy taking care of my daughter and making money. But now I've been researching Costa, and I know your father is very old-world, very conservative. Am I right on that?"

She nodded. "Very."

"But I know men like him. I grew up with them. If they come up against someone they respect, their attitudes aren't necessarily written in stone. I haven't even met your father yet. Let me meet him, Gabriella. Let me get to know him, and get to know you, too. We can take this very, very slowly if you want. I'm not rushing you into anything. I just"—Cliff's voice briefly caught—"I just can't let it go without trying, do you understand? I have feelings for you. Unexpected ones. Bear with me, please."

Her smile wavered, and then it broke across her face again, like sunlight spreading across the sea. "I think . . . I think I can do that."

Teddy had received an invitation to the christening and had managed to squeeze a day out of her schedule to fly to Costa.

Jac sent a polite bouquet of flowers to her hotel room but had not called her, and she'd read in one of the local tabloids that Lady Philippa had flown in from London and would be accompanying him to the ceremony. *Far be it from me to interfere,* she thought stiffly. Besides, she did *not* want him to know how much she still thought about him.

In her hotel room, she dialed Auggie's number at the hotel in Melbourne where he had arrived early to prepare for a benefit tournament for a wildlife preservation organization.

"Tee," he exclaimed, obviously glad to hear from her.

"Tee, how does it feel to be hobnobbing with the royals again?"

"Oh, great. . . . The whole country is covered with flowers and streamers and bunting, and Prince Henri has been giving one speech after another. Everyone is going crazy."

"Good, good," Auggie said, launching into a long discussion of his practices, and a contractual dispute he was having with one of his sponsors. "Those people are witch doctors," he told her angrily. "They've gone back on their word. Don't they know how overscheduled I am?"

As usual, she listened to Auggie's self-involved monologue, wondering when he was going to say something tender to her, something that would make her feel how deeply he missed her.

"Auggie," she said after a while, "Auggie, do you realize all we ever talk about is your problems, your complaints, your contracts, your tennis game?"

"Oh, Jesus, have I been doing that?" He laughed cheerfully. "Teddy, Teddy, Teddy. Well, I sure didn't mean to. I love you, baby, have I told you that yet today? More than the world. Even more than my tennis racquet." And he laughed, making it clear this was just his little joke. After a few more frustrating minutes, she had to hang up since she was already late for a shopping date with a palace escort.

Teddy had been invited to tea with Princess Kristina, and spent a few hours shopping the boutiques on Princess Lisse Street, carefully choosing an outfit she thought would be suitable to wear to the Vendôme Palace and then to the christening. She was lucky; it fit perfectly and needed no alterations.

"Oh, Teddy, Teddy!" Kristina didn't stand on ceremony, just rushed toward her and swept her into her arms for a hug. "You look fabulous! Your hair—it's blonder than ever, nearly as blond as mine now."

They settled down for a long talk. Kristina told her all about her acting classes, her restless discontent here in

Costa, her plan to get a divorce and go straight to Holly-wood.

"But what will your father say?" queried Teddy.

"He'll hate it—but Teddy, I have a life to lead, too," declared Kristina.

Accompanied by a bevy of nursemaids, with Mary Abbott carrying Princess Charlaine Lisse, Kristina and Gabriella walked together toward the portico of the ancient church where privileged royal guests were waiting to enter with them. Awkwardness hung between the two princesses, but they kept their public smiles. They'd done little but argue with each other since the baby's birth.

The organ music was beginning the prelude that would signal the royal family to proceed to their pew, an enclosure marked off by elaborate carvings glistening with gilt and embedded with precious stones.

"Kristina . . ." began Gaby, as they reached the vestibule. "I know I haven't been— I mean I didn't congratulate you properly. Maybe I've been a little jealous. . . ."

As Kristina's smile became cooler, Gaby hurried on. "But please accept my congratulations now."

Kristina nodded reluctantly.

"Please!" Gaby begged. "I know we have our differences and don't always get along as sisters, but we . . . we should. Please."

"I told you I accepted your congratulations," said Kristina, softening. "Now they are all waiting for us."

A week later the Paris newspapers reported that lawyers for Prince Henri and Jean-Luc Furnoir had been closeted in the palace for several days, working out the myriad details of the complex divorce settlement. Princess Charlaine, of course, would remain with Kristina. There was no question of the father getting custody.

Wearily, Prince Henri took a telephone call from Queen Elizabeth II, an old friend of his.

"My sympathies," the Queen of England told him, calling from her office in Buckingham Palace on her scrambler line, which she routinely used so as not to be overheard.

They discussed their mutual problems with children and failing marriages.

"These young people," sighed Henri. "They don't respect the crown anymore . . . not the way we did."

"We are the last of an era, Henri," declared Elizabeth. "It isn't as it used to be. They want their own lives now."

Kristina had ordered Jean-Luc's clothes and personal belongings to be packed by one of the servants. Now she walked back to their apartment to say a brief good-bye to her husband.

"I wish to keep this quiet and dignified," she said.

Unhappily, Jean-Luc nodded. "I would like to see my little girl once in a while, Kristina. I deserve that."

"You'll see her when she is ten, according to the agreement," Kristina said coldly. "Considering the circumstances, we've already been too generous."

Jean-Luc reddened. "You Bellinis think you are next to God, don't you? If you want a divorce, you just get it, and damn the consequences. Well, you're not so great, Kristina."

"What?"

"Oh, don't look at me that way. I have my ear to the ground, I hear things." Jean-Luc moved closer to her. "I heard you've been taking acting classes. Well, you haven't got any talent. Do you hear me? *You* haven't got any talent at all. You're going to be the *laughing stock* of the world."

MAY 1990

In MAY THE PORT-LOUIS FILM FESTIVAL BRIEFLY
crammed the country with more than ten thousand film-
makers and their entourages, wheeler-dealers, and groupies.
The event was even bigger than the rival Cannes Film Festival, also held in May, although some managed to put in
an appearance at both.

Kristina loved her baby—no, she *adored* Charlaine—
but she yearned to be among film people, be part of their
lives.

She attended several parties, one hosted by Mike Eisner,
of the Disney Studios. The private rooms of the pink stucco
Costa Grande Hotel were jammed with warm bodies.
Shouting to be heard over the din, people discussed the
merits of various films. Michael Douglas was in town to
promote his latest picture, and Kristina was surprised to run
into Bret Thompson, the actor-director she had met at the
Academy Awards.

Bret was even better looking than she had remembered
him. He was wearing his hair longer, pulled back into a
short ponytail, and wore a diamond stud in one ear, giving
him a sexy, rakish look she found tremendously intriguing.

"We meet again," he said, smiling. His downward
glance took in Kristina's slim, black spandex Missoni
jumpsuit worn with a jacket embroidered with silver-and-
gold threads—an outfit that emphasized her fragile blond
beauty and made her look reed-slim. Thank God the diet
and exercise program she'd followed faithfully had given
her back her former weight and slender figure.

"All these people," she shouted back. "Such amazing
crowds!"

"Are you in films now?"

"Possibly," she said. "Actually, I hope to be."

Thompson's expression changed, his sexual appraisal vanishing, to be replaced by sharp, keen interest. "Wow, what a trip! I'm putting together a new picture, you know. I'm both producing and directing it myself, and I think I've got a real winner. It's called *The Congregation*. It's about a group of Philadelphia bluebloods who are split apart by religious scandal and murder. . . . You'd be just right for one of the roles. In fact, we're doing another rewrite of the script now. Are you interested?"

Kristina blushed violently. "Yes. Yes. Oh, yes."

"Good. I'll take another look at your screen test when I get back to L.A., but Mike Ovitz tells me it's fabulous. . . . Jesus!" Bret said, smacking his hand on his forehead. "Wouldn't that be something? A real princess. . . . I assume Ovitz is still your agent?"

Kristina nodded, but the mention of Mike Ovitz was bringing her back to earth with a rapid crash. She already knew she couldn't possibly leave her beautiful baby daughter for more than a week or so, not even to star in a Hollywood picture, and then there was the problem with her father.

"My head's starting to ache from all this noise. Let's go somewhere quiet, and we can talk about all this in detail," suggested Thompson, gazing again at Kristina's curves.

She moistened her lips. It *was* more than just a movie role, wasn't it? Damn . . . a complication.

"I—I really should be getting back to the palace. I want to say good-night to my baby."

Thompson sensed her change of mood. "Princess Kristina? Why do I get the feeling you're slipping away from me?"

"I'm not. I *want* to be in your movie, I really do. But, please, I do need time to think about it. It isn't easy for me, you know. I have obligations. If I'm going to do this, I have to rearrange my life. Please. . . . Check with Mike in about ten days."

* * *

Kristina and Jac went on one of their long motorcycle rides, then began walking the boardwalk, where a turquoise May surf splashed and pounded the jetty.

"But, Kris, have you thought this through very carefully?" Jac said, as they sat down at a table in a small café near the boardwalk. "Taking Charlie to Hollywood with you . . . living the life of a movie star . . . How will you manage your security requirements? Will you even be able to live a normal life in California?"

Her laugh was silvery, tinged with bitterness. "I don't live a normal life *here*. I'll take a staff of bodyguards—I suppose I'll have to—and Charlie will have her own guard, too. I'll lease one of those houses with the electrified fence and all the security trimmings. . . ." She leaned forward intently. "Barbra Streisand, Elizabeth Taylor, Cher—they all deal with that kind of thing all the time. It's part of *their* lives, Jac, and *they* manage, so why can't I?"

"But they aren't princesses."

Kristina hesitated. "Jac, when I stood there at Charlie's christening and I looked out into the cathedral at all those people, and all the press, something inside me began to question it. Just like Charlaine, *I* was born to that sort of life, but I've always felt restless . . . as if something were missing."

"I've felt that way, too," Jac told her. He was frowning. "I imagine most of the royals have. Papa. Even Queen Elizabeth, I suppose, when she was younger. And I *know* Prince Charles has felt out of synch sometimes."

"I want to be *out* there in the world," cried Kristina. "I have to be! I have to try! I want to do something with my time—something more than just going to royal ribbon-cuttings and getting adulation just because I was born a princess, something that isn't me at all."

Jac sat very still.

"I wish you weren't going to do it," he said. "But somehow . . . I respect you for it, Kristina." He leaned over the table and took her hand. "I'll talk to Papa for you, Kristina. I'll try to make him see."

She nodded. "It won't be easy. He's a pretty fierce old thing when he wants to be."

Jac smiled knowingly. Looking at him, Kristina had a premonition of the way he would look when he was much older and more settled . . . the way he might look if he were the Prince of Costa del Mar.

The contract negotiations for *The Congregation* had been settled. Kristina would receive an unprecedented $8.2 million to play the role of Hillary Page. Location filming would begin in two months, and the interior shots would be filmed on a Warner Brothers soundstage in Burbank.

"My assistant has found you a house to lease in Los Angeles," said Bret Thompson over the transatlantic phone. "It has a full security system, of course, and there's a live-in couple who will cook and clean for you. Additional servants, maids, and gardeners complete the staff. There are three servants' apartments. It's in Bel Air, on the same street as the homes of Carol Burnett and Warren Beatty."

"Fine," said Kristina, who had met Carol several times.

"I'll take you to see the place when you arrive. If you don't like it, we can find you another one. *But*, this place comes with a high price tag," added Bret flirtatiously.

"Oh?"

"Dinner with me. A dinner where we do *not* talk business." Then Bret seemed to realize he was speaking to a princess, not an ordinary actress, and continued, "Of course, that would be entirely up to you, Your Highness. I know you'll have a very busy schedule."

"I will have a busy schedule," declared Kristina, wondering what it would be. "But dinner would be delightful. Is it possible for you to send me a script, Bret? I'd like to look it over."

"We're having another story conference tomorrow, but

as soon as the script is whipped into shape, I'll fax it to you," he said. "We'll make any changes you want—within reason, of course. We're just delighted to have you on board, Princess Kristina. I can't tell you how thrilled."

Kristina hung up, bemused. She was being given script approval—she, who had not yet spoken one line in front of a camera. That was because of her royal status, she realized. Because she was a princess. That fact would always follow her, no matter what she did. But once she was in front of the camera, she'd show them she could act.

"You will *not* take Charlaine with you!" raged Henri, too angry to keep his voice low. "I forbid it! I absolutely forbid it!"

"Papa, she's my daughter, and I think it would be wrong to have her brought up by nannies. She belongs with me."

"You're right, of course. You should be here attending to your responsibilities. The baby has a heritage here! You're robbing her of her birthright! Do what you will with your own life, but leave her here."

Kristina sighed. This scene was far worse than she'd ever envisioned. Prince Henri actually had moisture in his eyes, and his voice had become so strident that she was afraid he was going to have a heart attack.

"Papa," she pointed out reasonably, "I will leave her here while I am on location, at least for my first picture. I'll have plenty of time between pictures to come back to Costa. I don't have to live in Hollywood all the time—I can come back for long visits. Charlie will have her own bedroom here, too. It will be as if she has two homes. I promise, honestly."

Henri nodded, slightly mollified. He cleared his throat. "You are assuming that you will have an extended film career. My darling daughter, have you considered the very real possibility that those people, the studios there in Hollywood, are all just using you, using *us,* for the royal cachet? You will appear in a few movies, you will create tremendous publicity for the film—then the novelty will be over. They may not want you anymore.''

"Papa, I've thought about that. But I'm willing to take the risk. *I* think I have real talent. I need to prove that. I won't be happy until I do.''

Henri sighed softly. "Daughter, I have never told you this, and I wish you never to reveal this outside this room, but you have been my favorite of all my children. You look so much like Lisse. . . . You are like your mother inside, too. You seem delicate, but you have a backbone made of steel. It's just that I will miss you and the baby. I love her.''

"Oh, Papa," Kristina said, breaking down. She went into Henri's arms, and father and daughter stood for a long time together, her head bent into his shoulder.

"We will have an enormous party to send you off,'' Henri decided. "I will have a press conference to announce it. I will . . .''

"She's really going to Hollywood?" asked Nickey Skouros, gazing at his press assistant with barely concealed anger.

"She is leaving next week with the baby. All the arrangements have been made.''

"I thought that Prince Henri would put a stop to it," said Nickey. He was at his private island off the Costan coast, working out on the electronic Nautilus equipment he'd just had shipped in from the States. Proud of his hard body, he was pushing himself today, testing the new machines.

"Well, he didn't, sir. In fact, he is giving a bon voyage party for her," continued the assistant, uncomfortable at being the bearer of unpleasant tidings. "Your invitation arrived at the office today by fax.''

"Yes, yes," said Skouros, recovering his composure. "All right. Call the palace and tell them I *won't* be able to

attend. Make my apologies. Tell them I have pressing business in California.''

When the man had hurried out of the room, Skouros
stopped walking the treadmill. He stepped down from the
machine and wiped his perspiring forehead with a towel,
then moved to the window, where he stared out at the vista
of tossing waves. His private sources had informed him
several weeks ago that Bret Thompson, the movie star, was
interested in Kristina.

He had wanted Princess Kristina out of the running for
the throne of Costa and now he felt sure this goal was
accomplished. Still, he didn't want her becoming involved
with another man, especially one who had a reputation for
being attractive to most women.

He paced for a few moments, considering his options.
Finally he showered in the large bathroom adjoining the
exercise room, then strode into his office, where he buzzed
his assistant and began issuing quick orders.

''I want you to contact the best detective agency in Beverly Hills. Remember, the best! Tell them to start researching Bret Thompson's background. I want them to find out
everything they can. I want weekly reports, and it is to be
kept completely confidential. Second, I want you to find
me a house to rent in Beverly Hills. Something pretentious,
impressive, perhaps one of the stars' old homes. Yes. That
would be perfect. Something that makes a big statement.''

He didn't intend to let Kristina go that easily.

The Ferrari looked like a curved red bullet.

Prince Jac stood in a large factory bay, gazing at the car
that boasted the new, semiautomatic gear box. The Ferrari
had a Patric Head chassis and was a sensational package
of curves and raw, top-end power. It was hot and had cost
$5 million. It was possible that this car could make him the
top F1 driver in the country, in the same class with Nigel
Mansell or Emmo Fittipaldi.

''Nothing can stop you in that one, Your Highness,''

boasted Giotto Bizzarrini, the Italian race-car designer. He
and his son, Giuseppe, had traveled all the way from Turin,
Italy, to deliver the car to Jac. Of course, there would be
weeks of road-testing and additional enginework still to
come.

Jac walked around the car for the dozenth time, inspect-
ing it from every angle. The car thrilled him deeply. It was
beautiful, exciting—but should he be driving it at all?

For the first time in his life, he had begun to have doubts
about the choices he was making.

After the meeting with the designers was finished, Jac
walked out to his low-slung 1988 Ferrari Testarossa, which
was his personal car, slid into the driver's seat, and started
the powerful engine purring.

He aimed the car along the E80 highway that stretched
from the French town of Nîmes, where the car had been
delivered for modifications by a local designer, southwest
along the Mediterranean coast, then inland through Tou-
louse back toward Costa del Mar. He pressed down on the
accelerator, enjoying the incredibly responsive surge of
power under his foot.

Why did he defy death? Why was he so stubbornly in-
sistent on racing, when only a few months ago he'd come
within inches of being incinerated alive in his car? That
was what his father wanted to know, and Jac could not
really answer.

For months after his mother's death he'd suffered nightmares, waking up in a cold sweat. Finally Prince Henri had
insisted he see a therapist, but Jac had stubbornly refused
to tell the doctor his innermost, terribly painful feelings.
That was the same summer he had begun free-diving to
thirty feet or more in the clear blue waters of the Atlantic,
sometimes staying down in the water until his lungs
screamed for air. Once . . . twice . . . Jac had actually
thought about never coming up again. But his healthy, thir-
teen-year-old body had kicked to the surface, lungs exploding.

"Why do you do it, why do you play with your life?" Henri had demanded some years later.

"Papa, don't I have every right, since it is my life?" he had told his father, but now he was beginning to think about it again. Kristina's leaving for Hollywood had only exacerbated his discomfort.

With Kristina going to California, with Gaby traveling to promote her jewelry, and now with Papa's health beginning to fail—who was left to rule but himself? Jac felt a sudden heaviness, a sense of some huge, inevitable thing closing down on him. Not yet, he thought. Maybe in ten or fifteen years. He wasn't ready to make the commitment yet.

Jac banged down on the accelerator, neatly negotiating a turn around a lorry loaded with Bordeaux wine.

"Teddy," said Princess Kristina, her voice made reedy by the transatlantic cable, "I just called to tell you—today's my bon voyage party. I'm really leaving!"

"Wonderful," said Teddy.

They began gossiping, and Kristina started telling Teddy about a near accident Jac had had several months previously at Le Mans.

"*No*," said Teddy, shocked. "I guess I didn't read about it."

If she'd known that while she was actually in Costa, she would have been even more uncomfortable than she'd already been, watching Jac sitting in the royal pew with Lady Philippa.

"Well, his car clipped another one and rolled toward the wall. It caught on fire, but Jac jumped out before he was hurt. Papa was livid," Kristina went on. "They had a terrible fight, and then Jac drove off in his Ferrari. I think my brother likes to flirt with death," Kristina added. "We're all terribly worried he might have another accident, a worse one next time."

Teddy swallowed, thinking the same thing. But, of

course, Jac's life didn't concern her so much now that she had Auggie. Still, she could not help wishing the best for him.

They talked for twenty minutes more, then Kristina asked about Auggie.

"We are nearly engaged," admitted Teddy.

"Nearly engaged! But that is wonderful!"

"Yes . . ."

"But there is a problem, then?"

Teddy hesitated. "No, of course not. It's just that Auggie and I are on the road so much, we conduct most of our romance by telephone. It's . . . well, sometimes it's hard to keep a romance going that way."

Kristina was silent for a moment. "Do you really think there is such a thing as love, Teddy? I mean true, deep, and wonderful love, the kind that they write about in the novels? *I* think it's all a myth myself. At least sometimes I do."

"I think I do believe in love," said Teddy.

"Well, I wonder," said Kristina. "I have a strange feeling, Teddy, that *I'm* not going to find it."

"What?"

Then Kristina laughed. "Why am I saying such things? I'm going to Hollywood—a city full of lovers. I think I'm getting a little nervous!" She added, "But I do want love to happen to me."

"You'll win, I'm counting on it," said Houston Warner as they stood near the security checkpoint at JFK Airport one Tuesday morning. She was leaving for Melbourne to play in the Australian Open—and see Auggie.

"Dad," said Teddy, clutching her carry-on, which contained her regular racquet and her spares, which she did not trust to baggage-handling. She was wearing Guess jeans and a cotton pullover, the gold racquet pin Auggie had given her affixed to a gold chain that dangled just outside her collar. "I just want to thank you for all you did when

I broke my ankle. Without you I wouldn't have made it back.''

Warner smiled and hugged her. ''Now don't forget to phone me every night while you're Down Under. I want to know everything—I'll help you figure out your strategy.''

''Don't you always?'' Teddy giggled. ''Oh, they're calling my flight.''

Seated on the aisle in the Quantas first-class cabin, waiting for the beverage cart, Teddy closed her eyes and tried to relax.

''Something to drink, Teddy?'' said a smiling flight attendant, recognizing the tennis star.

''I think a Diet Pepsi, please.''

She found a paperback in her carry-on and opened its pages, but instead of reading, she began fantasizing about Auggie. He was going to meet her at the airport. They hadn't seen each other in more than a month, although they'd talked on the phone every day, and she missed him painfully.

She could hardly wait.

In Melbourne it was hot, breezy, and humid at only 11:00 A.M. The gate area at Tullamarine International Airport was already overheated by summer sun streaming through the windows.

Exhausted from her sixteen-hour flight, with an hour stopover in Honolulu, Teddy walked down the jetway.

She stepped into the gate area, looking around for Auggie. In the milling crowds, he was conspicuously absent. Disappointment stabbed her, but she knew Auggie wasn't known for his promptness.

''Well, Tee, are you gonna knock 'em dead or what?'' said a voice behind her. It was Auggie, looking resplendent in blue cotton pants and a yellow, open-throated shirt, his blond hair glossy, his suntan the color of a lightly-browned Belgian waffle.

''Auggie! Auggie!'' Teddy ran to him and threw her

arms around him. "Auggie, I'm so glad to see you. See, I'm wearing your pin. Are we staying at the same hotel? When are you playing? Oh, Auggie—I've missed you *so* much!" She was almost crying in her joy.

"Babe—" he began uncomfortably.

"Let's go to the hotel," Teddy bubbled. "I want to hold you and love you forever!"

For a brief second Auggie seemed oddly reluctant, but then he smiled, taking her hand. "For you, I'd cross the Alps on my bare feet."

Teddy was staying at the Regent Hotel again. In her room, they fell on the bed, rolling around together like two happy puppies, deliriously happy to see each other.

"God, I love your new hairstyle," Auggie said, running his fingers through it and following with a nibbling kiss at her nape. "And your shoulders . . . and your back . . . and that wonderful, firm ass . . ."

"Oh, Auggie," she purred, "I have so much to tell you. I'm so glad we're together." Her hands slid all the way down Auggie's muscular body. It was going to be a wonderful afternoon.

After they had made love twice, they ordered room service. They moved the trays to the bed, sitting naked and cross-legged as they ate broiled lobster, crisp French fries, and a Caesar salad, licking their fingers as if it were a picnic. Despite her tiredness from the flight, Teddy felt wonderfully elated! She was back to normal, her ankle healed. And now she was with her man. . . . One day, perhaps, they would be married. They would travel to tournaments together, and when they were much older, she supposed, they might open a tennis academy and teach young tennis players to be stars.

"Oh," said Auggie, "do you know who's also here in Melbourne?"

"No, who?"

"Your old nemesis, Roxy Eberhardt. She's only seeded

tenth, though, and she probably won't make it through the quarterfinals. Maybe you'll even draw her to play.''

"I hope not," said Teddy, who had had more than enough of Roxy.

"She's been—well, I wanted to warn you before anyone else told you," said Auggie. "She's been kind of coming on to me. She and a few others."

"What?"

"Of course, none of them are as pretty as you—especially not Roxy," declared Auggie with a laugh. "She's too skinny and muscular for me."

Teddy pushed away her tray, a spurt of jealousy rippling through her. And she didn't particularly enjoy his humor.

"Baby, baby," said Auggie, stroking her bare knee. "Now don't get the wrong idea here. I just like to tease you a bit. Roxy Eberhardt isn't even my type. She's got absolutely no appeal for me. *You're* my type. I haven't touched her—I only want you, you, and more you."

"Roxy, of all people. I'd hate it so much if you did," Teddy said with a sigh.

"Well, didn't I just tell you? I didn't. So quit worrying, beautiful golden girl, and let's put these trays back on the table so we can make love again. Then I have to go to the health club in the hotel—I have a trainer meeting me there."

She had the fleeting thought that he "doth protest too much," but quickly suppressed it. Auggie's hands were all over her again, and she didn't have time to think.

Finally her bon voyage party was winding down. Kristina had endured the evening festivities for two hundred guests at the palace: the long, formal dinner, the dancing afterward—her father's idea of a farewell party. He had even arranged for Bruce Springsteen, on tour, to make a brief appearance and sing several songs. Kristina had always loved "The Boss," and Bruce and his new girlfriend seemed equally intrigued by the palace.

But now she was slightly high on wine and bored with the celebration. She wanted to have a little fun, raise a little hell, do something to cap off the evening and declare her independence. But what could she do? Then she remembered the casino—the famous, glittering Casino de Palais, which she'd never set foot inside. Not even once! She and Gaby were strictly forbidden to go, although Jac frequented it occasionally. She ought to go there, just one time before she went to Hollywood. Break the barriers!

British rock star Johnny Coates, a friend of Springsteen's, had been invited to the party, and impulsively Kristina walked up to him.

"Johnny, I know you go to the casino all the time," she said. "I want to go tonight. Will you be my escort?"

The long-haired Britisher looked at her. He'd partnered her in the disco, and she knew he was smitten with her blond looks, but the palace and all the royals intimidated him.

"Please, Johnny," she begged. "Just as friends," she added. "Good friends, nothing more. I just want to prove something, that's all."

The rocker nodded. "You sure that his royal nibs won't object?"

Kristina giggled. "He won't know . . . not until it's too late. Hurry downstairs and wait for me by the outside gate, the arch by the guardhouse. I'll meet you there in ten minutes. I want to change my clothes first."

The Casino de Palais was a huge, rambling building of bisque-colored stucco that had been cantilevered on a rocky bluff looking out over the ocean. Crashing at the wall were huge, Atlantic combers. As Johnny's white Rolls-Royce Corniche pulled into the parking lot, he and Kristina could hear the pounding of the surf.

As they walked in, a group of arriving guests stared at them apparently trying to figure out if the young woman in the curly brown wig was someone they should recognize.

Giggling, pleased with her disguise, which she occasionally used to avoid being recognized, Kristina took Johnny's arm, and they hurried past.

The casino was a vivid, glittering, sensuous feast for the eyes—so exhilarating that even the most jaded of visitors became excited.

The floor was covered with Aubusson carpets woven in jewel tones of ruby red and sapphire blue. Huge crystal chandeliers sparkled overhead, the walls were swagged with lustrous red satin brocade, and there were priceless antiques collected by four generations of Bellinis. The famed gambling rooms echoed with the clatter of chips, cries of the croupiers, and sudden bursts of excited laughter. A room to one side held shiny rows of slot machines, which added their own coin-clatter to the general cacophony.

"I love it here already," declared Kristina, breathing in the ambience. "Why haven't I ever come here before? But do you know"—she struggled hard to say the words—"I think I'm, well, a bit *paf.* Plastered. Drunk."

As they started across the floor, a casino manager came hurrying by. He glanced at Kristina, stared again, and then his eyes widened. No female Bellini had ever entered the casino before, not even the headstrong Princess Lisse.

"Your Royal Highness . . ." he faltered. "Is there something we can do for you? Would you wish me to call for your car?"

"That won't be necessary," said Kristina grandly. "I only want an hour here. I believe that will be sufficient."

As the manager stood motionless, stunned into silence, Kristina swept past him, into the main gambling salon.

"Bank has two, player four. Player wins," said the dealer, a small man with a drooping mustache.

"I win? *I win?*" Kristina stared incredulously down at the pile of chips that the dealer had just thrust in her direction.

"It's all yours, Princess," said Johnny, taking a patronizing attitude toward her beginner's luck.

Kristina stared down at the money, realizing that she had just won $8,000. Suddenly she wasn't tipsy anymore, or even high. *She had won.* It seemed a wonderful omen . . . a signal for the rest of her life, which lay ahead of her in Hollywood, beginning tomorrow.

She could hardly wait.

"Your Highness?" someone said.

Kristina turned. A man in a dark suit stood beside her. He was one of the security men she'd seen roaming around the salon, observing the play at the tables.

"Your Highness, a driver is parked at the VIP entrance past the *chemin de fer* tables to take you back to the palace," the man said in the stiff manner that Kristina had heard all of her life from nannies, governesses, and security guards when they were conveying her father's wishes to her.

"I'm not ready to leave yet," she told the man, smiling back at him radiantly.

Teddy Warner ran off the court, perspiration giving a sheen to her smooth, toast-colored skin. The crowd was still yelling, and flashbulbs were popping all around her. The tournament had been a long one—nearly fourteen days— but she'd beaten Roxy Eberhardt, and it felt terrific. Now maybe Roxy would leave her alone, and she could concentrate on Auggie.

They'd decided to take a few days off—a rare treat for both of them. They would do some sightseeing together, maybe fly to New Zealand. Tonight they'd promised themselves dinner at Fanny's on Loorsdale Street, but upstairs, in the restaurant's luxurious, private dining room.

She hurried into the locker room, dodging the swarms of reporters and media people, eager to feel the relief of a hot shower. But she was stopped in the doorway by a petite, energetic woman she recognized as Judy Seivers, a reporter for the AP wire service.

"Teddy, how does it feel to be back again after your injury?"

"Great, it's just terrific. I'm so happy."

But oddly, Judy didn't seem all that interested in the match Teddy had just won. "I understand you and Auggie Steckler have just broken up," she went on.

Teddy stared at the woman, wondering if she'd heard her right.

"You mean you don't know? I thought—I mean, Ingrid said—" The reporter seemed to become more eager and took a few steps closer. Teddy realized that something terrible was about to happen.

"Please, I . . . I'm late for a meeting."

Teddy hurried into the shower room, slamming the door behind her, her face flaming. She half ran to the back of the shower room, and fumbled with the combination lock on her locker. *Ingrid? Ingrid who?* There was a new German tennis player called Ingrid Hertzlich, a tall, slim blond, only seventeen, who had been playing the circuit for only three months.

No, it couldn't be, she assured herself, forcing herself to calm down. She and Auggie had been together all week. Hadn't he told her how much he loved her, how he wasn't attracted to other women and wanted only her? Tennis gossip could be vicious: Rumors got started . . . then they just snowballed. . . .

Auggie wasn't in his hotel room. Teddy rang his phone over and over, until the desk operator came back on the line and told her that the party didn't answer.

"But he has to. I was supposed to call him there!"

"Mr. Steckler is out at the moment," said the operator.

Teddy hung up, still trying to reassure herself that everything was all right, but beginning to feel waves of anxiety again.

She reached for the chain she wore around her neck and touched the small, gold tennis racquet engraved with both

of their names. Her "pre-engagement" present. But even
on the day he'd given it to her, Auggie had admitted that
he was still afraid of the big "M" word. Teddy, on the
other hand, had for some time now been having fantasies
about getting married to Auggie and making a life together,
the two of them traveling to tournaments all over the world.

She paced her room for a few minutes, then decided to
go down to the lobby and have a drink. She needed something to settle her nerves.

The bar off the lobby was crowded with tennis players
and their entourages—the parents, coaches, agents, and
other hangers-on who accompanied most players on their
travels. Teddy spotted several people from ProServ, International Management Group (IMG), and Advantage International, agencies that handled most of the top-ranked
players in the world. And, there were also some players she
knew from the tennis circuit, along with a few members of
the press.

"Give me a wine spritzer," she said to the young, good-
looking Aussie bartender. "No," she said, changing her
mind. "Make that a grasshopper."

She found a table by herself and began pensively sipping
the frothy green crème de menthe. In a few minutes she
got up and went to a telephone and dialed Auggie's room
again. He still didn't answer.

She ordered another grasshopper, and the room began to
assume a soft, hazy glow. Several other players joined her,
and they sat around discussing the matches.

No one said anything about Auggie, but it seemed to
Teddy as if they were all watching her knowingly. Finally
she excused herself. It had occurred to her that Auggie
might possibly come into the bar—with someone—and she
didn't want him to see her here waiting for him.

She ordered room service, and then watched TV, seeing
replays of the day's matches. Narrowing her eyes at the
screen, she thought she saw Auggie's blond head, but the

camera switched to another shot before she was able to tell for certain.

Auggie, I'm going to kill you, she said to herself, finally collapsing into tears.

At eight A.M., after dialing Auggie's room several more times throughout the night, Teddy was finally able to reach him.

"Auggie," she cried, "I thought we were going to dinner last night—weren't we going to go to Fanny's?"

"Oh, babe," he said, "I completely forgot. I had a meeting with my agent. Did you wait very long for me?"

"I waited all night."

"But I thought I told you I had the meeting. Then it was too late to call. Honey, I've got so much going on in my mind right now, I can't remember everything. Look, I can make lunch today. How would that be? Then I've got to hop on a plane for France."

"France?" He had told her absolutely nothing about going to France. "Auggie—I don't want lunch. I want to come to your room right now. We need to talk."

His laugh was nervous. "Honey, I'm just showering—"

"I don't care. I'll be there in two minutes," Teddy insisted.

She ran a comb through her hair and quickly put on some lip gloss, then let herself out of her room and went to the elevator. A few minutes later she was knocking at Auggie's door on a lower floor. Was it her imagination or did she smell a cloud of cloying perfume in the air?

"Tee," said Auggie, coming to the door with a towel slung around his middle. "When you say two minutes you really mean two minutes, huh?"

The fragrance was even stronger in the room.

"Auggie," said Teddy, feeling sick as she looked around, half expecting to see a woman emerge from the bathroom or closet. "I've heard something. . . . I hope it's just gossip."

He shrugged, giving her one of his warm, sweet Auggie smiles that always caused her heart to tumble inside her chest. "You know me, honey, people like to talk about me. It's just part of tennis, Tee."

"Is it? Someone told me that we've broken up. Is that true? Someone said that you have a new girlfriend now, a girl named Ingrid. Maybe an Ingrid who wears a particularly musky brand of perfume?"

Auggie smiled; then the smile faded from his face as he realized that she knew. "Honey . . . I didn't mean for it to happen like this."

"How *did* you mean for it to happen?" Teddy snapped.

"I was going to tell you when you got here, but you threw your arms around me and looked so cute that I couldn't resist you, and then—every time we made love, it got harder and harder to tell you."

"Oh, Jesus." Teddy slumped into a chair, crushed by the news, and too exhausted by her night without sleep to move. "Auggie . . ."

"I'm sorry, Tee. I really am. I really care about you."

"I can see how much."

"It's just that when you broke your ankle, well, I guess I kinda withdrew from you. My health is so important to me, I didn't want your bad luck to rub off on me. I know that's crass, but, hey, tennis is a tough game. Ingrid is good for me. She's a strong, young player, and tough, *really* tough."

"Tougher than me?" Teddy whispered, somehow more hurt by this than if Auggie had said he loved Ingrid. Slowly she rose, pulling her dignity around her. She didn't want Auggie to see her cry.

She stopped at the door and turned. "I wish you all the luck in the world, Auggie. You're a totally selfish person, and arrogant, but that's probably what you need to get ahead. You're a real bastard! I enjoyed what we had—it was great, we had fun—and now it's over. Maybe we can be friends, but I doubt it.''

When she reached her room, she closed and locked the door behind her, and waited for the tears to come. Auggie had been a shit, but he'd been nice, too, and kind and funny, and she *had* loved him. But it never would have worked, would it? Auggie was too self-centered and would have made a bad husband, an even worse father. She was lucky he'd dropped her for Ingrid.

She walked to her window and pulled back the drapes, looking down on the street in front of the hotel. A taxi was pulling up, disgorging a well-dressed couple. The woman threw back her head and laughed, the musical sound carrying clearly up to Teddy's window. The woman's laugh reminded Teddy, fleetingly, of Princess Kristina.

She decided to give Kristina a phone call. Find out how she liked Hollywood.

Then, just as Teddy started to dial, the tears came in a flood.

TWO YEARS LATER . . .

Her FATHER, MISSING IN THE CHOPPY GRAY WAVES of the Atlantic.

No, not missing, he was drowned . . . murdered.

Teddy felt numbed, then angry, then numb again as the *Olympia*'s launch raced across the harbor to the royal quay. Wind whipped at her hair, but she didn't notice. So much had happened so suddenly. Her father's disappearance and then Prince Henri's heart attack and his evacuation by helicopter to the hospital in Port-Louis, with Jac and the princesses accompanying him.

''Please, Teddy, let the doctor give you a tranquilizer,'' said Skouros, who stood beside her.

''I can't—I really can't.''

"It would calm you, my dear."

"*No.*"

Her eyes still probed the waves, hoping somehow her father would still be found. His body had not been recovered, and she had been told that the chances were slim that it would ever be washed up on shore. How could it have happened? The *Olympia* was one of the safest ships afloat. Houston Warner hadn't been seasick, nor had he drunk too much. And she knew he hadn't committed suicide. He was a successful entrepreneur generally feeling good about himself and happy with what life had handed him. Maybe one day, he would have even married again.

But had someone really pushed him overboard? The thought was too horrible. Maybe her father *had* fallen, but how could it have happened? *Daddy,* she reflected. *Oh, Daddy, I love you so much.*

As the boat pulled up to the royal quay, Skouros put a protective arm around her shoulders. "Teddy, there are already reporters gathered on the public docks near the Royal Quay. I'm sure you do not wish to talk to them now, so I will see you are escorted directly to my private car. Where are you staying?"

"The Hôtel Île de France," Teddy gulped. "But I can't . . . I don't think I can . . . It would make me think of him." She collapsed into tears again. Skouros pulled her close, comforting her as he would a small child.

"I will arrange for you to stay at another hotel," he told her soothingly.

"I have to fly back to Connecticut. There are people to notify, a memorial service to arrange—how am I going to get it all done? I barely know where to start."

"Please use my executive secretary," responded Skouros. "He can make all the arrangements. I will have you flown back to Connecticut in my private plane. It is the very least I can do."

"Thank you . . ."

As they stepped onto the quay, reporters swarmed toward them. "Teddy, what happened to your father?" "Teddy, was your father suicidal?" "Were there business problems?" They surged aggressively around her, cameras rolling. Instinctively Teddy put up her hand to shield her face.

"Please . . ."

Skouros issued an order to several of his crewmen, and Teddy was spirited away to a waiting Rolls-Royce, Skouros jumping in after her.

Teddy buried her face in her hands. "They're such *awful* people."

"It is what happens when an important man dies under peculiar circumstances," said Skouros. "Teddy, I know how badly this hurts, but please stop crying for a moment, right now, and look at me."

Numbly she raised her head.

"I want you to know that I personally will do everything I can to find out how your father died. I have already started an investigation, and you may rest assured that no stone will be left unturned. We will have some answers."

"Thank you," said Teddy. Then the anger surged back again. "I want to know why this happened! I want to know why he died!"

"I don't know if we will ever find an answer, but I will do everything I can," said Skouros in a manner that Teddy suddenly saw as placating.

"I'm *going* to find out," she cried hotly. "I will! I'll go to Connecticut and take care of the funeral, and then I'm coming back here!"

"Of course you will," soothed Skouros in a condescending way. "But I am sure by then we will have more information, and such a trip may not be necessary."

The car took Teddy to the Hôtel Normandie, where Skouros owned a penthouse suite and kept another of his offices. His executive secretary, Stavros Andreas, was waiting for them. Skouros excused himself, telling Teddy that he wanted to get back to the *Olympia* and begin questioning his crew, under the supervision of the Costan police.

"Mr. Andreas will assist you in any way possible. You have only to ask."

"Coffee, Miss Warner?" the secretary asked politely when the Greek had left.

Teddy nodded. She'd calmed down a little, and her practical nature was beginning to assert itself. First, she'd call her father's sister, Alicia, Warner's only other close relative, who was now living in Palm Beach, Florida. Aunt Alicia would be heartbroken. There were numbers of cousins and dear friends to call, too. Then the executive vice president of WarnerCo, Reginald Luden. He would take care of what needed to be done at her father's company. Then she'd have to call Justine Ravitz, the family attorney and Russ Ostrand, her agent, who would start canceling her tennis engagements.

She gave the assistant a list of the phone numbers she wanted, and pensively sipped her coffee, barely able to think.

Three hours later, Andreas drove Teddy to the Costan airport, where she would board Skouros's 747 for the trip back to the United States. The radio in the limousine gave constant updates on Prince Henri's medical condition.

The prince's condition had stabilized. All three of his children were at the hospital. Prince Jac would take over as temporary head of state for several months until Prince Henri could either resume his throne or other arrangements were made by the Privy Council.

Teddy shook herself. She'd been so concerned with her own loss, she hadn't had much time to focus on Prince Henri.

The radio went on to say that Warner's disappearance on board the *Olympia* raised the question of whether her father had committed suicide because of recent business reversals.

"Never," cried Teddy, clenching her hands in her lap, tears beginning to flow. "How can the press get away with such allegations? They're just malicious gossips."

As she was sitting down in the airport's luxurious VIP lounge, she was surprised to see Princess Kristina enter the room, her face ashen and strained.

"Teddy, I was afraid you might already have left."

"No, the plane takes off in ten minutes. Kristina, I'm so sorry about your father. I just hope everything works out for the best."

The two women hugged, and Teddy could feel the tremble of Kristina's body. "He's not going to die until he's ready," Kristina said in a muffled voice. "Such a tragedy that you have to leave like this."

Teddy and Kristina withdrew to a corner of the room and stood facing a window. They could see the pilot and crew boarding the elegant silver-and-red aircraft emblazoned with the Skouros Shipping Lines logo.

"I'm going to come back," whispered Teddy. "I have to prove the rumors wrong."

"And you think the answer is here? In my country?"

Teddy flushed. "It's a place to start. I don't know what else to do."

Kristina looked thoughtful. "Teddy, as soon as my father is well enough, I have to fly back to Hollywood. The shoot on my next movie has already been delayed several days because of me. I should tell you this . . . I don't know if it has a bearing on your father's death or not. There are many political factions in my country, some of them quite militant. Perhaps your father inadvertently became mixed up in our politics, which are extremely volatile now. The issue of whether Costa will be re-annexed to France has become hot, but almost everything seems to spark one controversy or another. It's just crazy."

"But why would he do that—and how?"

"He is—was—an important man. He had money, connections. Who knows?'' Kristina's shrug was pure Gallic grace. ''I can give you the number of a man who might be able to help you. He moves in mysterious ways and is extremely discreet. I'll have my secretary call you with his number.''

''A detective, you mean?'' Teddy stared at the princess, bewildered.

''Yes. His name is Frédéric LaMarché. We've used him with our own security people and have always found him to be reliable.''

Teddy narrowed her eyes, staring out the window, watching as baggage handlers finished loading her luggage on the plane, along with her father's, which Skouros's servants had carefully packed. Skouros had treated her wonderfully, but how could she completely rely on information he might provide her? He might be involved in Costa's politics, too.

''I want LaMarché's number,'' she decided.

The flight attendant was approaching, to escort Teddy onto the plane, and the two women embraced again.

''Anything,'' said Kristina tearfully. ''I'll do anything to help.''

''Papa,'' said Gabriella, clutching her father's firm hand. She could hear the gathered crowd through the window, chanting Henri's name. She glanced anxiously at her father, who'd just been taken off the critical list.

''Don't be worried, dear,'' said Henri, speaking in a muffled voice through the oxygen tube affixed to his nose.

''I love you so much.''

''I know you do. And I love you.''

''Papa, I'll postpone my trip to Dallas. It's more important for me to be here with you.''

''I will be fine,'' said the prince. ''Make sure that Teddy Warner has everything she needs. And tell our people . . . I love them.''

The palace physician hurried in, accompanied by Dr.

James Tranh, the famous Vietnamese heart surgeon, who had been flown in from the DeBakey Clinic in Houston on Cliff Ferguson's private jet. The two doctors informed Gabriella that she would have to wait in the lounge, as her father was tiring.

"He is holding his own nicely," Dr. Tranh added, in perfect French. "He is a very strong man."

She left the room, passing the two royal guards who stood stiffly at attention outside the room, and found Jac pacing the floor in the lounge. He had shaved and changed his clothes, and looked frazzled but in control. With him was Anatole Breton, her father's chief advisor; Raoul Labatt, Henri's press secretary, and Henri's brother, Prince Georges, scowling and looking anxious.

"When do you wish to have a press conference, Your Highness?" Labatt was saying as Gaby entered the room.

"In one hour," said Jac. "Please notify Drs. Blanchet and Tranh of the time."

"Yes, Your Highness," said the press secretary.

"That will be all," said Jac, dismissing the officials. Within seconds they had bowed and left the room. Georges also excused himself, sensing that Gaby and Jac wanted to be alone to discuss their father. For the first time Gabriella noticed the light film of perspiration on her younger brother's forehead.

"I don't want Papa to die," Jac said.

"I don't either," Gaby gulped.

"I hate this."

"I know."

"I want him well." Then Jac drew a deep breath, straightening his shoulders.

Jac walked out on the third-floor balcony, gazing below him at the spectacle of people. As he stepped forward to the railing, a shout went up.

Turning to Henri's secretary and Prince Georges, who had walked out with him, Jac took the portable microphone from the secretary's hand and turned to face the swelling crowd.

"As you all know, my father, His Royal Highness Prince Henri, has suffered a heart attack. I am here to tell you that he is improving by the hour and is now out of danger."

A cheer rose, filling the air, reverberating against the hospital walls.

"I would like to thank you . . . " Jac continued, but could not make himself heard over the shouting and clamorous applause. Finally he just held on to the mike, moisture dampening his eyes.

When the shouts had died down slightly, he tried again. "My father wishes me to tell you that he loves you all and he—"

Jac unashamedly wiped away his tears as thousands of unrestrained voices started to sing the Costan national anthem.

Within hours of her arrival in the United States, Teddy held a press conference at WarnerCo, whose headquarters were in New York.

"Everyone was most kind, especially Mr. Skouros, and I am certain that all questions will soon be answered," she said into the microphone, beginning to read a prepared statement.

When she had finished, so many people shouted questions at her that she could not hear, and Reggie Luden, who stood next to her, had to ask for silence.

"Teddy! Is it a fact that your father had recently been advised by the SEC in Washington that a group was preparing a bid for a hostile takeover of the company?"

"There is no truth to that whatsoever," said Teddy, looking at Luden. Actually, there had been an attempt, but her father had managed to defuse it within the past month by enacting "golden parachute" provisions.

"Miss Warner, is it true that your father was despondent

because your tennis career no longer required his full attention and he felt . . . well, let's say, like a third wheel?''

Teddy stared at the woman who had asked the question, her expression hardening. "Where on earth do you think up those questions?" she blurted. "My father loved me. I loved him. We were very close. I—"

"Do you think there was any reason to suspect foul play?" shouted a man in the back row. "Will there be an official inquiry?" the same reporter continued.

Teddy froze. "Of course not."

She answered five or six more questions, then they ended the conference. There was so much to do: a church memorial service . . . the reading of Warner's will . . . and then she had to phone Frédéric LaMarché, the detective in Costa del Mar.

The memorial service for Houston Warner was devastating. Even though hundreds of people attended, including her agent, Russ Ostrand, and Jamaica DuRoss, nothing could lessen Teddy's sense of loss.

Now she felt so alone and by herself.

"Houston Warner was a man who never stopped giving, whether it was professionally, or to sports, or to his family and friends," said the minister, Dr. Lamont Norwich, beginning a long and glowing eulogy.

When it came time for her to say a few words about her father, Teddy broke down.

"Everything I am in tennis, everything I've accomplished, I owe to him," she finished, her voice cracking. "And I think he's still somewhere nearby, watching over me. He'll always watch over me."

Seated in the second row, Jamaica was openly sobbing.

"Teddy, please call me," Jamaica told her later, after the service was over and people were returning to their cars. "I know we've kinda grown apart, me in college, you with your tennis, but I still consider you my best friend."

Teddy clung to her. "I think something bad happened

to my father. I think . . . Oh, it's just too horrible to say out loud.''

Jamaica nodded dubiously. The press had openly speculated about Warner's death, coming up with a dozen theories, including the ''conspiracy theory,'' which seemed to be currently in vogue to account for the deaths of public figures such as Warner and Robert Maxwell, the publishing magnate. But suicide was still the most popular theory, a suggestion Teddy vehemently rejected.

Teddy told her friend about her plans to return to Costa and investigate her father's death.

''Teddy, don't get yourself into something dangerous,'' Jamaica said. ''I mean you're a tennis player, not a detective.''

''I won't.''

''Now promise me, Teddy. Promise?''

Teddy forced a hollow laugh. The service had taken a lot out of her. ''I swear it. I'm not a fool. Besides, I *am* a tennis player, and that's what Daddy really wanted me to do. So I won't be able to stay there forever. I have the U.S. Open coming up in a few months.''

But before she could even think about Costa del Mar, she had a million things to do. And one of the most important was a meeting with Russ Ostrand.

''Teddy, I'm sorry that all of this had to happen,'' said Ostrand who had really become much more than just her agent over the past several years. He had become her friend as well. Russ Ostrand with his short-clipped gray hair, hazel eyes, and ruddy skin was far more youthful looking than his fifty-five years, but had a mature way of approaching difficult situations that provoked confidence with his clients and friends. The two of them had just completed a three-hour meeting where Russ had advised her on both financial and personal matters involving her father's considerable estate. He had made suggestions as to the law firm she should begin consulting with in the immediate future.

''I don't want to think about such things now,'' she murmured, her throat closing painfully and her eyes welling up with tears. But, of course, she had to.

It was a week before Teddy could return to Costa, which was still in the middle of its ''high'' season, the ranks of its wealthy guests augmented by hundreds of reporters who sensed some sort of scandal. Her invitation to stay at the palace had been made formal by a note from Prince Henri's personal secretary.

As she followed a servant through the long corridors of the palace, passing open doors that revealed rooms of surpassing beauty, filled with priceless antiques and Old Master paintings, Teddy's awe was tempered by memories of her father. She could never forget that he had been with her the first time she had seen the palace.

Her apartment was a suite of breathtaking rooms with walls covered in ice blue damask. Its Aubusson carpets were pale cream and blue, with a design showing nosegays of flowers interspersed with *fleurs de lis*. A carved four-poster bed was covered with a blue silk trapunto quilt. There was a wonderful Seurat on the wall and a collection of ivory fans, centuries old. The suite also contained a small library, a living room, and an antique armoire that opened up to reveal a television set, VCR, and telephone.

The majordomo, Claude Boufait, showed her the pink marble bath, the adjoining dressing room, and the intercom service that would connect her with the other palace numbers, including housekeeping, the kitchen, and security.

''Thanks, it's all great,'' Teddy finally said. When Boufait left, she walked to the cabinet, picked up the phone, and dialed the number of the private investigator that Kristina had given her.

''Miss Warner, I can promise nothing,'' said Frédéric LaMarché. ''In my work, there are no guarantees, and there are often unpleasant surprises.''

His office was tucked on the second floor over a sta-

tionery shop called Cassegrain, a branch of the Paris sta-
tioner, which had carried the royal Costan warrant since
1852. The detective himself was a wiry man of about forty,
with a typical French appearance of dark hair, dark eyes,
and voluble hand gestures.

"I understand that."

"But I will do what I can. You will pay me a retainer
of five thousand Costan dollars, and I will bill you at one
hundred dollars per hour plus all expenses for my services.
You will receive weekly reports, daily reports if they are
appropriate. Naturally, our relationship is confidential."

"Yes, agreed—" said Teddy, flushing as she wondered
just what kind of reports she might receive, and what kind
of surprises there might be, if any. "When can you start?"

"As soon as I receive your check," said LaMarché.
"Just one thing, Miss Warner."

"Yes?"

"I understand you are staying at the palace. You may
not be aware of this, but the Vendôme Palace, like Buckingham Palace in England and the palace at Monaco, is a
small community unto itself. It is also—how do you Americans say it?—a hotbed of gossip. Servants hear everything,
and sometimes they look where they are not supposed to
look, *N'est-ce pas?* Keep my reports in a safe place."

A week after Teddy returned to Costa del Mar, the doctors decided that Prince Henri was out of danger. The old
prince urged his children to resume their normal lives, saying he didn't wish them to hover over him.

"Are you sure, Papa?" asked Gaby.

"Go . . . go now, daughter. I wish to look over some
papers."

She flew to Dallas and was met by Cliff Ferguson.

Despite being separated by an ocean and some three
thousand miles, Gaby and Cliff had managed to see each
other at least once a month over the past few years. Their
differences often got in the way of their relationship—his

expansive American tastes, her more restrained European sensibilities. His thousands of acquaintances, her smaller circle of intimate friends. His enthusiasm for contact sports, her preference for long walks on the beach. She knew a man like Cliff would be completely stifled living in a small country like Costa del Mar. But Cliff was warm and loving, and although Gaby occasionally had doubts, there was no man she wanted to be with more. They had become very close and still had learned to respect each other's views.

The ride from the airport to his fifty-thousand-acre ranch, Jacaranda, named after the tropical tree with lavender blossoms, took over an hour, and they filled each other in on what they had been doing during their separation.

She shared with him the story of Houston Warner's unexplained disappearance from the *Olympia*. His body had never been located.

"Do the authorities suspect foul play?" asked Cliff thoughtfully.

"No. I don't think so. I'm not sure. Since the body hasn't been found, nobody can be sure. There have been terrible rumors he could have suffered a heart attack and fallen over the railing," she went on painfully. "He was a workaholic, and apparently he once had a slight heart attack that he kept secret, even from Teddy. Oh, Cliff, you should have seen how devastated Teddy was. She just tore at my heart."

They discussed the tragedy for a few more minutes, and then Cliff proudly announced, "I'm throwing my usual once-a-month Sunday night barbecue for you, so I hope you've brought barbecuin' clothes."

Gaby smiled. "That will be lovely, darling. How many guests?"

"Just a few friends. Six hundred or so." Cliff laughed. "You know we Texans don't do anything on a small scale. Rebecca can't wait to see you, by the way. She wants to show you her triple axle. She's been practicing for weeks."

They drove under the tall wooden gate, embellished with the name and cattle brand of the huge spread, and it took another twenty minutes to actually reach the ranch buildings. The ranch house was big and white, shaded by spreading green trees and purple jacarandas and surrounded by decorative white fences overgrown with climbing roses and vines. There were a number of corrals and outbuildings as well as bunkhouses for ranch personnel. A blue swimming pool sparkled in the sun, and there were two tennis courts, plus a large indoor ice-skating arena for Rebecca, who was planning to compete in the upcoming U.S. Championships.

Gabriella took a deep, contented breath, realizing she never tired of coming here. She usually lived in jeans during her entire visit, free from intrusion by reporters or the need to wear makeup and look and act like a princess.

"I understand a little incident happened at the airport. Your security guard mentioned it to me," Cliff said, clearing his throat. A crowd had become unruly, pushing and shoving to get closer to Gabriella.

"Oh, Bernard took care of it quite nicely, and after all, I'm used to it."

"It worries me, those kind of incidents."

Gaby shrugged. "Those kinds of things have been happening most of my life, to my whole family. Once Jac was mobbed by a group of American girl students. Another time a man got into the palace and tried to find Kristina's bedroom. Even Papa was once approached by a man who began swearing at him and shouting obscenities. But we can't let those kinds of things stop us, Cliff," she went on, as he looked dubious. "Otherwise, we would never go anywhere except surrounded by bulletproof glass and bodyguards. We would have no contact with the people we rule, and our own lives would be the lives of virtual prisoners."

"Of course," he agreed at once. "I didn't mean to imply . . . Anyway, you are very, very safe here at Jacaranda. The most dangerous thing here might be a loose bull at rodeo time or a Texas rattler. And that's the way I like it.''

As they drove toward the large, five-car garage, a teen-aged girl came running out of the arena. She was clad in a blue warmup suit, her brown hair flying out behind her.

''Daddy! Gaby!''

Sixteen-year-old Rebecca Ferguson ran up to the car, pulling open the door and rushing to Gabriella for a kiss and a hug. ''Gaby, Gaby, you're here! There's so much to show you. My coach says my triple axle is perfect, and I have four new costumes! And I'm going to wear the neck-lace you sent me at the championships. Daddy said I could!''

Gabriella couldn't help laughing as she hugged Cliff's ebullient teenaged daughter. Rebecca looked like a pretty, female version of Cliff, and her personality was just as outgoing as his.

They walked into the ranch house, Cliff's arms around both Gaby and Rebecca.

''I want to show you the beautiful new little colt we have,'' Cliff was saying. ''He's reddish chestnut, with a white blaze across his forehead, and his bloodlines are sen-sational. I had him bred out of Lexington—that's in Ken-tucky—and I think he'll be even faster than his great-great-granddaddy, Secretariat. Why, Secretariat won the Derby back in 'seventy-three, you know. Lexington breeds more great winners than any other place in the coun-try. It's really famous, Gaby,'' he continued excitedly. ''I'd like to race him, Gaby. What do you think? I think I'm going to build a practice track out beyond the lake. It'll be the exact replica of Churchill Downs just like my friend Danny Galbraith built for his horses at Darby Dan Farms outside Columbus, Ohio. The idea was that if his horses trained in the exact same conditions as the Kentucky Derby, they'd have a better chance of winning—and his horses have been really successful.''

Gabriella sighed with peaceful resignation. This ranch in Texas often seemed like her second home.

Cliff had lit dozens of candles in his huge master bedroom suite. Their glow flickered against the pecan paneling of the walls, from which hung Frederic Remington paintings. A stereo was playing an old Johnny Mathis record, the singer's voice like warm honey.

Gaby threw her head back, exposing the slim column of her neck for Cliff's kisses. He was a tender lover, taking endless time and patience, and she knew he would not hurry.

"My beautiful, gorgeous Gaby," he murmured, kissing her collarbone, the warm puff of his breath against her skin unbearably sensual. Gaby ran her hands down the smoothness of his back, loving the coiled feel of the muscles just underneath his skin.

The kisses went lower still, and Cliff licked the aureoles of her nipples, hardening them with his tongue until they stood up in taut, excited peaks. His hands cupped her small breasts, kneading their softness, and Gaby began to moan. With infinite care, Cliff fastened his mouth tightly upon her and began to suck, creating a delicious, pulling sensation that created answering chords of pleasure deep within her groin.

Then Cliff pulled away, lowering himself onto her. "I can't wait," he groaned. "God . . . Gaby—you drive me crazy, and I can't ever, ever get enough of you."

She came swiftly, in ripples of joy that became crescendos. Within seconds, Cliff's body had stiffened as he was swept away by his own climax.

She collapsed on his chest, and he held her tightly, then Gaby rolled off him and lay beside him, the sensual odors rising around them in a musky haze.

"I missed you so damn much," said Cliff, sighing.

"I feel the same." She sighed contentedly into the soft spot of his neck.

"This seeing each other once a month or so—it's got to stop," he said. "We get together, just start knowing each other again real close, then one of us has to leave again. I want something better for us."

Gaby caught her breath. "I suppose . . . I could spend more time in the States."

He rolled over on one elbow to look at her. "A *lot* more time. Gaby . . ." He sighed. "I don't want a long-distance romance with you anymore. I don't want to be the guy mentioned in the tabloids as Princess Gabriella's Texan friend. I want us to get married."

For many months Gaby had known this was coming; Cliff had increasingly been dropping hints about marriage. Still, the shock that traveled through her body was profound. She felt a gasp strangle itself in her throat.

"Silence?" said Cliff. "Oh, Gaby, maybe I didn't phrase it right, I'm not the best guy in the world with words. I love you, I adore you, I couldn't imagine life with anyone but you."

"Nor I you," she said slowly. "I feel exactly the same way. . . . But, Cliff . . ."

What was she going to do? Although Prince Henri had come to like Cliff a great deal and to respect him, he had told her privately that he would prefer her to marry a man with more ties to Costa—a man with a Catholic upbringing, an ancient title, and keen awareness of Europe's traditions and its politics. Gaby believed that Henri would be disappointed if she announced her engagement to Cliff. After his heart attack, she dreaded upsetting him, and yet didn't she have a right to her own life, too?

"What is it, Gaby? Jesus, honey, don't tell me that you're going to say no." Cliff was holding on to her very tightly.

"No . . . no . . . I'm not going to say no." Gaby's laugh turned to a muffled sob. This was the most wonderful moment of her life, and she was having doubts. "I'm saying yes. But, Cliff, I know there are going to be so many problems. Our differences—''

Cliff clasped her to him for a joyful bear hug, not having heard her last few words. "Gaby—darling—we'll be married in a few weeks, I can't wait any longer!''

"A few weeks?'' She sat up, pulling the sheet over herself. "Cliff, we can't get married in a few weeks. It's going to take months! I'll have to fly back to Costa. There are a thousand arrangements. We'll be married in the cathedral, of course—''

"Oh, boy.'' Cliff sat up too. "You're right. The important thing is, we're going to be married. I can't tell you what courage it took for me to ask you at all. You're a princess, I'm just an ordinary guy lucky enough to have made some big bucks. . . . Sometimes I think meeting you was just a Hans Christian Andersen fairy tale, but then I look at you and you're so real.'' He reached for the bedside table and pulled out a small silver box. "Here. I want you to wear this, darling, if you would. With all my love and adoration.''

With a shaking hand, Gabriella reached for the box and opened it. Inside was a ring with a flawless, blue-white ten-carat diamond surrounded by diamond baguettes in a star shape. It glittered brilliantly, catching the candlelight on its complex facets.

Gabriella looked at it again. The design was her own— a style she had been hoping to release as part of her next fall's collection.

Cliff seemed very proud of himself. "I went to New York and had Kenny Lane show me all of your sketches, honey. He helped me choose it, and he had his own artisans do all the work. It has you in it—that's the way I wanted it. Isn't it the most beautiful ring you ever saw?''

Gabriella slid the ring on her finger. It fit perfectly. She looked down at it, tears springing to her eyes so that the flashes of light from the huge diamond had a mystical, surreal beauty. "It's beautiful," she whispered. "Just like you."

"Papa," Gabriella said over the telephone to Costa del Mar, twenty minutes later. Her voice was light with happiness, and yet part of her felt apprehension, too. "I have news . . . such wonderful news! You're the first to know."

"Then by all means tell me," said the old prince wryly. "I think I am ready for some wonderful news . . . for a change."

"Cliff and I are getting married!"

Henri did not seem surprised. "That is very good news, Gaby. But," he added, as Gabriella began to sigh with relief, "have you thought it through very carefully? When a man marries you, he takes on many responsibilities. He is aware of our rules regarding marriage and divorce, isn't he?"

"Yes. . . ."

"I assume you will be living in Costa most of the time."

"No. . . . Papa—" She shook her head. "We haven't really talked it out yet, we just now decided. But I am sure that we'll live in both places. . . . Papa, be happy for me! Don't find things wrong with my choice. I want you to love him! He is such a good man, and he—"

"I know he is a good man, daughter. I have observed him over these years, and I find him honest and reliable— but very American. Are you quite sure you wish to marry an American rather than a European man?"

"Why not?" she blurted recklessly. "You married a Scandinavian, didn't you? Cliff is going to make a wonderful husband. He has great respect for us. Give him a *chance,* Papa!"

"Then I am happy for you," said Henri firmly. "Very happy."

The GRAY LIMOUSINE EXITED THE FREEWAY AND continued through the maze of manicured roads that led upward into the famed Beverly Hills, burning with the last reddish orange hue of the setting sun.

Kristina, holding a sleepy Princess Charlie on her lap, was exhausted from her long flight, the tragedy on the *Olympia,* and her worry about her father's health. And she wasn't looking forward to the problem she now faced here in Hollywood, one that had to be dealt with, and soon.

The *Hollywood Reporter* had phrased her dilemma very well: *Hollywood's Own Royal Merger,* the headline proclaimed. *Are Princess Kristina and megastar Bret Thompson going to tie the knot? Royal-watchers have placed bets on wedding bells. . . .*

Kristina winced. Bret Thompson.

Handsome, rakish, talented Bret, a sex object for millions of women. He'd been her lover off and on for the past two years, and once more they'd be working together in a film. Recently he *had* begun to hint about marriage. But then he'd change his mind.

Did he or didn't he want to marry her? She had thought about it all the way from Costa, and she wanted to settle the matter. Even Henri, recuperating in the palace, had mentioned it to her. The old prince had told her he wanted to see his daughter settled with a man who would love both her and Charlaine.

Her house, on Lago Vista Drive, had been owned at various times by Debbie Reynolds, Sherry Lansing, and Anthony Newley. Its architecture was Spanish style, with a red-tile roof and curved stucco arches. Two large wings wrapped around a turquoise swimming pool, its bottom tiled in a blue mosaic pattern. There were splashing fountains and a rose garden that contained a white gazebo.

The limo pulled up to the gate, and the driver activated the automatic opener. The sleeping three-year-old blond princess didn't stir as they drove through to the capacious five-car garage, whose second floor provided studio apartments for her two bodyguards and Mr. Nakamura, the gardener.

As the limo whispered to a halt, Kristina felt her spirits lift. Here, exactly, was where Bret Thompson had parked two years ago on the day he'd first brought her to see the house. . . .

. . . "Really a very decent price," said Bret. "Considering all of the amenities." The real-estate agent had given him a key, and he proudly opened the front door on an entrance hall that gave a view of a huge living room with oak flooring, a brick fireplace, and acres of French doors that overlooked the rose garden, ablaze with pink, red, white, and yellow blooms.

"Oh, the roses," cried Kristina, running to the doors.

"I can give you the name of a good gardener. As I told you, there is plenty of room for live-in help, and the location is perfect. The house is as beautiful as you are," Bret added.

Kristina turned. The actor was standing behind her, gazing at her with a soft, melting yet intense expression. Suddenly she was very conscious of being alone with him.

"Kristina," Bret said huskily. His eyes searched hers. "I've been so attracted to you ever since we met at the Oscars. It was like karma or something. In fact—"

"I did find the Academy Awards fascinating," she smiled quickly. "We Europeans don't have anything quite like it. And it is wonderful of you to take the time to show me this nice house. Now, how many rooms does it have? I want a large room for Charlie's nursery, an adjoining room for her nurse, and I will require a large dressing room for myself."

She strode ahead of him, exclaiming at this and that, forcing Bret to walk faster to keep up with her. Inwardly she felt a burst of elation. A famous movie star wanted her . . . but, of course, she had no plans to have an affair with him. After the humiliation of her divorce from Jean-Luc she felt somewhat wary of men. Besides, she didn't want Henri to read about her in some tabloid and order her back to Costa del Mar.

Wardrobe fittings, meetings with the hair stylist, the makeup artist, the cinematographer, and others connected with the picture had taken nearly three weeks. Kristina was given a script, and painstakingly studied her lines. Then the script was polished again, and she studied the new revisions. A voice coach was brought in to work with her on the fifties torch song she was expected to perform in the movie.

While she practiced, her bodyguard sat in a chair near the door, looking bored. Kristina had begun to find his presence annoying. She'd grown up with servants and bodyguards—she had known nothing else—but now she could look around and see beautiful women her own age who, despite their celebrity status, drove cars and moved about freely, doing whatever they wished.

She already loved the film business, but there was one major drawback—she missed baby Charlaine, Princess Charlie, desperately. She'd reluctantly agreed to leave the infant in Costa until her first picture wrapped. Then she'd fly home and get her daughter.

One day after she'd rehearsed the musical number, Bret took her to lunch at Bistro Garden, a favorite eating spot of L.A. power brokers, with its outdoor fountain, festive umbrellas, and white lattice-back chairs. People seated at other tables tried not to stare too obviously at the sight of Hollywood's major sex symbol dining with Europe's most beautiful princess.

"I didn't realize you could really sing," remarked Bret, smiling.

"I had voice lessons at school," said Kristina, forking into her baked sea scallops with muscat ginger sauce. "I gave a recital, and Papa said I was another Edith Piaf."

"My dear Kristina, your voice sounds just like you . . . soft and incredibly sexy."

"I'm glad you like it."

Yes, Kristina thought. He *was* coming on to her, but she could handle it.

They talked casually about Gaby's jewelry line, which was becoming immensely popular, especially after Liz Taylor had bought more than a dozen pieces. As they were completing the meal, Kristina heard a familiar deep voice and looked up.

"Princess Kristina. Ah, how marvelous to see you here today. Your presence glows throughout this lovely restaurant, making it even more charming." It was Nickey Skouros, dressed in a light blue sport jacket and darker navy shirt, colors that emphasized the striking silver of his hair and the piercing blue of his eyes.

"Nickey!" she cried, delighted to see someone she knew. Her voice warm, she introduced the Greek to Bret. The two men exchanged greetings, but seemed cool.

"You must treat this delightful princess with care on the set," murmured Skouros. "She is used to receiving the best of everything."

Bret reddened. "Princess Kristina will receive every courtesy possible; it has been written into her contract."

"Ah," said Nickey. "Excellent." He extended his hand to Kristina. She took it, feeling the warm dryness of his palm. "Your Highness, if there is anything you need, any problem you may have, no matter how small, you have only to telephone me. I have taken a bungalow at the Beverly Hills Hotel until my house is ready. I am having a place on Bellagio Drive remodeled. I will be spending some time in Los Angeles over the next two or three months."

"How nice," smiled Kristina. Seated beside her, Bret bristled even further.

"I am your friend in Beverly Hills if you should need one," Skouros finished suavely. "Now, if you will pardon me, I have guests waiting upstairs."

After the Greek had left, Bret Thompson raised an eyebrow. He drawled, "Nickey Skouros, the third-richest man in the world, or is it second-richest? There was an article about him in *Forbes* last week, but I found it rather boring."

"Nickey is an old family friend," Kristina explained lightly. "Now, tell me more about the locations, Bret. How did you ever find that beautiful church in Philadelphia? And authorization to film at The Country Club in Brookline . . . isn't that rather unusual?"

Later, as soon as he left the Bistro Garden, Nikos Skouros picked up the telephone in the back of his limousine, punching in the numbers quickly.

"It's Skouros. What have you got for me on Thompson?"

"I'm having my secretary type up your weekly report now, sir," came the reply. "The man has had a string of girlfriends, mostly actresses, but there have been a few rock singers. He usually becomes bored with them after a month or so. He's had a succession of one-night stands, too. He's quite a Lothario."

"I know that," said Skouros dryly. "What else have you got? What about his business interests? That chain of hamburger restaurants he owns? His bank relationships? His health? I want a thorough investigation, not just rumors. If this is all you can give me—"

"Sir, I've already sent a man to his former home in Dearborn, Michigan, and we're digging deep, but the man appears to cover his tracks well. If there's any wrongdoing, we haven't been able to find it so far."

"Hmmm," Skouros said in displeasure. "Keep me

posted. When you come upon anything important I want a phone call immediately.''

''Yes, sir. Immediately, sir.''

''Princess Kristina,'' said the ABC/CAP Cities syndicated columnist Shirley Eder, who had arranged to meet with Kristina at her hotel for a brief interview. Eder wore a knee-length, heather-colored Perry Ellis suit and carried both a notebook and a small tape recorder. ''Are you excited about coming to America and getting into films?''

Kristina's smile was warm. ''I'm much more than just excited, Shirley. I'm terribly nervous, too. I want to do well. The whole world will be watching, which puts a great deal of pressure on me.''

''Your Highness, I imagine it is tough to follow your mother, Princess Lisse, who got three Academy Award nominations if I remember correctly.''

''Yes. But this film, *The Congregation,* is a wonderful vehicle for me. . . .'' Kristina went on at some length, describing the plot of the picture and her feelings about the character she would play, a well-bred young woman with deep, hidden passion.

''One more thing,'' Eder said as she prepared to leave. ''Rumors here in Hollywood connect you with two attractive and influential male friends—Nikos Skouros and Bret Thompson. Is there any truth to those rumors?''

''My family has known Nikos since I was a child,'' said Kristina smoothly. ''As for Bret, we only have a professional relationship.''

Later, after Eder had left, promising to devote her entire column to Kristina, the princess walked to the window. She stood gazing down at Sunset Boulevard, where traffic whizzed back and forth, $150,000 Lamborghinis overtaking BMWs, Mercedes, Ferraris, and Cadillacs. Only in Hollywood did so many splendid cars crowd the roads.

She felt herself tremble slightly. The columnist had unerringly picked up on her biggest fear—could she ever measure up to Princess Lisse?

Kristina closed her trailer door behind her, wondering what she was to do next. The Winnebago had been carpeted in dusty rose plush and was full of magnificent flower arrangements. She moved toward a bouquet of dark red roses and pulled out the card.

All good wishes, luck, and love, from Nickey, it read. Kristina smiled; she did care about Nickey, even love him in a way. But he wanted to own her, and she wasn't ready for that. Maybe she never would be.

To the most beautiful princess in the world. So glad to be working with you at last, read another card, this one from Bret Thompson.

There was a knock on her door. Kristina hurried to open it.

"Your Highness," said her bodyguard, Thierry, as if he were announcing a visitor to the palace. "Mr. Bret Thompson."

The actor was standing on the step, wearing a fifties-style jacket with oversized shoulders and lapels, pleated pants, a white shirt, and a bold paisley tie. Bret's hair had been brushed back into a pompadour with Bryl-Cream in the look popular in the fifties. On him, the style seemed astonishingly attractive.

His smile was warm. "Welcome to the set, Your Highness."

"Call me Kristina," she said. " 'Your Highness' is too formal on location, don't you think?"

Bret nodded his approval. "That'll make things a hell of a lot easier. I just want to fill you in on what's going to happen. You'll go first to the hair and makeup trailer. The costume designer wants to see you, too. We'll start with an easy scene today—just you getting out of a car. You're running after me, you're angry, but you only have two or three lines of dialogue. We'll have a rehearsal before we start shooting. I hope to make things as easy for you as possible.''

Kristina nodded gratefully, hoping no one guessed how terrified she was.

Kristina was permitted to join the select group, consisting of Bret, Fred Wiseman, the co-producer, and Hitch Birnkrant, the famous cinematographer, who had gathered in Thompson's trailer to watch the ''dailies,'' a video cassette copy of the footage that had been shot the previous day. A small theater could have been used, but this was easier.

Stunned, Kristina stared at herself on the TV screen. She looked . . . different. All of her characteristics were slightly exaggerated, giving her the smolder of Rita Hayworth, mixed with the fresh blond grace of Princess Lisse.

''Nice . . . nice,'' Bret kept murmuring, as they viewed take after take. ''Each one better than the last. . . . Sensational. She photographs like a dream. Projects like a goddamned hand grenade.''

The others were nodding agreement.

''But I thought—'' Kristina began, remembering how Bret had repeatedly criticized her as the scenes were being filmed.

''You're gonna be a big, big star, dear,'' said Bret, smiling with satisfaction. ''No doubt in my mind whatsoever.''

At the same time that Kristina was making her first film in Hollywood, the breakup with Auggie had sorely wounded Teddy. She made up her mind that there wouldn't be a repeat. No man was going to toy with her emotions again—especially not any male tennis player.

So she slogged on, methodically winning tournament after tournament, then going home to an empty hotel room, or dinner with her father or her hitting partner, Manuel Muñoz, a very nice man who had become a close friend.

When she read in *USA Today* that Jac had just broken

up with Lady Philippa and had embarked on a series of short romances, she didn't even feel a pang. Jac was a royal playboy. Why should she care about him?

Christmas came, and Teddy flew home to Connecticut to be with her father, who wanted to take her window-shopping on Fifth Avenue and promised a twenty-foot tree in their living room, glowing with lights. He hinted at glorious presents and cross-country skiing in Vermont.

"It'll be just us, and maybe we'll invite Jamaica and her family for Christmas Eve," promised Warner. He seemed thinner this year and told Teddy that his doctor had put him on a diet to lose about fifteen pounds.

"You haven't been sick, have you, Dad?"

"Me, sick? Teddy Bear, I've never felt better," her father declared heartily. "Oh, did you hear—Princess Kristina is making another movie. She gets more like Lisse every day, don't you think? Princess Lisse was a great representative of an era that's gone now. In fact, the whole country of Costa is rather like that—something out of the past, a sort of modern-day Camelot. Its history is quite surprising."

He proceeded to give her a rather detailed history of the small country, finishing with a discussion of its heroics during World War II, when more than five thousand Jews and members of the French Resistance had escaped through its ports.

"Daddy," she said, grinning, "I didn't know you were that interested in Costa, let alone that you had an encyclopedic knowledge of it."

He seemed to blush. "I guess I surprised you, huh?"

One night while her father was working late at the office, Teddy struggled to wrap the dozen large packages she'd splurged on as gifts for her father and Jamaica. Rummaging around for more ribbons, she walked into the room her father used to store old boxes, wrapping paper, and various hobby items, as well as all of his old tennis memorabilia. Her curiosity got the better of her, and instead of searching for ribbons, she began leafing through a file cabinet, pulling out old letters from agents, yellowed clippings, reading them and smiling. Her dad had once been quite the aggressive pro—in fact, something like Auggie, with a definite way with women! Looking at these things made her feel close to her father, and she began to enjoy herself immensely.

A cardboard box in the bottom drawer of the file caught her eye, and she pulled it out. More tennis stuff, she supposed, or maybe even some love letters. Then she saw that the box was labeled *Costa*. She hesitated, then finally opened it.

Inside were stuffed hundreds of clippings about Costa, some recent, others several years old. They covered every aspect of the country, but most seemed political in nature, outlining the various controversies that had rocked the tiny principality over the years.

No wonder her father had seemed like such an expert on Costa, she realized, her breath coming fast. He was! Apparently he had been collecting these clippings for years and had never told her about it.

It was odd. . . . Usually her father was very open with his opinions, but he had kept this secret from her, and now Teddy wanted to know why.

Later that evening, as they were sitting in front of the crackling fireplace, he with his briefcase full of papers, she with a novel, Teddy told him about the box of clippings.

To her shock, Warner seemed annoyed. "You were looking through my things?"

"Dad, I wasn't 'looking through your things,' I was looking for some Christmas ribbons, and then I found the tennis stuff and I just started browsing. Why would you have collected so much stuff about Costa? You never seemed that interested before. At least if you were, you didn't tell me. I don't understand, Dad."

Warner hesitated. "It's . . . just a hobby I have."

"A hobby? Costa? Dad, it still doesn't make sense to me."

"Why not?" he said testily. "Do you think that I only focus on business and your tennis career? I have many more interests than that, darling Teddy. What else did you find?" he added sharply.

"Why . . . nothing. Should I have found more?" Teddy was beginning to get a little angry. She couldn't believe it, but she and her father seemed to be having an argument, over a bunch of silly newspaper and magazine clippings.

"Well, I wish you wouldn't just prowl through my things without my permission," her father grumped.

"Dad . . . !"

"All right," he finally said. He began to explain to her how he had been snubbed at the palace several years ago by Prince Georges when he mistakenly asked the prince for directions to the telephone. He'd become interested in Costa then. It had started as just curiosity, but gradually it had become an obsession.

"But *why*?"

Warner gazed into the fire. "I don't know. I've asked myself that, too. I've found some things—well, you don't want to know them, and anyway, there is no proof, only rumors. I suppose," he went on with difficulty, "I suppose this has something to do with you and Prince Jac."

"Me and Prince Jac?" she stared at him. "Dad . . . I'm *not* interested in Jac. Truly I'm not. We—we just had a little flirtation, and it was over in a few days, and he went on with his life and so did I. We *do* live in two different worlds, and I don't think a tennis player is exactly what he is looking for."

"Tennis players are as good as anyone," began Warner in a slightly truculent tone.

"Of course." Teddy giggled. "Dad, you always get so protective when it comes to me. That was great when I was fifteen, but now it's getting a little old. Look—would you like to make some popcorn? I bought a new microwave brand with cheese on it. It's supposed to be wonderful.''

So the topic of Costa passed, and neither her father nor Teddy ever mentioned it again. In fact, Teddy forgot all about it. Within ten days she was back on the tennis circuit again—back to her round of spectacular wins and lonely hotel rooms.

Some things never changed.

Kristina slipped on the sheer silk negligee and turned to look at herself in the mirror. Elegant and sexy, the gown, designed by Scaasi, was as suggestive as it could be without Kristina being totally nude. Its white lace bodice plunged between her breasts, the sides cut away so that the outer quadrants of her breasts were emphasized. When she moved, more than half of them would be exposed.

''It's not what I expected,'' she murmured, turning to the wardrobe mistress, who stood with a small sewing kit and a pincushion.

''Your Highness, it's gorgeous! It will photograph like *fabulous*.''

Kristina raised her arms, observing the way the chiffon fell away, nearly revealing her nipples. Angrily she realized that this was the studio's way of getting around a contract that specified no nude scenes.

''No,'' she said flatly.

''But the costume has been approved by the director—''

''I don't care who has approved it. My contract says no nudity,'' Kristina snapped. ''I'll wear this *if* it's modified. I want full approval first.''

''I'll talk to Mr. Thompson, Your Highness,'' said the wardrobe mistress reluctantly.

The bedroom was decorated in ice-pink, the satin bedclothes were in sensuous disarray, and lights were blazing on overhead dolly tracks. Kristina wrapped her arms around Bret Thompson, her lips playfully nuzzling his ear. He was bare-chested, clad only in pajama bottoms, and smelled faintly of pancake makeup. She wore the altered lace negligee, made less revealing after several discussions with Bret.

"Closer," boomed the first A.D.'s voice through a microphone. "Kristina, I need your head angled to the right. . . . Don't block Bret's face. . . . Yes, that's more like it. And, Bret, when you kiss her, I wanna see a busy mouth."

Kristina stifled a nervous giggle. Millions of American women daydreamed about doing a love scene with the sexy Bret. Little did they know what a difficult procedure it was, barely sexy at all. Because of the close quarters, one had to constantly think about positioning, and the constant, intrusive presence of the camera. Then there was the embarrassment of being in an intimate position in front of a mostly male crew. The skimpy gown was revealing enough, and although Kristina had been assured that the most revealing angles would be cut later, she still felt uncomfortable.

"From the top," said the assistant director.

"Darling," breathed Kristina, opening her mouth and beginning to nibble at Bret's neck again. As they moved in the carefully choreographed sequence, she felt something hard press against her thigh.

Kristina gasped, then felt herself shiver deliciously.

"You were turned on, too," Bret murmured, as they put on robes and stepped off the set, walking into the huge, hangarlike sound stage.

"I—" Kristina began in embarrassment.

"It's all right, Kristina. I felt the same way, as you might have noticed. Any chance you might like to come to my house tonight, maybe take a steam in my Finnish sauna and then a dip in the pool?"

He wasn't asking her to swim in his pool . . . that was clear.

"I must go home and call Costa," she told him. "I always talk to Mrs. Abbott to find out what my baby is doing. I miss her so much. This is the last time I'll ever leave her in Costa while I'm shooting. But after that, perhaps . . . if I'm not too tired."

He grinned. "You won't be too tired, and if you are, I know something that will wake you up. Trust me."

"As the old showgirl Blaze Starr told her boyfriend, Governor Earl Long of Louisiana, I never trust any man who says, 'Trust me,' " Kristina responded provocatively.

"She was absolutely right!"

Bret's bedroom suite took up an entire wing of his magnificent house. Kristina had a vague impression of lots of dark blue brocade.

There was no foreplay—there had been enough of that all through the day as they did sixteen takes of the steamy sex scene. Now they fell on the bed, pulling at each other's clothes.

He was a silent, intense lover, and very attentive to her sexual needs. He knew all the right moves . . . knew every one of a woman's erogenous zones, from the tender skin on the back of her knee to the soft, sensitive flesh in the creases of her inner thighs.

Kristina longed for him to say something warm and tender, but Bret lifted her up, positioning her astride him. She lowered herself onto the hard, blunt end of his cock, and they began to move together. She didn't expect to come immediately; she seldom did unless the man used his tongue for forty minutes or longer. Still, she moaned as she circled herself on his shaft, moving up and down in short, teasing movements. Bret reached upward with his hands to squeeze her nipples, thumbing them to taut erection.

He thrust harder, pounding into her, rocking her up and down.

"No—not yet! Don't come yet," he ordered her as she threw back her head, a cry beginning in her throat.

He reached into the bedside table for a small, plastic envelope, removing a narrow glass tube with an outer cover of burlap. "Amyl nitrite," he told her. "A popper. It'll heighten everything for you."

It did.

Afterward, Kristina curled up beside Bret and napped for half an hour. The noise of the telephone ringing elsewhere in the house woke her. Bewildered, she looked around at the unfamiliar room. Then, glancing over at Bret's nude body, she realized where she was. She'd made love to a man who had not uttered one word of affection, just pillow talk.

Disappointment and remorse consumed her as she slid out of bed and jumped into the white jeans she'd worn, wriggling into a green cotton sweater, and thrusting her feet into her huaraches. The room now seemed cool, and she shivered. Her sexy, loving mood had vanished totally in the wake of frustration. Why had she done it? she wondered. It had been chemistry . . . sex . . . nothing more. He didn't know anything about real love, and maybe never would.

"I've always been into sexual prowess," Bret told her the next evening. They had dined at Towers, in Laguna Beach, nine stories above the pounding surf, and now were walking on the beach. Barefoot, they held hands as the sun sank over the waves in bursts of fuchsia, salmon, gold, and lavender. "Women complain about it. They want to hear sweet nothings, they want tenderness, and instead, I give them hard exercise."

Kristina's laugh was restrained. "You certainly gave me that. I'm really sore all over today."

"I want to change. I want to be more tender for you. I know I can be—if you're patient."

Kristina stopped and looked at Bret. "The feelings come first, then it's easy to be tender. Women want to be cherished, Bret. Most of us would rather have that than mega-star sex any time.''

Bret flushed. ''Kristina . . . I don't want to lose you.''

''I'm not sure if I'm ready,'' Kristina whispered after a time. ''My marriage to Jean-Luc hurt me very badly. There are things about that marriage no one will ever know.''

''I do know. . . . I had a painful divorce, too. Divorce hurts like bloody hell.''

''Do you have children?'' she asked.

''Three little girls. They live with their mother in Michigan. It's painful—I seldom see them.'' He sighed. ''I always wanted to start a second family, make up for my previous mistakes.''

They walked for a long while, talking about their lives, until the sun sank behind the waves with one brief, greenish flare, and purplish light stole over the curls of foam that washed up on the damp sand. Holding Bret's hand, Kristina began to feel a deep, warm relaxation, a sense of well-being.

Maybe their first lovemaking session hadn't gone one hundred percent right, but now Bret was beginning to relate to her as a person, not as a sex object. Maybe, after all, she could fall in love with him.

The wrap party for *The Congregation* was held on a Monday night at Spago's, on Horn Avenue in West Hollywood, the starstruck eatery presided over by superchef Wolfgang Puck. The cast and crew milled around, congratulating each other on producing an ''opener''—a real moneymaker. Of course, the picture had not yet gone through postproduction, when editing would be done, the music track laid in, and sound effects dubbed with the Foley added, but industry gossip predicted that the film would be a major hit. And insiders were saying that Princess Kristina was a sensation, even better than Lisse.

Kristina was in a state of euphoria. It was everything she'd ever dreamed. . . . By Christmas her face would be on two thousand movie screens. By the following April—who knew? But she pushed thoughts of an Academy Award out of her mind.

"Dear Kristina," said Bret, bringing her a fluted glass of wine. He slid his arm around her in a proprietary manner. "You're gonna set this town ablaze, I know it. I've been in pictures a long time, and I can just smell a winner."

"*And* the little gold fella, God willing," added Michael Ovitz, who had just worked his way through the crowd to join them. The mega-agent was with another man, tall, blond, with a deep suntan. "Princess Kristina, I'd like to introduce you to one of our partners at CAA, Will Camden."

Kristina looked into a pair of serious gray eyes, their corners fanned with laugh wrinkles, more deep laugh lines scored at the corners of his mouth. Camden, about forty, looked like a type of man Kristina had already seen often in America—the kind of man whose job gave him easy power.

"It's wonderful to meet you, Princess Kristina. I've already heard the good rumors about you from Mike. You must be very pleased."

"I am," she said, flushing as the deep gray eyes seemed to stare straight into her. Bret had moved away, and Kristina found herself talking to this new, interesting man. She knew that being a partner of Mike Ovitz made him one of the most powerful men in Hollywood.

"Was it difficult all these years, being Princess Lisse's daughter?"

If the question had come from someone else, Kristina might have found it intrusive. But from this man with a warm smile and his respectful demeanor, it came across as very genuine.

"It was extremely hard," she admitted.

They talked for more than twenty minutes, and Kristina found herself telling Will about her toughest challenge, which was getting past the criticism of the crew on the set, which she found difficult to take.

"I don't imagine that a princess has much experience dealing with criticism," said Will, grinning.

"That's not so." She giggled. "If you knew my father—"

Suddenly Bret was back, taking her arm possessively. "Darling, I hope you don't mind if we leave early—I have some phone calls to make," he said. "My apologies," he added to Will.

"Of course," the agent murmured politely, his glance taking in the way Bret's glance rested on Kristina. "Well, Your Highness, it has been great to talk with you, and I'm sure we'll be running into each other again at the agency or . . . somewhere else. This is a very small town."

As Kristina left the party with Bret, she experienced an empty pang that she recognized as disappointment in leaving so early. She'd liked Will—he had made her feel comfortable. If Bret hadn't been with her . . . but he was. And she was having a relationship with him now, and since half of Hollywood knew it, she assumed Will Camden did, too.

Five minutes later, she'd forgotten all about Will Camden.

MAY 1993

Kristina HAD RECEIVED AN ACADEMY AWARD nomination for her role in *The Congregation*, although the "little gold fella"—Oscar—had gone to Jodie Foster. But now it was two years later, and everyone was saying that Kristina's latest picture, *Mafia Ladies*, might put her up for another nomination.

Her romance with Bret, although it had had some rocky moments, had survived and deepened, and now they were a recognized couple and frequently entertained together.

Bret occasionally flew to Las Vegas on business—he owned a national chain of thirty-five restaurants called Hamburger Hacienda with corporate headquarters there—but otherwise they saw each other at least twice a week.

She entered the house, carrying Princess Charlie. Mary Abbott came hurrying to greet them, and Kristina turned her three-year-old daughter over to her expert care. The two bodyguards began carrying in Princess Kristina's considerable luggage, plus several large boxes of toys and other items. Marie-Claire, Kristina's personal maid, supervised the unpacking.

Kristina walked into her downstairs study, closed the door, and made a quick call to Costa to check on Prince Henri's condition. He was resting comfortably, thank God. She thought about Teddy Warner, wondering how she was holding up after the tragedy of losing her father. Tomorrow she'd phone.

Then she punched in the numbers of Bret's private line at home.

"Yo," said her lover, coming on the line.

"Bret," she said, "I'm back. I can't wait to see you, and I want to talk. We need to talk, darling."

"Sweetheart, can it wait ten minutes? I'm on the phone with Sly."

Kristina bit her lip. Bret hadn't flown to Costa, either for Nickey's charity ball and cruise or to be with her when her father was so ill. He'd been deeply engrossed in finishing a picture called *Bush League*, which had gone over budget and become a big problem. She understood the huge pressures of a big-budget picture. Still, she was annoyed that he couldn't even drop his phone conversation to greet her. Why did he do this to her? Just when she'd lowered her defenses enough to fall in love with him, he became elusive.

"Baby?" he said.

She drew a deep breath. "In ten minutes," she finally agreed.

But when she dialed him again in ten minutes, his personal assistant picked up the phone and told her that Bret had just left the house, not saying where he was going.

"He's done what?" she said angrily.

But before she could get an explanation from the man, her maid knocked on the door and told her that she had a visitor. "It's Mr. Thompson, Your Highness."

Kristina's anger vanished.

"Where is he?"

"I've put him in the living room, madame."

Kristina felt her heart do a deep twisting turn, and she flung open the door and rushed down the corridor. Bret never did the expected, did he? Maybe that was why she'd fallen in love with him.

"Kristina, Kristina," said Bret, holding her tenderly. "God, I missed you. This movie business is sheer hell. I worked twenty hours a day getting that movie in the can. I wish I could have been in Costa with you. God, did I miss you!"

They hugged again, shamelessly wrapping themselves around each other.

"My heart is pounding," Kristina laughed.

"Mine is slamming."

"I was miserable without you."

"Then hug me," he ordered, drawing her close for another ten delicious minutes of caressing and embraces. But when the maid crossed the corner of the living room to get to the stairs, Kristina drew away.

"I've missed you, too, so much," she said in a low voice. "Especially with all that went on, I really needed you. Bret ..." Then she laughed nervously, her old fears returning. "I'm not going to be diplomatic or coy about this. I'm not that kind of person, and I want to know rather than just guessing."

He looked at her fondly. "You want to know what, darling?"

"You've been dropping strong hints recently about marriage. Are you planning to ask me to marry you?"

Bret stared at her, then threw back his head and laughed. "Sorry. Oh, Kristina, only a princess would propose to a man first. Yes, darling, I was planning to ask you to marry me. In fact, I have been shopping in New York and Amsterdam. I want you to have a *huge* diamond, darling. I can afford it, and I want it to outshine any of those royal Costan jewels, the crown jewels, whatever you call them. Hollywood is where we're going to live, and I want us to be married here, maybe at the Bel Air Hotel."

Kristina stared at him. He looked so earnest and loving. It was as if his previous vacillation had never even existed. "Bret," she said, gazing into his eyes, "are you sure? Very, *very* sure?"

"Of course I'm sure. I love you so much, darling. I adore you. Every inch of you."

"But why— I mean—"

"I don't want to wait." His smile comforted her. "Baby—oh, Jesus—I don't want to wait."

He pulled her into his arms for a long, sensual kiss, mixed with more "I love you's," and "darling Krisses." Kristina sighed, allowing happiness to sweep over her. Bret could be a workaholic at times, and his playboy past was somewhat lurid, but she felt certain that he did love her.

"Teddy, are you *sure* you're all right?" said Kristina over some static on the long-distance wire to Costa. It was the following day, and she still felt tired from the all-night lovemaking with Bret after his surprise proposal. But she couldn't forget Teddy Warner and her problems.

"No, I'm not sure. But I'm hanging in there," Teddy said. "I've given a press conference, and there are dozens of people to call ..." Her voice caught.

"I would be there if I could. Is there anything I can do? Anything? I just wish— It's so hard to know what to say.

I know I would be devastated if my father—if anything happened to Papa. . . .''

"I'm sure nothing will happen to him," said Teddy generously, catching the quiver in Kristina's voice.

"I've become engaged," Kristina said after a moment.

"What? Do you mean to Bret Thompson? Oh, Kristina, but that's wonderful!"

"Yes, it is. I *am* so happy. I know he isn't perfect, but—'' Kristina paused, struck by a sudden feeling of apprehension, as if her dream was too wonderful and might be unexpectedly snatched from her.

"But about eight million women think he *is* perfect," finished Teddy. "I'm so glad for you. Really."

Kristina's apprehensions seemed to melt away, and she began sharing the details with Teddy, telling her everything Bret had said and done.

"Teddy . . . I know we haven't seen a lot of each other, but I've always liked you. I wish we could be closer friends. Could we? I would love it so much."

Two days later, Kristina had her ring. The perfect twelve-carat solitaire of a rare, deep yellow glittered on her finger like sparks of captured sun.

"I want us to be happy," he whispered, kissing her over and over. "I'm going to do everything in my power to make you deliriously happy. This ring is only the beginning."

She flung her arms around him, whispering into the crevices of his neck. "Bret, I never thought that after Jean-Luc I'd ever really want anyone again."

"Well, now you have me. . . . Honey," he went on, "I do have to make just a short trip to Vegas. I have to meet with the operations V.P. for my restaurant chain and dream up a few new ways to make hamburgers. But I'll be back by Friday, and we can start making our plans. I want you to wear the most delectable white-lace dress with plenty of ribbons and furbelows and sequins, maybe long, white gloves, and a veil with flowers—something nice and elaborate—or whatever *you* want, baby," Bret added hastily.

"A honeymoon," Kristina sighed. "I'm really going to have one. Where shall we go, Bret?"

"Where do you want to go?"

"I've never been to the Far East. I think it would be so lovely there . . . cherry blossoms . . . Mount Fuji . . . the baths at Hakone."

"Then Japan it shall be. Darling, I'd do anything for you. Anything. I've always told you that, and it's the truth."

"My dear and charming princess," said Nikos Skouros, his voice thinned by the long-distance phone transmission. "I was hoping I could catch you. Thank God that I have."

"Why, Nickey," she said, swallowing, "is something wrong? This isn't about Papa, is it? Or Teddy's father?" She felt a sudden burst of fright.

"Dear Kristina, I don't know how to tell you this. I only wish it were not true."

Kristina's heart gave a terrible thump. "It isn't Papa! No! Nickey, tell me it isn't Papa. I can't stand it if Papa—"

"No, my darling girl, your father is fine, already doing some work in his office against his doctor's orders. I myself talked to him on the telephone only this morning. No, this is about another matter, Kristina, a matter of some delicacy. You see, it's about Bret Thompson."

"It's about Bret?" She shook her head. "What do you mean?"

Over the past two years, Nickey Skouros had made it clear that he disapproved of Bret and disliked him. He was obviously jealous of the other man, although he tried to hide it behind a facade of charm.

"My informant tells me that the man is not free to marry you."

"What?"

"He is already married, my dear. I'm so sorry," Nickey added, as Kristina gasped, clinging to the telephone.

"But it can't be. Who told you such a thing? Nickey, what informants are you talking about? Who told you such a lie?"

"It is not a lie, Kristina. When you first came to Hollywood, I had suspicions about Bret Thompson, so I hired a detective agency to investigate his background. For a long time we found nothing incriminating, but—"

"You what?" Kristina gasped. "You hired a detective to investigate Bret? How dare you invade my privacy, Nickey? And his? How dare you—"

The long-distance wire hummed as it carried Skouros's voice all the way from his private Greek island, Tílos. "Please, do not be upset. I was only doing it because I value my long friendship with you and your family. If we had found nothing, I would never have told you any of this. I would not have dreamed of upsetting you in such a manner. But the truth is that your Bret Thompson is—how do the Americans call it?—a very slippery guy."

"What do you *mean*, Nickey?" She was almost crying. "How can he be married? He's divorced! He has three little girls! He told me so himself. I'm wearing his r-ring, Nickey, a huge r-ring."

"He was divorced, my dear. That much is true. But on the day his divorce was final, he flew to Las Vegas and married a woman called Ronna Sue Drexel. She is one of the executives of his Hamburger Hacienda Corporation and a former *Playboy* model. He visits her perhaps once a month. She satisfies some rather kinky desires of his—acts that other women usually refuse to perform. She told my representative that he asked her to keep their marriage a secret because his fans would not like it. She agreed; after all, he supports her in very high style."

"A restaurant executive? *Playboy* model? Kinky?" Kristina felt nausea spill out of her stomach and up into her throat. "Nickey, we're engaged, we're holding a press conference today. I—"

"Do you wish me to take care of it?" Nickey softly inquired.

"What—what do you mean?"

"I can have the woman paid to keep silent. I'll go to Thompson and talk to him myself. I'll force him to divorce her. You can't afford any scandal, Princess Kristina. The tabloids—"

Hot tears had begun to flow down Kristina's cheeks. "Nickey, if he wants to be married to that woman, then let him be. I don't want any more embarrassment. I'll just break it off with him, quietly and finally. But why did you do it, Nickey? Why? You had no right to meddle in my life like that."

"Kristina, I'm your friend—" For once Nickey Skouros seemed to lose his equilibrium.

"Friendship is caring, Nickey! Friendship is allowing people their privacy! Friendship is not hiring some damned detective agency to spy on someone's lover! You were jealous, weren't you? Jealous of Bret. You didn't want him to have me. That's why you hired the detective."

"My darling Kristina, it's not as it seems—"

"It is!" she snapped. "And one more thing, Nickey. If you would do that to *me,* what else would you do . . . to other people?"

She slammed down the phone. Then, her body shaking, she sank into a chair. Bret was another Jean-Luc! *Mon Dieu!* If she'd married him . . .

Hanging up from his conversation with Kristina, Nikos Skouros frowned angrily. The bitch. She was so stupid . . . and so arrogant! If she were not also devastatingly beautiful . . .

He began thinking about his plans for Costa.

A huge hotel-casino called The Breakers would contain twelve hundred rooms as well as four hundred suites, in-

cluding twenty deluxe penthouse apartments. The entire
ground floor would be a Vegas-style casino. Next door
would be the first phase of his four-hundred-unit condo-
minium complex. Naturally, side businesses would spin off
from these: exclusive shops, gourmet restaurants, a cabaret,
a follies revue, and more. The type of tourists he wanted
to attract would patronize such establishments. He would
make billions!

All he needed were the authorizations, and these were
almost in his hands. *If* Prince Georges fulfilled his prom-
ises, and *if* Prince Henri ''cooperated'' by remaining pre-
occupied with his infirmities and other problems. If, if . . .
a dozen ifs, but Skouros felt sure that within the next eight
to ten months, he would be breaking ground on his new
casino.

His cellular phone rang, wakening him from his reverie.

''Yes?'' snapped Skouros. ''Yes, yes. . . .'' His voice
changed. ''Yes, I see. Then you must do as you see fit.
Now, today.''

He hung up, his heart beginning to pound faster.

The house in Malibu was perched on a promontory,
wedged on a narrow lot between two similar dwellings, all
three with a view of the beach and the shimmering blue
Pacific. A redwood deck wrapped around two sides of the
house, and a flight of wooden steps gave access to the
white, furrowed surf. It wasn't the biggest house in Malibu,
but it had been appraised at $5.5 million, and was one of
the most beautiful.

Omar Faid, the plump, aging Egyptian star who had
been on the *Olympia* at the same card table with Prince
Henri and Houston Warner, hurried out of his house, carrying a briefcase that contained some papers he wanted his
accountant to look over.

It was a warm, windy day, and Omar could hear the
crash and pound of the surf only a hundred feet away. He
lifted his head and sniffed the exhilarating salt tang as he

walked across the gravel driveway to the three-car garage where he had parked his newest car, a white 911 Porsche Targa.

He entered the garage through the side door, not noticing that it was already unlocked. The Porsche sat in its bay, its powerfully curved fenders gleaming with a deeply lacquered shine.

Faid fumbled for his keys and pulled open the driver's door, slid into the curved, high-back bucket seat, and turned the ignition on.

Light exploded in his face, inside his head, shattering his body and mind into fragments of blood, bone, and pain. The small, powerful bomb that had been wired to the Porsche's engine blew up in a display of pyrotechnics, pulverizing the car and its owner, and driving the fragments into the garage roof, which collapsed from the force of the explosion.

Prince Jac welcomed Teddy to the palace, offering his sympathies again, but he seemed guarded despite his cordial conversation. "Teddy, this is a difficult time for us, too, as I'm sure you can appreciate. My father's illness affects the entire country. You are welcome to stay here as long as you wish." He paused. "What is it, exactly, that you hope to find here?"

She flushed. It had been barely a week since Houston Warner died. While on the *Olympia,* back before her life had been shattered, she'd been terribly excited about the prospect of seeing Jac again, but now that all seemed a hundred years ago. Now all she could think of was her father.

"I don't know," she admitted honestly.

Jac frowned. "Do you think that someone in Costa is to blame for your father's death?"

"I don't know. I'm confused. I just know that I can hardly sleep or eat for thinking about him . . . and how he must have felt. I have nightmares, Jac. I wake up sweating, feeling as if I'm strangled for air.''

"His death was very strange," Jac remarked thoughtfully.

"*Why* did he die? It wasn't suicide, I *know* it wasn't. It seems as if I can't put him to rest until I find out.'' Her eyes had filled with sudden tears. "Your country is so beautiful, Jac, and I had such happy memories of it. Now this happened, and I—I—'' She broke down.

Jac put his arm around her, steadying her, the actions not those of the carefree boy she'd known five years ago, but of a young man beginning to take responsibility. "I want you to come to me with any information you find," he told her.

Teddy looked at him. Jac's blue eyes seemed darker than she remembered, and there were frown lines on his forehead now.

"I promise," she said.

Teddy settled into the Vendôme Palace. The place was so huge—it had over one hundred rooms—and its long maze of corridors wound around so much that she became lost again and again. Gabriella told her that art treasures and priceless furnishings, some of them centuries old, were occasionally rediscovered tucked away in some out-of-the-way corner, where they had been overlooked for many years.

Teddy racked her brain, trying to recall everything her father had ever said about Costa. Damn!—she should have paid more attention!

And once she'd thought they were being followed. But, of course, even if that was true, it probably had nothing to do with Costa, she assured herself. After all, her father had been the CEO of a large corporation, and maybe the man was her father's own security man, following them at a discreet distance to keep them safe. Or even a business rival, checking up on him.

She decided that she needed a plan. If Kristina was right,

and her father's death *did* have something to do with Costan politics, then she ought to talk to as many people as she could. She was anxious to receive the first report from the detective she had hired.

On her first morning in Costa, Teddy decided to go back to the quays and attempt to talk with some of the crew of the *Olympia,* which was kept permanently anchored out in the harbor of Port-Louis. But the harbormaster told her that she would not be permitted to board the ship without permission of Monsieur Skouros.

Teddy had noticed a small bistro located just off the quay nearest the yacht. Outside, empty half-barrels, shaded by umbrellas, had been set up to serve as tables. On impulse she went inside. The place was small and dark, with rough stone walls and wood beams. The large selection of wines leaned to the Loire Valley, and there were huge platters of cheese, ham, sausage, and bread.

She ordered wine and cheese and asked the young French waiter to tell her when any of the crew of the *Olympia* came in. To ensure his cooperation, she slipped him a $20 bill in Costan dollars.

Her patience was rewarded forty minutes later when two suntanned young men entered the bistro. One of them strolled over to her table and sat down. He wore a spotless white uniform decorated with gold trim.

"I am Jacques Millet; I am the steward aboard the *Olympia,*" he explained in accented English.

Teddy explained who she was and told him that she just wanted to know more about her father's death—any detail, no matter how small, that he might remember.

"But what is there to remember? We knew nothing. We merely heard he had gone—how you say?—overboard, and then there was the confusion, *un chahut.*" The word, Teddy vaguely remembered, meant racket or uproar.

She leaned forward desperately. "Maybe someone else saw something."

"*Non.*" The man shook his head.

Teddy thanked him, asking if he would tell the other man she wished to speak with him, too. But the second crewman—small, dark-haired Emmanuel Lefèvr—was just as vague.

"We have told everything we know to Monsieur Skouros, but no one saw anything. Your father had ordered a bottle of wine that night, and he was—how you say?—perhaps a bit plastered?"

"What! My father wasn't. He never drank more than one glass of wine at the most."

Lefèvre shrugged in the French manner. "Who knows? It is only what I heard. It is not the first time such a thing has happened."

"What! On board the *Olympia*?"

"Of course not, mademoiselle. But on other ships, surely, and there is your Bermuda Triangle, most interesting."

Frustrated, she waited another two hours for more crew members to show up, but none did. Finally she walked back up the cobblestoned street, uncertain what to do next. Was it true that the crew members knew nothing, or had they been instructed not to talk? If that was true, then they had undoubtedly been silenced by Nikos Skouros himself. After all, her father had disappeared on board his ship, and Nickey would surely wish to protect himself legally.

Perhaps Prince Jac would allow her to interview the Costan officials who had talked to the crew.

She walked slowly up the hill, passing a small beauty shop situated on the first floor of an old, timbered building with flowers growing in window boxes. Although it was small, she knew it was very posh, and its famous customers had included women like Melanie Griffith and Catherine Deneuve. Through the glass, she could see several stylists bent over customers in chairs.

Teddy paused. Beauty shops . . . gossip. The two were practically synonymous.

* * *

"Mademoiselle Teddee!" The elderly female shop owner came hurrying forward, having recognized Teddy. All the other heads in the shop were turning as well. "I am very honored. . . . We have just now had a cancellation, and so our most prestigious stylist is available to serve you— *Monsieur* Adrien Marivaux. He has often dressed Princess Kristina's hair at the palace. And Princess Gabriella as well. He is most expert."

Teddy looked at the short, slender man who came forward at the owner's request. About thirty, he had a dark mustache and bright, knowing eyes.

"Monsieur Adrien Marivaux will suit me perfectly," she said, smiling.

She decided to have a permanent, together with a cut and styling. The process would take several hours, giving her plenty of time to prod Marivaux for any information he might possess.

And within minutes, in response to her questions, he was talking volubly about Costa. Who was who, who had villas here, what celebrities had been seen partying on the beach, and more. She learned that David Letterman had just purchased a villa in Notra Patria, one of Costa's three cities.

"I suppose everyone is wondering who is going to be the next prince," she mentioned after half an hour or so.

"*Mais oui,* without question. We are all so concerned," Marivaux told her. "But, *naturellement,* it will be Prince Jac. Who else? He does not want to rule—that is why he does crazy things, his car racing, his danger, eh? He wishes to tempt fate. But he will settle down, yes? He is still young . . . and besides, it is his destiny."

Teddy felt a red flush steal over her face, and for a moment she was silent, thinking of Jac and his destiny! Ruling Costa would be like running a conglomerate corporation, but with permanent, lifetime obligations and much more glamour. Teddy wondered if she would ever be part of Costa's future, then felt a dash of panic as she was called back from her thoughts by Marivaux's chattering.

The talkative *coiffeur* had finished putting Teddy's hair in gray and pink rollers and now was adding the perm solution.

"You must hear a lot of rumors around here," she said to him. "I mean, you probably know just about everything, right?"

Flattered, he smiled affably and nodded.

"I know you've heard about the man who fell overboard on Nikos Skouros's yacht . . . my father. Have you heard any talk about it? Any gossip of any kind? I need information. Anything I can find."

"Ah." The busy hands stopped pouring the solution. "Teddee, I *have* heard a whisper." The man lowered his voice. "Some say that Houston Warner was pushed. Of course, it is only talk. . . ."

"Pushed!" She'd known—suspected—but now here was someone confirming her own suspicions.

"*Oui, mademoiselle.* One of our other stylists does the hair of Alexis Belcouri—she is housekeeper on board the *Olympia.* I overhear her talk. She says she opens a housekeeping cupboard and gets a big surprise. She finds contraband explosives in there. So just then the purser finds her and questions her, and she is afraid, so she tells lie and says she does not know what the materials are."

Teddy stared at the coiffeur. *"Are you sure?"*

The hairdresser shrugged. "But then, why was she suddenly transferred to Skouros's private island in Greece? Poof!" He made a gesture. "One day she is in here, getting her hair frosted. The next . . . she is gone. Away. In Greece. Where she cannot talk."

Two days later Teddy received her first report from Frédéric LaMarché, the detective.

"Whatever happened, the trail has been thoroughly sanitized," LaMarché said. "But, Mademoiselle Warner, there is something else I must tell you."

"Yes?"

"I have been retracing your father's day on board the *Olympia,* and it is the bridge game that I find most interesting. His partner was Prince Henri, and his opponents were Nikos Skouros and Omar Faid."

"Yes, I walked by their table and saw them. But why do you find it interesting?"

"Because Omar Faid was found dead last week, mademoiselle. Someone blew him up with a car bomb out in Malibu."

"What!"

"It was on the AP wire-service news. I phoned California and talked to the Malibu police. They say it was definitely a professional hit. The assassin used a small bomb combined with plastique, an illegal explosive, extremely powerful, that was ignited by either the car's engine or radio waves from a distance. Terrorists use it all the time."

"B-but," she stammered, "who would have done this? And why?"

The detective shook his head. "It makes perfect sense to the person who wanted Faid killed. Think about this for a moment, mademoiselle. There were four men at that bridge table. Now two of them are dead."

Teddy was shaken and frightened. "But my father hadn't met Faid before that night, I'm almost sure."

She told LaMarché what the *coiffeur* had said, and he agreed to try to contact Alexis Belcouri in Greece. "But don't expect much. Skouros owns an entire island there, much like Aristotle Onassis did. Those who live there, even the servants, are isolated from the rest of the world."

"How medieval," said Teddy.

The detective nodded. "Mademoiselle Warner, there is something you must understand about Costa. It *is* exactly that—medieval in some very important ways. For instance, the throne. You live in America, where they elect their officials, but here rulers inherit the job, and the Bellini fortune is a huge one for a small principality—more than several billion if you count the antiques, paintings, and the huge collection of crown jewels. And there's a total family allowance of over seventy-five million Costan dollars yearly."

"I . . . I see."

"That could make for some nasty rivalry, and there *is* someone in Costa who would be extremely happy to become the ruler, who has been slavering for the opportunity, and rumors say that he is now mixed up with some very powerful bedfellows."

Teddy frowned. "Who is this?"

"It's Prince Georges—Henri's younger brother. Please don't discount him. He is sixty years old but very vigorous, and he has resented his older brother since childhood. I have been talking to some of his servants at Royal House. They tell me Georges has had several clandestine meetings with Nikos Skouros."

"Nickey?" Always, it seemed, it came back to Nickey.

But then the detective shrugged. "I don't have anything more definite, but when I do, I'll tell you. I'm not sure just how this would fit in with your father's death anyway. Any small country is full of politics. And there is still a strong probability that the two deaths are only coincidence. That your father was perhaps despondent—"

"No," Teddy said. "Never."

She knew she had to tell Jac what she had learned. But when she dialed the private number that Jac had given her, his secretary told her that the prince was out. Teddy sat staring at the telephone and finally went downstairs, finding her way to the secluded gardens of the palace.

Strolling in the beautiful formal gardens, she felt her distress mount. *Had her father been murdered?* She stopped by a splashing fountain and stared into the bubbling depths of the water. *Daddy,* she whispered, *I'm going to find exactly how you died. And I don't care what I have to do.*

Walking in the gardens, she suddenly had an idea. She decided to phone LaMarché. . . .

That evening Teddy dressed for dinner, putting on a simple blue cocktail dress for the royal family's formal meal in the Gold Dining Room. She hurried to the dining room early, hoping to encounter Jac before the rest of the family and guests arrived.

She was rewarded when she passed a sumptuous room and through the open doorway saw the young prince seated inside, speaking on the telephone. Teddy knocked on the open entrance.

Jac waved to her, finished his conversation with a few short words, then greeted her with a smile. "Teddy, you look wonderful tonight. Blue complements you."

"Jac, I— May I speak to you for a few minutes?"

"Of course." Jac rose and walked behind her to close the door. Teddy hesitated, looking around.

"Sit down," Jac invited. "This is the Small Library. It used to be my grandfather's favorite. Do you see his pipe collection on the wall? But you seem nervous, Teddy. Is there anything wrong?"

Teddy sank into a red brocade chair. "Yes. I think so— but I'm not quite sure! I've heard the most awful things. I'm so upset."

Jac pulled up another chair and sat down beside her. "Then you must tell me everything, Teddy, because I too have had a feeling . . ."

Teddy told Jac everything she knew, all the gossip and rumors she had heard, the way her father had collected information on Costa for the past five years, even the way the crew of the *Olympia* had been disturbingly vague, refusing to talk. When she told him about Faid, the young prince seemed horror-struck.

"Omar, dead?" He gazed into the distance, his eyes moistening. "He once gave me a pony, did you know that?

I was four, and I rode him until I grew too big. I knew it . . . I knew something was wrong. I have been suspicious of Nikos Skouros for years, but I have never had any proof to back up my suspicions. When I tried to talk to my father about it, he became angry. In his view Nikos has rescued our country from financial disaster, and my father even thinks he would make a wonderful husband for Kristina.''

"But it seems so strange to think that Nikos . . ." Teddy wasn't shocked, but she found it hard to imagine the handsome, charming Greek involved in anything so sordid as murder.

Jac's expression hardened. "I know he wants to control too much of this country, that he has been trying to buy up huge amounts of property here, but I have no proof of any wrongdoing."

Teddy sighed. "I see. . . . And a few bits of gossip don't prove anything—I've watched enough TV detective shows to know that! Jac, I *know* my father didn't have an accident. More strongly than ever, I feel that his death was deliberate. But I've got to think about leaving Costa by next week—I have to start practicing for the U.S. Open again. Daddy wouldn't have wanted me to miss it."

"Teddy, I'm going to start my own investigation! We'll start by taking new written statements from the crewmen on the *Olympia*, and if you don't mind, I'll send Frédéric LaMarché to California to investigate Omar Faid's death."

Teddy felt herself wilt with relief. She knew she did not have the authority to question the crewmen on board the *Olympia*, nor was she equipped to deal with the intricacies of the Costan power structure, but Jac was. She started to tell Jac what she *did* intend to do, then changed her mind. He might try to stop her. "And I'll continue asking questions too," she finished.

"We'll work together," Jac said.

They looked at each other. Electricity seemed almost to leap between them, causing Teddy's heart to jump into her throat. She noticed for the first time that Jac's blue eyes had brownish rays in the irises, and they signaled a soft, gentle strength. Flushing, she remembered the time they had made love in the boat, five years ago. She could still feel the sun hot on her bare skin and hear Jac's groan of passion as he pulled her on top of him. His body was so beautiful, his arms so wiry and strong. . . .

"Teddy? Is anything wrong?"

"No, nothing."

They couldn't seem to stop looking at each other.

"Are you sure? I've been worried about you."

"Please . . . don't worry about me." She turned away from him.

The magnificent dining room contained priceless treasures, including a pair of solid gold candlesticks. There were six seated at the long table: Teddy, Gabriella, Jac, and Anatole Breton, Henri's chief advisor, and his elderly wife Eugénie. Prince Henri, who had aged considerably since his heart attack, had been brought to the dining room in a wheelchair, and presided at the head of the table, pale but composed.

Jac was scheduled to race the following week in Buenos Aires, and the table was alive with debate about the Formula One racing circuit. "My new car makes me a top contender," Jac insisted. "If the engine performs to specifications—"

"Enough," snapped the old prince. "Must we talk of a death wish at the dinner table?"

Jac shook his head. "We were talking about Formula One racing, not death."

"I do not wish to discuss it any further."

"Racing can be extremely safe," cried Jac. "It's only a matter of reflexes and timing and the best engine—"

"Enough," thundered Henri. He turned to speak to Teddy, his angry expression instantly vanishing. "Teddy, what tournament will you play in next?" inquired the prince politely.

"The U.S. Open in September," she explained, embarrassed for Jac and eager to smooth over the violent emotions she'd sensed in the room.

During the rest of the meal, Jac sat glowering, and he responded to conversation only when directly addressed. As soon as the meal was over, the young prince excused himself and stalked out of the dining room, and he did not appear in the library for coffee with the others.

There, Princess Gabriella came up to Teddy, radiant in deep apricot, the huge engagement ring that Cliff Ferguson had given her sparkling under the light of the room's crystal chandeliers.

"Do you ever get to Texas?" she inquired. "If you do, please visit us at Cliff's ranch. Nearly every month when he is in town, he gives an enormous barbecue. Cliff has bought me a Stetson hat to wear at Jacaranda and a wonderful pair of snakeskin boots, too."

"I love the western look," said Teddy.

"I only wish I could wear western gear more often, but it wouldn't do in Costa, I'm afraid. By the way, I'll be in New York again in September. I'm meeting with Kenny Lane, and also going to a publishing party. Betty Prashker at Crown has approached me with an idea for a book. And we'll announce the project at the party. You're invited, Teddy, if you're going to be in New York."

Finally Gaby drew her into an alcove, and they sat down on facing chairs, their talk becoming more intimate.

"You met Cliff Ferguson that time in New York, didn't you?" Gaby began in a low voice. "What did you think of him, Teddy?"

"Why, I thought he was extremely nice," Teddy said, guessing where the conversation was leading.

"He is. Very nice," said Gaby, biting her lip. "And I'm so excited about marrying him. But sometimes—sometimes I'm afraid, too. He is so typically American."

Teddy couldn't help smiling. "He is, isn't he? But don't you think that's part of his charm?"

"Teddy, I haven't had anyone to talk to about this. My friends here in Costa were shocked that I would consider marrying a Texan. Even Marie-Paule, my press secretary, was surprised. To them, he seems rough-hewn. They were all horrified when I told them he wants me to live at least six months of the year in Texas."

Teddy nodded. She'd already seen the blaring headlines in the European tabloids: *Princess Gaby to Become Texas Cowgirl?*

"Do you *want* to live in Texas?" Teddy said.

Gaby nodded. "Yes, I think I really do. I love the privacy of the ranch—it's wonderful! I can walk free for miles, and there is a pretty little lake where I—where Cliff and I . . ." She blushed. "Teddy, perhaps you aren't aware of just how public my life has always been. Until I left Costa, I was constantly surrounded by servants and bodyguards. I never realized how refreshing it could be to go for a walk by myself, to gallop a horse in the wind."

"You ride?"

"Oh, yes, I've always ridden, but now I do it Western style. I even roped a calf a few weeks ago. It was quite amazing." Gaby seemed proud of her accomplishment. Then she grew serious again. "But my father is pushing for me to spend much more than half of the year in Costa. I sense he is thinking of something else, something that worries me deeply. He is going to abdicate soon!"

Teddy drew in her breath.

"Jac hasn't said whether he would like to rule. He is too wrapped up in his racing. That's why Papa is so angry with him. And Kristina is solidly committed to Hollywood now. Which leaves me."

"You?"

Gaby reached out both hands and clutched Teddy's, squeezing her fingers. "I don't want to rule Costa! *Mon Dieu!* I can't! Cliff isn't a European man. He has his department stores, and he adores his ranch. He would never consent to living here, and besides, there has always been a small group here who don't like me. I don't want to sacrifice my life for Costa. . . . Is it wrong for me to think that way? But it's the way I feel. I love my country, but I want a life for myself, too.''

Later that night Teddy felt restless. At midnight her call from LaMarché came through. He had been out earlier in the day, and she had been unable to reach him.

"I want to go on board the *Olympia*," she told the detective.

"Now, Mademoiselle Warner, that's my job," he told her. "Unfortunately, Skouros runs tight security and—"

"I think I know how I can get past security. I'll just phone up that male secretary of his and tell him that I have misplaced some of my tennis things on board the *Olympia*—a racquet, warmup gear, and several pieces of jewelry. On the night my father died I was so distraught I couldn't remember exactly where I put them, but if I could go back to my room, I might remember. I'm sure they will let me back on board.''

"Even if you do get on board, they will watch you like a hawk—especially if they have something to hide.''

"I have to try," she insisted. "I want you to tell me what explosives look like and what signs to look for.''

LaMarché hesitated, then sighed. "Very well, mademoiselle, I certainly can't stop you, but I want you to remember one thing: You are not to attract their attention by doing *anything* unusual or suspicious, do you hear me? This isn't 'I Spy.' If you behave like someone confused and still slightly distraught, you'll probably be all right.''

After hanging up, Teddy sat up late reading. It was past 2:30 A.M. when she finally decided that she'd like something to eat. Feeling adventurous, she put on jeans and a T-shirt and a pair of Reeboks, and plaited her newly permed hair into a thick blond braid down her back. Then she left her room to find the kitchen, making her way down the long corridors.

She heard the trill of a telephone, the sound making her jump.

"Aha," said Jac, stepping out of a room she recognized as the Small Library. "You were spotted on the closed circuit TV, Teddy. The security guard just telephoned me."

"Oh . . ." She uttered a nervous giggle. "Well, I wasn't up to much mischief. I was just going to stage a commando raid on the kitchen. But if you think I shouldn't . . . ?"

"No, I'll join you," said Jac. "You'll need help finding the kitchen."

They descended a staircase, walked down more hallways, finally pushing open an unmarked, solid wood door. Jac began switching on lights, revealing a huge room lined with granite-topped counters, equipped with Gaggenau appliances, including two huge walk-in freezers.

As Teddy gasped, Jac laughed at her reaction. "We prepare state dinners for as many as two hundred fifty people here, Teddy. My father's first act when he took over as prince was to modernize the kitchen." Then a sudden thought made Jac frown. "Let's see what snacks are available," he said after a moment.

They walked into one of the freezers, a large room lined with plastic mesh shelves, on which had been arranged hundreds of food items, everything from frozen sorbets to prime beefsteaks.

"What looks good to you, Teddy?"

She searched on the shelves, but didn't find anything that appealed to her.

"How about if I make you an omelette?" suggested Jac.

She laughed. "You can cook?"

"When I was a small boy, I used to wander in here, and one of the cooks took me under her wing and allowed me to assist her. I was her favorite. Do you wish cheese? Fresh mushrooms? Perhaps some onion and garlic?" Jac left the freezer and began to investigate the contents of a huge refrigerator. "And there are fresh *escargots,* I see."

"Mushrooms and cheese will be wonderful," said Teddy.

The omelette was slightly soft, prepared in the French fashion, and to Teddy it tasted perfect, and even more perfect was the way that Jac served her, pouring them glasses of chilled white chardonnay wine.

"For you, mademoiselle," he jested, finding a chef's hat and clowning around as he put it on.

As they ate hungrily, Jac began to talk about his racing. "You have no idea how it feels to drive an automobile faster than any other person alive—and even beyond that. One feels alive, a part of the hot metal and pulsating engine . . . even part of the wind itself." Jac sighed. "It is the most exciting feeling in the world, and I will confess something to you, Teddy. It is addictive, too."

"Addictive?"

"Some men, once they have experienced it, cannot easily give it up. Racing is . . . like cocaine. It feeds something in them. I am afraid I am that sort of man. It is most inconvenient. My father senses it too, which is why he is so angry at me."

"But what about your being prince? Ruling Costa del Mar?" Teddy dared to say.

Jac's eyes flashed, and he stopped eating, pushing away his plate. "I will probably rule. One day. But not now! I am not ready. It seems like a walled fortress to me, Teddy, a fortress I can't enter yet."

She persisted. "But won't you *have* to? I mean—"

They were suddenly interrupted by a member of the kitchen staff arriving to begin preparation for breakfast.

Teddy gasped, looking at her watch. "Jac, it's nearly six. I have to go and practice in one hour!"

"I will walk you to your room."

This time, as they walked through the long corridors they encountered several sleepy-looking maids, who glanced discreetly away as they passed. Jac did not take her hand or touch her, but Teddy was electrically aware that she was walking through the palace at this early hour of the morning with Prince Jac.

"Teddy," Jac suddenly said, stopping. "Do you think I am wrong to keep on racing?"

Teddy hesitated. She knew her reply would affect the way Jac felt about her. If she said the wrong thing, he would be upset with her, perhaps even drop her friendship.

"We each do what we must," she replied briefly.

Jac nodded. Apparently she had said the right thing. They had reached the door of her bedroom, and Jac put a hand on the doorknob, then looked into her eyes, giving her another of those long, searching looks.

"Teddy," he whispered.

Her heart caught.

"Teddy, Theodora, you are so beautiful. I've never forgotten you."

"I thought you had." Her words were barely a whisper. "You never called."

"No, *you* never returned my call. I left a message with your father, and—"

They looked at each other, and Teddy felt a tiny rush of anger at her father for keeping the message from her.

"I was wrong, wasn't I?" said Jac. "I should have called again. But, Teddy, we were both so young, and our closeness frightened me. I didn't know how to deal with it, and I think I just wanted to play. I was not good for you at that time."

Teddy's laugh was strangled by a flood of conflicting emotions. "No, you were *not* good for me. That's the major understatement of the twentieth century! But, Jac, how do I know you are any better for me now? I'm not—that is, I can't ..." She was floundering. "I couldn't be just your lover anymore, someone you just play with. Not this time."

He gazed into her eyes for a long, long time.

"I'm not going to be anyone's toy," she blurted. "Not even a prince's."

Jac touched her cheek with his fingertip. "Teddy, did I ask you to be my toy? I confess I have had my share of lovers. Anyone who reads the tabloids knows I have not been exactly a recluse. But this time . . . this time it's different."

He leaned forward and gave her a gentle kiss on her lips, a kiss so soft she felt it as an exquisite caress, sweetened by his breath. "I know you are going back to New York soon, but may I call you there? And not just to discuss your father or our investigation."

"Yes," she whispered.

Jac kissed her again and left, telling her he was leaving for Buenos Aires later in the day, and first he needed to do some office work and make some telephone calls to make sure his racing car had arrived safely in Argentina.

Teddy went into her bedroom, closing its door behind her. Brilliant Costan sunlight was streaming through her partially opened drapes. She raced into the center of the room, wanting to burst with happiness. Jac really cared about her! He wanted to see her!

The bay was choppy, waves pounding the hull of the launch that had been sent from the *Olympia* to pick Teddy up. She sat in the stern, wind whipping at her hair, which she had tied back with a head scarf. She was nervous, but assured herself she would be perfectly safe. After all, Nikos Skouros wasn't even in Costa.

When she reached the *Olympia,* a hydraulic cage was lowered alongside the yacht to pick her up.

"Miss Warner, I see you arrive right on time."

The purser was waiting for her on a lower deck, a man more than six foot three, with jet-black hair, a bulky body, and heavy muscles. The glowering scowl on his face made her think of a gangster. A name tag pinned to his white uniform said his name was Stavros Papadopoulos.

"Yes, I have to fly back to New York in a few days, and I just realized that I must have left several items some-

where in my room. One of them was a small pin that had
great sentimental value.''

Dark eyes glittered at her, and she hastily added, ''I was
so upset when my father . . . I just couldn't think. I'm sure
that no crew member would have taken them, of course,
but I have a habit of putting things in odd crannies. I can
be silly that way.''

He nodded and began escorting her through the ship to
the upper deck where her quarters had been. Before, when
the royals had been aboard, the ship had bustled with life.
Now, it seemed almost deserted, with only a few crew
members on board. In his ear the purser wore a headset,
which occasionally burst out with bits of static. The ship
was so big, she surmised, that this was the best way for the
crew to keep in touch with him.

As they walked along, she saw dozens of storage areas
marked *Staff Only.* Which one should she look in? Teddy's
heart sank. For the first time she realized just how foolish
her trip here was. Even if Papadopoulous were to leave her
alone, which seemed unlikely, how would she know where
to pry?

While the purser stood in the doorway, arms crossed in
front of his chest, Teddy made a show of searching the
room she'd been given before. She had come prepared with
a small tennis pin, which she pretended to ''find'' in a
potted plant.

''Ah! This means so much to me! I won this at my first
U.S. Open!'' she cried, but Papadopoulos was already
speaking into the headset in Greek.

He scowled with annoyance, then bowed to her and told
her, ''Minor engine problem. I must go below for a few
minutes. The room your father used is two doors down.
Why don't you look around there, too, and I'll send a steward to assist you.''

Teddy nodded, and the purser left. The moment he had
disappeared behind a corner, she ran into the hallway, hop-

ing she might have time to inspect the *Staff Only* areas before Papadopoulos's replacement arrived.

Five minutes later she was staring into the depths of a housekeeping cupboard that contained large shelves piled with expensive Porthault and Laura Ashley linens, scented British soaps, and boxes of chocolates to be put on guests' pillows. But there was a large empty space on one of the shelves, as if something had been removed.

Glancing down at the floor, Teddy saw a small scrap of wire and a bit of red-and-black paper. She bent down and picked up both objects. The piece of paper, slightly oily in texture, had three letters on it: IQU. Teddy frowned. When she was young, her father had insisted she work the *New York Times* crossword puzzle. Could the IQU possibly belong to the word *plastique*?

"Miss Warner, what are you doing here?" came a voice behind her.

Teddy jumped, her heart knocking violently. She turned, to see the purser standing there. Instinctively she closed her fist around the scrap of wire and the bit of paper.

"I thought my tennis racquet might have been put in this closet. The housekeeper told me they keep spare racquets on board, and I thought mine might have gotten mixed up with the others. It's extremely expensive. It was made just for me, and it's irreplaceable."

"You were not given permission to look."

"Hey, I'm sorry, that steward you said was going to come and help me never showed up," she said, smiling her prettiest smile. "I can't help that, can I?"

"Mr. Skouros does not like people on board his ship when he is not here, especially those who seem to be extremely inquisitive. You come to *my* office. *I* ask you questions, and you give me straight answers this time. Maybe we keep you here for a while and wait for Mr. Skouros to return from New York."

Teddy felt a spurt of real panic. *Keep her prisoner here?* That's what it sounded like!

"No," she cried, "I won't! As a matter of fact, if I'm not back at the palace in half an hour, the police will know where to search for me."

By the time she was stepping into the launch again, Teddy felt weak with a release of tension. She'd gotten away with it, and even better, she had the wire and the scrap of paper buried deep in her pocket.

"What is this piece of paper from?" she said later that evening to LaMarché, who had agreed to meet her for a glass of wine at a small hotel near the boardwalk.

The detective studied it, then looked up at her. "It appears to be from a plastique wrapper. The stuff is made all over the world, but this could come from Israel. It's what the military uses to bomb bridges and other installations. Terrorists find uses for it, too. It's highly illegal to have it in your possession."

Teddy could feel the blood drain from her face as her fears were confirmed. "And that bit of wire?"

"From a bomb, perhaps. Or simply from some shipboard appliance, who knows? I can trace this piece of paper, though, find out where it was purchased, maybe even who bought it." The detective looked worried. "Mademoiselle, you got on the ship and you got off again. You were tremendously lucky, but don't push your luck again."

She drew in her breath. "I'm going to have to phone Prince Jac."

Buenos Aires, overlooking the blue bay called the Rio de la Plata, is frequently labeled the Paris of South America.

Prince Jac was staying in a hotel near the Plaza de Mayo, in the center of the city, where a number of offices and government buildings were located.

He hung on to the telephone, straining to hear over a

bad connection. "Teddy? Is that you?"

"Yes . . . Nikos Skouros . . . on board his ship . . ."

"Stop, stop—the connection is very poor. Shall I phone you back?"

". . . plastic explosives," he thought he heard her say.

Swiftly he hung up and dialed the palace switchboard, asking to be put through to Teddy.

When they were reconnected, she told him what had happened on board the *Olympia*. Jac let out his breath in a long sigh. "Teddy, I want you to promise me you will do nothing further—*nothing!*—until I come back."

"But we're so close now! I feel it, Jac! I want to go and talk to Nickey Skouros. I want to ask him—"

"No," Jac practically shouted.

A small silence hummed over the wire, and he knew that he had hurt Teddy's feelings. "For God's sake," he went on in a lower voice, "Teddy, you must realize that finding explosives, or evidence of explosives, on board Nickey's yacht is still not solid proof of his implication in your father's death. It is only one piece of evidence, and it needs corroboration from other sources. I know you're eager to know more, but I have to be very careful about making accusations, especially when it concerns such a close friend of my family as Nikos Skouros. I need to find out more. I'll talk to you at the palace in a few days."

He could tell how disappointed she was. "All right," she said.

"Teddy," he pleaded, "please don't be hurt. You did wonderfully. I'm so proud of you. You were very brave."

"I don't care about being brave. I want to *know,*" she cried.

"And we will know, I promise you. I'll be back as soon as the race is over. Just stay away from Nickey Skouros," Jac pleaded. "Teddy, I . . . I don't want you to get hurt."

The practice track, located outside the city near the town of San Isidro, was dusty and noisy, and smelled deliciously of barbecuing meat. Several dozen vans and trailers were parked near its pit area, which was serviced by gangs of locals hawking everything from Coca-Cola to *parrillas,* the Argentinean national delicacy, a mixed grill of prime steak bits, chicken, small sausages, lamb, and pork slices, all tantalizingly grilled by colorfully dressed gaucho chefs.

Prince Jac, clad in a red coverall sewn with the Skouros Shipping logo, strode toward the pits, where his sleek, low-slung racing car waited. It was on blocks. He was angry; the car had been damaged in shipping, and now he had to send for an engineer from the manufacturer to fly down and supervise the repairs.

Several cars were whizzing around the track, blurs of color as they sped past.

Jac watched them, shading his eyes, impatient at being sidelined and eager for action. It would be at least a day before his own car was fixed, and he didn't want to lose his edge. Furthermore, his conversation with Teddy had alarmed him. Nickey Skouros! Not that Jac believed Nickey would directly participate in anything of a questionable nature, but he certainly had plenty of employees. . . .

When another of the Skouros cars pulled in, a Ferrari driven by Paul Belmondo, the actor's son, who had shown talent on the track, Jac started toward him.

"I need to warm up, do some laps," he said.

Belmondo nodded. Everyone on the Skouros team catered to Jac, whose royal status was bringing them much publicity.

Within minutes Jac was strapped into the car, wearing his crash helmet, suit, and gloves. Joining several other cars, he lapped the track, sun glaring into his eyes as he completed loop after loop. He passed Stefano Modena's Yamaha V-12, then Gerhard Berger's McLaren-Honda, clipping out around them; first 110, then 120, and now he pressed for 130 m.p.h. on the circular track. Jac clenched the steering wheel, laughing as he began to experience his usual racing "high."

This was living—this was being fully, totally alive!

Then another car, a red-and-white McLaren chassis, edged aggressively up his left side. He hadn't seen it in his mirror until it was almost on him; it must have entered the track only a few minutes before. It immediately began challenging him, pushing closer to his fender.

Jac pressed down hard on the accelerator, swerving his own low-slung vehicle out.

He felt the shuddering sensation as metal tapped metal. His car spun out of control, careening toward the sandbags that lined the track.

He hit them with such violence that his car shot over them, flipping twice, then slamming onto its side. He was vaguely aware of the impact; then he slid into unconsciousness.

"Prince Jac! Your Highness!" Jac heard voices, smelled something so sharp and repugnant that he twisted his head away from it.

He opened his eyes. He had been pulled out of the car and was lying in the dirt. Belmondo, Berger, and six or seven mechanics were crowded anxiously around him, and a doctor bent over him, waving smelling salts under his nose.

"I'm all right," Jac said sharply. He shoved the salts away and sat up.

"Your Highness, you must not move too quickly. You have a concussion. You have been unconscious for more than five minutes."

"I'm fine," snapped Jac, fighting dizziness and nausea as he got to his feet.

He walked over to a set of wooden bleachers and sank onto one of the seats, staring incredulously across the track. The car he had been driving was nothing more than a twisted pile of chrome and metal. Black smoke churned up from it, staining the blue sky.

Staring at the sight, Jac felt his stomach squeeze hard.

He must have been pulled out of the car just before it went up in flames.

Thinking of all the burned children he had helped, their facial and body scars, their agony as tissue was debrided and their dressings were changed, he shuddered.

Beads of perspiration broke out on his forehead as he buried his face in his hands and wept with relief.

The summer spent in Costa del Mar hadn't yielded any new information about her father's death.

Teddy was back at the U.S. Open, but now everything seemed totally different. For one thing, there was Jac, back in South America for another sanctioned race in São Paulo, Brazil. *"Teddy, I . . . I don't want you to get hurt."* In her mind she replayed their few encounters and their past conversations over and over again, reliving each touch, each kiss, each word.

She floated on a dreamy haze, unable to stop fantasizing as her thoughts took wing. Jac had told her that he worried about her. So that meant he was serious . . . didn't it?

Maybe he would ask her to marry him! Or did he think that they would have only an extended love affair?

Her heart hammering in her throat, Teddy tried to bring herself back to reality, but found the fantasies kept tantalizing her. She waited impatiently for Jac to phone her again, leaving messages at her hotel desk, exhorting the staff to be *sure* to transmit any phone messages to her immediately.

Then Jac called. He wanted to know what she had been doing and she told him, truthfully, that she'd been practicing her tennis and doing a lot of swimming and shopping. She was behaving.

"Good," he said.

But then there was one of those awkward pauses when two people want to say more but don't know quite how to begin. Teddy found herself asking lamely about the weather.

"Cool but sunny. The sky is incredibly blue." He went on about the car's most recent engine problems, sounding much more like a race driver than a prince. He added that he'd had another slight injury. "Nothing serious, I haven't thought twice about it, even though the press wrote about it for days."

Teddy had read about Jac's bruised shoulder in the tabloids. She clung to the phone, thrilled that he'd called, but disappointed, too.

"Good luck at the Open," he finally said, telling her he had to go. A group of them were going to visit Ca D'Oro, one of the famed restaurants of São Paulo. Afterward they were going to a disco club for South American salsa music.

"I'll be thinking about you, praying for your good luck," Teddy said, wondering what sort of girls would be at the club, and if Jac would find them attractive.

"I'll be thinking about you, too," he said, and seemed about to say more.

But then she heard voices on the other end, and Jac hastily said good-bye. He promised to phone her again after the race, which would be in another three days, assuming his car's engine was fixed by then.

Bemused, Teddy hung up. She'd hoped for a closer, more intimate conversation, but there had been others in Jac's room. Of course, she remembered, he traveled with an entourage. How naive she was! She still had so much to learn about the royals. Would she have a chance to learn, or was she only deluding herself?

That night she lay awake until almost dawn.

She easily breezed through the quarterfinals and the semifinals, but when the semis were over, a sense of loss settled over her.

Daddy, she thought, *I won! But it wasn't the same without you.*

Sitting in her hotel room, freshly showered, her damp hair curling in tendrils, Teddy felt a fresh wave of grief.

She realized that there were really very few people on this earth that she cared deeply about. She had hundreds of tennis acquaintances, but she'd never formed any deep friendships except with Jamaica.

She suddenly longed to talk to Jac. She could call him . . . but she decided not to. She didn't want to class herself with the other women who chased him.

Which left only Jamaica. Teddy fumbled in her purse for her small address book, riffling through it until she located Jamaica's phone number at the apartment in Ann Arbor that she shared with two other girls. Jamaica was now a first-year law student at the University of Michigan.

"Teddy!" cried Jamaica into the phone. "How did the semis go? And what about Costa? Did you find out anything? And, my God, how are you doing since your father . . . ? I mean I'm so glad to hear from you I can't even think straight."

"I'm okay, Jamie. Actually I didn't find out much, nothing that's solid, anyway." Jamaica had probably read about Faid's death in the papers, but she didn't want her friend to worry.

She told Jamaica something of her visit.

"You stayed in the *palace*?" Jamaica squealed.

"Yes. . . . As a matter of fact, I do have something to tell you, though. Something exciting. *Really* exciting!"

"Like what?"

"Like I've fallen in love—I think."

"Mmmm . . . who with?"

Teddy's laugh went high with nervousness. "You're not going to believe this."

"Teddy, it's not who I think it is? It's not *him*? Prince Jac?"

"Don't tell a soul, Jamie. Please promise me you won't. He doesn't even know I love him, and it's all so new yet. I *think* he cares about me, too, but I'm not certain, and he's in Brazil right now and—Oh, God, Jamaica! All these years I've thought about him. I've had a crush on him from the first time I met him. And he says the same about me, too!''

"Teddy," said Jamaica warningly. "Earth to Teddy. Earth to Teddy. Come on down off your cloud.''

Teddy laughed. She knew she was on an enormous high of adrenaline. "I know it sounds fantastic and unbelievable, but I swear to you that he told me he cares about me. He's so handsome, Jamaica! You know that old saying about you have to kiss a hundred frogs before you find your prince? Well, I haven't kissed a hundred of them, but I've kissed a few, and I finally got lucky.''

"Teddy, listen to yourself," Jamaica said, emphasizing her words. "What exactly happened between yourself and Jac? Did he ask you to marry him?''

"No. . . .''

"Teddy, we've all read those magazine articles about Prince Jac. Didn't *Cosmopolitan* call him Europe's Most Eligible Hunk, or something like that? He's dated dozens of women . . . models, countesses, that British lady—the whole royal-stud thing. Worse than Prince Andrew before he married Fergie. What does he say to them? Does he make them think that he's seriously interested in them, too?''

Hurt, Teddy was silent for a moment. "Jamie—''

"I don't mean to burst your bubble, but, honey, you have to face facts. Prince Jac might be wonderful and all that, but he runs on a pretty fast track. Why should he settle down now? He'd be a fool to. Besides," Jamaica added, "how will you see him? He's traveling all over the world racing, or else he's in Costa, and you're on the tennis circuit.''

Teddy held on to the phone, suddenly irritated at her friend warring with her over Jac. Yes, Jamaica *had* burst her bubble.

"Oh, Teddy, you're not mad at me for saying those things, are you?" Jamaica queried.

"No, of course not.''

"I only want what's best for you, Ted. Why don't you

try to visit me some weekend in Ann Arbor? There're tons
of gorgeous Michigan men here, lots of grad students, doctors, and assistant professors, and I know quite a few of
them. I'm sure they'd love to meet you.''

"All right," Teddy agreed reluctantly, then changed the
subject and told Jamaica about the Open and the gossip
over some players Jamie had known in her tennis days.

She ordered room service, then sat watching TV while
she ate, suddenly in a despondent mood. Jamaica had implied that Jac had a string of girlfriends, telling each that
she was special and that he was "serious" about her. Teddy
began to remember how Jac had used her the first time, and
then dumped her. It seemed plausible that he might do it
again. . . . What was to stop him?

The next day at 9:30 A.M., Teddy emerged from the
clubhouse at the National Tennis Center and made her way
down the paths of the outdoor courts until she came to court
sixteen, her practice court. She was to meet Manuel Muñoz,
her practice partner.

It was a warm morning, the pale blue sky dotted with
fluffs of white clouds, crisscrossed by jet trails from the
planes taking off from nearby La Guardia. The sounds of
ponging balls, punctuated by occasional shouts, filled the
air.

The scene was so familiar that Teddy barely saw it, her
thoughts on Jac again.

"Someone sent a package to you, Teddy," said Manuel,
handing her a package about the shape of a shoe box.
"They stopped me at the front desk, said this was for you."

"It's probably the new shoes I sent for," Teddy said
casually. Manuel nodded, putting the package on the court
floor near the entrance as they walked in.

Two hours later, Teddy was loosened up, her skin run-
ning with the pleasant perspiration of vigorous exercise.
She'd worked on her serve, too, powering out balls that
Manuel grimly chased toward the net.

As they walked off the court, Teddy stooped to pick up the package. When she shook it, the contents didn't feel like shoes.

They started toward the locker rooms, but then Teddy spotted a vendor selling iced cans of soda and natural oatmeal cookies. "Let's get a Diet Pepsi—I'll buy," she said to Manuel. "And I'm dying for a cookie."

Carrying their sodas, they walked to an area that contained umbrella tables, near the court where Gabriela Sabatini was practicing. Teddy was slated to play Gabriela tonight in the finals and wanted to watch her in action.

As they sat down on opposite sides of a table with a red umbrella, Manuel took the package from her. "No shoes in here," he declared, shaking it. "Probably a surprise from one of your boyfriends."

"Hah! Since you're so inquisitive, why don't you open it?" said Teddy, who was trying to unwrap her cookies. "At least tear the paper off for me, Manuel, be a sport."

As Manuel moved slightly away from the table in order to unfasten the fiberglass tape with which the package was strapped, he said, "That is strange. I see a—"

There was a small red fireball that flashed up around him, accompanied by a horrifying bang. It knocked Teddy backward, slamming her onto the ground.

Teddy was sobbing. "Manuel! Manuel!" She tried to rush toward the bloody, blanket-covered mound, but hands held her back.

She was shaking all over so violently that her teeth chattered. Waves of frigid iciness rippled through her limbs. *The package had been addressed to her.*

"Shock," someone said. "She's in shock. Get her a blanket."

Teddy sat on the grass, huddled in two blankets. She'd known Manuel for eight years. They'd been friends. He had a young wife; he'd gotten married just last year. She kept shaking her head, shocked to the core, barely able to assim-

ilate what had just happened. Photographers rushed forward, swarming over her to snap picture after picture.
"Teddy! Teddy!" they kept calling. "Teddy, were you
hurt? Why do you think—"

She shook her head numbly, gesturing them away.

*The package was meant for her. She was the one who
should have been dead.*

"Back, dammit, back, I'll have you assholes thrown
out," said a gruff voice. "Damn vultures." She heard the
man calling out orders, and the reporters dispersed.

Then a man sat down beside her. Teddy dully looked
over and saw a man in a cheap pair of navy blue polyester
slacks, yellow open-collared shirt, and sagging blue-and-
white checkered sport jacket. A holster was hanging from
his belt, along with a pair of handcuffs. A gold badge
flapped from his shirt pocket. Another man waited nearby,
dressed similarly.

"I'm Detective Piersante, NYPD," he told her, holding
out the badge for her to see. "And this is my partner, Detective Marchetto. Let's go in the clubhouse, where we can
talk."

Inside the clubhouse, Teddy was led to a small office
with walls posted with tournament schedules and member-
ship rosters.

"Can you tell me what happened, Miss Warner?" said
Piersante. "From start to finish, if you would."

She was shaking now, even more violently. *Had this
happened because she went on board the* Olympia? Horror
filled her as she wiped away tears. "It was the p-package.
Manuel had it with him when we came to practice. He said
someone gave it to him at the desk, it was addressed to
me-me. . . . I shouldn't have let him open it. . . . I was trying to unwrap a cookie . . ." She started to weep again.

"Miss Warner, do you know of anyone who might want
you dead?"

She froze. The yacht . . . the purser who'd glared at her,
threatened her. She didn't think he knew she'd found that

wire and the scrap of paper. She didn't intend to tell anyone about that, not even these two detectives.

"I'm . . . not sure," she said miserably. Deep fright squeezed her stomach, and she felt as if she might be sick. "Oh, I'm not the only one. . . . There's Omar Faid."

"Faid?" said Detective Piersante sharply.

"We were both on the same boat. Nickey Skouros's yacht. But I'm sure it doesn't mean anything. I don't know why anyone would want to kill me, I'm just a tennis player," she babbled on.

The two detectives kept Teddy in the office for more than two hours, asking questions, then repeating the same questions from a new angle. Through the window they could hear the noise of the reporters crowded around the front entrance of the clubhouse, waiting for her to come out.

"What will I tell them?" Teddy finally asked.

Piersante looked sour. "I guess you'll have to give a press conference, but I want you to keep it short and non-committal, Miss Warner. Don't name names, don't give theories, just say how sorry you are that Manuel died, something like that."

She gave a short, ten-minute press conference, fielding questions with shakes of her head and "I don't knows," until exhaustion swept over her.

"That's it. This little lady is tired. Go and write up some hogwash that passes for news," said Piersante, steering Teddy back into the clubhouse.

"Teddy—are you afraid?" called a woman as she was leaving.

Teddy turned, staring at her with burning eyes. "Wouldn't you be?"

"Now, Miss Warner," said Piersante, taking her into the office again. "Don't open any packages, any mail of any kind," he told her. "And switch to a new hotel immediately. Let me know where you are, and I'll have someone from the bomb squad sweep your room. We'll also give you twenty-four-hour protection for the next few days, until the tournament is over, and after that I suggest you hire a private security service.''

Numbly, Teddy waited for a young police officer to escort her. He drove her back to her hotel, where she checked out, and then checked into a different hotel. Even though Manuel was dead, the final match hadn't been canceled so she was going to have to play Sabatini or forfeit the tournament.

Finally entering her new room, freshly swept for bombs and incendiary devices, Teddy stripped off her clothes. She was horrified to discover that her shirt and shorts were covered with specks of Manuel's blood. She shuddered violently, then rushed to the bathroom and threw up.

Finally she went to the phone and dialed Manuel's wife, Katie. She had already been notified of his death by the police, and was crying so loudly and continuously that she could barely talk.

''I'm so sorry,'' Teddy whispered painfully.

''I don't understand,'' Manuel's wife kept saying.

''I'll . . . make sure you're all right. I'll start a trust fund for you,'' Teddy told her. ''I'll have Russ, my agent, set it up for you. Manuel earned it.''

Finally she hung up, and after taking several deep breaths to steady her nerves, she dialed the number of Jac's hotel in Buenos Aires.

''Jac,'' she said weeping as soon as the prince came on the line, ''something awful has happened! Manuel's been killed—he's my hitting partner—and the bomb was meant for me!''

''I know. It's already on TV here. I tried phoning your hotel but they said you had checked out.''

She went over the day with Jac, who didn't conceal his horror. ''*Mon Dieu*, Teddy,'' he kept saying. ''This has gone too far. Why do you think someone would do this?''

Teddy guiltily hesitated. Jac would be furious if he knew

she'd gone aboard Skouros's yacht. "Maybe I've been asking too many questions about my father's death. I . . . well, Jac, I went on the *Olympia,* and I nosed around a little bit. In fact, I found something! I found evidence that—"

"You went on Skouros's yacht?"

"Well, yes, but it was perfectly safe—they gave me permission to go on board. I said I needed to find a pin I'd lost—"

"Oh, Teddy."

His voice was so appalled that Teddy stopped chattering, feeling another pang in the center of her stomach. "I'm sorry," she gulped. "I know I shouldn't have."

"I'm flying up there to be with you."

"No," she said weakly. "What about your race?"

"I can get back for it. Teddy"—his voice seemed to shudder—"I don't want anything to happen to you."

Teddy did not win the Open.

As she played the voraciously powerful Sabatini, she was still weak from the shock of witnessing Manuel's death, and her usual crisp, aggressive game was slightly off, her coordination less than razor sharp. But afterward, as she walked off the court, thousands of fans stood up, shouting her name. Everyone had heard about her nearly being killed that morning, and they wanted to show both their support and respect. Sabatini herself came over to Teddy and put her arm around her opponent's shoulder.

The cheers continued. She shaded her eyes, gazing into the stands.

"Thank you," she called, overcome.

The cheering intensified as she ran into the locker room, where she was mobbed by reporters. Drawing a deep breath, she decided to give another, impromptu press conference.

"Manuel Muñoz was an excellent tennis player," she said into the mikes that were thrust into her face. "He was my friend for the past eight years. I'll do everything I can

to help his family. The New York police are working on
the case now. And I've already started things in motion
with my attorney to fund a trust for his widow.''

"Teddy! Teddy! Are you going to get another hitting
partner? And what about a new coach, now that your father
is gone?"

"I probably will, but I can't think about any plans right
now," she said, hearing her voice give out. She ended the
conference and felt her knees wobble as she walked into
the locker room. Suddenly it seemed as if there were people
everywhere, tennis players, friends, agents, coming up to
her, patting her shoulders, touching her, offering their com-
miserations.

"We love you, Teddy," said someone.

"We care about you."

Teddy choked up again.

Jac arrived fourteen hours later, immediately buzzing
Teddy's hotel room although it was only 5:30 A.M.

"Jac . . . Jac . . ." She threw herself into his arms. He
was deeply suntanned, and seemed even more handsome
and blue-eyed than Teddy remembered. He was wearing
casual pants and an open-collared shirt. He must not even
have bothered to change.

"Teddy." He seemed as choked up as she was, and he
hugged her tight, crushing her to him. "I watched the news
as we were flying in for a landing. That terrible video of
the explosion. They've been running it nonstop."

They hugged again for a long time. Then the hug intensified, and they clung to each other, Teddy wrapping her
arms around Jac's neck, trying to get her body as close to
his as possible, wanting to be protected by him, safe.

"I can't believe what happened," Jac whispered
hoarsely. "You're so alive, Teddy. So beautifully alive.
Thank God. You just don't know."

Somehow they fell on the warm, mussed-up bed. Jac
pulled her to him.

"I don't even want to make love," he groaned. "I just need to hold you."

She murmured something, and then she was crying again. Jac brushed away her tears and stroked her gently. He began pulling off her clothes, and she helped him, until they both were naked. He caressed her body, adoring her with his gentle hands. Their nourishing touches were love-making far beyond sex, far deeper. Teddy had never experienced anything like it, and she wondered whether Jac had, either.

"If you'd died, I would have died with you," Jac said solemnly.

"I missed you so," Teddy said, weeping.

"And I missed you."

"Jamaica said that—that I was fooling myself, that you're just my f-fantasy," she began.

"I'm not a fantasy, Teddy dearest. I'm real. So real." Finally Jac lowered himself on top of her, and Teddy opened her legs wide, allowing him to slip inside her. They caught each other's rhythms immediately, beginning to move together in a deeply intimate motion.

Jac's thrusts became deeper, stronger, as Teddy arched upward to meet him, thrusting as hard as he did. She desperately needed to blend herself with him, to become one with him. Their skin became moist, and Teddy clutched Jac's back, then moved her hands down to cup his buttocks, firm, muscular, smooth. As he pumped into her, she could feel his muscles undulating.

"Teddy . . . God. . . ." Jac's deep thrusts shook her body, pummeling her, carrying her with him, and she began to moan with her approaching climax.

Her orgasm began deep in her groin, exploding outward, carrying her on spasms of pleasure that pulsated and then pulsated again and again.

Then Jac came, too, his body shuddering into hers.

"I almost lost you forever," he said into her shoulder, his voice so low she barely heard him. "In Argentina—

Teddy, I have told no one—the car I was driving crashed. I was . . . so surprised. I never thought it could happen to me. I was nearly burned to death. I begged my friends and rival crew members not to sell this story to the tabloids but it still may be printed.''

"Jac," she said, horrified.

"I don't know if racing is my destiny. I'm not sure anymore. Maybe I should be going in a different direction."

She sensed what a difficult admission this was for him to make.

Holding Jac in the morning darkness, Teddy began to feel a beatific sense of happiness, mixed with a growing sense of safety and security. Jac did love her—she'd been right. Even if he wasn't fully aware of it yet, he really did love her. And she loved him, too.

They loved each other. Now, what were they going to do about it?

Jac lay in bed holding a sleeping Teddy in his arms. He was listening to her soft breathing, but unexpectedly grim thoughts consumed his mind.

Was Nickey Skouros a killer? He was certainly capable of ordering someone killed. Or was the assassin someone else? And even worse, who would be next? Was someone trying to launch a terror campaign against the royals? Extort something from Henri? Force him into giving up his strong hold on the country? Even abdicate . . . in favor of who? Who would gain from such action? It could only be—

"Jac. This is real, you're here," murmured Teddy sleepily, turning over at 10:00 A.M.

Jac smiled and kissed her.

Teddy who had slept naked, reached out for a skimpy T-shirt, pulling it on over her head. Her tousled, thick hair streamed down her shoulders. Her clean blondness, her freshness, excited him. In the morning light her tanned skin seemed to glow.

"I want you to rest today in the hotel," he told her. "I'm going to go and talk with the police."

"Not without me, you're not," she said, starting to dress. "This is America, Jac, and women don't stay at home anymore."

At first the police didn't want to cooperate, but Jac talked to the State Department in Washington, and through diplomatic channels he eventually got what he needed. They were even allowed to look at photos of Omar Faid's demolished car and garage, a sight that made Teddy shudder.

"With Muñoz the explosive was plastique again, Your Highness," said Piersante, looking speculatively at Jac and then at Teddy. "Someone professional did these two jobs—someone who knew exactly what the hell they were doing."

"I see."

"Any reason you can think of why someone would want to blow away both Omar Faid and Teddy Warner?"

"No."

"Well, shit, there has to be a reason, pardon my French, Your Highness and Miss Warner." The burly detective floundered. "I mean these two people have one thing in common, they were both at that big shindig of yours, on Nikos Skouros's ship, the *Olympia*, right?"

"It seems so."

"I want to talk to this Skouros."

"I can give you a telephone number to contact him, but I am not sure how much cooperation you will receive since he is not an American citizen," said Jac.

"Hey, we'll bring Interpol in on this if we have to."

Jac asked to be allowed to use a private telephone. The detective pointed out an empty office. Within minutes he was speaking to Prince Henri.

"Papa, I have some bad news, and we need to talk about it. It seems that someone tried to kill Teddy Warner."

"*Sacristi!*" cried the prince. "Good God!"

"Papa, are you all right?" Jac could hear his father gasp and then start to cough. "Are you strong enough to hear this?"

"*Oui, oui.* Give me your number. I will call you back on a secured line," said Henri in a heavy voice.

Five minutes later the phone rang, and Jac picked it up.

Jac told Henri everything. "Somehow it is connected with Nikos Skouros, Papa. I feel very sure of it. Both Teddy and Omar were on his yacht. And so was Houston Warner. And then later Teddy went back to the ship. Papa, something happened on that ship! Involving all three of them. Do you know what it could be? Do you have any idea at all?"

The silence was so deep, so profound, that Jac thought his father had hung up, except for the continuous, slight hum of the cable.

"Jac," said Henri heavily, "this is a tragedy."

"Of course, it is. Teddy nearly died. Three other men did die. Papa, *do* you know something?"

"I am not sure."

"Anything," pleaded Jac. "No matter how slight, no matter how small. What thing could connect them? Papa, the deaths were no accident. There had to have been some valid reason. What?"

Henri cleared his throat. "I had too much wine to drink that night," he finally said.

"Yes? Yes?"

"I do not remember everything I said. I was angry. . . . I was talking about Costa, how someone has betrayed us. I am not sure who even now. I did not name names. Well, perhaps I might have named one name—one of my ministers. I suspect he has been taking bribes, helping someone to form offshore corporations in order to buy up our land. I have no proof, of course."

Jac shook his head. "But this makes no sense. You named a name. What does this signify?"

"I was sitting at the bridge table with Houston Warner, who was my partner," Henri went on. "We were playing against Faid and Nickey Skouros. We had all been drinking quite heavily, I might add. But I do not know about Teddy Warner. She was at another table. She might have walked past us. Or perhaps they are afraid she is asking too many questions. . . . I'm just not sure anymore."

Jac felt a profound heaviness drop over him. "Papa, I have been suspicious of Nikos Skouros for a long time. Why didn't you tell *me* about this minister?"

"Because I am responsible for Costa, not you . . . not yet," said Henri. "I have been friends with this man for over twenty-five years. How could I suggest his name until I had solid facts? It would destroy him, and he may, in fact, be innocent of any wrongdoing."

"Anatole Breton?" said Jac, his voice rising.

"He is my friend," said Henri.

"He is your enemy! He and whoever he was working with," snapped Jac. "Papa—I am going to forget about my race. This is far more important. Today I will return home, and I will get to the bottom of this. You have been too complacent," he accused. "You have been reluctant to take effective action, and now our country is threatened."

"I love Costa," said Henri. "I would give my life for it."

"So would I," snapped Jac.

Heads turned and flashbulbs popped as the two Costan princesses made an entrance, Kristina in strapless red chiffon, Gaby in a yellow Tarquin gown, a stunning hammered-gold necklace around her neck.

The publishing party was being held at Le Chantilly on East 57th Street. The guests included an elite group of Doubleday authors and editors, and, of course, there was Kenny Lane, who had arrived with his close friends, Sid and Mercedes Bass and the Alfred Taubmans.

Betty Prashker, an executive editor at Crown, was giving the party to announce a new project. Ms. Prashker had just signed Gabriella to do a book on her fashion secrets, and now she glided over to greet the princesses, asking warmly about Prince Henri, whom she knew well.

When the conversation turned to Teddy's narrow escape from the bomb, then the New York publishing world, Kristina excused herself. Teddy had called with regrets about not being able to come to the party, and she missed her. She just wasn't in the mood for a party. She drank a second champagne cocktail; even as its bubbles tickled her throat, the wine seemed to rush to her head, coloring the room with bright glitter.

Bret Thompson. She knew her emotions were still raw. How could Bret have done it to her? He'd been such an unprincipled liar—a total asshole. Kristina knew she was never going to forgive him. She hoped his *Playboy* bunny/hamburger executive wife took him for everything he owned. And Nickey, too, how dare he interfere in her life?

The party grew noisier, and Kristina drifted from group to group, more bored than ever. She found herself talking to Gaby again. Gaby wanted to introduce her to some men Cliff knew, in particular a wealthy Dallas heart surgeon.

"Texans? With cowboy hats? I don't know," said Kristina, shrugging. "Not unless I have them checked out with a detective agency first. Anyone with more than one previous marriage need not apply." God, she sounded bitter.

"I've only got one previous marriage, do I qualify?" said a voice behind her. Kristina turned to see Will Camden, the Creative Artists Agency partner she had met several years earlier. The one with the interesting gray eyes.

"I didn't say I was offering a job. In fact, I'm definitely not."

Will smiled, evidently taking her words for party banter, but then he looked at her more closely. "I see a quiet alcove over there, Princess Kristina. Would you like to join me there? I think I can flag us down a couple of drinks."

She didn't really want to, but it was easier just to follow him.

They began with the usual Hollywood shoptalk, and when the conversation turned to Bret, Kristina gazed into her drink, then tilted it up and swallowed most of it in one long gulp.

"You haven't heard? Bret and I are finished. It was a mutual decision."

But when Will didn't say anything, his eyes fixed on her with warm sympathy, Kristina somehow felt encouraged to talk further, and poured out the entire Bret episode. Will was the first person she had told the whole thing to, and with each word she felt a tiny part of her burden lift.

"Can you imagine?" she said bitterly.

Will nodded. "Fortunately you found him out in time."

"Yes, from a man who has ulterior motives, I suspect." Kristina stared into her drink. "I don't want to marry Nickey, either. Sometimes I get tired of relationships. Sometimes I wish— I don't know what I wish!"

Will hesitated. "Kristina, don't take this wrong, please. I'm forty-two years old now, and like everyone else, I've had my share of problems, but at least I've learned to be open about my feelings—as open as most men can be, anyway."

She looked at him suspiciously.

The gray eyes searched hers. "I'd like us to be friends, Kristina. That's all I'm asking of you right now. It never has to go any further than that if you don't want it to. It's totally up to you. But I really like you as a person, and I'd like to explore it further."

"Friends," she repeated. "I don't think I've ever had a male friend. I'm not sure it's possible!"

Gabriella and Kenny Lane talked in a corner, taking time off from party chatter to discuss some business.

"With you getting married, I want us to go all out," the

jewelry designer was saying. "I think we should have a line of really romantic pieces—maybe a whole series of wedding jewelry. And I think it's time we launched a perfume line. I've already made inquiries in Paris, I've found a perfumer at Lancôme who can originate for us a very elegant scent, floral with a bare hint of musk."

Gaby nodded excitedly. "We'll call it Princess Gabriella."

"Or we could call it just Gaby. Gaby is short, sexy, romantic, *very* French, and the name is synonymous with you. What do you think?"

They discussed the perfume line for twenty minutes more; then Gaby sighed and glanced at her watch. "I really should go back to my hotel, Kenny. Cliff has promised to phone me from Boston."

"We'll meet tomorrow for breakfast, then," said Lane.

Gabriella excused herself and phoned her driver, beeping him on his pager.

As the bodyguard appeared, she greeted him with a smile, her mind still musing on the new perfume. It would have to have a decorative bottle, of course—something that suggested glamour, perhaps with a faux jewel on its lid. Yes, she could design something that would be perfect. . . .

Pierre escorted her across the lobby and out to the sidewalk, where the limousine was double-parked, waiting with its motor running. As she started toward the car, a man came running up to her along the sidewalk. There was a muffled explosion, and Pierre went down, sprawling violently.

As Gabriella screamed, another man grabbed her arm and tried to shove her in the back of the limo. She yelled, trying to twist away, as she saw Pierre roll over onto his side, reaching for his gun. Shots rang out, and her assailant staggered backward, his knees folding.

The bodyguard aimed another shot at the limo, but it was already speeding away, tires squealing on the rain-wet pavement.

* * *

"What?" Prince Henri, in Costa, stared at his personal press attaché, the blood leaving his face. "Attacked by terrorists?" He began fumbling for his nitroglycerine pills.

"Your Highness, Princess Gabriella was not hurt. It was a minor incident—she merely has a scrape on her left arm and has suffered shock," said the attaché. "The bodyguard was shot in the shoulder but is in stable condition. The limousine driver has not been found, though, and may have been killed by the terrorists. Your pill, Your Highness," he added. "Take one now."

"Which group was responsible for the attack?" Henri growled as his heartbeat steadied.

"The New York police think the attackers were from a Costan dissident group," said the attaché. "It could have been much worse but for the quick action of her bodyguard."

"Thank you. Now please leave me," said Henri. "I do not wish to receive any calls for the next several hours."

When the attaché had left, closing the door behind him, Prince Henri wiped droplets of perspiration off his forehead and pondered what steps to take.

The death of Houston Warner . . . the killing of his old friend, Omar Faid . . . the bomb meant for Teddy Warner . . . now his daughter.

Something was terribly wrong.

The old prince slowly rose from his chair and moved across the large office to a twelve-foot-high bookcase that had been built against one wall. Pulling out a book, he touched a slight indentation in the wood.

Almost soundlessly, a section of the bookshelf began rotating outward. Henri stepped back, allowing it to open fully, and then walked into the vault. He touched a light switch, and rows of overhead lights sprang on. The room was large, windowless, completely lined with steel.

It contained rows of wooden cabinets with long drawers, each one laden with pieces from the Bellini crown jewels.

The famous fifty-carat Yemeni Diamond, set in a brooch ringed with smaller diamonds. Tiaras of sparkling magnificence. Necklaces of rubies mined in Burma. And more.

Henri walked to a cabinet at the far end of the room. Reaching into the deep top drawer, he pulled out a silk-wrapped object, peeling away the cloth with an indrawn breath.

There it was. The Costan crown, worn by Henri when he was invested, and earlier by his father, and before him, by a line of Bellinis that stretched into the distant past for several hundred years.

Henri held up the crown, made of white gold and platinum. It glittered with more than four hundred brilliant-cut diamonds set in an ornate festoon-and-scroll pattern, its eight points surmounted by large rubies surrounded by circlets of pearls.

Soon, he thought, sinking into a chair with the ornate crown still in his hands. *Very soon.*

Ten minutes later he was back in his office. He rang for his secretary and told him to contact the princesses. Jac had already decided to fly back to Costa today, and Prince Henri wanted Gabriella and Kristina to return immediately, too.

The doctors had just made their early-morning rounds and pronounced Gaby's condition as "very stable and improving all the time." Two U.S. State Department security agents stood guard outside Gaby's hospital room, insisting that everyone who wanted to enter, even doctors and nurses, present valid identification.

Cliff Ferguson showed his driver's license and business card, then hurried into the room.

"*Gaby, thank God you're all right!* I jumped on my plane as soon as your secretary phoned me, darling."

He wore his usual well-tailored business suit and his trademark cowboy boots, and in his arms he carried a bouquet of red roses so huge that it nearly obscured his face.

"Hello, Cliff," Gaby said, sitting up in bed. Her left

forearm was bandaged, and she felt slightly woozy from the medication.

Cliff set the bouquet down on a table and hurried toward her, scooping her off the mattress and into his arms. Gaby snuggled into his warm strength.

"Oh, Cliff," she sighed, "I need you so much!"

"Well, I'm here. And I'm going to take care of you. I couldn't believe it when I heard. . . . Oh, Gaby. Those men were serious. They would have held you for ransom!"

Gaby's eyes widened. "Ransom?"

"They would have held up your country for millions, darling, and then there's no guarantee that they ever would have returned you alive."

Gaby had never seen Cliff so upset. His cheeks had reddened, and his eyes seemed to flash with anger. She swallowed. "They wouldn't have dared . . ."

"You know how serious kidnapping has become in South America and some of the Third World countries, and now it's hitting the rest of the world. You have made yourself a target, honey, by traveling all over the country as you do."

"But I didn't—I only went to a party."

"I know that's all you did. But you're not just any ordinary woman, you're a princess. You don't seem real to a lot of people. To them, you're more like a symbol of wealth and western power—of something they hate."

Gabriella shook her head. Damn! She still felt so fuzzy. . . .

"I want to move up our wedding date," Cliff went on. "We'll have a small garden wedding right on the ranch, and I'll stop traveling so much. We'll spend a lot more time at Jacaranda where you'll be protected. I'll hire extra bodyguards for you, I'll add security to patrol the perimeters of the property—"

"No," she said.

"What? Gaby, you're not thinking clearly. This wasn't just a little fracas, it was far more serious—"

She drew herself up. "I *know* how serious it was. Cliff, do you know what you're saying? You want me to drop my jewelry business, don't you? You want me to run and hide on your ranch, wall myself behind your barbed-wire fencing, safely away from everything. Papa wants me to do the same thing, only in Costa."

"It wouldn't be that way," he protested. "You could still design your jewelry. It's gorgeous, honey. You've got a great talent, and I'd never deprive you of that. We'll build a little workshop for you right on the property. I'll hire artisans who can fly in—"

She stared at him, alarmed by what he was suggesting. She loved her jewelry business—her life of travel and adventure, the television appearances, fashion shows, and media interviews. It made her feel free, competent, more than just another royal who had inherited her position in life. She had finally broken away from Costa, and now Cliff wanted to put her behind barbed-wire fences at Jacaranda.

"*No,*" she said firmly. "I can't live like that. How could you ask me to?"

"But you're being foolish—"

"I'm *not* being foolish. If I come to live on your ranch under those circumstances, I'll feel like I'm back in Costa, something like a prison. You must understand the way I feel."

"Me? Keep *you* a prisoner on Jacaranda?" Gaby realized that Cliff was very angry at her. "You insult me, Gabriella. I can't believe you said that. Jesus Christ!" Cliff jumped to his feet and stood glaring down at her. "I'd better leave, I guess. We both need a cooling-off period, and you should think through what I've just told you."

"I don't have to think about it. I *won't* change my whole life because of this," she cried. Angrily she grabbed the ring on her finger and yanked it off.

"Take this back!" she cried. "I can't wear it!"

"You keep it. Put it on later when you've calmed down," said Cliff, turning white.

"Never!"

She held out the ring, but he had already turned and stalked out of her room.

Gaby slid down on the mattress again and began to cry.

"Such beautiful roses," said Princess Kristina.

"Take them away," said Gaby, teary-eyed.

"What?" Startled, Kristina stared at her sister. "Gaby, what's the matter? Why are you crying?"

"It's finished." Gaby sniffled. "I thought I was going to marry Cliff, but now I'm not. He—he wants me to give up everything just because of those terrorists. I can't. I won't do it."

Kristina laughed. "Oh, don't listen to him. He's just being overprotective now. He's probably scared out of his wits. You know, like Papa gets. Give him a little time to adjust to things, and he'll be fine. Men have to be babied *until* we get them to understand us."

Gaby blinked and opened her eyes wide, staring at her sister. "That's how you look at it, Kristina? That I just need to baby him, and everything will be fine? No wonder your romances have all fallen through."

"And no wonder this is your first big one," snapped Kristina, but then she immediately softened her tone. "Anyway, sister dear, you can't break your engagement just because Cliff wants to protect you. Any man would!"

But Gaby had stiffened stubbornly. "I won't give up what I've worked so hard for. Why should I? I've finally broken loose and have some independence, and believe me, I'm not going to give it up for Cliff—or anyone else. And I told him the same thing just a few hours ago."

The telephone rang. Gabriella wearily reached for it. "Yes?"

It was the hospital switchboard, with Prince Henri on the line.

* * *

"Gaby," said Cliff Ferguson, reaching her on a private phone line a few hours after he'd left her earlier, "are you feeling better now?"

"I'm feeling the same." She had been crying off and on ever since Cliff had stalked out of her room. And now she would have to fly back to Costa del Mar.

"Gaby, I do love you," said Cliff. "I'm sorry about our disagreement. But surely you can see my position."

"And I love you, too," she said, as tears filled her eyes again. "But I *can't* live my life your way, Cliff, or anyone else's. I must be my own person."

"Oh, my darling Gaby," he groaned. "I'm not the one who tried to hurt you. I'm not the terrorist. I only want to protect you, keep you safe."

"And I only want to live my own life," she whispered, hanging up.

The following morning Gaby gave the ring to her secretary to send back to Cliff, then dressed herself in a beige silk pantsuit the woman had brought over from the hotel.

Seated in a wheelchair, escorted by four bodyguards, she took the elevator down to the hospital's main floor, where a large conference room had been prepared for a press conference. She winced as she saw that the room was packed with reporters and TV crews.

One of the bodyguards wheeled her over to the mikes, where Gaby rose and began to read from a short prepared statement.

"I was attacked by some men whom the police believe were international terrorists," she read aloud. "We aren't sure at this time who they were *or* exactly what they wanted with me. I will be more careful in selecting my public appearances now, but will continue to live my life without fear. I believe in a kind and merciful God who watches over all of us, and I believe that the good Lord will protect me from harm."

She fielded several questions on the attack, but then was

interrupted by a man wearing credentials from CNN news.

"Your Highness!"

"Yes?"

"Your Highness, can you confirm the rumors that you have quite recently broken your engagement with Cliff Ferguson?"

She hesitated somewhat taken back by the question. "My relationship with Cliff Ferguson is private."

The hubbub rose, everyone shouting at once. "Your Highness! A hospital source confirmed the breakup!" called a woman from the *New York Post*.

"I will not discuss my personal life at this time."

"But didn't you send Ferguson back his ring? The delivery service confirmed it. Isn't it over, Your Highness?"

Gabriella was swaying, her face drained of blood and color. "This press conference is over."

That day Cliff Ferguson flew back to Texas on his private jet, devastated by the breakup with Gaby.

How could she be so stubborn, continuing to put her life in jeopardy. For what? They didn't need the money . . . or the public adulation that so many celebrities craved. She was just being foolish and headstrong!

He spent the flight brooding, his depression interrupted by several business calls, which he took on the plane's cellular phone. But he could barely force himself to concentrate. He felt as if Gabriella had taken a sledgehammer and smashed away at his heart.

Several hours later he was pulling through the main gate of the ranch, driving up the paved road past arroyos where he'd ridden horseback with Gabriella, past the small lake where they'd swum nude, laughing and making love on the sandy banks. He slowed his four-wheeler, passing the stable where Gaby's favorite horse, Lady Fawn, was stabled. She'd never ride Lady Fawn again. . . .

Tears blurring his eyes, he drove up to the house.

His daughter, Rebecca, came racing from the skating

rink as he got out of the car, and threw herself into his arms. Her eyes were red, her face streaked with tears.

"Daddy, Daddy, I saw it all on the news—Gabriella almost got killed! And, Daddy, is it true that she broke up with you?"

He nodded.

"Daddy, why? Why?" the teenager wept.

"I'm not sure, punkin. It was one of those things," he said with difficulty. "Here, let's walk into the house, have you had lunch yet? I'll ask Mrs. Henderson to fix us something."

"I couldn't eat. I'm not hungry. Oh, Daddy, I just don't get it," Rebecca kept wailing. "Why would she do that to us? I love her so much. I wanted her to be my new mama. . . . Please don't let her go. . . ."

"I know, baby doll," said Cliff, feeling as if his entire stomach was one raw, aching wound. "But I said the wrong things. I was too protective of her. I told her she had to stay here at the ranch, and I'd take care of her. She resented me for it. I . . . I don't know, baby."

"Then call her!" cried Rebecca. "Call her right now. If that's all it is, she'll take you back. Daddy," she pleaded, "if you love her and she loves you, then you can't let it just fall apart like this. That's stupid!"

"I know," sighed Cliff.

"Then call her!" Rebecca's slim hands urged him toward the telephone.

"No," Cliff said. "Becky, this is more than just a stupid fight. She is a princess. She comes from a completely different world. The royals have always lived in the public eye. They've had to, and there's always been the risk of attack by crazies. . . . The threat of violence is something the royals have to live with, just like the President. To me, though, it's a threat to everything I hold dear. I can't live under that kind of shadow."

"Daddy, please," she cried.

But Cliff wouldn't talk about it anymore.

* * *

The royal Costan jet was buffeted, hitting a pocket of turbulence.

Teddy tightened her seat belt, drawing her breath in uneasily. Her skin felt oddly hot. Since the bombing she'd had a persistent cough, and now she wondered if she was also getting a fever. Since Manuel's death her whole life was turbulent.

She'd decided to drop all her tennis plans and go back to Costa with Jac. She *had* to settle this. She knew she'd be too terrified to walk into another tennis club until she had some answers. Jac had promised her full security measures for the time she was in Costa, and, in fact, a burly ex-NYPD officer now sat in a seat behind them.

"You seem so tense, Teddy," said Jac, seated beside her in the elegantly furnished private cabin.

"I am tense. I was almost killed right there at the tennis club," she said, choking. "Jac, I want to confront Nikos Skouros directly. I want to accuse him. I want to see his face when he replies. I won't need any further proof than that."

Jac spoke slowly. "Teddy, I don't think you realize yet just what sort of man we are dealing with here. Nikos Skouros is smooth. He charms people into thinking he's wonderful and harmless, but behind that charm is the soul of a Mafia godfather."

"I hate him!" she muttered, clenching the armrests of her seat. "He had my father killed. I know he did. One of the crew on his ship did it. Maybe that terrible purser. I *know* it."

"I feel you are right." Jac paused. "But we need more proof, and even then we will have to tread very carefully. We don't want any more 'terrorist' incidents, do we?"

"No, of course not."

"I have been thinking," he said slowly, "and I believe I have a plan."

* * *

The pilot turned off the cabin lights, and they both tried to sleep, but Prince Jac kept turning restlessly, unable to find a comfortable position.

All three of them—Jac, Gaby, Kristina—were proceeding to Costa, but the two princesses, at Jac's insistence, had taken the Concorde. Jac didn't wish to alarm his sisters, but he didn't want all three of them aboard the same aircraft.

He shuddered and forced the thought away. He knew what his father's command to immediately return home meant. He looked at Teddy, seated next to him, her head resting on the window, her blond braid falling over on one shoulder, golden tendrils of curls escaping from it. As she breathed in and out, her eyelids fluttered slightly, giving her a vulnerable appearance.

He loved her.

He knew that now—had known it from the first moment he heard about the bomb that had been meant for her. He couldn't live without her. He had had many women, and some had touched his feelings, but he had loved none of them until Teddy.

But she was American, a tennis star at the peak of her career. If she married him, she would have to give up much of that, playing only an occasional tournament. He was certain that, like Princess Grace of Monaco, and then his mother, Princess Lisse, and later Princess Diana, she would become an immediate icon—photographed and idolized, made a symbol of Costa. Could the rebellious Teddy handle that? Jac wasn't sure Teddy could put up with the lack of privacy, the ever-present bodyguards, the constant scrutiny.

He wasn't even sure that he could. So why should he ask such a thing of her? And did she even love him? Jac swallowed, feeling a burst of real panic. He would soon find out.

"I miss Cliff already," said Gaby, gazing out of the small window of the Concorde at the blue Atlantic waters, fifty thousand feet below. Her lip was trembling.

Kristina looked at her sister. Gaby's eyes were dark pools of grief, and under a light covering of makeup, her skin appeared translucent.

"You'll get over him in a month or two," lied Kristina, who hadn't gotten completely over Bret yet.

Gaby shook her head. "I won't. *Why* did they try to kidnap me? If they hadn't, Cliff would never . . . I wish he— I wish I—" She stopped.

"One does get over these things."

"Did *you* get over Jean-Luc that easily? And what about Bret Thompson? One moment you were madly in love and going to marry him, the next you wouldn't even talk about him."

Kristina shifted uneasily. She hadn't confided in anyone about Bret being already married; only Nickey knew about that. And now Will Camden. Her new friend.

"Men," she said contemptuously. "I'm not even sure if I ever want another one. Except for Will Camden. And that's not love, it's only friendship."

The flight attendant came through the cabin with a cart of scrumptious hors d'oeuvres and Dom Perignon champagne. Pensively, Kristina sipped hers. "Why do you suppose Papa wants to see all of us?" she began.

"He—he must be ill," said Gaby, biting her lip again.

"No," decided Kristina. "If he was, we would have been immediately informed. I think it's something else. I think it has to do with . . . the crown."

"Oh," said Gaby in a small voice.

They sat for several minutes in silence while each contemplated her own thoughts.

"*I* can't possibly," said Kristina, but her voice was hesitant. "I have my career, my life in Hollywood. I can't give those up."

"I don't think you'll be asked to," said Gaby with just a touch of sharpness.

* * *

Arriving in Costa, Teddy was again given the VIP guest quarters at the Vendôme Palace, and she settled into the familiar surroundings with an odd feeling of homecoming. It felt safe here in the palace, being near Jac.

"Tomorrow we'll meet with Breton," Jac had told her. "But today my father has asked my sisters and me to meet privately with him. I hope you won't be offended."

"Of course," she murmured. Actually, she would be glad of a respite. Her head had begun to pound, and she wondered if she was coming down with something. But she couldn't get sick now, she told herself.

She rang for the maid and asked the woman to unpack her things and run a bath for her, deciding that there were some royal luxuries that were very nice indeed.

Bending over stacks of documents, as he prepared for the meeting with his three children, Prince Henri felt his age more than ever before. He was almost three-quarters of a century old. Europe had undergone a major depression and a world war since his birth. His country had seen turmoil and controversy, and now once more was embroiled in economic and political chaos.

Prince Henri received the three young royals in his favorite room, his large office, which was hung with portraits of Bellini ancestors and lined with oversized books bound in Morocco leather.

Nervously Kristina took a seat in a red chair, and Gaby chose a chair beside her, upholstered in darker red. Jac chose to stand. They were all solemn, sensing the seriousness of the occasion.

Henri regarded them for a long, unsmiling moment. He knew each of their weaknesses only too well. None of his three children was perfect, but they carried the royal blood of the Bellinis, and only they could be responsible for the perpetuation of the country's heritage. Could he depend on them?

"I am happy that all three of you could be here," the

old prince began, his eyes fixing on each of them in turn. "Gabriella," he said to his older daughter, "you have been at my side with loyalty and kindness since the death of your mother, and you have brought Costa del Mar to the attention of the world with your successful business enterprises."

"Papa," she said, gulping.

"And you, Kristina, daughter of my heart, you have shown the world that royals have talent as well as beauty. You have matured well, recovering from your marital problems, and you deserve much commendation."

"Oh, Papa." Kristina, too, swallowed hard. Her eyes brimmed with unshed tears.

"And Jac, my son, my only son. I have watched you grow up from a daredevil youth who lived for danger into a young man able to assume responsibility."

Jac nodded stiffly, his face pale and solemn.

There was a long pause while Henri considered his words. "I am presented with a difficult problem," he finally said, taking a deep breath. "I intend to abdicate the throne in six weeks."

There was a lengthy beat of stunned shock. Jac drew in his breath sharply, while Gaby uttered a tiny cry. Kristina, always the most emotional of the three, jumped out of her chair and went running to Henri, throwing herself into his arms.

"Papa! Oh, Papa! You can't mean that! What will we do without you! You aren't—you aren't— Papa, you aren't sick, are you?"

Henri held her, his face contorted. "My heart condition is under control, according to my physicians, and I have many more years left if I am careful. But I am not able to give this country the strong leadership it needs in these times of crisis. It is not enough for Costa to have a frail ruler in precarious health. It needs someone younger, a monarch who is prepared to devote a lifetime solely to its needs and who is vigorous and determined enough to *pull it out of its present dilemma.*"

Another silence followed, as the young people looked at each other, realizing what the prince had said.

Jac was the first to speak. "You have made a choice then, Papa?"

Henri nodded. "I have chosen you, Jac."

Jac's face went white. He said slowly, "This is an honor beyond compare, but I do not know—"

"You must know! You must feel it in your heart," said Henri vehemently. He rose, his eyes focusing on the face of his son.

"Costa needs strength. It needs courage. It needs an influx of young blood, a new generation. I am the old generation, I am finished. I have done my best, I have struggled, but it was not good enough to—"

He swayed.

"Papa!" exclaimed Jac, stepping forward to catch his father as Henri, exhausted from emotion, toppled backward into his chair.

Henri had suffered an anxiety attack, the doctors informed the three young royals an hour later.

"He is resting comfortably, under sedation, and there is nothing to be unduly alarmed about. His health is fragile, but with care, he will live many more years. However, he is not to be subjected to emotional stress," cautioned Dr. Blanchet, the palace physician. "It could kill him."

The three young royals adjourned to the small library, where they dismissed all secretaries and bodyguards. For a long, silent moment they stared at each other in amazement and shock.

"You *must* rule," declared Kristina, staring at Jac. "You have no choice now! You're the one Papa wants, and you're the best one for the job."

Jac was silent, his face grim.

"Jac . . . please!" cried Gaby.

He paced the room, going to stand by a portrait of one of the early Bellini princes. Jac stared at his ancestor, wondering if he had faced the same tormenting decision.

They'd all assumed it would be him.

In his heart, he also had known he was the logical choice.

But it meant giving up so much. He wasn't ready! When he was forty, he might be better prepared for the throne. What should he do?

"I need to think about this overnight," he finally said, walking out of the room, immersed deeply in thought.

Jac couldn't sleep. He paced his room for hours, thoughts racing through his head. He loved his country. He loved its people. He would never forget that day when he'd walked out on the hospital balcony and heard them sing the Costan anthem while tears ran down his face.

He knew the people could be as loyal to him as they were now to Henri. But he would have to earn their trust. He would have to pull his country out of debt, he would have to find and punish its enemies. Skouros . . . Anatole Breton . . . *if* Breton was the traitor.

At a little after eleven P.M he decided to go down to the pool for a swim. The palace corridors with their high, arched ceilings gleamed with lavish touches of gilt. As he passed somber Renaissance portraits and gay rococo murals, Jac felt the essence of the Vendôme Palace surround him.

The sky was deep indigo, and violet shadows cloaked the night. The stars were tiny, glittering jewels while misty clouds partially obscured the huge, three-quarters moon.

As Jac approached the pool, he saw a lacy splash of white. On a deck chair a T-shirt had been flung which said *U.S. Open, 1992.*

He pulled off his robe and dove into the water, catching up with Teddy in a few strong strokes.

"Jac . . ." She turned to face him, her hair wetly slicked back, water droplets running down her face. She had been wearing a pair of goggles, which she pushed up on her forehead. "I didn't think anyone else would be in the pool at this hour."

"I had to think," he told her.

"Oh. . . . I'm sorry if I'm disturbing you. I can leave."

"No. Don't leave. I would love your company."

So they swam laps together, passing each other several times. After Teddy had climbed out of the pool, drying herself off and sinking into a lounge chair, Jac continued to swim until the hard exercise cleared his mind, and at last he felt a kind of peace.

Finally they were seated side by side in two chairs, the pool area lit only by a few lights. Summer would be ending soon, and already the night air had turned chilly. Jac got up and went into the pool house, returning with four or five thick sheared beach towels, which he spread over both of their legs.

"There. That should be more comfortable."

Teddy smiled at him, her teeth very white in the darkness. Without makeup she looked ethereally beautiful, and Jac felt his heart turn over in his chest.

Teddy told Jac how helpful Russ Ostrand had been the past weeks in working out the details of the trust fund she was setting up for Manuel Muñoz's widow. Then they talked casually about tennis, a book Jac had recently read, some gossip about Princess Di, a movie they both wanted to see. Jac began to talk knowledgeably about Costan politics, answering Teddy's questions, but finally he lapsed into silence. It was almost like he had used her the past hour as a sounding board in clearing his own thoughts.

They sat for a long time, neither of them speaking. The only sound was the slight, subterranean hum of the pool filter.

"My father is going to abdicate and has named me as his successor," Jac said suddenly.

Teddy gasped. "You mean . . . you're going to be prince? *The* prince?"

"Yes. You're not surprised, are you? It's what I was born for."

"I know, I realize that. . . . It's just that it's such a—I mean . . . *you're going to be the prince.*" Teddy clasped both of her hands tightly in her lap. "Jac, this is very, very serious, isn't it?"

"Yes. Teddy, it will change things. So many things."

She shivered as a slight wind came up. "Jac, there's no question you have the strength to lead your country, and I think Costa needs you very much."

She began to shiver harder, so he rose, taking several of the towels off his knees and spreading them around her. "There," he said softly. "Teddy, this is my decision alone to make, but it will affect you, too. I wanted to talk to you first."

She was looking at him, her eyes dark pools now, with an expression he could not read. She responded in a low voice. "What do you mean?"

"I don't know if you could ever live this kind of life." Jac gave a wide gesture that took in the ancient walls of the Vendôme Palace, the smart shops and luxury hotels of the capital, and the countryside beyond.

He could see the astonishment in Teddy's eyes as she became aware of the meaning of what he had just said. She stared at him, her entire body tensing. "What are you saying?"

"I'm saying, Teddy, that I—"

Just then a palace security guard entered the pool area. Seeing the two figures by the pool, he shone his flashlight toward them. Realizing it was Prince Jac and Teddy, he gave a stiff, embarrassed bow. Jac moved slightly away from Teddy, unwilling to have the staff see him in a moment of such deep intimacy.

"Teddy," he whispered when the man had left, "will you be my wife?"

* * *

Teddy could scarcely breathe. Her heart had begun to slam. It was as if every fantasy she'd ever had suddenly burst into a thousand colors, like Fourth of July fireworks.

"You're asking me to marry you? You—you can't be," she blurted.

"I am." His smile was gentle.

She shook her head back and forth. Tears were running down her cheeks. "But I—I'm an American."

"Darling Teddy. Beautiful, wonderful, darling Teddy. I know I'm asking a great deal of you, and perhaps you can't make the sacrifice, but I love you so much."

She laughed weakly, seeing him now only through a prism of glittering tears of happiness. "But that means I'd be—"

"A princess. My princess."

"I can't believe it. I always loved you. And now you're . . . now we're going to—" She broke down again. "Things don't happen like this. I *never* thought we would— Oh, God."

Jac moved to the chair she was sitting in, stretching his long, lean body out on the canvas and taking her into his arms. She cuddled close to him, clinging to him in shock.

"Teddy, I realize that it would be difficult for a while, but you could learn to handle it, and my sisters would help you."

Teddy was weeping openly as she threw herself into Jac's arms. "I love you so much. You're all I've ever w-wanted."

"Hush," he said, stroking the tears away with his fingertip. "You're going to live here in Costa, and you're going to add so much to this country." His laugh was low, chuckling. "The people will probably love *you* much more than they will me. I'll never love anyone but you, Teddy, for as long as I live!"

* * *

They had their arms around each other, Teddy leaning her body into Jac's as they walked through the palace to her apartment.

"I know there will be much to work out, darling. Your tennis, for one thing. I can't deprive you of that."

"Jac, I love tennis, but I've pounded out a lot of hours on the courts for a heck of a lot of years, and now I want to start living the rest of my life. Maybe I could start a Costan Open," she mused aloud. "Maybe a tennis academy here. . . ."

"We must tell my father first," he said. "Then in a few days we'll make the official announcement. Teddy, you may not realize it but you are going to become one of Costa's most important national assets."

Before breakfast the next morning, Jac led Teddy to the West Wing, where his father's private quarters were, and within a few minutes they were being ushered into a huge bedroom papered in a muted brick color, its large, four-poster bed swagged with dark green satin. Prince Henri was seated in the bed, propped up on five or six pillows, wearing a white nightshirt of the type that Teddy had seen only in old movies.

"Papa, I hope you had a good rest," Jac said quietly, going forward and bending his head in a slight bow. At the same time Teddy curtsied deeply. She could feel her face turning bright pink.

"My son," Henri said, gazing questioningly first at Jac, then at Teddy, then at Jac again.

"Papa, I am here to tell you that I have decided to accept the investiture as ruling Prince and Sovereign of Costa del Mar," Jac said formally. "And further, to ask your permission to make Theodora Warner my wife and princess."

Prince Henri broke into a beatific smile. "Son," he said, breathing out a long sigh of pleasure and relief. "Son, you have made me so very, very happy. And as for you, Theodora, you will make a wonderful addition to our family.

I am most pleased to grant this request. Most pleased. Now let a grateful old man hug you a few times.''

Henri actually had moisture in his eyes.

''Thank you, Your Highness,'' Teddy said, touched. She embraced the old prince, who held her tightly.

Henri turned to his son. ''Jac, you must now choose a ring for Teddy, and I wish to give her the Princess tiara as her wedding gift from me.''

The Princess tiara had been given to the Bellinis by Queen Victoria and had been worn since then by all the sovereign princesses, including Princess Lisse. It was shaped in the form of interlocking hearts and encrusted with hundreds of diamonds. Teddy had seen it in dozens of photographs of Jac's mother, and thought it was one of the most beautiful pieces of jewelry she had ever seen. Astonished and delighted, she could only stare at Henri.

''My dear,'' the old prince told her gently, ''you will wear it for state occasions—and I am certain you will wear it beautifully. Welcome to our country . . . and to our hearts, Princess Theodora.''

The tiara! The wedding! Henri wanted Jac to be crowned first, and several weeks later he and Teddy would be married.

''I love you,'' Jac whispered, as he walked her to her door.

''I love you, too.'' Teddy slid her arms around him.

Jac enfolded her in his arms for a kiss as soft and sweet as it was thrilling—a kiss that promised much more tenderness to follow. Teddy moaned, pressing herself as close to him as she could get. Suddenly she needed his comfort—his support. She was scared!

''Don't worry about it all,'' he told her, sensing her distress.

''I am, though. I'm petrified.''

Jac's laugh was low in his throat. ''Now you know how I feel. We can muddle through this together. Teddy, I can't tell you how much this means to me, that you would do this for me. Having you with me will make it all so much easier.''

''*I'll* make it easier? Bold, brash, all-American me?'' But Teddy laughed, her nervousness quickly ebbing.

''The Golden Girl of Tennis is exactly what I want,'' Jac whispered.

Teddy wanted desperately to share this news with her father . . . but he wasn't there.

Finally she opened her briefcase, where she always carried a photograph that had been taken of them after her win at Wimbledon.

She pulled out the photo and looked at Houston Warner's laughing face. ''Daddy . . . Oh, Daddy—I'm going to marry him,'' she whispered. ''I'm so excited. I'm so happy. It's just so incredible.''

But she could almost hear him saying, ''*What about tennis?*''

Teddy held up the picture. ''I love tennis, Daddy,'' she whispered. ''But I've given twelve hard years to it. I'll still play two or three tournaments a year. . . . Daddy, I can still do so much for tennis, but I want to do it with Jac. I'm gonna be a princess, Daddy!''

Gazing at the picture, she imagined she saw Houston Warner nod slightly. Then, smiling even as tears streamed down her cheeks, she put the photograph down.

Shivering suddenly in the coolness of the early morning, she rummaged in a drawer until she'd located a favorite Teddy Bear sweatshirt that her father had given her once for her birthday. It said *Bears Have More Fun.* She shivered her way into it, then pulled on a pair of sweatpants.

She *must* be coming down with something, she decided with annoyance. Crawling into bed, she pulled all the coverlets over herself, then reached for the phone again.

''Jamaica,'' she said, when she had dialed the number

in Ann Arbor. "Jamie, you're never going to believe this.
I don't even believe it myself, but . . ."

Gabriella was in her room, sketching some ideas on an
artist's pad, when her telephone rang. It was Jac, asking if
he could come to her room for a few minutes.

"Of course," she said. "Jac? Is anything wrong?"

"No," her brother told her. "Everything is fine."

Ten minutes later she was staring incredulously at Jac
as he told her that he and Teddy Warner were getting married.

"As my older sister, I wanted you to know first," said
Jac, his cheeks flushed with excitement.

"Why, that's wonderful," said Gaby, overcome. She
sank into her chair, feeling as if she'd just been struck by
a massive blow. She liked Teddy—that wasn't the problem.
But Jac's news made her painfully aware of how much she
missed Cliff Ferguson. She swayed, her body trembling violently.

"Gaby? Are you all right?" Jac asked.

Gaby realized that she was weeping. "I'm so happy for
you," she sobbed. "I am! It's just that Cliff— We broke
our engagement. I'm so miserable."

"Sis," said Jac, fiercely hugging her. "Was it him? Did
he break it off? If he did, if he hurt you, I'll—"

"No, no. It was me. He wanted me to stay behind walls
and guards. He doesn't understand how we have to live."

Jac continued to soothe her until finally Gabriella
stopped crying. She wiped her burning eyes. "I'm sorry. I
didn't mean to dump on you with my problems."

"Gaby, I'm marrying an American, too, and there'll be
some major adjustments for Teddy and me, but I am sure
we can work out our differences. I'm certain you and Cliff
can do it, too."

"No! It isn't the same. Don't you understand?" Her
voice rose. "Teddy understands what it is to be in the public eye. She's lived that way for the last twelve years. Cliff

hasn't ever lived that way. He wants to be protective, he doesn't understand that for us, every day of our lives poses some kind of a risk. We have to live with that risk, or we might as well be prisoners forever."

Jac nodded. "I know, but tomorrow it will all look much better."

"No," said Gaby, crying again. "It's over! I humiliated him. He would never take me back now."

Teddy barely slept that night. She was so charged with energy that her mind kept running in circles. At six A.M. a coughing spell brought her sharply awake. Her heart was thumping heavily, and there was a strange pain in her chest when she breathed. Her skin felt hot.

She crawled out of bed and went to the pink marble bathroom, where she stepped into the shower, turning under needle-sharp pinpoints of spray. She *couldn't* get sick now, she told herself. Not with so much to do. She didn't even know all the duties her future entailed, but she felt sure that it would be awesome. The invitations, Jac had told her, would be sent to more than twelve hundred guests, a number that seemed astronomical to Teddy.

Looking in the bathroom cabinet, she found some aspirin and swallowed two pills.

She decided against breakfast and dressed in jeans and a long-sleeved T-shirt. Then she left her room and found her way to the west entrance of the palace, the one closest to the beach. A blue-uniformed sentry nodded to her and carefully wrote down her name and the time. She remembered briefly that she was supposed to have a bodyguard accompany her, but it seemed foolish so early in the morning. Besides, she wanted to be by herself.

The sky was a soft, mild blue, the surf swirling gently up onto the golden sand. It must have rained sometime during the night, for the air tasted of wetness, and there were small puddles on the wooden boardwalk, which was nearly empty except for a few fishermen. The rows of beach cabanas stretched out, deserted.

Teddy found her way to the surf line and began to walk on the damp sand, swirls of water occasionally dampening her sneakers. A princess! She knew she still hadn't really absorbed the amazing thing that had happened. Would she live a life something like Princess Diana's, full of "official" trips and engagements? She would live in the palace, she found herself thinking. She would be mistress of a house with more than 120 ornate rooms, a household staff of more than 250 people.

God . . . was she ready for all that?

But Jac had told her he didn't feel ready either, so maybe it would be all right. . . .

She continued to wrestle with her thoughts as she passed the cabana area, heading toward a section of the beach that had not yet been commercially developed. A hundred yards farther down the sand Teddy spotted two men in slacks and shirts standing together talking. One carried a briefcase and notepad, while the other one was talking fast, gesturing toward the vacant land that stretched back from the beach.

Absorbed in her thoughts, she paid them no attention. But then, looking up as she walked past, she realized to her shock that one of the men was Nikos Skouros. She recoiled. He had not paid her any attention, as he was busily pointing out something to the other man.

A burning anger began deep in Teddy's stomach and rose up swiftly into her throat. She reeled a little, almost feeling sick. Nickey Skouros!

She didn't stop to think. Nor did she remember to feel fear. She strode through the sand until she had reached the two men.

"Out early, I see," she said to Skouros, her breath coming fast.

"Good morning, Miss Warner," Skouros said, giving her one of his famous, charming smiles, as the sea wind ruffled his silver hair. The second man, the one with the notepad, whom she now recognized as Skouros's executive secretary, Stavros Andreas, stepped back deferentially. "I see you are out early, too. Isn't it a glorious day? The sun is going to blaze hot by afternoon."

Teddy drew herself up. Hatred swirled through her.

"I know what you've done," she snapped. "I know all about it—and other people know, too."

"Miss Warner, what is it that other people 'know'?"

"I—you—my father," she said painfully, fear beginning to ebb into her mind now. Why hadn't she brought her bodyguard?

Skouros kept his smile. "Your father's disappearance is still under investigation, but the preliminary findings by the Board of Inquiry of the Costan Coast Guard affirm an accidental death. I know how difficult all of this has been for you—"

"Difficult!" Teddy cried incredulously. "Difficult? Mr. Skouros, my father is dead! Someone tried to kill me with a bomb that exploded within a few feet of me and killed a man I'd worked with for eight years. I think you had something to do with it."

"And I think *you* are very distraught, my dear Teddy Warner," said Skouros smoothly. He moved forward, taking Teddy's arm as if to support and guide her. She tried to jerk away, but his fingers were surprisingly strong and held her tightly in his grip.

"Let go of me!"

"Miss Warner, you appear to be somewhat hysterical, probably as a result of the stress you have been through."

"No! No!" she cried.

He continued, his voice silky. "Because of your hysteria you're making frivolous accusations that have absolutely no basis in fact and are, I must tell you, slanderous. But in deference to your condition I will forget about it—and I suggest you do the same. Now why don't you return to your hotel and seek some medical assistance for your nerves? If you need a recommendation, I will be happy to provide the name of an outstanding physican who might be able to help you.''

Teddy twisted violently, managing to pull away from him. She backed away, her footing awkward in the sand. They stared at each other, their eyes locking.

"Mr. Skouros, I am not hysterical, nor do I want to visit *your* doctor." Her voice rose angrily. "You are currently under investigation, and if there are any more attacks on me—or anyone else—you'll be charged with murder!"

She was amazed at what she'd just shouted, but the words could not be taken back now. She saw Skouros's eyes darken almost to black.

"You little bitch," he said in a low voice. "You stupid little bitch."

Teddy lifted her chin. "No," she snapped. "*You* are the one who is stupid. You want your power so much—you want to control this whole beautiful country, don't you? Well, you're not going to. I promise! And when I'm princess—"

She stopped, choking off her words.

"Princess, eh? So you think you are to marry Prince Jac?" Skouros's smile began to widen almost to a grin. "In this world of ours, my dear, nothing is certain!"

Teddy stared at him, appalled and afraid. He had threatened her, hadn't he?

"Leave me alone, Mr. Skouros, and leave this country alone, too," she blurted with forced bravado. Then she turned and hurried along the sand again, in the direction of the palace, aware of the two men behind her, watching her every move. A brisk wind began blowing over the waves, chilling her to the bone.

Nikos Skouros watched the blond girl jog down the beach. Then he turned to his secretary.

"That girl is dangerous, Stavros. She's got a loose tongue, and her wild accusations could cause exactly the type of trouble we don't need."

Stauros nodded.

"I want you to find out where she's staying and have someone follow her. I want to know everywhere she goes and everything she does."

"Yes, Mr. Skouros."

"I want this property, and I want it now. It's time to start putting real pressure on Prince Georges and on Breton, too" he snapped. "We can't afford to wait any longer. Get me Breton on the telephone."

The man produced a cellular phone from his attaché case, punched in some numbers, and then handed the phone to Skouros.

When the phone rang Anatole Breton was bathing, stretched out in his large, marble bathtub, while his twenty-two-year-old mistress, Anaïs, scrubbed his back with a scratchy loofah sponge. She was naked, too, her voluptuous body already exciting him.

Playfully Breton reached out and squeezed one of her pinkish nipples, tweaking it between his thumb and forefinger. His wife was visiting Paris for one of her shopping sprees.

As the phone rang, Breton was extending his caress to include the girl's ripe, curved stomach and buttocks. He was already partially erect.

"Merde!" he swore as it rang repeatedly.

Finally he motioned for Anaïs to hand him the phone. When he heard the voice on the other end, he gestured her to leave the room, and he stood up in the tub, reaching for a towel to drape around his waist.

On the other end of the line, Skouros spoke in a low, controlled voice. He told Breton that he had moved too slowly, that he had not obtained the necessary permits, that he had reneged on several of their agreements, delaying Skouros's plans and creating havoc. Although Skouros never raised his voice, anger hardened his tone, bringing beads of perspiration to the forehead of Prince Henri's chief advisor.

"I did my best. You do not understand, Mr. Skouros. In this country, everything goes back to Prince Henri. He does not permit any building along the shore unless it is done exactly according to his wishes. He dislikes foreign corporations. He has set up certain safeguards that thwart attempts to circumvent the rules and corporate regulations—"

"I want those permits issued first thing tomorrow morning. I plan to break ground next month," snapped Skouros. "And I expect your full cooperation."

Holding on to the telephone, Breton felt his entire body tremble with fear.

"Jac," Teddy whispered later that morning. She had rested in her room, exhausted by her run on the beach. The aspirins were making her feel light-headed. Now Jac had met her in the main hall, preparatory to their leaving for their meeting with Prince Henri's chief advisor, Anatole Breton.

"Jac, I may have done something I shouldn't have."

"What do you mean?"

She told Jac everything that she and Skouros had said to each other. "I blew it," she said. "I was just so angry, I didn't think clearly. I accused him, and he was furious. I could see it in his eyes."

Jac scowled. "Don't worry, Teddy. I'll get to the bottom of this. Meanwhile, you are to keep your bodyguard with you at all times, and it would be best if you stayed inside the palace, except when you're with me."

Teddy nodded, a cough suddenly racking her for several minutes. Ordinarily she would have argued with Jac's protective logic, but right now she didn't feel all that great— light-headed, warm, clammy—and she had no energy.

Anatole Breton lived in a large villa perched on a hill overlooking the sea, about a half kilometer away from the Vendôme Palace. The fifteen-room home, built in the

1920s, was made of pale bisque-colored stucco, with a Spanish-style roof, and fountains and statues in front. It reminded Teddy of a house in Beverly Hills.

As Jac's driver pulled the Rolls-Royce up the steep driveway that led to the property, Teddy murmured, "Jac, why are we coming here rather than going to Breton's office?"

"I want to see him at home. I think it may be better this way."

"I don't understand."

"If I'm right, you'll understand a great deal in a few minutes. Trust me, Teddy."

The chauffeur waited in the car while two bodyguards accompanied them into the house. They were admitted by a servant, who led them through rooms crammed with expensive French paintings.

Breton received them in a study that faced the sea. The room was as luxurious as the rest of the house.

"Good day, Your Highness," said Breton, coming forward to greet them. He was a distinguished-looking man of sixty-two, who appeared much younger than his years. A nervous smile sought to conceal his tenseness.

Breton, after acknowledging Prince Jac, turned to greet Teddy. Although he had greeted Jac in French, he now spoke in nearly flawless English. "And, Mademoiselle Teddy, I am delighted to see you in my home. I have ordered some wine. It will be here in a few moments. . . . Are we not having beautiful weather? But a little chilly at night now, don't you think?"

Teddy could sense Breton's nervousness at this unusual royal visit.

The wine arrived, and they were served on a patio overlooking the high promontory. Jac turned the conversation to the topic of new construction in Costa, including the recent arcane sale of an eighteen-acre tract of prime beachfront property to an unspecified foreign investor.

"And it is not the first such sale, is it, Monsieur Breton?

Isn't it true that there have been several large land sales in Costa in the past five years to some well-insulated cartel, some group that does not wish its identity known to us? Such sales could only have taken place with your knowledge and permission.''

Breton's hands convulsively squeezed his linen napkin, his sweaty fingers squashing the carefully ironed folds.

"The Crown is totally aware of what has been going on," Jac continued. "You are violating the trust bestowed on you, aren't you, Monsieur Breton? Your actions also happen to be in clear violation of the law. They are dishonorable and illegal.''

Breton paled. "Your Highness, to what do you refer?''

"I have been using private investigators for some time, and they have given me a full report of your activities,'' Jac said. "We now have irrefutable evidence of your insidious behavior.''

"*No,*" said Breton. The blood had drained from his features, and he looked suddenly like a tired, frightened old man. "No, Your Highness, it is not—you are mistaken—I would never—''

"All the evidence has been carefully documented, and you face an indictment on criminal charges, heavy fines, and a long prison term, monsieur,'' Jac went on coldly. "All of your possessions, including this house and your art collection, will be confiscated by the government and held in escrow . . . unless, of course, you wish to cooperate with the Ministry of Justice and earn clemency.''

"Clemency! Your Highness, please—''

"Talk to me now,'' Jac said flatly. "Otherwise I will have you arrested today, Monsieur Breton.''

"I—I—'' Then the minister slumped in his chair, spreading his hands wide. "I am an old man. What do you wish me to do? I will do it!''

"Tell me who is buying up the beachfront property. Also, the name of those you've been working for during the past three years. I wish to see your financial records, receipt books, all documents, letters, or other materials. Otherwise . . ." Jac let the threat hang.

"I can't. . . . This group is— This man is powerful, very powerful."

"His name," snapped Jac.

"Nikos Skouros," mumbled the advisor. "But, Your Highness, he threatened me, he threatened my family. He said that if I did not cooperate with him my wife and grand-daughters would be involved in a horrible accident. He even threatened to harm my m-mistress! I could not permit it, Your Highness."

"If, in fact, you cooperate with me fully and your statements check out, then that will be taken into consideration at your trial, and the Crown's counsel will recommend that the court take this into consideration. But there are more names, aren't there? I want them all."

Breton swallowed, running his tongue over dry lips. Then he reluctantly said, "Yes . . . there *is* someone else. It is your— Your Highness, it is your uncle. Prince Georges."

Wearily Jac rose, indicating to Teddy that she should come with him. He lifted the cellular phone he had been carrying in a briefcase and spoke a few words into it. Then he turned to the elderly advisor. "Monsieur Breton, you are under house arrest. The police will be here within five minutes. You will go with them to your office and help them locate all incriminating documents."

As they left the patio, Teddy darted a look of sympathy at the elderly man who was still slumped in his wicker chair.

As they reached the Rolls, police were already arriving in their blue-and-white government vehicles. Jac stopped and looked at her.

"My bluff worked admirably, didn't it, Teddy?"

"Yes, but I— He *is* elderly, Jac. Surely he wouldn't have to go to prison."

Jac shook his head. "He is a traitor to the Crown. He

tried to destroy everything that has meaning for us here in Costa. I cannot countenance that, nor can my father. It is not always an easy job to rule. Sometimes one must do unpleasant things, such as now. I don't particularly enjoy this, but there is no choice. I hope you can understand that.''

''I—I do,'' she gulped.

''Besides, don't you understand what this means?'' Jac went on. ''Breton is only an accomplice. He is not the real power behind what happened; neither, really, is Prince Georges. Skouros will stop at nothing in his efforts to turn our country into another Las Vegas, including the use of Georges's envy.''

Teddy stared at him. ''But what does this mean?'' she said in a low voice. ''Is Nikos Skouros the one who killed my father? Or had him killed?''

A muscle knotted in Jac's jaw. ''I do not know yet. After Prince Georges is questioned, I think we may have a few more answers.''

Earlier in the day Prince Georges had been notified of Prince Jac's expected visit to Breton's home, and during the past forty minutes he had waited for a report, tensely pacing through the rooms of his villa in the hills.

Why was Prince Jac suddenly paying a call on Breton? Did the Crown suspect? His stomach was tightly clenched as he worried that Breton might talk and implicate Georges.

The phone rang. Georges hurried into his office and answered it himself, dismissing his secretary with a furious wave of the hand. The man hurried out of the room, closing the door and leaving the prince in privacy.

Georges clicked the door bolt shut.

''Yes, yes, yes?'' he snapped into the phone.

''Georges, it is too late. They know everything,'' came Breton's voice, high, alarmed, on the verge of hysteria. ''I only have a few minutes before the police arrive.''

"What did you tell them?" Georges's voice held a deathly chill.

"I told them . . . about you. I had to! He knew! Jac knew everything—he has been using investigators. I am waiting now to be arrested! I don't know what to do! You must hire lawyers for me. You must see to it that I am protected! I can't go to prison—I'm too old. I must—"

The muscles of Georges's arm seemed to turn to water, and he felt the telephone fall away from his grip. He stared out the window at the beige towers of the palace, flying Costa's blue-and-white pennants.

They knew.

His hands moving quickly, as he placed a call to Skouros's villa.

"They know," was all that he said, but he was forced to swallow rapidly in order to avoid sobbing like a child.

"What? You can't be serious," said Skouros, but his voice was hard, giving Georges the feeling that he already knew.

"They know, I tell you. They know it all. And you do not know my brother or his son. They can be vindictive. They will hunt you down, Nikos. They will take their Bellini fortune and use it against you. I know them! Please . . . you have to do something! I don't wish to go to prison. I cannot go to prison."

"You can rot there for all I care," snapped Skouros. "You stupid fool. Did you really think that you were going to rule Costa? *I* would have ruled Costa. It was all just your fantasy, Georges. The fantasy of an old royal who has never done anything for sixty years but envy his older brother."

"And *you* are a murderer," cried Georges.

"No, my good man, you are. Aren't you the one who ordered those deaths?"

"But I—I didn't. Not those deaths."

"I advised you not to. I told you that you could not prevent the gossip, plug all the leaks, but you insisted on trying to do so anyway. If you had not condoned those

murders, we would not have attracted so much attention,"
the Greek went on silkily.

"But you're lying. It's all a lie—"

"Is it? If there is ever a trial, who will they believe?
You, who openly plotted against your own country, who
had a finance minister killed along with his wife? Or me,
a respected Greek businessman?"

The phone went dead in Georges's hand.

Slowly he lifted his head and opened the lower right
drawer of his desk, pulling out a .38 pistol.

By the time they had returned to the palace, Teddy was
breathing rapidly, and she could feel the blood pounding
uncomfortably in her veins. A headache skewered her temples, and occasional fits of coughing had begun to rack her
body.

"You have a bad cold," Jac said.

"I guess I must," Teddy said between coughs. "I've
been doing too much. I ran along the beach this morning
and got wet. I guess I shouldn't have."

"I want you to get in bed right now, Teddy. I'll call the
palace physician and have him come to see you."

By the time she entered her room, Teddy suddenly felt
exhausted. She crawled onto her bed and lay there, too tired
even to get under the covers. She wondered just what kind
of a bug she'd picked up. She was shivering again, having
cold chills.

Five minutes later Dr. Blanchet, the physician on staff
at the palace, arrived, accompanied by his nurse in case he
needed assistance. Blanchet listened carefully to Teddy's
heart as well as tapping her chest and taking her temperature.

"I've been feeling punk for several days now, but I
thought it was just a cold," she told him. "All the stress,
and then flying over here and jet lag, and then I accidentally
got wet this morning while I was running on the beach."

She saw him frown. "You have a fever of over thirty-nine degrees," he told her in perfect English, adding that this was more than 103 degrees Fahrenheit. "Have you been suffering chills?"

"Oh, yes."

"Rapid breathing? Coughing?"

"Yes."

"Headache? Nausea? Vomiting?"

Teddy sighed. "Yes, the headache, but I'm not—"

Suddenly she was. She had to jump up and lunge for the bathroom. After a while, weak and chilled, cold sweat standing out on her skin, she returned to the bedroom.

"I want you to come to my office immediately for a chest X ray," said Dr. Blanchet. "I want to have a better look at your lungs. I suspect you may have advanced pneumonia."

Teddy rode in a motorized wheelchair to the doctor's office, located in a distant wing of the palace. She started having another cold chill as she was standing with her chest pressed in front of the X-ray machine.

Dr. Blanchet frowned as he came into the examining room a few minutes later. "You have pneumonia. It would be best if we put you in the hospital for the next ten days, Miss Warner. I can treat you much better there since the hospital has the very latest technology. Now, don't worry," he added as Teddy gave a little cry of dismay. "There are excellent antibiotics to deal with this problem, and in a few days, you'll be feeling much stronger."

Teddy was taken to the Royal Costan Hospital, where the entire ninth floor was divided into luxurious suites with bedrooms, lounges, and special kitchens where gourmet meals could be prepared for the invalid royals or other VIPs. Already Mack Douglas, the ex–NYPD officer who was now her bodyguard, had posted himself at the door to her suite, along with a Costan bodyguard. The sight of them brought her a feeling of relief.

Teddy undressed and got into bed. Pneumonia? Is that what she had? She'd have to get over it quickly. She and Jac had so many things to do now . . . announce their engagement, choose a dress; she would have to study Costan history and constitutional law, and improve her French. She also needed to phone Aunt Alicia, her only living relation. . . .

Her thoughts drifted. She closed her eyes, falling immediately into a feverish sleep.

Prince Jac heard the news of Prince Georges's suicide with a dulled shock. "Are you sure?" he asked when the chief of palace security brought the news to him. "Are you *sure* it was suicide?"

"There is no doubt, Your Highness. There were fingerprints on the gun and powder burns all over his hand. His office door was bolted from the inside, and the windows were also locked."

"I see," said Jac, who possessed a Catholic's horror of suicide, which would prevent a believer from being buried in consecrated ground or ever entering the Kingdom of Heaven. "I wish to go to Royal House immediately."

"But, Your Highness, the scene is— It is most unpleasant."

"Immediately," insisted Jac. He telephoned LaMarché, the detective who had worked for him and Teddy, and requested that the man accompany him to his uncle's home.

Prince Georges's body had been removed, but Jac felt a deep sense of revulsion and depression close over him as he and the detective began their search. He realized now that Skouros would have used his power to place Georges on the throne. Georges then would have been a puppet ruler with Nikos Skouros pulling the strings.

As for himself—Jac felt a sudden hollowness in the pit of his stomach. They would have had to get rid of him, of course. How could a young, aggressive prince be permitted to threaten their plans? No, Jac had already driven in Formula One races—and for Skouros Shipping Lines! He had already suffered several minor mishaps. What more simple than that he should have another accident?

Jac shuddered as he realized what an easy target he had been.

The detective and Jac spent hours going through Prince Georges's study, sorting through his letters, papers, notes, hoping for a clue, something tangible, that would lead them to Nikos Skouros. Solid proof was what they needed, and without it Skouros would go free.

"Merde," said the detective as he closed the bottom drawer of a large file cabinet stuffed full of papers, many dating back twenty years. "This man saved everything, but it's all innocuous. Nothing out of the ordinary here that I can see."

"Georges could be a very clever man," mused Jac. He remembered his father's office, the bookcase that had a secret door, leading to the palace vault.

He walked over to a bookshelf that lined one wall and began pulling out books, pressing sections of the wood, hoping to trigger a secret button or lever. But nothing happened. If there was a doorway behind the bookshelf, Georges had had it hidden well.

Jac then moved to the wall and began pushing pictures aside, hoping to find a secret safe. But again, there was nothing, and he was about to give up when he saw a slight crease in the leaf-green brocaded wallpaper that lined the walls of the study. Curious, he walked over and began running his fingers up and down the break. One indented area interested him, and he pushed down on it.

A two-by-two section of the wall slid open, revealing a small wall safe with a combination lock.

"Call palace security," Jac said excitedly. "I want to get into that safe."

While he was waiting for security to arrive, Jac placed

a call to the palace physician, and was informed that Teddy had been taken to the hospital with bronchial pneumonia.

She twisted and turned, fighting the sheets that bound her.

"Mademoiselle Warner, you must lie still. The antibiotic is going to make you better, and we don't want that intravenous line to slip out now, do we?" said a nurse.

"I'm sorry," she muttered.

"His Highness is here to see you."

Vaguely Teddy was aware of Jac sitting by her bed, holding her hand, murmuring to her about a safe they had found at Georges's house.

"He kept detailed notes of everything he did," Jac told her triumphantly. "A diary in his own handwriting! Meetings with Nikos Skouros, an agenda of everything that was said. Even a meeting with the French president. And details about D'Fabray's death. Apparently Skouros has been plotting for years to get control of Costa. He was using both Georges and Breton, and was close to completing his master plan. He intended to reward Georges by making him the sovereign prince."

Teddy tried to smile, but instead doubled up with a knife-sharp cough. "Did he . . . my father . . . ?" she managed to say through chattering teeth. She clutched Jac's hand.

"Teddy, are you all right? I'm worried about you."

"I'm f-fine," she chattered. "T-tell me, Jac. Tell me what else you learned."

"According to the diary, Georges already knew your father had uncovered damaging information about his activities and might discuss it with the wrong parties, so he went to Skouros with his suspicions. Skouros decided to silence your father and Faid, too, because both of them had overheard my father talking on board the *Olympia*, naming the advisors he felt were betraying him. As for you, you were asking too many questions, and they were afraid your father might have talked to you. Teddy?'' Jac added. ''Teddy?''

''I want him punished,'' Teddy moaned. *''Please. . . .''*

''It's already being done. Teddy!''

But Teddy had sunk back on her pillow, her eyes closed. Her skin was so hot it throbbed.

''Dr. Blanchet,'' said Jac anxiously, ''tell me what her condition is. She's burning up with fever! Why haven't the medications taken effect?''

''I don't know, Your Highness, but be assured we're doing our best,'' said the physician. ''When I took her history, it became evident that she has had this infection in her system for some time now, and it's hard to break it. We're doing our best, but it depends, in large part, on her body's ability to fight the sepsis.''

''But she *has* to be all right,'' cried Jac, starting to panic. ''We're engaged, we are going to be married.''

''Your Highness, permit me to speak frankly. We will try to bring down her temperature with an ice bath and drugs, and the antibiotic will reduce the bronchial infection, I hope, but Mademoiselle Warner is gravely ill.''

''Do you mean—?''

The doctor nodded.

''God, please, no,'' said Jac hoarsely.

When word of Prince Georges's suicide reached Nikos Skouros, he moved through his villa, gathering up papers and stuffing them into his briefcase, snapping orders at Stavros as he went. ''Have the car waiting—five minutes! We can call from the car and have them ready my plane for flight. . . . No, they'll be waiting at the airport. Charter a helicopter under another name. Move it! Move, move!''

''Yes, Mr. Skouros,'' said the frightened secretary. ''Will I . . . ? Will I be coming with you?''

''Of course, you will. And hurry! I have no intention of spending a single minute in jail.''

* * *

Jac, Kristina, and Gabriella were keeping vigil in a mag-
nificently furnished lounge, waiting for word on Teddy's
condition.

"Jac, I think it is wonderful that you're marrying her,"
Kristina kept saying encouragingly. "She will make a wonderful princess. She'll recover. Don't worry."

"Yes," agreed Gabriella. "The antibiotics will cure it.
They have to!" added Gaby.

"And *I* love her," said Kristina. "Even more than you,
Gabriella. Because I know her much better."

Both princesses sighed, their expressions anxious.

"I don't want to lose her," muttered Jac. "I can't. Not
now, just when I've found her again." He turned away so
his sisters wouldn't see the tears that streamed from his
eyes.

An hour passed. Then two. Jac paced the room, his anxiety growing with each step. Teddy! She was so young, so
strong and vital, he couldn't believe that pneumonia . . . that
she might not make it. *She had to make it.*

Restlessly he continued to pace. He had already telephoned Paris, at the American Hospital for Dr. Sanford
Sklar, a prominent specialist in pulmonary medicine, who
was being flown in. He was due momentarily, and Jac had
been assured he was one of the best in his field.

Teddy, he thought desperately, *I love you.*

Dr. Aldo Masci moved quietly through the hospital
lobby, proceeding toward the elevator, where he punched
the button for the ninth floor. He wore a white doctor's
coat and an ID tag.

Emerging from the elevator, he walked briskly down the
corridor to the nurses' station, where two nurses sat conferring over records. When one of the royals was a patient
on the ninth floor, an extra doctor and two nurses were
assigned to the floor exclusively for their benefit.

One of the nurses looked up appreciatively as he paused.

He was gray-haired, distinguished-looking, with an aquiline nose and confident stride. Only a slight paunch detracted from his good looks.

"Good day," he greeted her. "Dr. Masci here. Miss Warner's room?"

"Number 901." She handed him Teddy's case file. Carrying it, he continued on his way.

Teddy aroused from her feverish doze long enough to hear voices at the door of her room. Mack Douglas, her bodyguard, had stopped someone, asking to see his ID.

"Can't be too safe, Dr. Masci," said the ex–police officer. "Sorry for the inconvenience." The Costan security officer stepped aside to allow entrance.

The doctor walked into the room and approached Teddy's bed.

"I am Dr. Aldo Masci from the American Hospital in Paris. I have been asked by Prince Jac to supervise your medical treatment," he told her. His voice had an accent, maybe Greek; she couldn't place it.

She twisted in the bed, moaning a little. "I'm so hot," she whispered. "Feverish. Doctor . . . am I going to be all right?"

"You're going to be just fine."

He examined her with the stethoscope, his fingers fumbling slightly, she thought, as he pulled open the front of her hospital gown. Then he fussed with her bed a little, telling her that he wanted to raise the head of the bed so he could examine her better. She thought she heard him fumbling underneath the frame of the bed.

"Ah. My mistake. Your bed is electrical," he murmured. He had found the control that could be used to raise the mattress. Teddy felt herself tilting up to a sitting position. Wearily she closed her eyes. She couldn't keep them open anymore, not even while she was examined by the doctor. She felt as if she was floating above the room . . . not really part of it at all.

* * *

Jac was sitting in the waiting room when one of the nurses, the younger one, came in to inform him that the doctor had arrived from Paris and had already been in Teddy's room, examining her.

"Good! Wonderful!" Jac was relieved.

"He'll have her well in no time," said Princess Kristina, the relief showing on her face, too.

"Dr. Masci has just left her room," the nurse added. "He said he needed to look at her X rays."

"Dr. Masci?" Jac felt a heavy thump in the center of his chest. "The man I called is named Sanford Sklar. Dr. Sanford Sklar!"

The nurse stared at him, her face going white. "But, Your Highness, he was in the room with Miss Warner for nearly twenty minutes."

Jac began running.

Teddy was having another feverish dream, but suddenly she heard pounding footsteps. Someone was in the room, shaking her shoulders, prodding her.

"Teddy!" Jac shouted. "Teddy! Wake up! Are you all right? My God!"

Teddy struggled to open her eyes. She tried to look at Jac, but all she saw was a round shape and his fiercely blue eyes blazing at her.

"You're all right, you're alive, thank God." He hugged her to him, and she felt moisture on his face and knew by the shaking of his body that Jac was crying. "Oh, God," he moaned. "He didn't hurt you. Teddy, I thought I'd lost you. I thought you were gone from me forever."

"I'm here," Teddy mumbled.

"I love you," Jac whispered. Then, almost in the same breath, he spoke to both Mack Douglas and the Costan bodyguards. "She hasn't been harmed, but I still have a bad feeling. I want her moved to another room—*now*."

Suddenly there was more activity in the room, a great

deal of it. The bodyguards, nurses, hospital security, Jac, Kristina, Gabriella, all of them milling about, talking at once. Teddy heard the sound of wheels, and then she was being lifted up, transferred to a gurney covered with a white sheet. She felt the delicious cool chill of the sheets as she was laid down. The IV pole came with her.

"Another room," she heard Jac say. He was holding her hand, gripping her fingers. In her filmy daze she smelled his spicy aftershave. "Someplace where you'll be safe."

Safe? Wasn't she safe?

Why were they moving her? she thought groggily. It had something to do with that doctor who'd been here . . . the one who'd said he was from Paris.

She struggled to think clearly, but her head felt so hot and achy, her skull throbbing and painful. Teddy blinked her eyes open as a feeling of urgency came over her. There was something she had to remember . . . something terribly important. Something so dangerous that—

He had sat down on her bed. Used the stethoscope. Fussed with the bed, saying he had to raise it. Hadn't he put his hands underneath the bed?

Teddy licked her dry, cracked lips. Why would he have made such a point of fussing with the bed?

Unless—

"Jac," she managed to croak, "there might be a— *Get everyone out of the room. There may be a bomb.*"

The explosion shook the hospital with the shudder of its blast, red fire blasting out of the room that only five minutes before had been Teddy's.

Security had managed to clear the floor, and the guards were now evacuating the rest of the hospital. Fortunately, it looked as if no one had been injured.

Jac had carried Teddy out of the hospital in his arms.

On the hospital lawn, Jac tenderly laid Teddy on the grass and commandeered blankets to wrap her in. All around them there was chaos. People ran back and forth, sirens wailed, and policemen and soldiers swarmed, making sure that all the patients had been removed from the hospital. Most of the patients sat quietly on the grass, but a few wandered about. Some were staring at the prince and the pale young woman, others were too dazed to realize that Prince Jac was among them.

"Darling Teddy, my darling," he kept murmuring to her as he clasped her tightly.

"Jac," she whispered through dry lips.

"If they had killed you, they might as well have killed me. It would be the same thing. Teddy, I adore you. I love you beyond compare. Beyond everything. You *have* to get well."

Teddy did not reply.

"Teddy? Teddy?" Jac's voice was close to panic.

"I love you, too," she whispered, and then she managed to smile.

Later that night the real doctor from Paris arrived, and changed Teddy's medication. Within hours, her fever had started to tumble downward. Three days later, she was sitting up in bed, feeling almost herself again.

Jac filled her room with flowers, and placed in one of the bouquets was a priceless pearl necklace that had been in his family for 150 years.

In the ornate cathedral, in front of a private audience of sixty, including more than forty-five royals from all over Europe, the Archbishop of Costa del Mar, and other high church dignitaries, Prince Jac knelt on one knee on a purple velvet cushion. The coronation ceremony had already stretched on for more than an hour, and the television crew's intense lights were making even the lofty nave warm.

Prince Henri held the glittering crown high in both of his hands, speaking the same words his father had spoken twenty years before, during his own investiture. He read off a list of titles with which Jac was being invested, 130 in all.

Jac was perspiring slightly.

Prince Henri placed the crown on Jac's head.

Prince Jac, the sovereign ruler of Costa del Mar, rose, making the sign of the cross, and murmured his assent to the proceedings. He turned, smiling, to face the room. His eyes searched until he found Teddy.

After the coronation and the public appearance for the thousands who had been waiting for hours, there was a private reception for five hundred at the Vendôme Palace.

Prince Henri stood in a receiving line beside his son, his complexion reddened with pride and pleasure. He had taken a nitroglycerine pill before the coronation, and he was feeling relaxed now that the reins of the principality had been placed in his son's hands.

Now he felt almost giddy with relief.

"Your Highness, you must be feeling so joyful," said Queen Beatrix of the Netherlands, when the receiving line was finally finished and Henri could have the solace of a glass of wine.

Henri nodded. "I have been waiting years to see my son take responsibility, praying for this moment. Thank God it has arrived. But I'll feel even more happy when his marriage to Teddy Warner is consummated. Grandchildren," he explained.

"She should give you some good ones," said Beatrix, nodding. "Good, strong, new blood will freshen a line."

Henri nodded vehemently, agreeing. "Teddy is a fine young woman." The two stood side by side for some time, discussing royal lineages.

"I haven't been this happy in years," Henri told Beatrix. "Now I'll have time to work on my stamp collections, and I'm thinking about breeding Arabian horses."

* * *

It arrived in a thick, cream-colored vellum envelope, the address hand-lettered in a beautiful, scrolled script. The stamp was blue, engraved with a portrait of Prince Henri. On the back of the envelope was the crimson seal of Costa's royal family.

The royal invitation. Twelve hundred people had received one.

In Connecticut, Jamaica DuRoss raced back from the mailbox, waving the invitation over her head as if it were a flag. "It's here!" she yelled to her mother, who was planting bulbs in the garden. "It's really here! It's really happening! I'm going to Costa del Mar!"

In Beverly Hills, Michael Ovitz slit open the envelope with a silver letter opener and stared down at the engraved invitation. *His Serene Highness Prince Henri of Costa del Mar Requests* . . . Ovitz read the words, then reread them, his pulse quickening. How many in Hollywood had received similar envelopes? Only a few, he would imagine. Those who had known the royal family for a number of years.

Just at that moment his intercom buzzed loudly. Will Camden had received an invitation also.

In New York, jewelry designer Kenneth Jay Lane was on the telephone to one of his most famous clients, Elizabeth Taylor. He'd received an invitation to the Costan wedding, and now he wanted to find out who else was going. Elizabeth had just received hers—she had been the first Hollywood star to befriend Princess Lisse years ago, and she sounded nearly as excited as he was.

In Texas, at his Jacaranda ranch, Cliff Ferguson was having an argument with Rebecca.

"Daddy, we *have* to go! Daddy, we just have to!"

But he shook his head regretfully. If they attended the wedding, he would see Gaby. How could he gaze at her face and not want her? No, he couldn't possibly attend.

In Palm Beach, Teddy's Aunt Alicia had just come in from shopping. She dropped her bags from elegant Worth

Avenue onto the table top in order to scoop up the letters that had been left on the table by her maid. When she saw the vellum envelope, her heart jumped. She tore open the envelope.

In Monaco, Princess Caroline was meeting with her press secretary to go over her schedule. Smiling, the secretary handed her the cream-colored envelope. Caroline let out a small squeal of excitement. She already knew what was in the envelope—and she wouldn't miss the wedding for the world.

At Buckingham Palace, Queen Elizabeth II, seated in her office, was also sorting through her mail. Seeing the Costan invitation, the Queen sighed and thought ruefully about her own children's weddings. Still, she would attend this one. She looked forward to seeing Henri again. . . .

In Santiago, Chile, Nikos Skouros settled in the backseat of the black stretch limousine, unfolding a copy of *Paris Match* he had just purchased at a newsstand.

Royal Wedding of the Decade, its headline blazed.

He studied the official, color engagement portrait of Teddy Warner and the newly crowned Prince Jac. Teddy wore a deep pink satin gown, her throat encased in a stunning diamond choker, a huge sapphire engagement ring on her left hand. Jac stood tall beside her in his Costan military uniform studded with medals. For a moment Skouros felt a cutting pang of regret. Then he dropped the newspaper on the floor of the limo. Life went on. As long as one had money, it didn't matter where.

"La oficina del presidente," he snapped to his driver in perfect Spanish.

Narrowing his eyes, he gazed out at the sun-splashed streets of Santiago, the capital city of Chile, nestled between the Andes Mountains and the Pacific Ocean. The city was wide open: bribery was a way of life here in Chile, as it was elsewhere in South America. Cocaine trafficking was common, and fabulous fortunes, unlimited power, were there for the asking.

He might expand his holdings a bit in this area. He already possessed ample avenues for laundering the funds, and if he played his cards right, he might be able to parlay this asset into an alliance with a powerful member of the capital's cartel.

Yes, it was risky. There was always the possibility of sudden death, but he himself was too powerful to be touched.

Nikos Skouros leaned back in his seat, smiling confidently.

"Mr. Ferguson, I'm so glad I reached you," said Princess Kristina into the telephone, speaking in her low, husky, smoky voice.

The man on the other end of the line sounded slightly out of breath. "Yes, this is Cliff Ferguson. I was out doing some bronco-busting. How may I help you, Your Highness?"

"You've received your invitation for the wedding, of course?"

"Yes. But unfortunately I had made a prior business commitment, and my daughter and I are unable to accept," he drawled. "I deeply apologize."

"But you *must* come!" Why was this stubborn Texan making her sister's life so miserable? "It's of vital importance!"

Ferguson hesitated. "Princess Kristina, I cannot."

"But you have to! Gabriella has barely eaten in the last six weeks. She's fading away to a shadow, and it's all because of you," Kristina argued. "She loves you, and you've broken her heart."

"On the contrary, she broke my heart. But does it really matter who is at fault? I appreciate your concern, Your Highness, but it would be best for all if I . . ."

Kristina gritted her teeth and took a deep breath. Playing

cupid was hard work, she was discovering, and her sister
hadn't been any more cooperative than Cliff Ferguson was
being now.

"I *insist* that you come. I'd send the family's jet for
you, but I know you have your own. Still, I beg you to
accept our invitation. My father will take it as an affront if
you do not," she improvised. "Gaby needs you. She has
been ill."

"I thought Teddy was the one who had been ill."

"She was; she is fine now. But it's Gaby who's sick
in her heart, Clifford. I know my sister. She has only
loved one man in her life, and it's you. I wish you could see
her. . . . She is so sad, Cliff. I truly am worried about her.
You owe it to Gaby to at least talk with her again. Just a
little talk," Kristina wheedled. "Ten minutes with her.
Maybe fifteen. Then you'd be free to leave."

There was a long pause, and finally Kristina heard what
she'd been waiting for: Cliff Ferguson's soft chuckle.
"You're asking me to fly across the Atlantic to attend a
royal wedding and then talk to Gabriella for ten minutes?
That's *all* you want?"

"That's all."

"Would I be permitted to talk with her for twenty
minutes if the timing is just right?"

"As long as you wish." Kristina laughed, her voice
fairly tinkling. "Please. Gabriella and I haven't always gotten along very well—sometimes we've fought like cats, as
you probably know, but I want to do this for her."

"Does she know about this call?"

Kristina shook her head. "No. Of course not. It's going
to be a surprise."

"I see. Well, I hope your little surprise doesn't back-
fire," said Cliff after another pause. "I'll be there!"

Wedding presents by the hundreds were being delivered
to the Vendôme Palace, where they were arranged for display in the Grand Salon. Queen Elizabeth had sent an in-

scribed silver salver. Ivan Lendl, Steffi Graf, and Whoopi
Goldberg had all sent gifts. A rare, seventeenth-century
grandfather clock had come from billionaire John Kluge.
Prince Rainier of Monaco had sent a delicate table service
of handworked porcelain. A miniature model of the palace
in gold and semiprecious stones was the gift of the Federation of Costan Athletic Associations.

"Amazing," said Teddy to one of the secretaries, who
was helping her open all the gifts, catalog them, and begin
the arduous task of writing thank-you letters. "I can't believe it. It's like a fairy tale."

The woman nodded. "Mademoiselle Warner, do you
wish to open the package from President Clinton next?"

Three weeks later, Teddy rolled over in bed, moaned,
and then blinked her eyes open. For a second she didn't
know where she was. The ornate brocade draperies, the
priceless paintings and their heavy gilt frames, seemed part
of her dreams, not reality.

Then she remembered and felt her heart give an enormous thump against her ribs.

"Mademoiselle Teddy?" said a maidservant, knocking
discreetly on her door, then entering. "Your coffee."

Teddy sat up, pulling on a pale blue terry robe embroidered with crossed tennis rackets, and accepted the steam-
ing cup of *café au lait* and the tray of assorted pastries
prepared by the palace chef. She wasn't the least bit hungry,
but Kristina had advised her to force herself to eat. The day
would be a long one, and she'd need all her energy.

"Will there be anything else, mademoiselle?"

"No, that will be all, thank you."

Her wedding. *Today.*

Televised via satellite to four hundred million people.

Butterflies began to beat their wings in Teddy's stomach.
She sipped her coffee, hearing the saucer clatter as her
hands shook. She'd recovered fully from her pneumonia,
thank heavens. The antibiotics had worked wonders, but the

doctors told her to avoid stress for another few months. What did they think a wedding was, if not heavy-duty stress? And after she was married to Prince Jac, there might be a different kind of stress.

But what if she lost her own identity? What if she became submerged in all the duties, the ceremonies, and forgot about being just Teddy? But, Jac had already assured her, warmly and lovingly, that wouldn't happen.

There was another knock on her door.

"Yes?" Teddy called, swallowing a bite of brioche.

"Mademoiselle Teddy, His Royal Highness has just sent a package for you, and I was requested to deliver it immediately," said the same maid, coming back into the bedroom. She handed Teddy a small box wrapped in silvery gray paper.

Inside, nestled on white cotton was a simple gold key. She stared at it, bewildered. Then she noticed a small card tucked underneath the cotton.

"The key to so much," the card said in Jac's firm scrawl. "My heart, of course, and also a new tennis arena that will be given to Costa in your name. Forever, my love."

She stared at the card, her eyes filling with tears. It was Jac's wedding present to her, an arena where she could practice her own tennis, train talented young players, and stage international tennis tournaments for charity. She loved him for it. But she loved even more what it meant—his acceptance of her need for a life and interests of her own.

He wanted Princess Teddy—and *everything* that came with her.

The sun shone brilliantly, without a cloud in the blue sky. The Vendôme Palace was flying hundreds of blue-and-white pennants, and ornate bunting was draped along its cream-colored walls. Church bells had been ringing all morning.

Geneviève Mondalvi gazed out the window of her taxi,

tamping down a thrill of excitement. Even though she
hadn't received an official invitation to the wedding ceremony itself, she'd wangled invitations to several important
parties and had even arranged an interview with Teddy
Warner.

"Drive faster, *s'il vous plaît*. Just move the car, and the
people will get out of the way."

"*Oui, madame.*"

The whole principality was *en fête*. Autumn flowers
were massed everywhere. Three miles of blue carpeting had
been laid throughout the streets. Every hotel was packed as
wedding guests poured into town, and every available villa
was rented. The world's journalists had also thronged to
Costa, and they flocked everywhere, filming everything,
from the dozens of balls and parties, to a gala at the Casino
Opera that featured Costa's renowned ballet troupe per-
forming a new work entitled *The Princess Suite*, danced by
Mikhail Baryshnikov and Leslie Browne, both brought out
of retirement for this special occasion.

The taxi inched through the traffic-snarled streets, nearing the palace with great difficulty. Huge, boisterous
crowds had gathered, waiting for the bridal carriage to
emerge for the half-kilometer drive to the cathedral. Many
had camped in the street all night. Hundreds carried signs
that said *Princess Teddy*.

Genie's taxi driver leaned on his horn, and they finally
reached the sentry box.

"Geneviève Mondalvi, *Paris Match*," Genie said to the
young sentry as she handed him her press credentials.

"My apologies, madame, but you are *not* on my list."

"But I have a press pass! I am interviewing Teddy Warner!"

"Oh, *oui . . .*"

Teddy was in her bedroom, hands lifted over her head
while two female attendants, standing on chairs, carefully
lowered her ornate St. Laurent wedding gown over her

shoulders. The dress was a breathtaking creation of *peau de soie* and lace, and scattered down the length of the gown in glorious swirls were appliqués of embroidered lace florets trimmed with tiny seed pearls. Its scooped, sweetheart neckline, embroidered with bugle beads and pearls, was set off by a pearl and diamond necklace that had been worn by six generations of Bellini princesses. In her ears, Teddy would wear the pearl-drop earrings that her father had given her.

"Careful—watch my makeup!" Teddy cried, holding her face away from the billowing fabric. For a second she was surrounded by white lace, breathing in the subtle cloth fragrance, seeing the world through shaded white.

The gown was lowered, and the two women clambered down from their chairs and began buttoning tiny buttons, fastening hidden zippers, smoothing the silky bodice and adjusting the yards of tulle petticoats. The stunning, twelve-foot train would be added at the cathedral, then detached again for the reception. From now until the ceremony was over, Teddy would be unable to use the bathroom without taking off the entire gown.

"Mademoiselle," said Teddy's new social secretary, a woman in her forties named Adrienne. "Mademoiselle Mondalvi from *Paris Match* is here."

"Oh, yes." Teddy had forgotten all about the ten-minute press interview that had been granted to Genie Mondalvi.

The columnist was ushered into the room, and immediately began gushing over the beauty of the gown.

"Astonishing," said Geneviève Mondalvi. "Do you realize that you actually look like Princess Lisse? Not in the face, but the way you've chosen to wear your hair—your braids wrapped in a chignon. That was the way Lisse wore her hair when she was married."

Teddy smiled, too nervous to react.

"How do you feel on this important day?" the journalist began, whipping out a small tape recorder.

"I feel— I can't even explain it. Marvelous. Scared.

Nervous. And confident, too. Jac is a wonderful man, and I adore him. No matter what happens, with him at my side I know I'm going to be happy. I only wish my father could be here to walk me down the aisle.''

Teddy hadn't planned to cry, but somehow a tear began rolling down her cheek. One of the dressers quickly moved forward with a handkerchief and began blotting her makeup.

"Who is escorting you down the aisle, Teddy?"

"I have asked Russ Ostrand to stand in for my father. He has been my agent and loyal friend for many years."

Genie Mondalvi nodded impatiently. She already knew that. She'd read all the press releases and had attended the daily pre-wedding press conferences. She hurried the pace of the conversation, knowing she'd only have a few more minutes to get some "news" out of the interview—something exclusive that would drive the other journalists crazy with envy.

"Teddy, is it true that August Steckler, the tennis player, has not been invited to the wedding and that he is wild with jealousy and has phoned you repeatedly, asking you to reconsider marriage with him?"

Teddy stared at Genie, her mouth dropping open. Then she started to laugh. "Who told you that?"

"I—why, I—" Geneviève had made most of it up herself.

"Actually, he did call me to wish me luck. Believe me, he never asked me to marry him! I already have a wonderful fiancé—and I'm gloriously happy. Write that down, please. *Gloriously*. And I'm going to wear a blue-and-white garter," Teddy added. "It's my 'something blue.' My maid of honor, Jamaica DuRoss, made it for me herself and I've borrowed a blue hair ribbon from Princess Charlaine, I'm wearing it woven into my braid."

Rows of Costan soldiers had marched from the Vendôme Palace and arranged themselves in lines on either side of the gate, linking their arms together to form a human shield. Security men roamed the crowds with walkie-talkies. Photographers stood on roofs, on top of cars, and climbed trees in search of the best angles. A helicopter dipped overhead, its rotor blades whapping. A small plane flew above it, trailing a banner that said *Teddy and Jac.* It was pandemonium!

Someone shouted, "There they are!"

Crowds began pressing forward, hundreds of people surging against each other, pushing unmercifully as they shoved their way up to the rows of soldiers.

The palace gates slid open, and pairs of Costan cavalrymen rode out, mounted on matched black horses, whose tails and manes had been woven with blue-and-white ribbons. Dressed in blue and wearing tall bearskin hats, the soldiers were young, square-jawed, handsome. One carried a stirrup holder with the Costan flag, which flapped in the wind, its folds rippling.

Then came the first carriage, gold-encrusted and ornate, even its wheels glittering gold. Inside rode Prince Henri, Princess Kristina, and Princess Gabriella, along with little Princess Charlaine. Screams went up from the excited crowd.

Then came more soldiers, again paired on black mounts that pranced along the cobblestones.

A second carriage emerged, just as ornate as the first, but open to reveal Prince Jac in the full splendor of his Costan military uniform. The uniform's blue serge was set off by gold-braided cuffs and epaulets, a gold belt, shoulder cord and chain, and a ceremonial sword in a gold scabbard. Across his chest, from his right shoulder to his waist, was slung the blue-and-white sash of the Royal Costan Order of St. Etienne, and the left side of Jac's tunic glittered with gold and silver decorations.

Women shrieked and tried to press forward. They had to be held back by the rows of soldiers, now straining to keep the crowds in check. Television cameras whirred, and flashbulbs popped in one little explosion after another.

Last to leave the palace was the open carriage that bore Teddy Warner. It was flanked on both sides by mounted soldiers. The carriage, dating from the seventeenth century, had been carefully restored to show off its gilded carvings of *fleurs de lis* and lions rampant. Its wheels were encrusted with thousands of glittering tourmalines and garnets. In the backseat, her billowing white dress taking up almost every inch, Teddy looked like a fairy-tale bride. On her head she wore a lace headdress embroidered with pearls, her shining blond hair, pulled into a braided chignon, visible through the delicate tulle.

The crowd pushed forward. People screamed her name. "Teddy! Teddy! Princess Teddy!"

Teddy sat very erect, gazing at the tumult of excitement with the appearance of serene calmness. As the carriage progressed through the streets, she lifted her hand and waved to the crowd.

At the cathedral a cordon of honor consisting of a company of soldiers in dress uniform and a platoon of armed carabineers had formed on the steps. Cardinal Bartolotta, representing the Pope, was just arriving, dressed in colorful red robes. Monseigneur d'Aillières, Archbishop of Costa del Mar, greeted him and accompanied him in procession into the cathedral.

The bridal party entered the cathedral, mounting blue-carpeted stairs and passing underneath a billowing blue silk canopy. The gothic church was magnificent. Huge blue baskets of white roses, lilies, and snapdragons hung from every glittering chandelier all the way to the altar along the center aisle and along each side of the nave. The altar itself was banked with masses of white hydrangeas, lilacs, and lilies, which were emitting clouds of perfumed scent. Organ music reverberated through the vast stone basilica in counterpoint with the decorous murmur of the twelve hundred wedding guests who filled every pew.

Jac had insisted that photographers and TV crews be banned from the cathedral, except for NBC News, which was televising the ceremony live by satellite. He didn't want a repeat of Princess Grace and Prince Rainier's wedding, when TV and newsreel cameras had whirred noisily in the cathedral, and reporters, virtually lurking behind the altar, had caused a major distraction for the guests.

"I'm nervous! I think I'm going to die!" Teddy choked to Jamaica as they waited in the large vestibule with the bridal party, which included eight bridesmaids and four junior bridesmaids, chosen from daughters of prominent Costan citizens. Jac's best man would be the twenty-two-year-old Renard, duc de Saint-Michel, a school friend and heir to one of the biggest fortunes in France.

Ever since she'd stepped into the ornate open carriage, Teddy had been fighting repeated attacks of panic. Thank heavens, no one knew. She'd managed to appear calm; she'd even managed to wave to the crowd—a magnificent act of willpower.

"I can't believe I'm here. Pinch me, Jamie! Is this real?"

"It's real, all right," laughed Jamaica, who appeared even more nervous than Teddy. "Teddy, you look so beautiful."

"But will I be able to remember my lines?" Teddy gasped. "Jamie, I'm a basket case."

"Hey, hey," Jamaica said to steady her, "it's going to be fine. I'll prompt you if you forget—which you won't. Teddy, this is the end of the rainbow."

Gabriella and Kristina found themselves standing together, each dressed in a stunning variation of the bridesmaids' blue gowns. Gaby wore pearls and diamonds; Kristina, diamonds and sapphires.

"Kristina," Gaby said, "I saw—I thought I saw Cliff in the crowd. Is he here? I didn't invite him!"

"I did," said Kristina calmly.

"But—"

"I invited him for you, Gaby. Stop being such a fool. The man adores the ground you walk on. He's been miserable since you broke up. Can't you compromise a little? Be more accepting? He'll let you pursue your career if you just give him a chance."

Gaby shook her head, looking frightened. Her eyes had filled with tears. "Kristina, how could you—" Then she bit down on her lower lip, stopping the words.

"Maybe I was wrong, but, Gaby— Oh, why can't you see! I'm trying to make amends. For . . . so many things. I don't have to tell you I've had some bad relationships. I haven't had good luck with men, but maybe you will. One of us *has* to be happy. Why can't you just take the happiness when it comes your way, Gaby? Why do you have to be afraid of it?"

"Oh," said Gaby in a small voice.

Kristina moved closer. "Give him a sign, Gaby. In church. Somehow. It'll mean the world to him. Tell him you love him! That's what today is all about. Weddings are for love, all kinds of love," she added.

It was an apology. From proud, capricious Kristina, who had always played with life, never really taking it seriously.

Gaby stared at Kristina, then rushed forward, flinging her arms around her sister. "Kris! Oh, God, I love you, too." Impulsively she took a small pearl ring off her finger, a ring that had been given to her by their mother, Princess Lisse, only a few days before she died.

"I want you to have this. Mama's ring."

"Oh." Tears filling her eyes, now it was Kristina's turn to cry.

Princess Gabriella came up to Teddy, leaning forward to kiss her lightly on the cheek. "Teddy, you're going to be my sister now. I'm so glad you're coming into the family. Jac needs you, and so do all of us."

"Teddy, I feel the same," said Princess Kristina warmly. "You finally tamed my brother, and I think—" The organ had begun to play the prelude to the wedding march. "I think it's starting," Kristina added, turning pale.

The palace majordomo, Claude Boufait, who had been placed in charge of starting the wedding party, was hurrying toward them.

"Mademoiselle," he said to Teddy, "we will begin in five minutes."

Teddy felt her heart pound into her throat, the blood leave her face. For one wild moment black dots seemed to pass in front of her eyes. She knew she was on the verge of fainting. She drew in a deep breath, clutching Jamaica's hand.

Jamaica whispered, "I love you," into her ear, and suddenly Teddy felt calmness sweep over her, a sense of inevitability. All her life had been leading up to this moment, and it was right. The faintness receded, her head clearing.

Russ Ostrand approached her, and Teddy linked her arm through his.

"Teddy, I know your father is with us today," her longtime agent and friend whispered. "I am filling in for him, but I can feel his presence and I know he loves you very, very much."

"Thank you," she murmured. She touched the earrings Houston Warner had given her and closed her eyes for a second as she felt a sensation of warmth steal over her. Yes, her father was here somewhere. How could she have imagined he wouldn't be? *You did it, Teddy Bear,* he would have whispered to her. *Go for it, Teddy. Give it two hundred percent.*

Then she drew herself up tall, waiting to start the long walk down the center aisle.

Maréchal Frédéric de Panne, Commandant of the Costan Royal Army, had already performed the ceremony of having the troops drawn up outside the cathedral present arms to Prince Jac. During his procession down the aisle, Jac had been followed by his four witnesses, all titled young men with whom he had attended school and who were now officers in the Royal Navy. Nearing the altar, he had been joined by his personal chaplain, Father Jean-Charles La-Valle.

Jac breathed deeply, calmly, as he stared out over the sea of faces, containing dozens of royals, ambassadors, celebrities, and sports stars from all over the globe, as well as a host of aristocrats with ancient titles, Costa's most prominent citizens, and the entire palace staff.

Teddy, his Teddy, would soon be his princess.

He could hardly wait.

Two-year-old Princess Charlaine, adorable in pale blue, walked in front of Teddy, strewing rose petals on the white carpeting before her. Solemnly she performed her task, skipping once and grinning as she spotted Mary Abbott, her nurse, seated on one of the aisles, smiling with pride. There was Meryl Streep, Ahmet and Mica Ertegun, the Marchese and Marchesa Giuseppe di San Giuliano, the Earl and Countess of Haddington, Britain's Princess Anne. Mark McCormack, Jerry Solomon, Steffi Graf and Michael Chang were just a few of the tennis world notables in attendance.

For Teddy, it was all a blur. Faces turned to her as she walked slowly, majestically, down the aisle, the heavy train of her dress held up by two exquisite flower girls, daughters of Costan officials, but Teddy found it hard to focus on them.

She thought she saw Cliff Ferguson, smiling at her. And a group of tennis players. Her aunt Alicia, blond and young-looking despite her fifty-five years, accompanied by her handsome, gray-haired fiancé, Cruse Simms from Boston. Was that Bruce Springsteen? And Kristina's friend, Will Camden. And, dear lord, there was Queen Elizabeth II, in blue polka dots and a lace hat! Incredible. Amazing.

Her father would have loved this. *Daddy!* she thought. *Oh, Daddy.*

Then she saw nothing but the altar, hung with cloth of gold, banked with thousands of white lilies and roses, candles glowing everywhere. Waiting for her was Jac, his eyes locked on to hers, filled with love and awe.

Teddy floated toward him.

Seated beside his young daughter, overcome by the magnificence of the ceremony, Cliff Ferguson felt a burst of sadness.

He'd taken an aisle seat, hoping to catch Gaby's eye as she walked down the aisle. He'd thought she'd looked directly at him, her eyes brimming with tears, but now he was no longer sure.

"Daddy," whispered Becky beside him, "this is *so* cool."

This wedding was an event from another way of life. He had flown all the way over here, canceling several important business meetings, only to be confronted with the realization that Gaby lived in a world totally different from any he could ever offer her. Costa was a beautiful country, but he didn't want to live here, not on a permanent basis. What would he do here? He loved running his chain of stores, and he loved his ranch, and he wanted to be with Becky, to support her Olympic dreams as best he could. Now he regretted bringing the teenager here. He didn't want to raise his daughter's hopes—or his own.

Gaby, he thought, feeling that she was already lost to him.

Monseigneur d'Aillières intoned, "Jacques Louis Henri Bertrand Bellini, will you take Theodora Elizabeth here present for your lawful wife, according to the rites of our Holy Mother the Church?"

"Yes, I will," responded Jac in English, then repeating the vow in French as he and Teddy had planned beforehand. He gazed at Teddy, his eyes burning.

"Theodora Elizabeth, will you take Jacques Louis Henri Bertrand Bellini here present for your lawful husband, according to the rites of our Holy Mother the Church?"

Teddy gazed into Jac's eyes, fighting tears of emotion. "Yes," she whispered. "*Oui.* I will."

Following the Mass and rendering of another hymn, the Most Reverend Father Bartolotta read aloud the solemn best wishes of His Holiness Pope John Paul II.

Cliff Ferguson sat rigidly in his pew, his sadness growing more intense with each word. The glorious wedding only pointed up the huge disparity between Teddy and Jac's happiness and his own misery. Within minutes, he knew, the bridal party would be exiting the church, heading for massive picture-taking and three concurrent, huge receptions to be held at the palace. Gaby would go with them, of course, pursuing her royal existence, far beyond his reach.

Yes, there they came. Teddy and Jac were proceeding up the aisle. Teddy's veil was thrown back now, her face glowing, radiant.

Then the bridal party.

"*Daddy,*" whispered Rebecca, "there's Gaby!"

So beautiful, so lovely. She moved in the slow rhythm of the recessional, clutching her lacy bouquet of violets, lilies, and orchids. Her eyes darted across the crowd until finally they found his.

Cliff turned, half stepping out of the pew, his eyes locked on Gaby's. His heart began beating so hard he thought it would pound right through his starched white shirt. The world fell away, leaving only himself and Gaby. A thousand regrets pulsed through him. He'd been too harsh. He hadn't compromised. He'd blamed her for being royal, for wanting to have her own life.

And then it happened. Gaby's left arm reached out and thrust her flowers into his hands. Stunned, Cliff closed his fingers around the bouquet, and then he looked at Gabriella. Her eyes pleaded with him, asking him . . .

"I love you," he answered huskily. "God, how I love you, Gaby. Always! Come back to me."

Her smile was radiant.

Cascading torrents of church bells filled the air as every church in Costa let forth peals of musical chimes, and guns boomed a hundred-gun salute.

Teddy and Jac emerged from the cathedral into the sunshine. In the square a new, open, cream-and-blue Rolls-Royce was waiting to take them back to the palace. The car would stop along the way at the tiny Church of the Virgin so that Teddy could lay her bouquet on the altar as an offering to the Blessed Mother. There would be a full day of nuptial festivities, and Teddy and Jac would shake hundreds of hands until their fingers ached.

But now her eyes widened in surprise. Crowds of people surrounded the cathedral, thousands of them, but the carnival atmosphere that had pervaded Costa all week, especially earlier in the day was gone. Now the pushing and shoving had disappeared, and the thousands stood quietly, craning their necks for a glimpse of the royal couple. Some gawked, others were weeping with emotion. Teddy saw Jac lift his arm and wave it slowly to the right, then to the left, in the royal gesture she had seen in countless news broadcasts.

Teddy raised her arm and began to wave too.

Jac turned to look at her, grinning his rakish grin. "Princess Teddy, I think we have some parties to attend. Are you up for it? Let's run to the Rolls—just to show them we're not too stuffy."

"In this long dress?" They'd been coached in every step of the elaborate wedding protocol, and running down the church steps definitely wasn't part of it. Then Teddy caught the spirit of mischief. "All right," she whispered. "I'm a champion runner."

She reached both of her hands down and grasped huge, lacy handfuls of *peau de soie*. Her legs were clad in white lace stockings, and Jamaica's blue garter was just barely visible under the froth of petticoats.

Laughing, she turned to Jac. "Ready?"

"I love you," he whispered.

Then they were running, his hand clasping her arm, toward the Rolls-Royce, running toward their future.